MW00973763

FROG GIG

BY ROBERT SMITH

DORRANCE
PUBLISHING CO
EST. 1920
PITTSBURGH, PENNSYLVANIA 15238

The contents of this work, including, but not limited to, the accuracy of events, people, and places depicted; opinions expressed; permission to use previously published materials included; and any advice given or actions advocated are solely the responsibility of the author, who assumes all liability for said work and indemnifies the publisher against any claims stemming from publication of the work.

All Rights Reserved
Copyright © 2022 by Robert Smith

No part of this book may be reproduced or transmitted, downloaded, distributed, reverse engineered, or stored in or introduced into any information storage and retrieval system, in any form or by any means, including photocopying and recording, whether electronic or mechanical, now known or hereinafter invented without permission in writing from the publisher.

Dorrance Publishing Co
585 Alpha Drive
Pittsburgh, PA 15238
Visit our website at *www.dorrancebookstore.com*

ISBN: 978-1-6366-1442-7
eISBN: 978-1-6366-1629-2

FROG GIG

CHAPTER ONE

It was late on a Wednesday when the fateful call came in.

"Jeff, pick up line 5. Anonymous call. Something about endangered frogs and paving a bridge at OCC." George was answering the phone and rerouting the calls by department. I was finishing the last article for a series on salaries of public employees. I had agreed to cover in the News Department, hoping to get a lead on something. Not much of a sacrifice since I didn't have much of a life outside work.

"Jeff Stewart here."

"I'm not going to give you my name, but I have information that you should be interested in. Okay?"

"We can start there." This was a familiar start for any reporter on the job more than a couple of months. "What's your information?"

"You know the OCC campus?"

"Yeah. Is that where you are?"

"Well, not right now. But it's what I'm calling about. How about the H. George Buckwald Bridge; do you know it?"

"I think so. Is that the one on the cut-through road that gets closed when it snows?"

"That's it. Tonight there was tentative approval to pave the bridge, and the frogs under there are going to die. That's why I'm calling."

"Who approved the paving, and what's the big deal about the frogs? I like them. I grew up watching Kermit every day. But this is the Shore, and there's plenty of frogs."

"These are Pine Barrens Tree Frogs, and they're endangered. The Environmental Club at the college has been watching out for them. The county Board of Freeholders approved planning to pave"

"Are you with the Environmental Club?"

"That's not important. How will I know what's happening? Can I call you in a few days?"

"It might be easier if I call you. I'm not always in the office."

"That's not going to work. Nice try, though, to get some information on me. That's why I found a pay phone."

I gave him my direct line and some likely times I'd be in the office. I finished the job I was working on and went home. I'd tell my editor tomorrow about the frogs and see if he wanted me to work the story.

This was the "little things" start that would lead to something bigger. It was no big deal that I was covering the department while I finished the last article in the series. And my girlfriend wasn't available on many nights—a reflection of her large circle of friends and of my crazy work hours. That's what was happening when I got the call that pulled me into an investigation that led to uncovering the illegal action of a councilman and that also solved an old murder.

I learned later that the name of the caller was Vince Fallon. Before I knew his name, I learned that he was determined and persuasive.

Vince's stylish dress drew the attention of most people when he entered a room. The women continued to look at his face and build after checking out the clothes. He was on the tall side of average height—about six feet even. The contributions of his Irish father and Italian mother blended into a swarthy complexion with captivating blue eyes. His almost constant smile gave an early indication of the self-confidence that became obvious on talking with him. Broad shoulders capped a trim build, suggesting even greater viewing pleasure if he were found at the beach. Modeling for GQ was within the realm of possibility.

He was in his third year at Ocean County College, on schedule to complete his AA requirements at the end of next summer. College was a push for him: completing six credits per semester and six each summer while holding a full-time job doing computer repairs and filling in for the sales staff when the store was busy. Marty Schenk, owner of Jackson TV and Appliance, often felt the dilemma of whether to assign Vince the repairs where he was skilled and quick, or to sales where he readily established comfortable customer relationships, which usually led to a sale.

He always seemed to know where he was going and had a plan to enroll at Kean College for the next two years. The ultimate goal was to own a company that sells technology products. His interest in ecology on a global scale began with a high school science teacher who talked him into attending a Clean Ocean Action beach cleanup on a cold, damp Saturday in March while a sophomore at Jackson Memorial High. With his good looks, affable personality, and determination he was a natural to get elected as treasurer of his school's chapter as a junior and as president as a senior. During college orientation, he signed the interest sheet for the Environmental Club and since then had stayed active. He missed about half the meetings due to his job, so president was out of the picture this time.

There was a message on Vince's answering machine when he arrived home that evening in 2005. He felt the usual Wednesday night fatigue caused by back-to-back morning classes and then a full eight hours at work. Today's work had extended to nine hours because Marty's father-in-law had called at 8:45 with a problem with his new big screen TV. The swing past Mr. Schenk's house to unscramble the multiple commands sent from his remote was the reason for the extra hour. It helped that Marty told him to come in an hour later tomorrow and that Marty's dad had insisted on heating up two slices of pizza left over from dinner.

It was nearly 10:30 when his phone had rung.

"Vince. It's Keeshon. Call me on my cell phone when you get in. I'll be up till 12:00. You'll want to hear this one!"

With a sigh, he erased the message and dialed.

"Hey, man, it's Vince. What's got you so excited?"

"I thought you'd be home long before now. Some female action after work?"

"I wish! If that was the reason, I'd feel more energy now. It was my boss's old man, screwed up his TV again. I say let 'em drive till they're 80 but take away the remotes at 55. I finally unplugged the set and had it repeat the auto-program, then pulled the batteries on the remote and re-programmed it. I like Marty, and he is my boss. What's up?"

"It's about the club's concern with the tree frogs. I went to the County Board of Freeholders public meeting tonight as a club representative. Talk about boring! Except when they approved planning for an asphalt surface on the Buckwald Bridge. I called you as head of the sub-committee keeping a watch on the frog issue."

"Did I hear you right? That's crazy! Those frogs are endangered already. We did a lot to clean up the discharge in the creek. Why didn't you do something?"

"Man, we're friends. Don't get upset and put the blame on me. I spoke during the public comment section. Their engineer and Morrison in the Science Department told 'em there won't be an impact on the frogs. They're guaranteeing no use of salt. You may be able to argue with them, but I haven't been involved like you have with the frogs."

"Hey, man, I'm sorry. You're right. You did what you could. Thanks for speaking up and putting them on warning. Did you mention the club?"

"You don't need to ask that question. Before I spoke, I said I was there as a representative of the Environmental Club."

"Thanks, again. I'll pick up from here... Oh, wait! When's the paving?"

"Don't know for sure. I got the idea that it'll be in the next few months. The county has to work with the college. They talked tonight about needing to hire an engineer and then adding the job to a contract for some road work to be done some other place."

"I got a call to make. I'll try to catch you this weekend."

Keeshon Wilson was a second-year student. He seemed to be born to enjoy life. People who had only casual contact with him saw him as the typical class clown who used jokes and pranks to cover up some intellectual deficiency or inability to relate to others. They somehow thought it was possible to be dumb and clever at the same time, or to be both insecure and confident enough to risk embarrassment if no one laughed. Someone who had such a good time seemed out of place in a club filled with people committed to identifying and fighting threats to the future of the world. He was famous for his campus pranks and usually escaped censure because no harm was done and his talents were on display.

Vince hit the speed dial for Roxanne Freeman after hanging up with Keeshon.

He always enjoyed talking on the phone with Roxanne, starting with the lilting "Hello" with the second syllable a couple of notes higher on the musical scale. The sound of her voice was like an echo to what he imagined while waiting for her answer.

"Rox, it's Vince. I got bad news!"

"Why? What happened? Anybody hurt?"

"Three questions with only five words! Maybe a new record! A tribute to your curiosity and quick mind!"

She deserved to be in a more challenging school. She was the standout in most of her classes and carried a 4.0 GPA. She kept her grades up despite a part-time job at Lowe's home store and working her butt off as president of the Environmental Club. Her other major obligation was a full day and evening in church every Sunday. Grandmother Bessie and Auntie Lily (actually her great aunt) insisted that the next two generations maintain the strong African-American tie to the church: morning service 10:00 to 12:30, afternoon visitation (to "those less fortunate") from 3:00 to 5:00, and evening service 7:00 to 8:30. Enormous meals involving the whole family fell in between. Like other traditions that are faithfully preserved, everyone complied without question because it had always been a part of their lives. Back-sliding lives in other families were ready examples of the "descent down the long slippery road to perdition." Roxanne never hid the reason that she was a student at OCC instead of Princeton or Georgetown or U. Penn: Her family couldn't afford to pay the difference between the scholarships she was offered and the annual cost of tuition, room and board, books, and fees. She never saw herself as poor with the richness she felt in her family, her church, and her schoolwork.

It was her voice that Vince anticipated, but she also was strikingly pretty. Her skin was the color of cocoa, and you could see it was smooth as silk without ever touching it. Her hair was jet black with a tight natural wave that stopped short of being curly. Soft brown eyes sparked with flecks of light when she was excited, danced when she was amused, captivated when she listened closely to what you said, or opened directly to her heart when she connected with someone's suffering.

"If you're joking, I guess no one was harmed. So what's the bad news?"

"I just talked to Keeshon. You know he covered the County Freeholders for the club tonight. He said the fools approved planning to pave the Buckwald Bridge so they can keep it open when it snows. That'll finish the frogs!"

"Did I hear you right?"

"The same question I asked Keeshon. I hate to say you heard me right, alright. We should do something!"

"I still have the plan we used to try to stop the wetlands construction. Do you feel like 'Here we go again!'?"

"Yeah. But you said it best in your club presentation at the Freshman Orientation; the job will never be done in a consumer society that measures success by how big your house is and how much crap you have in it."

"A prophet in my own time! Problem is that after all my time listening to Bible stories, I know what happens to prophets! We gotta remember we didn't get into saving the world because it's easy. Are you ready to work beside me on this? They're your frogs!"

"I wouldn't have called if I didn't care. What's the plan?"

"I need to think more about it in the morning, but I have a tentative plan that centers around making the public aware and trying to get government intervention. I'm appointing you publicity chairman so that you sound official when you call *The Press*. Most of the people who drive over that bridge have no idea about the frogs underneath. And if they know about the frogs, they think they're like every other frog. I'll explore filing a complaint with the State Department of Environmental Protection. The DEP is an odd department. If we can find someone who's interested, they probably can be some help. It's just as likely, though, that the person I talk to will think I'm some nut who gets worked up about every praying mantis that's killed."

"I'll get right on this. I'll make the call if that part of the plan is solid."

"Yeah, go ahead. This is the wetland plan. I found it in the file while we've been talking. It should work again. We need to act and not spend time planning. I'll call DEP tomorrow.

CHAPTER TWO

It's amazing how little things make big differences in how your life goes. That's the way it's been with me. I mean I'm not famous like politicians or sports heroes, but there have been little things that made a big difference in my life. Like a change in the photography business that led to my family's move from central New York state to central New Jersey. After the move, the trail of my little things ran from Brick Township, to Rutgers University, to *The Asbury Park Press*. The secret under the H. George Buckwald Bridge on the campus of Ocean Community College was little as well, but it grew into something big.

Dad was a senior manager in the marketing division of a large photographic equipment and supplies company. Mom never worked a day of her life. I'm not bitter about Mom not working. That's how things were where we lived—in every home. She played tennis and golf with the rest of the wives and helped out with the big charity ball each year, but she loved to bake. Eddie and Pete loved to stop at my house in the afternoon because there usually was a fresh batch of cookies (chocolate chip was the favorite) or some other sweet. My all-time favorite was toffee bars—chocolate and caramel and something that made them crunch. And she drove us around more often than the other moms. Some of them stayed around the country club for hours after morning tennis and lunch or afternoon golf. Three martini lunches weren't restricted to business executives. Others had book clubs or volunteered in the hospital gift shop. We all liked knowing that Mom would be at home most afternoons.

Dad worked with a headhunter for Fortune 500 companies after his former employer let him go. He had several interviews but never got an offer. He said he was out of practice since he worked at the same company for eighteen years and had moved up through the ranks without an interview. After six months, he revised his expectations and tried several sales jobs. He wasn't satisfied with any. Then the job-jumping caught up with him. He probably worked six months out of the eighteen after he was "down-sized." The move to New Jersey gave him the opportunity to do what he loved—work with boats. He went to work at Water Rats. He whistled, hummed, sometimes even sang when he arrived home. I never heard any of that from him when he was in his old job.

Nine months after Dad was laid off, Mom used her college bio degree and a contact at church to land a sales job with Nolan Generics Pharmaceutical Corp. She did okay, but her heart was never in it. Then Grandma, Mom's mom living in Brick, had a bad stroke. Mom didn't have a choice but to go live there because Grandpa had the start of Alzheimer's. Grandma lasted two months. I guess it was good for Mom to have that time with her, but I know it was tough watching one parent die and the other lose his mind.

After Grandma's death, Mom and Dad put Grandpa into a nursing home. He got good care, but went downhill faster. He and Grandma had been married forty-eight years, and he couldn't understand why she was missing. The nursing home restricted his movement a little more every couple of weeks because he kept trying to leave. Mom flew back and forth over three-day weekends for three months, trying to resume her drug sales job in between. She always had a beautiful smile that was part of her personality. After Dad lost his job, the smile disappeared, and she developed a short temper.

After a trial period of three months, Mom and Dad took stock and then called a family meeting. The kids learned then that they would sell our New York State house, move to Jersey into Grandpa's house, take him out of the nursing home, put him in senior day care, and see how that worked. Dad would look for a job in the boat business. Some of the house proceeds would pay off the home mortgage loans that had supported us for two years. Some would provide living expenses for several months if necessary. Some would be used to start Mom in business with her own bakery. If anything remained, it would be saved for college tuition for the three children.

Although as the outsider I hated living in Brick the last two years of high school, I made the best of a bad situation, distinguished myself with high grades, and scored 1360 out of 1600 on the SATs. I went to Rutgers University on a scholarship because there wasn't much left of the New York house sale money after expenses connected with Grandpa's health care. So that Mom could get the bakery up and running, she and Dad hired a home health aide to be with Grandpa during the day.

Even as early as the start of the college application process, I knew two things about what I'd study. One was it wouldn't be math. The other was that I liked to read and maybe could do something in that area, probably not an English major because students in that major seemed so studious. At the start of freshman year, we were asked to indicate the subject that we thought we'd major in. We could change our minds, but the college wanted to assign each of us to a faculty advisor and thought it was a good idea to have the advisor be someone in the potential major. I said communications because it looked like there was a lot of flexibility in choosing courses and it might be easier to change majors.

High school senior year was a tough time for me and my family. My parents thought I couldn't do anything right, and I knew they couldn't. My dad had hopes that I'd get a big scholarship to a prestigious college. I was accepted to several places—NYU, Boston College, Georgetown, Cornell—but none of them offered a financial package large enough that we could afford the rest, even with a scholarship job and some loans. My mom kept pushing for me to go to Ocean Community College for two years and then transfer to NYU. We'd save money the first two years and then could afford the last two if I kept my grades up. I didn't like that plan. I needed to get out of the house. Some kids I got to know a little told me that the first couple of years can be pretty boring at a community college because your program's filled with required courses. And the transfer part depended on good grades, and I didn't know how well I could handle college work. Rutgers wasn't my first choice, but it was okay.

I got lucky with a roommate. Joe Hendricks was his name. He was from north Jersey, the town of Cresskill. Graduated from Northern Valley Regional and was on a scholarship too. He knew exactly what he wanted to do after high school so choosing a major was no problem for him. He worked on the school newspaper there—*The Communique*—and knew he wanted to major in jour-nalism. He was a nut about newspaper reporting because he got involved in writing a controversial series about the school administration that led to the replacement of a vice principal. The school first tried to stop him, but he went to the local advertisers' rag, *The Suburbanite*, and got on their staff and did his writing for them. One reason he chose Rutgers was because the daily campus newspaper, *The Daily Targum*, had a good reputation. Joe and I had comple-mentary personalities. He was hard-driving, knew quickly what he wanted to do, rolled up his sleeves and got started, and set everything else aside until he reached his goal. I'm more laidback, with a slower start, a more cautious gath-ering of the facts, a willingness to let things develop at their own pace, and persistence as strong as Joe's once I'm well into the project and have a good idea of where it's going. We had similar interests from the start: needing to be around people, reverence for the written and spoken word, interest in news reports, participation in less formal group activities—stick ball, ultimate fris-bee, hiking, going to a movie (the worse the quality, the better we liked it), and frequent midnight cravings for pizza. We also shared dislikes: formal re-ligion, major college athletics, fashion crazes and dressing "right," and aversion to most vegetables.

It was Joe who got me interested in news reporting. He forced his way onto the *Targum* staff as a freshman, an unusual accomplishment. It took me a year and a half to apply to be a staff member and then undertook it only as a trial to help me decide between print and non-print reporting for my future in communications. Joe talked me into taking a fabulous course on journalism from an historical perspective, "Reporting Current Events Through the Ages." That was first semester of sophomore year and was acceptable as a course in a communications major. My next course sealed the deal because it was a hands-on writing course that required a publishable article each week. It seemed to come easy for me. Now that I'm a couple of years away from college, I can see that a middle school English teacher, Mr. Accardi, hooked me on writing, and the one bright spot in the two painful years in Brick was senior year English with Josephine Sullivan.

My academic record was undistinguished: a C+/B average overall with a B in my major. Sophomore year slump lasted three years with me because I spent all my time at the *Targum* office. Some of that time was devoted to writing and proofing. Lots of it was just hanging out with whoever came around. I was there more than Joe and enjoyed the challenge of doing the investigative work to get the facts for my articles; it was like putting puzzles together. The editor would make an assignment and give me what he knew. I'd start by asking myself questions: Who was involved that I know about now? Who was involved that I don't know about? Where did this known information come from? What other sources are available for additional information? Why would someone do the things that I know about? How did the person do what he did? What were the results of what was done? Are there other things that could happen? My mom used to say that I had a million questions. Back then the fun was in asking the questions, and I expected her to answer them; now I know I'm the one that must get the answers and getting them is the challenge. The challenge requires long hours, abuse by people who don't want you checking into their business, some occasional physical risk, and lots of stress. But satisfaction comes from meeting the challenge. Choosing the words and arranging them in the best patterns to clearly convey understanding is pure pleasure.

Joe was miffed when I received the Ladley K. Pearson Memorial Prize after working on the paper for two years compared to his four and despite the fact that I took fewer journalism courses than he did to complete a major in the field. But with my average, I needed the award to get a job after college. Mr. Bieberman told me during my first year that it was the Pearson Prize that swung his decision to me because one of his all-time favorite reporters had won the same award.

So that's the trail from New York State, to Brick, to Rutgers, to *The Asbury Park Press*, to the secret under the H. George Buckwald Bridge on the Ocean Community College campus.

CHAPTER THREE

After the tip about the paving decision by the Freeholders, I had a restless night and car trouble the next morning. Sometimes it seems that things pile up on you when you're tired.

The bridge, the paving, and the frogs were pretty annoying in the beginning. It was the type of a phone call that usually didn't go anywhere, just some kid who had a beef with the college. I made a few of those calls during four years—mostly about grades in courses. But since the call was my only lead, I had to look into it. And despite my pessimism about the significance of college kids' complaints about the local college administration, I had kind of an itchy feeling that maybe this event was different

Anyway, I was feeling tired when I multi-tasked my way through a Pop Tart and bottled orange juice, as I put on a dress shirt and slacks, while watching CNN news. I dragged myself out the door and down the steps to my '93 Chevy Cavalier. It chose today to not start. Up to that point I had a good shot at getting to work close enough to being on time that I could redeem myself with my editor for several other days when I had been late, really late.

When I turned the key, there was no sound—nothing. Following some simple checks to find the problem, starting with a check of the dome light, I used emery cloth to clean the battery posts. Started like a charm afterward. As

I got angry for allowing too much time between the last cleaning of the posts, I thought of Edgar Allen Poe's short story "The Imp of the Perverse."

By catching a few breaks and entering intersections in the late stages of yellow on the traffic lights, I made up five of the fifteen minutes. Going up the stairs two at a time probably didn't save time over the elevator, but it felt good to tell myself that it did. Kim, the new secretary to the editor, greeted me with a coy smile and the suggestive comment, "Using the elevator would save that heavy breathing for another time." Why is it that the beautiful women with big engagement rings are the most appealing? I'm usually ready for a verbal contest, but she left me speechless most of the time.

"He said to send you in as soon as you got here. You must have something big going for you." I'm sure I blushed—doing so a second time in a space of a few minutes.

I knocked on the jam of the open door. Alex Speery, my editor, looked up and motioned to a chair across the desk from where he sat. "Come in, Jeff. I got your voicemail this morning. Tell me what's got the kids at OCC stirred up?" I liked Alex. We had hit it off well from my first employment interview.

"The caller said the Freeholders decided last night to plan to pave the Buckwald Bridge, and he's worried that the work will kill the frogs who live under it."

"I remember hearing that there are frogs over there. Are they some special kind?"

"They're the Pine Barrens Treefrogs. He said they're endangered. I think he's with the Environmental Club because he mentioned it. When I asked if he's with the club, he said that isn't important."

"There might be something there, and it might get bigger if a student club gets involved. People talk about the liberal press, but I was never more liberal than when I was in college. I also was ready to fight to the finish for a cause. Get over there and see what you can find out. Maybe someone in an office can connect you with a club officer."

"Right, boss. This tip has a different feel than others that went nowhere."

As I got up to leave the office, Alex said, "Jeff, nice work on the public employees' salaries series! This morning I read your copy for the closing article. You've tied the pieces together and summarized the highlights."

"Thanks, I feel good about it too."

I tried a wink to put Kim off balance as I left. She began fanning herself with the papers she was holding and said quietly, "Be still, my heart!" I didn't respond and didn't look back because I knew my face was red.

Leaving the parking lot, I noticed for the first time that the weather was nearly perfect. When my family moved to the shore area of New Jersey, I had a hard time adjusting. The weather was one of the factors.

In winter the seashore humidity made the mild temperatures seem cold without the benefit of snow and winter sports. There were whole winters when the ponds never froze thick enough to skate. Skiing required driving to the Pocono Mountains in Pennsylvania; "mountain" was a fancy name for a big hill.

It was the summers I first came to appreciate because the shore area came alive. Sailing, power boating, fishing, swimming, parasailing or water skiing behind a power craft, surfing and wind surfing, beach volleyball, kayaking, and just lying on the beach. But the weather was an adjustment. Most mornings in July and August began with overcast that burned off by 10:00 and was followed by intense heat. Often the overcast returned in late afternoon. The humidity rarely let up. If you were active outside and wore more clothes than a swimsuit, the sweat stayed on you.

The blue of East Coast skies is usually dulled by pollution that accumulates in the steady flow of upper air masses. This day was a pleasant change. A few small, puffy clouds drifted slowly across a sky that was truly azure in color. The humidity of the day before was gone and replaced by drier air that allowed perspiration to evaporate in the soft, steady breeze. I headed for the college with my AC off and windows open.

I planned my route so that I would cross the Buckwald Bridge. Believe me when I tell you the size of the structure falls way short of the attention focused on the bridge by this story and by the rustic wooden signs a half-mile away from either a westward or eastward approach, announcing that the bridge is either open or closed. The length of the bridge is a mere 100 feet. The wooden decking and side rails of the modest height of thirty inches are the only indications that a bridge separates the asphalt road on either side. I'm sure my conclusion is correct that the prominence of the signs are a tribute to the accomplishments of H. George Buckwald more than they are an important facet of the area's transportation system. H. George Buckwald had been the Mayor of Lakewood, an Ocean County Freeholder, and a Trustee of Ocean County College.

———————————————

The college had a luxury of space with its campus of 275 acres, including an arboretum and a pond attracting anglers intent on outwitting small fish. College facilities included twenty-five buildings that provided offices, classrooms, a performing arts center, a library housing 75,000 volumes, and indoor and outdoor athletic facilities for a program including soccer, baseball and softball, basketball, volleyball, lacrosse, cross-country track, and golf (although no golf course). The campus is a pleasant surprise in a sprawling municipality of 90,000 residents that has grown in numbers by 1,200 percent since the Garden State Parkway was completed in the 1950s, and even by 75 percent in the last twenty-five years.

CHAPTER FOUR

The parking lot was partially filled by a mixture of vehicles that couldn't be ignored. I was familiar with the diversity among the student body and the faculty. The cars were a mirror of that makeup. My short walk took me past a dented Neon, a mid-seventies brown Ford Torino station wagon, a silver Beemer with beach parking decal for Nantucket, and a convertible model of the latest VW Beetle. I headed for the library.

A visit to a library was like a field trip, a special gift—definitely not like work. For as far back as I can remember, I've loved libraries. I can remember visiting the library as a young kid with my mom or my dad. I must have been three or four, not reading yet, but being there to pick out something that would be read to me. It was quiet and peaceful. Displays of books with bright colors caught my eye and kept me turning one way, then another. Objects to draw attention to a special book—a stuffed animal, a toy truck, a doll, a baseball glove, a girl's hat—changed frequently. The librarian was always happy to see me, gave me a smile, shook my hand, and asked if she could help

College libraries of course are more serious and expect more independence on the part of the patron. I completed the material request form at the reference desk, asking to use the media file on the Pine Barren Treefrog. As the librarian took my ID and handed me two bulging files, I asked if she had information on the clubs on campus. She suggested I try online or go to the Student Center and the Campus Life office.

A half-hour of reading and note-taking was fascinating. The frog is only one to three inches long and is usually green with wide, dark stripes and—found in brushy areas, often near peat bogs or shallow ponds. The marking that distinguishes it from other green tree frogs is a lavender stripe with white borders on each side of the body.

As I returned the files and retrieved my ID, the library began to fill with the change of class periods. On my way to the College Center Building, I was enchanted by the mix of dress (in some cases, the mix of costume) of the students, displaying care, creativity, and indifference. From tattered jeans to Calvin Klein slacks, from precise color coordination to combined stripes and plaids, from modest necklines to scoop necks, and from muscle shirts to fleece jackets. The occasional older student with more conservative dress prevented me from being odd-man-out in my dress shirt and slacks.

At the Campus Life Office I was given a leftover brochure about Freshman Orientation and a list of clubs, and I was referred to the OCC website for information about current activities. I found the listing for the Environmental Club, citing Roxanne Freeman as president. Her email address was included. I decided to leave a note to her in the club mailbox and to send an email once back at the office. My note read,

> Ms. Freeman,
>
> I'm following up on a phone call from someone who may be a member of your club who reported approval to pave the Buckwald Bridge. Please phone,
>
> Jeff Stewart

I enclosed my business card.

On my way back to the office, I stopped at Cuzzins Pizzeria for lunch. There are thousands of these places throughout the state, a population greater than the famous Jersey diners.

I went to Alex's office, prepared for a verbal joust with Kim. I started speaking as my foot crossed the threshold, "I hope your temperature has returned to normal after my wink aroused you this morning."

She shot me her best flirty smile and answered, "There you go again, toying with my affections."

I managed a comeback. "I respect you too much to treat you like a toy. A doll to be admired would be more like it."

"You brute! You're setting me up for a fall off the pedestal," she said with a pout. "Mr. Speery is expecting you. I'll announce you."

She raised the phone, punched a button, and announced, "Jeff is here for you. This is twice he's come today." She looked down at her desk blotter as she said, "You can go in now." I know I saw her cheek muscles twitch like she was preventing a giggle.

"What's up with the college kids and the wildlife?" Alex knew when to be serious and when to have fun.

"I stopped at the library and researched the frog species. I think I upset that kid last night on the phone when I made reference to Kermit and suggested that the college frogs were the same as all the other ones at the shore. Now I have a new respect. Did you know that they're green and white and lavender?"

"Pretty interesting, but this isn't a feature on the frogs. What else do you know?"

"Not much yet. I left a note for the club president to phone me. I'll do an email when we finish here. I want to check if they have a plan of action and find out what to expect."

"Make sure you check for a college press release on last night's meeting. You may need to talk with the press officer because they may try to play down the paving. Do you still think this is going some place?"

"Yeah. No concrete reason for my prediction yet, just a feeling. I think it's going to play out with conflict over the environmental issues. The county has invested in an image of the college being environmentally friendly. There's the arboretum dedicated to preserving the flora and fauna, and the ponds are home to a large peeper population. Up to now they've enjoyed positive press for their environmental sensitivity and willingness to close the cut-through instead of using salt and chemicals to clear snow—all in the name of protecting an endangered species. This issue may put the county freeholders and the college at odds with each other."

"Sure is potential for generating lots of interest. While you're waiting for the call from the club president, get the freeholders' rationale. Use the background you found at the library. Check our archives for other information. If you haven't received the return call at that point, leave a place for what you hear from the club and write the rest of the article. Write it so that you can delete the lead into what you're waiting for if there's nothing by 7:30. Because by eight o'clock I want something, either a feature with all sides included or a straight news article that reports the vote of the freeholders and anything on the plans and timetable. Looks like another long day. After you finish the copy on what you have now, let me have a look. You probably will have time to grab a few things off the wire services and prep some short articles while you wait for the call."

"Piece of cake. Will you leave me on the college story?"

"The frogs and the bridge are all yours."

I made the decision to treat Kim as a business associate as I left the office. "Good afternoon. Thank you again for your prompt and courteous help. Have a good night."

"Thank you!" she said with a genuine smile. "You have a good night too." Then with a tilt of her head, "If you have strength left. Things seem to just keep coming up for you today."

Maybe I should limit my remarks to: "Hello," "Goodbye," "Yes, please," and "No, thank you."

I phoned Deena Johnson, County Freeholder Press Officer, for information on the freeholders meeting.

"Deena, it's Jeff Stewart with the *Press*. How's everything with my number one source for information from inside county government?" I made a practice of schmoozing every press officer I knew at least once every six months.

"Hi, Jeff. All's well with me. How are things with the APP's most persistent reporter?"

"I'm keeping busy and out of trouble. What's this I'm hearing about pavement of the Buckwald Bridge?"

"You'll have to tell me what you're hearing. I can tell you the related facts."

"I hear that after all these years of environmental concern that includes a bridge surface made of bongossi wood, a ban on the use of salt to remove snow, and bridge closures until Mother Nature got rid of the snow, the freeholders voted to look at a petroleum-based surface over the wood so that plowing would be possible."

"Wow! Sounds like your sources got you all worked up. It wouldn't be someone from the college's Environmental Club would it? They had a member at the meeting last night."

"You know reporters don't identify their sources. Are you telling me that what I hear is true?"

"The fact of the decision is true. The emotional overtones belong to you or to your source. The road over the bridge has become an accepted piece of the transportation network with as many as 500 cars an hour passing through there. Some are students on their way to the campus. As much as sixty percent of that number represents motorists taking a shortcut from Church Road to Hooper Avenue. It's a real inconvenience to faculty, staff, and students when they find the bridge closed and take ten minutes or more to go the long way and in the front drive. The late people delay classes by as much as twenty minutes."

"Surely you don't want to see a headline 'Stragglers Pressure College to Consent to Endanger Wildlife.' What's the real motivation here?"

"OCC is a growing school. With the costs of tuition, room and board as high as they are at both public and private four-year colleges, it's meeting a very real need. At the request of the County Engineer, one of OCC's science faculty members Dr. Morrison, has analyzed the threat to the Pine Barren frogs of the project of paving the bridge. His conclusion is that the asphalt will penetrate the first inch or two of the twelve-inch planking and will stop there. Continuation of the no-salt practice will protect the frogs. Those are facts without emotional overlay. As always, it's your editor's decision about what to report."

I responded to the icy tone of the last couple of sentences, "I sense you feel like I'm attacking you. I called for the facts, and you gave them to me. I'm grateful. My quip about the headline was intended to emphasize the questionable position of determining organizational practice on the basis of the people who cut corners so often that any change in routine causes missed deadlines

"I'll be preparing an article. The *Press* needs to be out in front and not following the other papers. Thanks for the information. Do you have an official release you can email me?"

"I'm working on it. I'll send it within the next two hours."

"I hope tomorrow's a better day for you. Goodbye."

It's strange how I sound more like my parents as I get older. It was a real jolt hearing myself comment that the corner-cutters shouldn't influence practice. Whether you have a good relationship with your parents or a poor one, they implant messages in your memory that get activated in certain circumstances.

I worked on a draft of the article, following Alex's plan to put together the notes from my phone call with Deena, supplemented by her press release, and my research notes made at the library. I left space for comments by Roxanne that would reflect her club's official position.

I spent the better part of two hours taking information off the wire services and producing short articles that might be used to fill space or might be held for another day's edition or be thrown away due to lack of space and expiration of timeliness. It's an interesting practice because a reporter competes with himself for space. If the bridge and frog article filled enough space, then the short articles might get trashed.

———

At 6:00 the Environmental Club President returned my call.

"Jeff Stewart here."

"Roxanne Freeman here. I'm returning your phone call. You probably took a call from Vince Fallon. He's the publicity chairman for the Environmental Club. What is it you want from me?"

"Thanks for calling. Your publicity chairman was a bit shy for that position, not being willing to give me his name. Is Vince's last name spelled: F A-L-L-O-N?"

"Yes, that's the spelling, and he's new to the position."

"I've been following up the call with research today. I have comments from the OCC press officer and a copy of the official press release. I read up on the frogs at the college library today. I needed you to corroborate that the person who phoned—Vince—is a member of your club, and you've done that. And I want to know what the club has planned."

Her exasperated reply was, "I don't know what the club will do now, but we have to do something. We have a mission, and the frogs are the local symbol for a global version of that mission. In the name of progress, the industrialized nations are destroying valuable resources. The U.S. has polluted tens of thousands of streams, rivers, lakes, and parts of the oceans. Much of the

Central American rain forests have been eliminated. I used to have hope for preservation by third-world countries. But they're following the lead of what most people call the most advanced nations. China's desire for electric power has displaced thousands of people along the Yangtze River and surely must be driving wildlife into or near extinction. We're trying to save a small colony of endangered tree frogs, but the change must begin locally and involve whatever is at hand. Within the next few days, we'll plan a strategy."

I got more copy from her than I had hoped. She obviously was bright and had a genuine concern. I finished my article and had it to Alex by 7:00.

CHAPTER FIVE

My first article was a straight news story, reporting the action of the Ocean County Board of Chosen Freeholders. It probably would have received little attention if the headline writer hadn't been at a party for several hours before crafting "College Club Croaks Caution." I don't have any proof, but I think my editor must have been at the same party. Kim, my nemesis and guardian of the door to Alex Speery's office, began, immediately after the article, to return my greeting with the exclamation "Ribbit. Ribbit."

The second article dug into the background of the bridge, the frogs, and the wooden roadbed, and added contrasting interviews with Roxanne and Gladys Helms, Director (effectively "President") of the Board of Freeholders. The difference of opinion was clearly progress (through improved traffic patterns) versus the environment. Mrs. Helms acknowledged that the frogs probably had a beneficial effect on reducing the insect population and was forthright in her insistence that the fate of Mother Earth was not dependent on the surface of the H. George Buckwald ("God bless his soul. A man of great vision.") Memorial Bridge.

As I approached the open doors of the auditorium for the regular meeting of the Environmental Club, the buzz of animated conversations poured into the hallway. Once inside the spacious room I noted an extraordinary amount of movement, in and out of the auditorium, from one seat to another, and up and down the aisles. The movement and a high level of noise as attendees spoke with one another, yelled across the space, and laughed heartily at comments by friends were consistent with my suspicion that tonight's meeting would be very important to my coverage of the fate of the frogs. I was there because Roxanne had told me there would be discussion about the decision to pave the bridge. I seated myself in my preferred vantage point, halfway down and in an aisle seat on the left side of the room. I was close enough to the front to hear well and to be able to see any audio-visual aids and near enough to the rear to be able to get a rough count of the audience. I had become expert at making quick counts of large gatherings. My count, made just before I sat, totaled 63. Another 40-50 arrived after my count.

Shortly after I seated myself and scanned the attendees, my attempt to find Roxanne was successful. We exchanged waves and smiles. We'd been in contact with each other several times since our first phone call. An interest in a set of events had expanded to a friendship. I was beginning to wonder if it was more than a friendship. My one phone call to her each week to check the progress of Environmental Club's concern about the threat to the frogs had gradually increased to two and then three weekly conversations, some initiated by her. I found myself picking up the phone to check an obscure detail as I wrote a second article.

Roxanne and I moved beyond phone calls to meeting at the Java Joint. Conversations moved from the Environmental Club and the frogs to our experiences as students—markedly different in terms of interests and academic success and for that reason intriguing to each other. We talked about our homes and families and early lives. Recently we had added our plans and dreams of the future. Sometimes I wondered about my ability to report objectively. Each time, I chose to ignore the issue.

Shortly after noting that Roxanne had disappeared from the front of the room, I felt a touch on my shoulder. As I looked up, she said, "I'm glad you could get this good seat." The smile on her lips and the bright twinkle in her brown eyes were signs of her pleasure at the size of turnout. "I'm so excited about the numbers here! I'll start in a couple of minutes. Can you wait at the end so we can get coffee and talk?"

"Best offer all day...to be honest, the only offer."

"I like that. See ya."

Three minutes later, she began the meeting on the nose of 8:00. "Welcome to this year's second regular meeting of the Environmental Club. I'm Roxanne Freeman, President. I'm thrilled to see so many people here tonight. We're always looking for more people to help us save our local part of the Earth. If this is the first time you're here, and that probably includes quite a few of you, please see me or one of the other club officers before you leave the meeting so that we can add you to our emailing list about club activities. Club officers have name tags like this one I'm wearing."

Roxanne continued her remarks, "Although this is a regular meeting, the agenda tonight is irregular. An important part of our campus environment is facing an immediate threat. Most people are unaware that there is an endangered variety of frogs living under the Buckwald Bridge. In fact, most people don't know even that we have a bridge." Some scattered laughs occurred, interspersed with short, quiet conversations as those who were aware of the bridge informed those near them.

Roxanne offered some help. "If you're leaving the campus and take H. George Buckwald Drive (the short road beside the large parking lot near the athletic fields) to Church Road, you cross one of the world's smallest bridges over the home of the Pine Barrens tree frogs. These frogs are on the list of endangered species.

"The plan of the county freeholders to pave over the wood road surface is a threat to those frogs. The surface is made of bongossi wood. Many years ago, it was installed in compliance with an agreement with the New Jersey Department of Environmental Protection. We believe that the petroleum base of any asphalt paving material will kill or will alter the gene structure of the frogs. We're here tonight to plan for action to reverse the freeholders' decision."

After Roxanne introduced him as publicity chairman, Vince Fallon moved quickly to the microphone. A ripple of comments moved across the surface of the crowd as Vince rose from his seat at the end of the first row and moved to podium at the opposite side of the floor. "Whatever he says, I'll pay attention!"

"He has my attention already!" Those remarks came from the females. Remarks by males revealed a different perspective: "I hope this is short! I don't need details on the frogs. I came to meet girls."

"This looks like the right place. There are about three of them for every one of us."

"We ought to know what's going on so we can decide if we're going to stick with this club."

Vince was always noticed for his good looks with an attractive face containing soft brown eyes and an athletic body extending over his six-foot height. After having seen, or at least having heard, him most people concluded that he was very smart and well informed.

Vince spread sheets of papers in front of the microphone and cleared his throat. "I'll keep my report brief. You don't need to be an expert on the topic, just informed enough to help make decisions. When the bridge was built in the 1980s, the DEP prohibited the use of chemically treated wood or other usual materials because the bridge stands in an area where the frogs, on the list of endangered species, breed. That's why bongossi word, a tropical timber with the hardness of mahogany, was used instead of concrete or asphalt."

Vince continued, "The frogs need a specific pH, a certain mix of acid and base, in the water. Both wood and concrete treated with creosote were banned so they wouldn't leech lime into the water and upset the pH balance. The DEP permit on the bridge prohibits the use of salt or chemicals for snow and ice removal on the bridge. The ban leads to closing of the bridge when covered by snow or ice because plowing would tear up the wood. These measures are covered in the DEP permit which was issued under terms of the Coastal Area Facility Review Act, usually shortened to the acronym 'CAFRA.' And now, our enlightened Board of Freeholders turned its back on the agreement when it voted to possibly pave over the wood so the bridge can be strengthened and can be kept open all winter. Last winter the bridge was closed a total of six days, one and a half percent of the days in a year! The Club officers are worried that the petroleum base of the asphalt will kill the existing frogs or will cause genetic changes in their future offspring. I say we need to do something."

Applause was punctuated with shouted comments: "Let's act now!"

"What are we waiting for!"

"We need to tell people of the danger!" Vince returned to his seat, and Roxanne moved to the podium.

She raised her hand and spoke energetically, "Wait. There's other information you should know. There'll be time for questions and comments and an opportunity to suggest action."

When the comments stopped, she continued, "Our next speaker is Hunter Markham. He became interested in the Club at the Freshman Orientation just this year and joined at our last meeting. He's taken an interest in the politics of this case and has some comments to share."

Markham had been very impressed by the Dean of Students during the orientation and took to heart her comments about a new level of responsibility. His failure to get accepted at any of the colleges his parents had chosen as good preparation for his law school ambitions was the source of many arguments in his home and was the prelude to his father's declaration that he had no intention of sending him to any school except OCC. Wilson Markham, a third generation of Markham lawyers, an English major graduate of Duke and on Law Review while in attendance at American University Law, had exploded as the final rejection letter was read: "You'll have to reap what you sowed! You know you should've done better. There's nothing wrong with your brain. It looks like you'll do it the hard way again! Your last chance to prove your worth will be OCC."

Dumb jock had been an easy role to play, and the attention from classmates had provided great satisfaction. Hunter had played the part with zest. His father was right; his brain functioned very well. It was the use to which he put it that was the source of the friction. Hunter kept an accurate set of grade books in his head, enabling him to calculate with lightning speed just the grade he needed on any given assignment in order to maintain an overall C-average. Attention from classmates and satisfaction from pinpoint precision in the production of inferior grades were two motivations for deliberately screwing up. However, they were secondary in importance to avoidance of the fear that gripped him when he thought he might pour all his energy into pleasing his parents and miss the mark. He preferred to not try. After all, what had been his sister's gain from finishing her high school career as salutatorian? She continued her grinding schedule of advanced courses in college, majored in education, and in her third year now as a second grade teacher earned a salary of

$49,000. He experienced the downside of his charade when his early athletic prowess peaked during sophomore year and others surpassed him in football, basketball, and baseball. His father's benediction following his last sermon on the sins of sloth was, "If you screw this up, you're on your own."

Hunter had joined the Environmental Club as a sign to his father that he was following a new path. Roxanne had sensed his leadership potential and wanted to test her intuition by assigning him the project of learning in depth about the county freeholders. His ability to connect the outcome of his investigation with the paving decision had led her to ask him to be a part of the presentation. Even though Wilson Markham was a Republican supporter, his desire to have his son get "back on track" led to his strong encouragement to seize a rare public speaking opportunity.

"I thought the freeholders would be a collection of intelligent men and women who were able to balance the needs of the county; the school; the interests of the students, the freeholder's own mission to make a college education available to a diverse student body who, for whatever reason, would not have it available otherwise; and the good of the world," Hunter began. "It seems to me they've missed the point with the last item on the list, the good of the world. They can argue that their decision in this case addresses the interests of the students, but that's only in regard to the academic program. We need to show them that this club speaks for a broader idea of our interests. That idea is that we are interested in the future of wildlife and a delicate environmental balance.

"The freeholders gave permission to continue planning for the paving when it met last spring. There were only two very short meetings of the board over the summer, and they were dealing with budget and negotiations. Last month, about two weeks ago, they met again and made a final decision to look into the paving.

"Let me backtrack some. There are five trustees on the Board of Freeholders. Of that number, three are Republicans; their names are Gladys Helms (also President of the Board), John Wilson, and Alberto Hernandez. Two are Democrats: Sam Ferguson and Maggie Thomson. Thomson is a self proclaimed Independent, although she usually sides with Democrat Ferguson. The Republicans usually vote to support the recommendations of the administration, and the others can go either way. This time the vote reaffirmed the party lines; the Republican members voting 'Yes' in favor of the resolution to proceed with the paving while Ferguson and Thomson voted 'No.'

"Hernandez owns a construction company, and his yes vote extended his unbroken record of supporting any project involving construction. He said at the meeting that he had based his stance on the advice of Assistant Professor Morrison in the Science Department and the engineer for the county, Barbara Macintosh. Both said there would be no impact on the frogs. I've placed a number of phone calls to Macintosh but haven't had an answer. I want to know what study she did to lead to the conclusion of no impact; I'm guessing there was no study. I waited outside Morrison's lecture earlier this month and asked to speak with him. He told me to phone for an appointment. I did, and so far nothing has happened. And that's all I have to report. I'll keep trying to get answers from Morrison and Macintosh."

"Thanks, Hunter," Roxanne said with a smile. "You've done a lot for the club. Now I have a brief report on my contact with the DEP and an outline of a general plan. Then we'll get to questions and answers and discussion of what we want to do as the Environmental Club.

"A few days after I learned that the freeholders had authorized the county administration to proceed with planning for the paving of the bridge, I phoned the New Jersey Department of Environmental Protection to alert them to the decision and to ask what action could be taken to stop the project. I was told that there was nothing DEP could do because it was an authorization for planning and not a final decision. I was told also that a complaint was out of the question for the same reason. I was talking with a department staff member who was very helpful. She sounded young, and I think she is fairly new to the department. She warned me that filing of a complaint and following up on it could be very expensive and very time-consuming. Nearly all complaints are filed by attorneys because the average person isn't well enough informed and has not had the experience to be able to complete all the documents and file everything acceptably. She offered to come to the college to speak to our club. I think we should ask her to speak.

"If we're going to have any success with reversing the decision made last month, we should pick up the pace of our work. We've been able to get two articles in the *Press* as a result of the interest of Jeff Stewart, a reporter, who is here tonight. Jeff, would you raise your hand or stand up?" she asked as she pointed in my direction and nodded.

31

I hate to be introduced. I'm often more effective in gathering information if people don't know my identity. Since my cover was blown, I waved and quickly put my hand down. There was some scattered applause. I made a mental note to talk with Roxanne about my preference to be unidentified.

She continued with her action plan. "I think we should get Kate McGuire from DEP to speak at our meeting next month. If anyone knows of an attorney who would consider pro bono work to file a DEP complaint, ask her or him and let me know if you're successful. We also should make contact with the Toms River Council, with the OCC Board of Trustees, and with all environmental groups we can identify to make them aware of our concerns and to ask for their help."

"Now it's your turn, time for audience input. If you want to speak, please raise your hand and be recognized so that we can hear each person."

The first speaker called on was one of those who called out earlier. He stood about 6'4" and probably weighed no more than one-eighty, producing a gangly look. His brown hair was cut short, and heavily rimmed glasses suggested a devotion to academic pursuits. As he spoke, he waved both hands. "We need to have a demonstration. Most people don't read the newspaper. Those who do don't pay attention. They're spectators and not actors. DEP will take too long. It's good to make contact with the Council and the Board of Trustees, but they won't do anything unless they're fired up."

Loud applause was the response.

Roxanne waited for the applause to die and then said, "Would you please state your name so that all of us can know who you are?"

The first speaker stood and called out, "Aaron Steltzin. I'm a third-year student."

Many hands were raised now that the ice was broken. Roxanne recognized others who followed with questions, comments, and calls for action.

"I'm Beverly DeAngelis of the *Shopper News*," began the next speaker, as she tucked her pen behind her ear. I had noticed her taking notes and wondered if she was an "outsider" like me or perhaps an older student. Her first statement identified her to be both an outsider and a sister journalist. She continued, "My question is for Hunter Markham. Mr. Markham, did you intend to imply that you think Assistant Professor Morrison and Engineer Macintosh didn't conduct any research study before stating there would be no harm to the frogs and that the freeholders voting in favor of the paving merely rubber-stamped the administration's recommendation?"

Roxanne gestured toward Hunter who walked quickly to the podium, starting his response at the same moment he arrived squarely behind the microphone. "I intended to report the facts without implication. It appears that you have inferred the additional meaning. I want to know what information Morrison and Macintosh considered in reaching their conclusions because I don't know of any to support their conclusions. That being the case, it may be that the freeholders voting yes for the paving have seen some more information than I have, or that they chose not to believe the information I have seen, or that they cast their votes without asking for supporting documentation. We need to know the strength of their convictions and any scientific support for those convictions."

Ms. DeAngelis replied, "Thanks for the clarification," and then moved out of the way for the next speaker to take over the mic.

The short and very attractive female with hair that had been bleached silver spoke with a mellow voice, "My name's Brittany Foster. Roxanne knows me, but for the benefit of the audience, I joined the Environmental Club last year. We have to do something to protect the frogs. I mean, the people who were elected as freeholders maybe don't care because they're too old and don't pay attention to what they're doing to ruin our world. They'll be gone when half the animals are extinct, and we'll live with the results, you know? I say I second what Aaron said; let's take action." She stood there for a moment as if expecting some audience reaction, and then walked to her seat when there was no reaction.

"Adam Worthington. I've been at this school for three years before this one. I haven't seen the student body stand up for any cause." The short, attractive, and well-dressed male spoke rapidly and with a soft voice. "No one lives on campus so there's limited social mixing. Most of us are off to jobs after our classes end for the day, or we come to afternoon classes after working the morning. I think we should speak up and demand a reversal of the decision. If you want a planning committee, I'm in." He walked back to his seat as fast as he had talked.

The next person to the microphone introduced herself, "I'm Colleen Townsend." Both those names were no surprise, coming from an obviously

Irish lass with dark hair and thousands of freckles. "I think we should meet with the person from the DEP. You said she's young and new with them. Maybe she'll relate to our group trying to do something that's ecologically sound. She could be a help."

As a two-person conversation was spoken into a microphone, Roxanne commented between speakers, "She may be young. She sounded like it. She was helpful. I'm planning to meet with her; it's a question of whether we want her as a speaker."

Colleen replied, "I meant we should have her speak."

"I'm Robin Gustafsen," began the next speaker whose tall, thin stature drew attention away from a plain beauty. She spoke firmly and without expression, "In Bio we just finished reading and discussing Rachel Carson's *Silent Spring*. That book's pretty old, and people are still doing stupid things. If we have a demonstration, I think my instructor would speak about the book."

Speakers continued to be recognized and come forward. I counted nineteen. At the end of forty minutes, Roxanne announced that she would recognize one more person and then end that part of the meeting. After the last speaker, who added nothing new, Roxanne said, "It seems clear what the majority of you want to do. I'm going to check to make sure. Everyone who's here can participate in this poll, not just official members. I hope we can count on most new people joining next month and staying involved. I'll give you three choices. One, decide now to have a demonstration. Two, don't demonstrate but take some other action to be determined by official club members. Three, wait to make a decision next month after hearing a speaker from DEP."

The vote came out as I had expected. Probably everyone there had expected the same thing; it was clear from Roxanne's comments that she had expected it. Fifty-one chose to decide then to have a demonstration. Seventeen wanted to take some other action. Fourteen wanted to decide at next month's meeting. I saw a few people vote twice and several who didn't vote at all.

I was impressed by Roxanne from our first phone conversation. Her next action was widely accepted by those at the meeting, while it maintained compliance with the club's charter. She requested that all official club members in attendance come to the front of the room and vote by recording on the current membership list either the number "1" (indicating authorization for the officers to plan a demonstration as soon as possible but with enough time to permit adequate publicity and with full obedience to college rules and local laws) or the number "2" (indicating postponement of a decision for action until next month's meeting). She promised to make the results known immediately. She asked that those in attendance who were not yet members and wanted to join and/or who wanted to be notified of meetings and other activities go to the side table and record their names and leave their email addresses.

Fifteen minutes later she called for attention and announced the outcome of the membership vote: Thirty-nine authorized the officers to plan a demonstration while seven voted to wait until next month.

═══════════

Shortly after 10:00, we left together. To say Roxanne was hyper would have been a gross understatement. Her smile was so continuous it looked permanent. She chattered about the bright future of the club with forty-six regular members showing up and voting and with an audience of more than 100 and twenty-eight non-members signing up to receive more information. She said she was hungry so we headed for Charlie Brown's in place of the Java Joint.

As we got out of our cars in the parking lot, she wrapped her arm around mine, kissed me on the cheek, and quietly said, "This is the happiest I've been in a long time. Many things are going right for me."

CHAPTER SIX

I love to write, but having the freedom to set my own schedule is another benefit of being a reporter. I slept later than usual the day after the big Environmental Club meeting and awoke thinking about what had happened. It was a big night for Roxanne and me also. We went out to eat, talked more than usual, and kissed for the first time.

Last night's kissing was kind of a surprise, not a complete surprise because we had been talking on the phone more frequently and had gone out for coffee. I had even met her mother—a chance meeting as I drove Roxanne home. Her mother was getting out of her car after a church meeting as we drove up. When she invited me for coffee, I couldn't very well turn her down although we had each finished two lattes at the Java Joint. I thought my meeting of her mother meant our relationship was moving beyond just a friendship.

It was her kiss on my cheek in the parking lot at Charlie Brown's that got things started. Her declaration of how well her life was going swelled my head. Then we held hands after finishing our food and during the walk back to our cars. Saying "good night" included holding each other, sometimes seeming desperate, including several long kisses. I wondered if I was ready for a new level of relationship. I enjoyed talking with her and looked forward to our trips to the Java Joint. I felt great as I got in my car last night. I guess my problem the next morning was that I had thought only about how good I felt and didn't wonder what our kisses meant to her. I warned myself to enjoy what was happening and to not ruin that with lots of analysis.

On my way up the stairs at work—slower this time so I wouldn't be out of breath—I made the decision to ignore, or appear to ignore Kim. It was a timely decision. With a coy smile, she greeted me, "You must have been getting your beauty rest. You're later than usual. Or maybe you did something special last night." The last three words were accompanied by a tilt of her head and were followed by biting the end of a pen.

"You might think I was having a good time, but I was working hard."

"I'm so sorry! I'd like your hard work to always lead to a good time."

I gave up, again. I should enter her office waving a white flag. "I think Alex is expecting me."

"He is. We expect a lot from you. Go in."

Alex looked up with phone to his ear and waved me toward his desk, pointing at the chair I usually took. "We can stretch the Middletown council report to make up the lack of news in *Wall*. It looks like seven inches and headline will fill the third page of the local section. I think it just walked into my office. Count on it unless I phone you in the next ten minutes."

He hung up, closed a folder, and looked at me. Alex was one of the few people I know who looks like he was crafted for his occupation. He dressed meticulously yet rarely wore the jacket of his suit while in his office. Each sleeve of his dress shirt was rolled twice. Bifocals perched toward the end of his nose verified that he was required to read heavily while on the job. His hair was turning white, but its light brown color disguised that development. His 6'2" height and fit torso gave him a somewhat youthful appearance. I spoke first, "So I've been reduced to seven inches and a headline? That's sad. I hope my folks don't find out. They're still paying off home equity loans for college."

"Hey, seven inches and a headline is testimony to achievement. It's a whole lot more than my next-door neighbor has to report, and his kid graduated a year before you. My nephew has changed careers three times in two years. You could get a longevity award in that crowd.

"Let me see the meeting article no later than 2:00. Tomorrow I'm also running your article on the cost of the new super ladder trucks and the number of fire departments that have added on to their stations to house them. That was clever detective work on the relationship between height of the ladders and the local building code height restrictions. You were so thorough that I had to edit out about four or five inches."

"Your cuts hurt a little, but they don't hurt as much as the job of adding a few inches." I stood and excused myself. "The clock's ticking. I'd better get at it."

———

It was on the weekend three days later when my schedule and Roxanne's enabled us to talk. She had spent hours on the phone working on details of the demonstration program. Her reliable members who had attended the lunch meeting were enthusiastically picking up their responsibilities. I remembered my college years and how easy it was to devote hours to a special project and ignore class assignments.

Roxanne was most excited about having gotten an agreement to participate by Kate McGuire of the Department of Environmental Protection; the agreement was contingent upon approval by the commissioner of the DEP. I was intrigued from the start by Roxanne's information about Kate: very bright, bachelors in science from Oberlin College and masters in engineering from New Jersey Institute of Technology, named assistant commissioner of DEP and head of the Wetlands Division at age 28, described by Roxanne as "a beautiful redhead who takes charge and doesn't let anyone stand in the way." When I reacted to the description with the question "What more could anyone want?" I got one of those looks from the corner of her eyes. I don't think she was worried, only having fun. We still were enjoying being together and finding our way through a developing relationship. Our conversations frequently were accompanied by touching each other and our walks by arms around each other. It was like electricity when my hand landed on her hip as I reached to pull her close. Her smiles and light laughter during these demonstrations of affection told me all was well.

———

We went to Surf Taco the next Friday for what was probably our first official "date." It was easy for me to say, "I'm impressed by your vision and organization in moving the demonstration forward. It takes special talent to get a group of different people pulling in the same direction."

"Oh, thanks! Your saying that is important to me. I like the way we're moving in the same direction."

I reached across the table and took her hands in mine and offered a long distance air kiss. She returned the air kiss.

Between exclamations of "Delicious!" "Oooo, that's really good!" and "Fantastic. I don't know what I like best," she said, "I got a report from Keeshon today about his visit on Wednesday to see the band he has known as "Jeep Space," "2 Bing," and "Wasted Spring."

"At the end of his report, Keeshon said, 'By the way, the band is good enough for the purpose we want.' He worked with them on a name for the event, and they'll call themselves 'Green Shade.'"

I couldn't resist saying, "I think they should call themselves 'Chameleon.'"

She laughed softly and replied, "That would eliminate all the fun of finding new names. Keesh's final words were thanks for giving him an assignment that found a new girl and one who can dance."

We ended our dinner with fried ice cream (a Mexican dessert) and coffee. While we ate the dessert, Roxanne said she was enjoying the evening so much that she hoped I would come into her house for a while.

I readily agreed that the evening was fun and that continuing it was a good idea. As we entered her house, her father called from the rear of the house as we heard his footsteps approaching the front foyer, "Is that you Roxie?" I saw her wrinkle her nose at the nickname that no one but her parents was permitted to use.

"Yes, it's me. Jeff is with me."

"Jeff, it's good to meet you." He extended his hand. He must have worn his big smile often because there were permanent laugh-line wrinkles beside each eye. His skin was darker than most African-Americans. A gleaming gold crown caught the light as his smiles grew. "I've heard about you, of course, from both Roxie and her mom. I'm glad to have a pleasant face to put with the name.

"Since Roxie met you, I started paying attention to bylines on articles in the *Press*. I saw your name recently on the public employees' salaries article. I liked that. I told the people at work that my daughter knows that reporter."

"Thanks for the compliment. I guess I have printer's ink in my veins. I can't imagine doing any other type of work."

"You put two men together for a few minutes, and they'll talk about work every time!" Roxanne said as she entered the living room. "Daddy, I'm skipping my ice cream tonight because we had a delicious meal and finished it with Mexican fried ice cream. I thought we might have some soda or iced tea. Will you join us?"

"No, I've been working on the photo albums and have had enough for tonight. I'm taking my magazine up and keeping your mother company." He started toward the stairs. "Jeff, you're welcome here anytime. I hope you know that."

"Oh, thank you, Mr. Freeman," I replied. And then with a slight laugh, "Be careful what you say!"

He laughed politely and finished with, "Good night."

Roxie asked, "Do you mind looking at family photos? I love to."

"Don't mind a bit. I'll get to know some other things about your family."

"Is soda or iced tea okay?" she asked as she took my hand and walked toward the kitchen.

"Make mine decaf soda. Otherwise I may not get to sleep tonight."

With glasses of soda, we moved to the family room, and Roxanne motioned to the couch. "That's where Daddy works on the photo albums."

There was a neat pile of photos next to an album. I had expected tape and scissors and a pen or two covering a substantial area. "Is he always this neat when he works on something? My apartment is messier than this after I've cleaned it."

"He's very meticulous, either the result of his years of work as a draftsman or the reason he chose that occupation."

"Your whole house is orderly, spotless, and beautiful."

"Thanks. I'll make sure I repeat that comment to both of them. Mommy says she's never happier at the store than when she's straightening up the merchandise."

"What store does she work in?"

"Boscov's. In women's clothing. They love her at work because she is happy straightening. The other clerks prefer not to do that job. It's all part of her philosophy for living: 'Share the load' or 'Do your part; It's much lower priority Lord.' 'Praise God for your life and the bounty you enjoy,' 'Treat others the way you want to be treated,' 'Serve God by serving your fellow Man.' I can't tell you how many times a day I hear her voice giving me direction."

"I hope you know that what you have is unusual and it's shaped you into a special person." We were seated on the couch, and I took her hand. "That's my assessment, and the other evidence indicates the same—chosen by your schoolmates to be president of the Environmental Club, high grades in your classes, and success with a job. A very consistent picture."

After I kissed her lightly, she used her other hand on the back of my head to prevent me from turning away. "I think you're pretty special too. I don't think you know how special." And she began a long and forceful kiss. I left an hour later with certainty that our relationship was on a new level. We never looked at a family photo.

———————

Vince Fallon phoned the next day while he was on lunch break. He said that because my article on the decision to demonstrate had identified him as publicity chairman, a source whom he couldn't identify had notified him that OCC President George had sent memos to others in the administration outlining procedures to be followed for approval of campus events and reminding them of the importance of maintaining a positive public image of quality education in a harmonious atmosphere free of politics and student unrest. He said he thought I would be interested and might know the way to get copies of the memos.

CHAPTER SEVEN

Roxanne sat up quickly as her alarm sounded at 6:00. When she raised her shade slightly, she was relieved that there was no sign of rain. She had chosen a light wool pantsuit in anticipation of a cold start to the day. After stepping into the maroon pants, she donned a white long-sleeve knit top to underlay the suit jacket, expecting a need to remove the jacket before the end of the demonstration.

A bowl of steaming oatmeal sitting at her place on the table surprised her, and she looked quickly to find her mother pouring a glass of orange juice for her. "Mommy, you should have slept in; it's Saturday."

"I know, sweetie. But I want to send you off right with a full belly and smile on your way to today's big event."

Roxanne gave her mother a hug and kiss. "You're the best, and I'm so blessed to be your daughter!"

After she sat down and said a silent blessing, her mother responded to her previous comment, "As a daughter you're a blessing in return. This morning you're going off to lead others in carrying out the stewardship that God assigned to humans. You live your faith daily. I won't be there in person today, but I'll be praying for you." Her mother read passages from the Bible while she and Roxanne ate. The readings attested to the responsibility of all people to protect Earth, the flora and fauna, and other people. At 6:45 Roxanne said a happy goodbye and left for her drive to the campus.

Roxanne was just starting to arrange some of the chairs on the stage when she heard, "Is this what it means to be chosen chairperson?"

She began talking as she turned to the direction of the voice, "I prefer Madam Chairperson." She started walking toward Jeff.

They kissed quickly and brought each other up to date as they moved toward the area for speakers, she telling him the length of her short night and how sweet her mother had been to get up to fix breakfast on a Saturday, he telling her about also having an extended Friday and asking if she had seen his photographer who had agreed to arrive by 8:00.

She checked her watch and said, "He's five minutes before he's late. I didn't expect you to be here two hours early."

"Today's photographer is female. For my article on today's demonstration, I want to capture the context by observing all the preparation. And that's a good excuse to spend time with you on a beautiful day like today."

Roxanne's smile grew, and she said, "That feels so good to hear!" She kissed him on his cheek, making a loud "Mmmmm" sound and finishing with an audible smack.

"I guess I should have caught that action on film. Sorry, guy." They turned quickly and laughed when they saw the approaching photographer.

"I'm happy you didn't catch that on film," Jeff replied. "We don't want a charge of biased coverage on my part. Janice Sims, meet Roxanne Freeman."

Janice Sims was attractive without being "pretty" or "cute." She shared with fellow photographers the use of a few small canisters in which to carry unused rolls of film (unused on the left side, each fully-exposed roll placed in an empty canister and then attached to the right of the strap).

Once back together with Jeff, Roxanne remarked, "I'm starting to wonder about Kate. She promised to be here by 9:00, but she's usually early. What car does she drive because someone just pulled in?"

"I think it's a Honda—something with good gas mileage."

She looked in the direction Jeff was pointing. "Yes, that's her. I can see the red hair. Come with me so the two of you can meet."

Jeff told Janice to wait where they were, and he walked with Roxanne. Once alone, she said, "I think she'll measure up to the expectations you have for beauty, brains, and success." The last was said with a lilt to her voice. When Jeff didn't respond, she pushed him playfully and said, "Lighten up; I'm teasing."

The three met halfway between their starting points. The two women embraced and exchanged pleasantries. Then Roxanne made the introductions. "Kate, this is Jeff."

The two shook hands, and in unison the two said, "I've heard so much about you."

They laughed, and Roxanne joined them, saying, "Great duet! Just needs accompaniment."

Kate looked up, spread her hands with palms up, and said, "Just look at this day! How did you arrange something so beautiful? Maybe we could have this every day if we all were as religious as you."

"I'm as pleased as you with this weather. If there were a way for me to call for it daily and have it happen, I'd do that," Roxanne replied. "I don't have that type of power, so I'll try to enjoy as much as you."

Jeff watched Kate closely, noting the soft red shade of her hair, which must have been strawberry blonde at some time in her life. His smile was like a sympathetic response as he watched her green eyes dance and the skin at their corners wrinkle. He spoke, "Kate, I need to interview you at some time this morning for the article I'll write about today's event. It might be easier for both of us if I do that soon before other responsibilities start to dominate our time."

"That works for me. Rox, will that work for you?"

"That's a good idea, sweetie," she said to Jeff as she placed her hand on his arm, causing him to stop staring at Kate. "The band should arrive anytime. Keeshon said they will be tuned up and ready to blast by 9:25. You two be good!" She kissed Jeff, turned, and headed for the platform.

Jeff opened his pad and pulled out the pen. "Rox has told me the basics of your background. I should confirm those things with you."

He ran quickly through the facts and then asked about Oberlin College. She replied, "I went to Oberlin undecided between a major in music and in science. I chose science after my first two years because I had some wonderful professors and because there seemed to be more likelihood of finding a job, especially since I was a woman in a field dominated by men. There were so many musicians at Oberlin, and the Career Counseling Department supplied information about the estimated number of music majors who are employed in other careers. I made my musical interest my minor. I first thought I'd do lab work or teach. A sophomore field experience in an education course led to the decision to complete coursework for certification to teach." She paused to let Jeff catch up with his notes.

"What was your instrument?"

"Violin—another reason to think there were too many people wanting careers in my specialty."

"Did you graduate with more credits than were required for a standard bachelors degree? With a music minor, lab courses required for your major, and completion of certification requirements you must have worked very hard."

"I had 145 credits in place of the usual 120. I averaged eighteen credits a semester. I worked my fanny off."

With a laugh in his voice, Jeff said, "Let me pause to consider that image."

With her eyes sparkling, Kate gave a sideways glance and said with sultry voice, "Take your time. I don't want you to lose focus."

"You're my focus, and that's an enjoyable task. What happened to the plan to teach?"

"I decided if I earned my credentials as an environmental engineer, I probably would have the opportunity for a greater impact on the present than I would preparing high school students to maybe fill the vacancies in that field. So I changed direction."

"I imagine you had many job opportunities available to you with your impressive and unusual background. Why did you go to work for DEP?"

"A cabinet-level department within a state government seemed to be a good place to have maximum impact on the present. My experience there has been consistent with that conclusion."

"Within the DEP, what are your major responsibilities as head of the Division of Watershed Management?"

"It's probably easiest if I define the territory first. A watershed is the area of land that drains into a body of water such as a river, lake, stream, or bay. It includes not only the waterway itself but also the entire land area that drains to it. For example, the watershed of a lake would include not only the streams entering the lake but also the land area that drains into those streams and eventually the lake. Drainage basins generally refer to large watersheds that encompass the watersheds of many smaller rivers and streams. Some of our primary concerns are ground water, storm water, pollution, and conservation."

"Give me a minute to catch up with my notes. That's a lot of information at one time."

As Jeff wrote rapidly, Kate studied his body. She concentrated on his head and what she could see of his face, then watched his hands before finishing with a glance down his body and legs. Her expressions showed interest and approval.

"There, I'm caught up. What have been the two most important cases in your division since you became head?"

"One is the continuing case of chemical infiltration of the aquifer in the western portion of Toms River, involving, first, the discharge by the Alliance Chem Products Corporation directly into one of the streams and, second, the continuing seepage from storage areas on the property which was reported to have been cleaned up. That case has led to periodic and then permanent closure of one of the major wells supplying water to the community. Another is also a continuing case, this one involving periodic accidents and antiquated equipment at the Oyster Creek nuclear power plant in Lacey Township. In addition to the usual questions about contamination and possibilities of meltdowns with an older plant, there are events where water temperatures during some of the accidents have become high enough to kill fish and other organisms in the creek."

"If you're game for more questions, I have only two more prepared. Then you can tell me anything you want, or we can end the interview."

"Fire away. I do want to get over where Roxanne is, but two more should take only a short time."

"What knowledge do you have about this case at the college?"

"Our department was involved at the time the original bongossi wood surface was installed. Of course, that was before my time with the department, but I've studied the background for today's…let's call it an event. The DEP was wholeheartedly in support and found it a responsible action. If we had had then the awards program we do now, it would have been a sure winner. The Pine Barren frog has been designated an endangered species for a long time. Following the report we received about the exploration of macadam paving of the bridge by the Ocean County Board of Chosen Freeholders, we made some enquiries and discovered that the only decision made was to continue planning. When they decided in September to go ahead with the planned paving, we increased our efforts and notified the freeholders of possible legal action."

"What do you mean 'legal action'? Are you talking about an injunction or fines or something else?"

"I can't elaborate. Our discussions have been privileged."

"I think I know your answer to this, but I need to ask. What is your conclusion about the action of the County Freeholders' decision to pave the bridge over the frogs' habitat?"

"If your prediction of my answer was 'No comment,' you're right on target."

"That's what I expected. I understand. Let's walk together."

As they started toward the speakers' platform, Kate said, "Now it's my turn to ask questions to learn about you. Your job must be fascinating. Did you always plan to be a reporter?"

———————

As Roxanne exchanged pleasantries with Colleen Townsend, she looked in the direction of the interview for the second time since she arrived. Colleen asked, "Who's that with Jeff?"

"Kate McGuire from DEP."

"From here she looks stunning."

"She's even more gorgeous up close!"

"I guess it's a good idea to watch your boyfriend when he's with a beauty like that!"

"Are you trying to feed my anxieties? I thought we were pretty good friends."

"Sorry," Colleen offered as she backed away.

Jeff and Kate talked animatedly and laughed periodically as she interviewed him during their walk to Roxanne's location.

———————

Roxanne moved to the mic and shouted, "That's Green Shade, our special band for the day." As she applauded, the audience joined her, the lead guitar struck a chord with vibrato, and the drummer repeated his flourish.

As Roxanne held up her hands, the applause and shouts ended. When eighty percent of the quiet had been restored, she began, "I'm so pleased to see people here today. I'm Roxanne Freeman, and I'm President of the Environmental Club here on campus." Over the sound of medium applause, she continued, "The club is dedicated to inform as many people as possible of the need to maintain the delicate balance in the ecosystems all over the world. Today we're here to try to reverse a decision that threatens an endangered species on our campus. The Ocean County government has voted to consider a project to pave the special wood surface of the bridge out here," she gestured behind her, "and we know that it's wrong! We need your help to get the word out and to express your opposition." The audience, which had grown by 100 or more within the last few minutes, cheered, yelled "Yeah!" and applauded.

A member of the audience shouted, "Save the frogs!" The audience turned the remark into a chant: "Save the frogs! Save the frogs! Save the frogs!"

In order to get back control, Roxanne raised one hand and then both. Her action, together with boredom in shouting the same phrase, eventually succeeded. Quickly she announced, "I give you as our first speaker Senator McMahon. The senator's position on the Agriculture and Natural Resources Committee in the State Assembly makes him an important leader. Give a warm OCC welcome to the senator!"

As he walked to the mic, the crowd enthusiastically applauded him. With a broad smile and both hands raised, he began his remarks and then repeated the start as the noise abated, "I'm proud to be here with all of you today... Yes, I'm proud to be here to share your concern about the protection of an endangered species. I know the freeholders of this special county, and I respect each and every one of them. I know they had good reason for their decision, but I think they were so intent on improving human lives through efficient and safe traffic flow that they didn't sufficiently explore the environmental issues. I commend your Environmental Club leaders and membership for providing this forum to educate the public and to draw attention to a small but important issue. Governmental decision-makers in the past have often overlooked consideration of how improvement of human lives impacts the total ecosystem. At the state level in New Jersey, we're getting better at this, and I hope we can provide a model for other governmental levels in the state, for other states, and for the national government. Make your appeal to the reason of the freeholders and the total community. I pledge to do what I can. Now I have to get to a meeting of state mayors, and I'll tell them what you're doing here today."

The crowd erupted into loud cheering and shouting. The senator clasped his hands and raised them above his head, then transitioned that gesture into two thumbs up. The noise which had begun to subside grew in strength again as he vigorously shook the hands of all other speakers.

"Our next speaker is a prize for us. He's an international expert and has traveled from north Jersey to impress on all of us that there are worldwide implications of local actions and our case is a good example. Dr. Max Eberhardt is the Victor Wilson Distinguished Professor of Environmental Engineering at New Jersey Institute of Technology. He has authored several texts and other books on ecology. One book I have here with me, *Nature's Chorus Silenced*, won recognition by the international organization Global Eco-action. Consider yourselves fortunate to hear such a renowned expert address the issue of our tiny frogs."

Loud applause greeted the blushing speaker. He ran his hands across his pink, high forehead and through his white hair. After straightening his glasses, he squinted into the sun. He coughed nervously and began with an apology, "I hope you don't mind my wearing this hat, but it helps me be able to see you." As he spoke, he removed a tan hat with floppy brim and placed it on his head.

"That's much better for me." Another cough. "You people here at the shore are giving good support today for action that needs to be repeated around the world in all places possible. Destruction of portions of the environment may have been excusable before we had knowledge that environments were being destroyed and knowledge of how the destruction takes place. Now that we have knowledge, such destruction is inexcusable. People responsible for destruction may have a rationale for what they do. But, if you don't support the rationale, their actions are inexcusable.

"Deciding where to start and how much to say is a problem within what otherwise is the rich opportunity provided by a forum of this type." He removed his hat, ran his hand through his hair again, and then replaced the hat. "I'll just dive in here and ask Ms. Freeman to signal me if I'm going on too long."

Following an extended presentation of highlights of the "Millennium Eco-system Assessment," a presentation whose significance was lost on an increasingly restless crowd, Eberhardt segued into his next strand of scholarly discussion:

"But I'm not all about gloom and doom." Professor Eberhardt moved his eyes slowly across the audience as he said, "I guess that's good news to most of you," a statement which drew laughter and expressions of surprise. "I want to conclude with a report of positive environmental change, which has had the impact of stimulating greater human prosperity in Costa Rica."

Eberhardt drew to a close. "My purpose today has been to emphasize the connections between the events in one part of an ecosystem and results in another part. Of course, the tree frogs on the college campus is quite different in scope from transformation of a Central American nation which had been devastated by slash-and-burn tactics and a gamble on a new agro-industry. I hope you see the balance within our environment. I especially hope you can help to educate others, including the government at your county. 'Turn the rascals out!' was a slogan of the past. 'Turn their actions around!' probably is more useful. So will you join me in repeating that directive?"

He began a chant that was joined by a large proportion of the audience: "Turn their actions around!"

"Turn their actions around!"

Initial cheers changed to the chant of "Go, Doc! Go, Doc!"

After he shook hands with Roxanne, he turned to the crowd with a huge smile, removed his hat with his left hand, and pumped his right hand again. The audience continued to applaud. He sat down but stood up twice to wave.

Kate checked her watch during the applause, caught Roxanne's attention, and Roxanne gave an exaggerated nod. When the applause stopped, Kate moved directly to the microphone. "Good morning!" she said and then waited, indicating a response was expected.

From the generally coordinated response a few voices stood out, clearly commenting on her startling appearance: "Good morning!" and "Goooooood morning!"

"I'm Kate McGuire from the New Jersey Department of Environmental Protection. Your warm reception quiets my anxiety about being on next after a rousing presentation like Dr. Eberhardt just made. I'm here to make some general remarks about the topic that brought us all together. I'll tell you up front that I'm limited in what I can say because we are in discussions with the County Board of Freeholders."

A low-level, yet audible, murmur spread through the audience.

"Senator McMahon said that the Board of Freeholders may have overlooked the consideration of how improvement of human lives impacts the total environment. My department was involved with the plans for construction of the current bridge. Bongossi wood is durable yet is eco-friendly. The use of dowel rods to hold the planking in place avoided the problem of oxidation and possible contamination that might have been the case with nails. The plan was excellent and gave protection to the habitat. DEP files gave us the background we needed on the current disagreement. The first call we received about the paving came after the freeholders had approved continuation of the planning process. We could take no official action because there was no approval of action. The August decision by the freeholders to advertise for contractors' bids for the paving took the project to a different level. At that point, the DEP could make an official inquiry.

"The DEP's responsibilities and authorization to act have changed over the years, but New Jersey has been in the forefront of protecting people and the environment. The protection of people is generally clear and usually uncontested. The responsibility includes pollution, historic pesticides in the soil, and chemical and radioactive contamination. Protection of the environment is where we encounter much of our controversy and, over a lengthy period, have often encountered controversy on both sides of a particular situation—too much protection and not enough protection. Included are flooding and erosion, tree and plant issues, sewage flows, oversight of energy sources, and protection of a wide variety of species. In New Jersey, the species range from endangered snakes and turtles through fish (whether fresh water, seafood, or shellfish) to birds and hunting of game (including deer and bears)."

With a broader smile and a change in tone of voice, Kate said, "That last part was a public service infomercial." As light laughter broke out, she looked at Roxanne who was on her cell phone briefly.

She continued, "Back to the action of the freeholders. After their decision to solicit bids for the paving, we began the official inquiry process. We also have had some face-to-face discussions that have reviewed the history, have reviewed the obligations of the DEP to oversee and protect, and have reviewed the full range of possible DEP actions."

She paused to close that portion of her remarks and then concluded, "That's all I can tell you because to go further with what we know and what we have done has potential for interfering with a process that is largely legal. On behalf of my department, I offer our services to provide information and to help in any way. I ask that you get progress reports on this issue by way of Roxanne Freeman and information released by the Environmental Club because you are likely to become frustrated in seeking information from DEP that we can't give you. Your local newspaper, *The Asbury Park Press*, is also a good source of the latest news.

"Before I leave I want to commend the college for permitting the Environmental Club to hold this forum. It promotes responsible participation in democratic action. Thank you."

Prior to a program break, which enabled early speakers to leave, Roxanne thanked the departees. During the break, the band played. Getting attention back proved to be a challenge, but she managed it successfully. As she held up both hands and said the same sentence three times—"Let me have your attention please"—she thought that the number of audience members who had left had been offset by the number who had just arrived. She introduced Hunter Markham and explained that he would be followed directly by College Trustee Mrs. LaRosa.

Unlike Vince's report, Hunter had new information to add to an abbreviated version of his report at the September open meeting. "The Board of Freeholders approved the paving by one vote with one member of the board abstaining. We may be able to change one of the yeses and get a revote that could go the other way. Since their vote, we've had representatives present at their meetings, and our representatives have signed up to speak and have spoken. We've also had some letters written, but nothing has changed.

"Following the August vote, I tried to speak with the County Engineer Barbara Macintosh and Assistant Professor Morrison in the college Science Department, both of whom made statements at the August freeholder meeting that there would be no impact of the paving on the habitat of the frogs. Both avoided me initially, but they couldn't do that forever!"

Applause followed, and several shouts of "Go, Hunter!" were heard.

"They both cited the same three recent studies of encroachment of humans on the habitats of endangered species, all of which seem to show that such encroachment has had only minor impacts."

He cited relevant details then moved to statements by Macintosh and Morrison, which were intended to cast doubt on the validity of reports of the damage by the Exxon Valdez oil spill in Alaska.

"At the same time that these two recognized scientists cited the three sloppily conducted studies, they also asserted that reports of the Exxon Valdez oil spill in Alaska in March of 1989 were grossly exaggerated due to the absence of baseline data regarding the populations of the animals for which great losses were reported. However, it is widely accepted that the most reliable of those reports were carefully conducted and closely analyzed, and they stood the tests. I have requested permission to speak at the freeholders regular monthly meeting on November 18th, and I will present this same information at that time.

"You heard Miss McGuire's report that the decision to pave is contrary to the original permit issued by the DEP in the 1980s. You heard Dr. Eberhardt state that ecosystems are balances of their components and that what happens in nature impacts our lives as humans. Assistant Commissioner McGuire was necessarily guarded in what she could say, but she did tell us that the original bridge construction was friendly to the environment and that the freeholders likely made a mistake because they didn't have the right facts. My report is consistent with what was said by the others."

Hunter placed his elbows on the podium, put his weight on them, extended his hands beyond the edge toward the audience, and clasped his hands as he leaned forward. With passion in his eyes and voice he said, "We've given you the background. Now we need... your... action. I ask you... no, that's not strong enough. I plead with you for the sake of the frogs, for the protection of our environment, or for the benefit of you, yourselves, in later life and for the benefit of your children, to get involved. Sign the petition. Stay in touch with us. Give us your email address. Go home today and write a letter to the Board of Freeholders. Phone the County Engineer. Join me on November 18th at the monthly meeting of the freeholders. As a group of committed and involved citizens, we will be very powerful!" He pulled a handkerchief from his pocket, wiped his forehead, and said, "Thank you for your support today!"

The loudest applause of the day followed the conclusion of his remarks. Mrs. Margaret LaRosa, a college trustee, was the first of the program participants to greet him as he moved away from the mic as she approached it. She took his hand in both of hers and spoke to him with obvious enthusiasm as she shook his hand vigorously.

LaRosa stood silently for a full minute as the applause continued. When she could be heard, she began, "My! My! What a way that young man has of speaking. I couldn't have been prouder than I am today.

"This subject of the decision by the Freeholders is very difficult. They do have their reasons for wanting to pave the bridge. I know that all of you students who were here last winter had some days when you planned to use the bridge and had to drive all the way around to Hooper Avenue and go through three traffic lights. You may have been late if you planned your schedule for arrival at class as close as I did when I was in college. Nooow, I don't want to hear anyone say that I rode to college in a carriage pulled by horses!" She turned her head shyly as she said the last word at a higher pitch and giggled slightly. The crowd laughed politely.

"But seriously," she continued, "the county's plowing of snow on both sides of the bridge took extra time with the crossing arms down. And it was confusing to motorists about whether the bridge was open or closed on days when the snow was light. But snow wasn't the worst of the problems. The county's biggest concern was for the safety of everyone. If there were an emergency that required police cars or ambulances or fire engines, God forbid, at a time when the bridge was closed, they all would have to take the time to go around, losing precious minutes. Or they would want the bridge road opened, and that would be a problem if it were covered by snow. Those things got me scared enough to think that paving was the best thing to do."

She paused, as if to let her words of wisdom sink in. "But the Environmental Club has its reasons to be concerned about these defenseless tree frogs. They're so tiny and cute." The last word was emphasized strongly. "Have you ever seen one?"

Mixed "yes" and "no" answers were shouted by a number of people.

"They're only about this big." She held the tips of both index fingers about three inches apart. "And some have nice bright colored skin."

She paused again and then resumed, "But that's not why we're here. I knew some of the things these experts said today. Especially I knew that all the parts of the environment were tied together. But I didn't know all that information about the delicate balance in the ecosystem. I was proud that you college students are so responsible to care about the environment and to hold this well-planned presentation. And that's what finally convinced me that the club is right that they need to try to convince the Freeholders to reconsider their decision. And all that information about the Alaskan oil spill and what happened in Costa Rica should be told to them. I wish everybody good luck in protecting the environment and good luck for the school year. I'm so proud of you."

Roxanne quickly introduced the next three speakers as college students, the first being the student body president and the next two being club members. Small in stature, extravagant in dress, and quick in movement, Alan Faber quickly took the mic. He spoke rapidly in expressing mutual pride for Mrs. LaRosa, admiration for the responsibility and dedication of Environmental Club members, and a plea for all to act now through signing the petition and taking at least one other step. Stylish Brittany Foster—blond hair shining and slacks and blouse which mixed luxury and provocation—praised the club for giving to members the opportunities to put their knowledge to work and repeated the slogan "Think globally; act locally." She ended with the declaration: The trustees'll be gone when half the animals are extinct, and we'll live with the results, you know? We need your help in a big way." Lana Olson—average height, average looks, average dress—next on the program quickly reviewed some commercial victories in applying scientific findings, principally the substitution of hydrofluorocarbons for chlorofluorocarbons in spray cans, and declared, "Scientists around the world have shown they can be very creative in finding ways to do things differently when necessary if decision-makers in government and corporations have the courage and persistence to force changes."

Roxanne hugged Lana quickly and introduced the final speaker.

Colleen deftly raised her hands and moved to the podium with a smile. As the first, slight decrease in sound occurred, she leaned into the mic and shouted, "Thank you! Thank you!" She waited for the next decrease and said in a somewhat softer voice, "I'm Colleen Townsend." She waited for near silence and them continued, "You're a great audience!" There was the beginning of more cheers, but she cut that off by saying, "There have been lots of stars here today. Everyone who has spoken, the band, and you! Each of you is a star of environmental awareness. You came here because you care, because you want to know more, and because you want to make a difference. I will be very brief because this is starting to become a very long morning. For the benefit of our planet in general, for your own benefit as an inhabitant of the planet, and for the benefit of the generations to come—the future inhabitants—take action! Put your knowledge to work! Cheer the others who are taking action! But get off the sideline and onto the field! You've heard it twice before today: Act locally! Please!"

Cheering was enthusiastic. Roxanne stepped onto the platform as Colleen finished, and she moved to the podium. She hugged Colleen and then kept her at the podium with her arm around her shoulders. "My message is very short, but first I want to thank all of you for taking time on a Saturday to show your support for environmental care in general and for the efforts of our Environmental Club to persuade the Ocean County Board of Chosen Freeholders to reverse its decision to seek bids to pave the H. George Buckwald Bridge, a decision which likely impacts the habitat of the Pine Barren Tree Frog, one of thousands of endangered species around the world. I ask you to make phone calls and write letters within the next few days asking for a change in that decision. There is nothing wrong with the bridge. There is no threat to safety that requires repaving the bridge. The paving is a misguided project. I kept Colleen up here with me as an example of involvement by today's young people. She has devoted countless hours to protecting the environment. She will graduate from here and go on to some occupation that may or may not be related to the environment. But I know that she will continue to protect the environment. For students who are here today and are not members of our club, I invite you… No, that's wrong…I implore you to come to our next meeting. For those of you who are not students, I implore you to get involved with one of the many organizations, both locally and nationally, such as Clean Ocean Action, the Sierra Club, Earth Corps, the Environmental Support Center, or some of the more than one hundred organizations listed at website 'earthshare.org.' Get involved. Take action. Support the efforts on campus to protect the environment. You'll be hearing more about our activities."

As Roxanne signaled the band to play, Colleen took the mic from her and shouted above the cheers, "Let's hear it for Rox!"

The crowd cheered, "Rox! Rox! Rox!" Roxanne elbowed Colleen playfully as she raised and waved both hands. Then she turned off the microphone and stepped away from the podium.

CHAPTER EIGHT

"Incomplete Information Guided Freeholders" was the headline over my article printed the Monday after the demonstration. The secondary headline, in smaller print, stated: "Senator Explains Traffic Flow Favored Over Endangered Species." Since my name appeared as a byline below the headlines, I expected to catch some flack within the next 48 hours. That afternoon, James Almwood, Ocean County Executive, phoned, starting the conversation abruptly after letting me know who was on his end of the line. "Your article is one-sided. You seem to have taken up the cause for those eco-nerds at the college who think we're trying to kill off the tree frogs up there. We're trying to improve the lives of the people and to do it now. Besides, there must be a million of those frogs around this area. Through June and July, the squeaks of the peepers is all you can hear in late afternoon along Hooper Avenue near the streams and standing water by the college and for about three-quarters of a mile east along Fischer Avenue, including the Cattus Island park area."

I was busy taking notes on the computer while he talked. When he stopped to breathe, I responded, "Do I understand you correctly that no one should be concerned about the possibility of killing members of an endangered species because you estimate the census for the Pine Barren Tree Frog to be approximately one million in the vicinity of the college? And that people who try to comply with the regulations designed to protect them are...what did you call them? Eco-nerds? I don't think I know that word, but the way you say it, it sounds like the people you're referring to have something wrong with them."

"There definitely is something wrong with people who put the lives of a few frogs above the efficient functioning of their own kind. The people who were put on the program of protest that the liberal college faculty and administration permitted to take place are what I call eco-nerds. That name means they are very smart and know a lot of facts about ecology but they make that their whole life. But my big problem is with you because your article makes it sound like the freeholders and county administration don't know what we're doing. Just read the headline."

"I think your problem with me is because I reported remarks that represent positions which are contrary to your positions. That's my job. That's what I do. I report things that take place. Your only criticism of me as a reporter should be misrepresenting what took place. And since you sound as if you weren't there, you have no basis for judging the accuracy of my reporting."

"Oh, I have no doubt that you reported very accurately what those liberal-thinking do-gooders said. You ignore another basis for someone to criticize what a reporter includes in an article, and that's whether he has given a balanced report, including ideas and opinions which are held by others. On that basis, you haven't met your obligation to inform the public of the opinions held by others. Your article should have been on the editorial page."

"What in your background makes you an expert on the press and reporting? My article purported to be nothing more than a report of what took place. And because what did take place was a demonstration against action taken by the freeholders, it was comprised of speeches. I reported those speeches. You can disagree with the opinions expressed at the event, but don't lecture me on how I should do my job. Would you answer the question about your background making you an expert?" I was hot and blasting away with both barrels.

He was hot to start with and getting hotter. "If you're asking if I ever worked for a newspaper, the answer is no. But I read newspapers, quality papers…and yours, and have some thoughts on the ethical obligations and standards of the press. In fact, my graduate school program in public administration included a three-credit course entitled "The Press in a Free Society." I highly recommend it to you and your editor."

I decided that our conversation was leading nowhere. "I see. We're into the old theory versus practice opposition. I think we're best leaving our difference of opinion as an agreement to disagree. I understand that you believe that I should have had a full discussion of the pros and cons of environmental protection. My point is that wasn't the purpose of the article. That purpose was to report what had taken place at the demonstration. I'm not moving from my position, and I think you're not moving from yours. I know we'll meet again on this topic. I'm ready to end this phone call. How about you?"

"I'm for ending the call, but not the debate. In the meantime, I think your article has had the effect of hardening the Freeholders' position. Thanks, at least, for taking my call." We both hung up.

The article that set off that skirmish also summarized the speeches of most of the others on the program. And highlighted the comment by Professor Eberhardt that he regarded the decision to pave as inexcusable in terms of environmental damage because he didn't agree with the rationale that traffic flow would be improved. Alex, my boss, added an editorial note at the end of the article that a more detailed presentation of information about ecological concerns discussed at the demonstration would appear in Friday's edition. I was assigned to work with the science editor on that article. Part of Almwood's anger probably resulted from my inclusion of a series of comments by the speakers and by randomly selected members of the audience in regard to the responsibility shown by the students for organizing and holding the forum to assure a frank discussion of the topic and the wisdom of the college administration for permitting the demonstration to take place.

My week as a reporter was controlled almost exclusively by the continuing development of the "frog fracas," as we came to call the events surrounding the topic. The college trustees held a meeting on Tuesday night to determine if they needed to make decisions after the demonstration. I guess they thought they might need to change policies or procedures or take disciplinary action. The president permitted the effusive Margaret LaRosa to provide her firsthand report. No other trustee had attended—a strategy planned in advance to avoid conflict and to permit "a dispassionate consideration of the event after the fact."

Margaret—Peggy—LaRosa was in her usual form. "I was so proud to be at the demonstration! The students who spoke represented the college so well. They were informed and informative. That's a combination I look for! The speakers were dynamite! Dr. Max Eberhardt on the faculty at NJIT presented some very important information. And our Senator McMahon took time from his meeting with mayors from throughout the state to make an appearance. He did say that the Freeholders probably hadn't sufficiently explored environmental issues, and that may be a bit of a problem. But he also said he respects each and every one of them and knows that what the Freeholders did was what anyone in the crowd would do if he or she was a freeholder. I'm so glad I was there. I know why the rest of you weren't, but you missed a good program... really good!"

College President Henson George Ill asked if there were any other reports. Trustee Glen Greenwood commented briefly that his neighbors who had attended had given him a similar report and likewise had praised the students for their responsibility. No other trustees had comments. President George spoke, "I must admit that I had my trepidations at first when there was talk of a student demonstration. We hadn't had one here, and I had never encountered one in my prior positions. But we have a great dean of students, Dean Emma Henderson. She conferred with the President of the Student Body, Stuart Faber, an energetic and level-headed young man, and then advised me. We concluded that one of our missions is to encourage students to raise questions as a critical component of their learning. Another mission is to encourage academic debate, reasoned give and take on the merits of an idea, an opinion, a plan of action, or a hypothesis for testing. The college campus must remain a forum for intellectual discourse. We decided to take a risk, and, happily, our faith in the intentions of the students and the possible outcomes of their attempt to influence local government was justified by the way in which they accepted their responsibilities and met their obligations. I commend all who were involved. I'm sure any future activities in regard to this topic will be planned and carried out at the same high level of purpose and accomplishment." There was light applause by some of the approximately thirty-five attendees in the audience.

Dr. George then concluded the meeting with the statement: "I believe we have met our obligation of due diligence in regard to this unique student activity. I see representatives of the campus *Viking News* and *The Press* in the audience and will be glad to talk with them. A motion to adjourn is all that we need at this time."

The reporter representing the campus newspaper was very aggressive in pursuing a line of questions regarding the memos by Dr. George, which my editor and the paper's attorney had obtained. She was outmaneuvered by a skilled practitioner who responded with expert evasion to each variation of the central question: "In light of your present commendation of the leaders of the demonstration, what was your motivation in clarifying for college staff the intent of maintaining a harmonious atmosphere free of politics and free of student unrest?" Essentially the president's response to each version of the same question was: "We have a set of procedures which we must apply equally in every case. I have the responsibility to preserve an atmosphere which maintains a high quality education. Some colleges have suffered a diminution of the quality of their educations as student unrest and protests have interfered. My present commendation recognizes the success of the student leaders in this case who honored the existing expectations and procedures and who, in the end, promoted the high quality of education. My clarification of the expectations is supported by the outcome."

In my article, I chose to pursue two questions: How did you know in advance of the demonstration that it would be helpful to clarify expectations and procedures? And, what types of outcomes would have led to the conclusion that the clarification was not justified? The headline on my article the following day was: "Student Demonstration Wins President's Praise." The secondary headline read: "Signs of Responsibility Raise Expectations." President George's answer to my first question was that he chose to issue his clarifications because no demonstration had occurred during his time at the college. In essence, his answer to the second question was that an absence of problems demonstrated that knowing the expectations and procedures was a good thing while problems would have demonstrated that the expectations and procedures either were not sufficiently clear or that the participants chose to ignore them.

CHAPTER NINE

With the advantage of hindsight, I concluded that the Board of the College meeting was a warm-up for the Freeholders meeting. That meeting of the Freeholders was standing room only in the meeting room for the approximately 200 attendees. When the emergency manager advised the county executive that the number of people exceeded the maximum allowable 125 occupants and was in violation of fire code, Roxanne quickly organized the voluntary exit of enough people to stay within the allowance and designed a plan to rotate people in and out of the meeting every few minutes. A high degree of concern could be seen on the face of James Almwood who, apparently, had planned on the fire code ruling as justification to cancel the meeting.

While the original intent of the demonstration was to provide a show of support by the people who opposed the paving plan, the greatest accomplishment was to generate activism, most obviously among those who attended the Freeholders meeting. As the meeting progressed, it became clear that there were others who took action by signing petitions, sending letters, and making phone calls to freeholders. Mrs. Gladys Helms called the meeting to order and after the opening activities of the flag salute and approval of minutes of the previous Freeholders meeting, asked for approval by the other members of the governing body to amend the order of business by placement of the topic of the award of a contract for paving the bridge at the top of the order prior to the committee reports so that the people who had come to the meeting for that part of the agenda could comment if they wished and could observe the action of the board. The only objection came from Almwood who said that a change in order of the agenda for the sole purpose of accommodating the audience may set a precedent that would encumber the ability of the board to conduct business in the future.

Helms brushed him off by saying, "I'm happy to have citizens attend the meeting so that they are informed. We have complained many times that there's a low rate of participation in local government, as exemplified by embarrassingly low rates of participation in elections. I'll do whatever I can to accommodate interested citizens. That's the essence of democracy."

Some new friction must have arisen between Helms and Almwood because she took a step that I never had observed when she called on him to give a brief synopsis of the bid action item. He looked surprised and made a couple of false starts initially. However, once he got rolling, he was on top of his game and was able to explain the scope of the project, the names of the bidders and the amount of each bid, the earliest and latest start dates and the latest end date, and the analysis of the bidders' qualifications in regard to the requirements. There were four qualified bids ranging in price from $95,000 to $135,000. The work would start no sooner than December 1st and no later than January 31st. The work must end no later than March 31st.

When Almwood called on the county engineer to add information, Helms replied, "That won't be necessary. I want to get to the business at hand at this point. I will entertain a motion to approve the contract resolution."

Alberto Hernandez said, "So moved."

He was followed by John Wilson who declared, "Second."

Helms then explained that there is a bylaw that states that public participation will be permitted for a maximum total time of thirty minutes, which could be extended by vote of the board for an additional thirty minutes and then again by vote for a final thirty minutes if necessary. In no case would the time exceed ninety minutes. Each individual would be limited to two minutes. She then offered advice as follows: "I was impressed by the quick initiation of a plan for reducing the number of citizens who could be present and remain within the fire code. I advise that either that person or some other person designate those people whose comments are of special import and therefore should be made first in order that they don't fall victim to the time limits. I'll wait five minutes to begin the clock so that the people can be identified and rotated into the meeting room."

Roxanne had a list in hand and had made certain that they remained in the room at the start of the rotation. She raised her hand and asked to be recognized. "Madam President." After she was recognized, she said, "My name is Roxanne Freeman. It was I who organized the rotation, and I have made certain that the people I want to have heard are currently in the room."

Helms responded, "Your planning is even more impressive. Are you ready to proceed?"

"Yes, we are," she answered. Then she continued, "I just want to remind each speaker that he or she should leave the room after speaking and send another person in to take that place. However, I want each speaker to please wait outside in the event that there is a question."

Roxanne remained at the microphone and addressed the Board of Chosen Freeholders, "I will repeat that my name is Roxanne Freeman. I'm the President of the Environmental Club at the college."

Almwood broke in, "Please include your address so that we can be certain that you are a bona fide resident of the county, a requirement for participation included in our bylaws."

Helms spoke quickly before Roxanne could answer, "Ms. Freeman, if you live within the county that is all well and good, and we'll discover that in a few moments. By the way, I haven't started the clock for the time limits. I'm going to ask my fellow freeholders to approve waiving the county resident requirement for this item on the agenda because it is so important to the college community, as evidenced by the demonstration which was held this past weekend."

Once again Almwood resisted a change. "Mrs. Helms, I advise against this. Our interest as a governing body is restricted to the geographical boundaries of the county."

With a louder voice and a measured cadence, Helms addressed the county executive, "Mr. Almwood this is your third attempt to delay this meeting and delay consideration of the action item of greatest interest. You asked the emergency manager to be present, a novel request. You advised that we not rearrange the agenda. And now you want us mired down in the designation of the legal residence of college students, some of whom normally live within the state and outside the county, and some of whom normally live outside the state but for the school term are living within the county. We can deal with the question of the legality of their participation, but if there is a challenge by a person whose permanent address is out of the county and whose temporary address is within the county, getting an answer will require hundreds of hours of legal work. I think the interests of the county residents is best served to hear all who want to speak tonight, realizing that some of them don't meet the usual residence requirement."

When Almwood chose not to rebut, she requested, "May I have a motion to approve waiving the usual residence requirement for the public comments on the H. George Buckwald Bridge paving action item."

Following passage of the motion, Helms said, "And now again, Ms. Freeman. I apologize for the delay, but it's best that we settle these procedural matters now.'

Roxanne began again, "I do live with my parents year round within the county boundaries in the town of Berkeley. I came here tonight hoping to persuade the Board of Freeholders to reverse its plan to pave and to persuade you to not approve a contract. I fear that the chemical composition of the paving material will harm the frogs and may have an impact on their reproduction. This also is the top concern of the club I represent. The bridge was closed a total of six days last winter. That's less than two percent of the total days in a year. I think that the human population of the area can be inconvenienced that small amount of time in order to protect one of the connections within the ecology of our community. While I know there is a desire to assure access by emergency vehicles at all times, that concern doesn't seem to have been present until this year. I don't understand why it's on the table now because there is no new emergency station. In the interest of time, I'll end my comments here with a final plea that you not award a contract tonight. Thank you for the opportunity to speak."

The next several speakers were lined up behind Roxanne and spoke quickly and succinctly. As each speaker finished and left the room, another person entered the room, like a superbly timed machine. I kept a tally of the number of speakers, as well as notes of remarks by some of them. A total of forty-seven people addressed the board. The average time taken by each speaker was less than two minutes. I learned later that Colleen stood at the front of a line outside and released the next individual or next five to ten, according to how many had come from inside.

Hunter, Alan, Brittany, and Lana reprised their comments from the demonstration. Vince delivered a scaled down version of the presentation I had heard twice previously, including the special bongossi wood surface as part of an agreement with DEP, issuance of the permit under the terms of the Coastal Area Facility Review Act based on the agreement, and the disregard of that agreement in the decision to move ahead with the paving project. He presented the petition with a reported 4,750 signatures, a figure I cited in my article.

Hunter set his sights on the County Engineer, Barbara Macintosh, and the faulty information on which she based her recommendation to proceed with paving. Loud laughter followed Hunter's question of what aspect of any of the three studies could be legitimately labeled as "scientific." Mrs. Helms's glance at the engineer seated in the audience was stern, if not scornful. Hunter concluded by saying, "At our demonstration last Saturday, we heard Dr. Eberhardt, internationally known faculty member at NJIT, state that ecosystems are balances of their components and that what happens in nature impacts our lives as humans. DEP Assistant Commissioner McGuire was necessarily guarded in what she could say, but she did say that the original bridge construction was friendly to the environment and that the freeholders likely made a mistake in moving ahead with planning to pave because they didn't have the right facts."

Mrs. Helms asked if either Dr. Eberhardt or Assistant Commissioner McGuire were available at the freeholders meeting to provide input. Hunter said neither was present because the disagreement was local.

Colleen had used information presented at the demonstration by Dr. Eberhardt. Terrence, Cheri, and Ramone also made use of the professor's remarks.

A surprise for me was the appearance of Wilson Markham, Hunter's father and also an attorney. He introduced himself as a county resident. "I'm an attorney by profession, a colleague of your esteemed barrister, Mr. James Denardo. Every attorney develops specialties over time on the basis of experience. Perhaps it could be said that the specialties develop out of necessity as we serve the needs of our clients. While we specialize on the one hand, we have areas in which our expertise is not at the same level. I, for one, would need help in the area of contract law. That's a prelude to my assurance that I'm here as a friend, offering my expertise in the area of DEP regulations and requirements, an area developed out of necessity. I offer the advice that there may be some gray areas regarding the county's legal standing in the matter of paving within the historical context of a CAFRA permit issued following the agreement your predecessors had with the DEP. My son spoke to you earlier, so I know how passionately some college students believe that the tree frogs are in danger if the paving goes ahead. I've offered my professional services to the club if they wish to pursue the matter in the event that you award a contract for paving. I'm here tonight because it's much more pleasant revealing my intentions in front of this audience than it might be in front of a judge. Thank you for listening."

Several members of the audience applauded and were immediately called to order by President Helms who commented, "This is a setting conducive to official business. It differs from a demonstration." As most of the same people sheepishly ducked their heads slightly and looked with nervous smiles at those around them, she softened her comment with, "Thank you. I know feelings are running high for many of you, and you may have forgotten where you are."

Mr. Denardo responded, "Will, I thank you for your advice. In the absence of a professional agreement governing your offer of such advice, I will assume that there is no charge."

A few audience members chuckled, but the large majority seemed uninterested in the humor. He continued, "While I respect your abilities as a colleague based on my direct observations and reports of others of your success in the past, none of your victories have involved DEP regulations. I believe you made an assumption about the depth of my knowledge in that area. I respectfully differ with that assumption. My advice to this Board of Freeholders has always been based on my due diligence, sometimes founded on late night study and collaboration with colleagues, I admit, but nonetheless diligently informed. I agree with your assessment of the relative degrees of comfort in the comparison of the present setting to a courtroom, but obligation prevails over comfort in my delivery of services."

Another highlight of the comments by the public was Dr. Carmelita Perez-Nelson, an environmental engineer and resident of the county. She quickly reviewed her credentials: undergraduate degree in biology from Universidad de Guadalajara, both an MS in Civil Engineering and PhD in Environmental Engineering from Texas Tech University. She had taught as assistant professor at Texas Tech while studying for her doctorate and had thirteen years of field experience working as a consultant in New Jersey, Delaware, and Pennsylvania. She cited her experience with delayed or denied approvals for construction in all three states in areas inhabited by Eastern Box Turtles and Atlantic Salt Marsh Snakes. "One specific concern in regard to the snakes is chemicals which are sometimes associated with embryos or to the development of defective snakes. To deny that there is a threat without extensive study is bad science. It is my professional opinion that the Pine Barren Tree Frog will be endangered by a project that introduces new chemical elements into their habitat. Two days ago I dispatched to the DEP a packet of research that supports my opinion. I urge you to delay the award of a contract."

Mrs. Helms responded, "Dr. Perez, on behalf of all members of the board, I thank you for your recommendation. Please rest assured that we study every recommendation on which we act. We have had input from the scientific and engineering communities. We will not act in ignorance on something this important."

Dr. Perez attempted to reply, getting out the words "If that scientific input was provided by Professor Morrison—" before being cut off by Helms who stated, "The purpose of this part of our meeting is to hear comments from the public. You offered those comments. I thought it prudent to counter the implication that this board acts without expert help. We aren't going to engage in debate, or in give and take. Would the next person in line share your wisdom with us, please?"

With a clear look of anger, Dr. Perez turned toward the audience, raised her hands in the air, and shook her head. A few utterances of "Booo!" were gaveled into silence.

With the exception of one other unusual testimonial, the other comments were a combination of rehashes of those comments reported here and challenges to the Board president for silencing those who tried to reply to her responses; there were no surprises. That exception was the report of Jeff Considine who was known by the freeholders from prior hearings. "Good evening, friends. I've been here so often that I do truly feel that salutation is appropriate."

Freeholder Wilson laughed heartily and exclaimed, "I for one don't share your opinion about friendship! I hope that one of the times when you address us you will reveal how it is that you believe that you know so much that you are an expert on so many topics."

President Helms turned to Wilson and said, "I understand your impatience as well as anyone, but I must ask you to listen politely and make whatever use you wish of the comments that are being made. Now, Mr. Considine, please continue with your remarks of no more than two minutes total, an entitlement to an additional one minute and forty-five seconds."

"Mrs. Helms, as a self-proclaimed statistics maven, I usually am in favor of precision. Tonight it works against me."

"One minute and thirty-five seconds," Mrs. Helms said with a smirk. Both hisses and chuckles were emitted from the audience.

"This problem," continued Considine at a brisk pace, "is yet another manifestation of the absence of a comprehensive master plan which, if one were in place, would include adequate infrastructure to prevent problems of traffic flow, would include a build-out plan that directs and limits the rampant tyranny of builders and politicians who hold tightly to the misconception that generation of tax revenue from additional and more expensive housing is the solution to all our problems. The plan also would include safe and quick pathways for emergency vehicles. In fact, the housing explosion is the source of many of the ills which we experience. I must have asked this question twenty times before, but I never get a definitive answer. When are we going to get such a master plan?"

Helms replied for the board, "Mr. Considine, I congratulate you for staying within the time limit. That may be the first time that has happened in the last twelve months. The topic tonight is the paving of the bridge and not the master plan. So we're not going to respond. The clock I've been watching shows that the expiration of the third thirty-minute period occurred five minutes ago. I thank all of those who spoke. The contributions of so many citizens take time, but this is a democracy. I would like to see this forum for comment used more frequently. I commend our college students who were clear in their expression of concern and at the same time were courteous. They were a model for democratic participation.

"We're going to take a five to ten-minute break. When we resume, I'll ask my colleagues to agree to take action on this topic before we return to the top of our regular agenda."

—————————

Roxanne went to the table and addressed the president immediately, "Mrs. Helms, thank you for your compliments about the Environmental Club and the nature of the demonstration. I hope your positive feelings about us will lead to reconsideration of votes to proceed with the paving project."

"I can't guarantee where this will end. We're going to spend some time talking about the subject after a motion is made to approve the contract. I can assure you that we will consider all aspects before we make a decision."

"I came here pretty hopeful that we would succeed with our quest to change the positions of the freeholders who voted before to proceed. I'm less hopeful now after the comments of the board's attorney."

"There are differences of opinion on the issue. We'll have to see where things go. Please excuse me while I freshen up." While she quickly moved toward the door, she was stopped twice by others from the audience. She excused herself in the same manner as with Roxanne.

—————————

Once the meeting reconvened, Alberto Hernandez stated his strong support to award the contract. "While I respect the information and opinions expressed by the audience tonight, what has been said hasn't changed my position. There are clear differences of opinion. One opinion is that everyone has his position and finds statements and statistics which support it. It's easy to shoot down the results of studies cited by Ms. Macintosh, as was done pretty effectively tonight. However, the studies have enough credibility to have been published and to have been used in graduate degree programs. When our engineer made his presentation to us, he gave us assurance that the DEP would have no problem with the project. Madam President, I suggest that we ask the engineer to respond."

"Mr. Hernandez, that's an excellent idea for us to hear from Ms. Macintosh, but it shouldn't be a response to any specific comment that has been made. We're not participating in a debate with members of the public. Our engineer will address issues of concern that have been raised this evening. My notes identify those issues as the introduction in the frogs' habitat of potentially harmful chemical substances, the likely effects of such an addition—be it death or modification of the gene structure—and the efficacy of interpolation of findings from research studies to the tree frog population. Ms. Macintosh, please give us your expert advice."

When Barbara Macintosh stood, she was not much taller than a tall person who was seated. Her small stature combined with her excess weight to give her a troll-like appearance. Her straight, medium brown hair was pulled back and gathered in a comb clip. The hairdo, octagonal eyeglass lenses with wire rims, and no makeup on her pallid face gave her a severe look, which was heightened by the way she held her lips in a straight line. Her voice was loud and an octave below the usual expectation for a female.

She cleared her voice and began in a monotone, "Mrs. Helms and members of the Board of Freeholders, thank you for giving me the time to address those issues. First, the chemical substances. There is no advance treatment, such as some form of spray, which is necessary prior to the paving. The paving material will be asphalt, the composition of which is natural or manufactured cementitious materials that are composed primarily of hydrocarbons. An ideal asphalt will retain some of its ability to flow and to be elastic at a wide range of temperatures so that it doesn't permanently deform and doesn't become brittle and crack. But at the same time, it should hold its form at high temperatures so that it doesn't form ruts during the summer. A number of manufacturing techniques have been developed which improve performance, such as blowing air through hot liquid asphalt and adding very fine rubber particles. We will be using a high-grade asphalt which has been modified to reduce solubility of component elements while retaining the viscoelasticity. In short, we will reduce the danger to plant and animal life as much as possible while providing a surface that is an improvement over the current bongossi wood." A number of whispered conversations were taking place. Many in the audience appeared to be confused.

Engineer Macintosh continued to deliver information, as if she were sure that others understood the technicalities as she did. Or, perhaps, she hoped that confusion would silence the critics. "The wood is so hard that nails cannot be driven into it. Therefore, dowels were used to keep the planks in place when it was constructed in the late 1980s. However, vehicles going over the bridge create vibrations, which, in time, loosen the dowels. When loosened, they move upward, requiring our maintenance staff to hammer them back in, when possible. When it is not possible to bang a dowel back down, we burn it off so that it is flush with the surface. After lengthy study, we decided that we had to pave the bridge to save it from eventually being shaken apart. We rejected the alternative of replacement with a new bridge after concluding that three factors mitigate against new construction. First, the construction process would be more of a threat to the frogs than would be paving. Second, use of bongossi wood would be prohibitively expensive, and cutting the trees, native to Africa and South America, would contribute to environmental problems of harvesting rain forests. Third, we failed to identify an alternative material which did not possess some potential threat to the frog population. Paving is the best option. If we had a better one, we would pursue it."

Helms, a look of satisfaction on her face, asked, "Are there any questions or comments about that report before we consider some other aspect?" She looked around, saw a hand raised, and said, "Mr. Wilson."

John Wilson rubbed his temples as he commented, "Ms. Macintosh, you lost me in regard to viscoelasticity. From all you said, I understood that we have to do something; paving is better than new construction, and there is a paving material which will reduce the danger from chemicals in the asphalt. Is that what you said...with much more completeness than I...but also with more confusion?"

"Yes, sir. That's the message."

"Then, Barbara, I think you can feel good that the essence of your message was understood," Helms commented as Macintosh nodded and smiled. "Are there other questions or comments?"

Thomson began, "We just heard that this is the best course of action to protect the frogs. As I understand, the reason for the initial construction of the bridge so that the access road could be constructed, someone found some frogs and discovered they were on an endangered list. That was in the 80s—twenty years ago. So our predecessors at the time made an agreement with the DEP, or whatever that agency was called then, to build what appears to have been a very expensive bridge for protection. Has anybody checked on those little guys in the meantime? Do we know if they're still there? Do we know if there are more or less of them than twenty years ago? It seems to me that in that amount of time, the tree frogs could have left and some other, non-endangered frog population has moved in."

Helms turned to County Executive Almwood and asked, "James, do you know anything in relationship to that question?"

Almwood replied, "I don't know that anyone has addressed those specific questions. I hope someone has been following up. Maybe Barbara has information about that?"

Macintosh responded by shaking her head.

Almwood said that he would check with the DEP since their rather unpleasant inquiry about the plan to move ahead with the bridge assumed that there was a need to protect the frogs.

"Madam President, I have a comment before we get to a vote on awarding the contract." Heads turned toward Sam Ferguson, and Helms nodded approval for him to speak.

"I think we're all too eager to believe that everything is okay. We need to slow down and maybe give ourselves a little space to get some more answers. The preponderance of the information that we've heard tonight came from well-informed and conscientious people who urge that we not proceed with paving because there is a very real danger that we may kill or alter the frogs. We heard from forty or fifty people during a period of over an hour and a half, and all but one asked us not to award this contract. In the last fifteen or twenty minutes, we heard again the information told to us before by Ms. Macintosh, which is that there will be as little threat as possible. I'm sure she believes the information that she has is accurate and is sufficient for her to make a decision of what to do. But earlier tonight we heard a presentation that some of the information isn't relevant to our local situation. And some of the other information we heard was from experts in their field who spoke last Saturday. Some of those people concentrate on the field of environmental science and engineering full-time. I move we table the resolution to award a contract."

"The chair is not ready to entertain that motion because doing so has the effect of ending discussion on the motion before us," Helms asserted her prerogative as the presiding officer. "Sam, I'm curious why you omitted from your rationale that you also are an environmental scientist."

Ferguson blushed as he replied, "I want to put the emphasis on the information presented tonight, information which represents the thoughts of many people, some—for example, the information presented at the demonstration by Professor Eberhardt and conveyed to us by students—who have reputations which eclipse mine. My position here is not influenced solely by my own experience."

"Now I understand," replied Helms. "I thank you for clarifying that for me. I assure you that I'll return to you for that motion prior to a vote on the award of a contract."

Turning her head so as to make her scan of the board members obvious, Helms continued, "I want to exhaust every question of all members of this board before we vote so that it is clear now and will be clear on the record that each of us voted with all the information that he or she wanted. Is there any other question on this topic?"

"I have a related question," stated Thomson simultaneously with raising her hand.

Helms included a quick smile with her recognition. "Please go ahead, Mrs. Thomson."

"I want to be on the record with my request that next month's agenda include a report and further discussion on the status of a master plan for our jurisdiction. Although our familiarity with Jeff Considine means that sometimes we don't listen well to him, he has a valid point that there is a relationship of the need to repair the bridge, the traffic congestion that occurs when the bridge is closed, the provision for safe and speedy response of emergency vehicles, and the absence of a master plan."

"Maggie, I have made note of your request and ask that James make a note as well," interrupted Helms. "But we're not going to respond to Mr. Considine tonight, as I stated earlier. Are there other questions or comments from other board members?"

She waited for less than sixty seconds, although the silence was noticeable. Board members and people in the audience began to look around and shift in their seats. Eventually, discourse was resumed when she turned to Ferguson and asked him to repeat his motion to table the resolution to award the contract.

He did so, and Helms declared that there is no discussion on such a motion. She turned to the secretary to Almwood and asked, "Mrs. Navarro, please record the vote." She asked for a show of hands in favor and then opposed. Ferguson and Thomson voted yes. The others voted no.

"The motion fails. Mrs. Navarro, please verify that we had a motion and second about two hours ago." After that step was completed, Helms addressed Navarro again, "Roll call vote, please, since the resolution authorizes an expenditure."

Hernandez, Wilson, and Helms voted yes. Ferguson voted no. Thomson abstained, explaining that her vote had been reinforced by the citizens' comments, but she needed more information regarding recent monitoring of the frog population.

"Madam Chairwoman," Hernandez said, "we have just authorized the expenditure of funds for paving the bridge. In order that we have sufficient time to plan and schedule the project, I believe that we should award the contract and get plans moving along. I move that the Ocean County Board of Chosen Freeholders award the contract for paving the surface of the H. George Buckwald Bridge to the low bidder, in this case, Baja Paving Corporation, at a cost of $95,000, with work to begin no sooner than December 1st and to be completed in full no later than January 31st."

Movement of some members of the audience was abruptly halted as Wilson spoke, "I second that motion."

Voting was swift with the same freeholders voting yes: Wilson, Hernandez, and Helms. Once again, Ferguson voted no, and Thomson abstained, the abstention followed by Thomson's explanation that she needed the results of the survey of the frog population.

Helms announced a recess of five minutes for the purpose of permitting people to leave if they wished. I stood in line behind four or five others waiting to talk with President Helms. As I waited, Roxanne appeared at my side and took my hand. I expected to see tears any second as she said, "What a set-back! One of our prior No votes became an Abstention. I don't know what we'll do now."

With a squeeze of my hand and a forced smile I tried to console her, "It must seem like defeat, but I wouldn't be concerned about Thomson's abstention. She said her vote in September had been reinforced by comments. I have confidence that you'll regroup and come up with a new game plan. What was Hunter's dad saying to you a minute ago?"

"He wanted to give me his business card for possible help with a legal challenge." She displayed the card for me. "I'm going to find Colleen and thank her for helping to coordinate the flow in and out of the meeting so that dweeb Almwood and his emergency manager henchman couldn't postpone the meeting."

I chuckled as I said, "Don't mince your words, dear! You don't want to re-press your feelings so much."

That brought a smile and a light punch of my arm.

When it was my turn with Helms, I asked when the report on the mon-itoring of the frog population would be brought to the board and on what basis the award of the contract could be challenged.

She replied that she couldn't give me a specific date for the monitoring report because a number of calls probably would need to be made. And then as a skilled politician, she turned it back on me. "If you have any contacts in the DEP and discover any information, I'll appreciate receiving it. Hopefully I could receive it by phone call or email or note before I receive it in your newspaper." She advised that I speak with the freeholders' attorney, Joseph Whitfield, at the meeting.

With the most charming smile I could muster, I replied to her answer about any help with the DEP, "Why, President Helms, has the efficiency of the county government operations reached such a low point that it's necessary to enlist the assistance of a journalist? If it is I who discovers the information about the monitoring of the frog population, I'll certainly give you the courtesy of a phone call before publication." Working on my smile again so that my words wouldn't sound so much like a threat, I added, "However, I won't permit failure to return my call as a reason to delay publication."

Always needing to have the last word, she answered, "I'll do my best to stay in touch."

I was able to broach the topic of my inquiry to Whitfield and ask if I could phone him for a discussion. His wizened reply was that he would not provide legal advice to a party who was not on his firm's client list or who was not a potential client. However, after I obtained advice from the newspaper's legal staff, he would welcome an opportunity to respond to any questions I had which were based on that advice.

I had just dealt with a couple of professionals and was not surprised that the reply of each was essentially: "I don't have information. You'll need to find it yourself. Then I want to talk with you before you publish anything."

While looking for Roxanne as I made my way to the exit after Helms rapped her gavel and called for the meeting to resume, I surveyed the greatly diminished audience. I found Roxanne at the center of a group of 15-20. Many were club members; many of the others looked familiar. I thought perhaps I was recalling their faces from the people at the demonstration.

Roxanne must have been looking for me as well because within a few minutes of my arrival she said she really needed to be on her way home. I saw Colleen elbow her and wink with a nod of her head in my direction.

"You look a little better than you did inside," I said as she wrapped her arm around mine and looked up.

"I am a little better. Encouragement from supporters helps tremendously. Mr. Markham told me again to give him a call, so I guess he isn't just trying to make me feel better and does want to help. I'm just usually such an optimist that I expect that everything will come out the way I want it to. Then when it doesn't...time and time again...I'm shocked. I guess I have to work on that."

"I hope the solution isn't that you become a pessimist. I hope you find a middle ground somewhere. You're successful enough that the expectation of further success is a realistic point of view."

"You're so good for me!" she almost whispered. I could not have missed the look of affection. Then she dropped her eyes and said, "I hope you stick around for a long time."

I reached over and with my index finger lifted her chin. "Where does that come from?"

With pleading eyes she replied, "I wonder sometimes if I can keep you interested."

"I'm very interested." I felt that maybe we weren't spending enough time together. "Is there something I've done or said...or haven't done or said?"

She leaned against me with additional force as she sighed. "Oh, no! It's me. I get these moods once in awhile." Then with a different tone of voice she asked, "Do you have time for coffee? I'll buy!"

"I can't pass up that offer. There's a Starbucks just around the corner. Let's go there...before you change your mind about paying. We can walk." I had planned on going home to work for an hour on an article due tomorrow afternoon, but Rox seemed so fragile that I was afraid that she might really get into a funk. As we walked, I asked if she wanted to go out to dinner on Saturday. She quickly agreed and immediately started to swing her hand that was holding mine.

CHAPTER TEN

I awoke before the alarm the next morning—a startling event. I tried to get back to sleep and then gave up. I normally sleep so soundly that I don't know how to catch forty winks. In less time than I had expected, I put the finishing touches on an article I had completed before going to bed, and I emailed it to Alex. To fill the half-hour before my meeting with him regarding the new development with the contract and the article I would propose writing this afternoon, I reviewed the DEP regulations on construction or rehabilitation work in areas containing endangered species and reread a copy of the original CAFRA agreement when the bridge was constructed. It seemed clear to me that paving would violate the agreement because it would violate the regulations. I felt confident that the basis existed for asserting that the start of work would constitute such a violation.

As I arrived in Alex's outer office, Kim commented, "That's a talent I haven't seen….or rather heard…before."

I guess in some way I knew I was whistling, but I rarely make a conscious decision to whistle; the sound just pops out of me. Immediately I made the connection to my thoughts of Kate. I had to cover in some way, so I replied, "I'm always happy about the prospect of seeing you again."

"You're toying with my emotions again, you brute! Where's this going to stop? I can't take it anymore!" She put the back of her hand to her forehead and faked a fainting spell.

I knew victory was within my reach this time, as I swooped in for the kill. "You must have been watching *Gone With the Wind.* That reminds me of Miss Scarlet."

With a syrupy Southern drawl and a sideways glance through batting eyelashes she asked, "Now, sir, would you be Rhett Butler or some Union tyrant coming to steal my silver and take advantage of me?"

"I have an appointment with Alex," I replied, returning to reality and feeling more like a Union soldier who had decided to turn and run after seeing who the enemy was.

"Go right in. I think you can find your way… It's been fun as usual."

———

"Come in, Jeff. I got your article. Good job again! What's the latest with you?" Alex turned from one of his computer screens, stood, and thrust his hand forward.

As we completed the handshake, I replied, "I was disappointed, but not surprised, as I witnessed the county freeholders hold a public hearing last night for ninety minutes and then vote to go ahead with paving the H. George Buckwald Bridge. This was after forty-six individuals commented against the project due to environmental concerns."

"Forty-six! That must be one of the largest crowds they've had ever. Did anyone speak in favor of the paving?"

"Forty-six was the number of speakers on the topic—all opposed to the paving. I estimate the total crowd as at least 200. There were so many that the Environmental Club president devised a plan to shuttle people in and out of the room to avoid a postponement due to fire regulations. No one in the audience spoke in favor. On another topic, there was one frequent flyer—and I mean that in more ways than one—who spoke about the paving project and traffic problems calling attention to the absence of a master plan for the county. I think there's something more about the bridge than what is obvious, and I want your okay to spend company time on investigating."

With a facial expression registering minor alarm, Alex asked, "What kind of something more do you think is going on?"

"At best, decisions made in advance of the meeting in violation of the Open Public Meetings Act—the famous Sunshine Law. At worst, corruption and graft."

"What reasons do you have for thinking something nefarious is going on?"

I sat forward in my chair and gave him the reasons so succinctly that he probably thought I had rehearsed the presentation. "For one thing, paving the bridge obviously would be a violation of the CAFRA agreement between the county and the DEP because it violates DEP regulations regarding construction or rehabilitation work in an area connected to the habitat of an endangered species. And that was said to them at the meeting by an attorney who also told them that he is willing to provide legal services for the club. Second, I've never seen the freeholders stand firm in the face of such a united front of opposition from citizens; they usually change their position or, at least, postpone action when they have twenty-five or so citizens oppose them. Third, it would be easy to postpone action on awarding a bid because there is no need to rush on this project. The work is scheduled for late winter or early spring. Let's say, five months from now."

"I'm going to okay the investigation, knowing that you realize that you will have other assignments as well—reduced in scope and number but other assignments, nonetheless. I trust your instincts and reasoning. However, you're moving to another level. We have to guard against libel. I want you to brief me more often than usual. We'll need to get Griffin Hess involved before we print any accusation and exposé. Where are you going to start?"

"I'm going to check the backgrounds of the freeholders to look for any possible factors which may be connected to their votes."

"Go ahead and keep me informed as you go. Make sure you investigate the backgrounds of all five freeholders so you aren't hunting a witch. You may limit your concentration based on what you learn, but you will have put all of them under scrutiny."

"That sounds like good advice. I'll follow it in order to stay out of trouble."

"I'll need your article on last night's action—without suspicions—by 3:00. That a problem?"

"No problem there. And thanks, boss."

"Good luck and be cautious."

I emerged from the office to Kim's whistling the dwarf's song from Snow White: "Hi Ho. Hi Ho. It's Off To Work We Go."

When I waved in order to avoid another losing verbal tussle, she stopped whistling and said, "That's a good Do Bee!"

I was energized enough by the approval to proceed with the investigation that I emailed my meeting article to Alex just before 1:00. We always had the option of suggesting a headline, so I included: "Freeholders Rebuff Paving Opponents." It remained intact in the next day's edition over the lead sentence: "Representatives of an overflow crowd urged the Board of County Freeholders to abandon its plan to repave the H. George Buckwald Bridge on the OCC campus prior to the board's majority approval of a contract with the Baja Paving Company on Tuesday night."

Wednesday morning was a day to grind out the work. I was coming to the end of my research into the backgrounds of the county freeholders who had voted yes to award the contract. The afternoon brought a pleasant surprise in the form of a phone call from Kate McGuire who was in Ocean County with her boss for a PR session regarding a beach replenishment project at Island Beach State Park. She expected the event would end about 3:00 and she would be free until a hearing at 7:00 with a group of sports fishermen in regard to a proposal to reduce catch limits for fluke. She asked if we could meet for coffee. I proposed a diner on Route 35 so that we were away from my usual coffee spots and so that she was within easy access of her meeting in Belmar.

I was excited enough that I decided to head back to the office and attack the freeholder profiles. I inserted my favorite Nickelback CD, cranked up the volume to where my car became an obnoxious boom box blasting music that no one wanted to hear, and then multiplied the annoyance as I sang along. I reduced the volume when I joined slower traffic back on state Route 66.

I stopped at Subway and picked up a salad so that I wouldn't need to go out again once I returned to the profiles. I took a break at 8:00, reading the latest wire service news releases and items posted on our internal network while I ate my salad and the eight-ounce bag of Sun Chips that had called my name as I waited to check out. I completed my project at 11:30 and emailed a copy to Alex with a request to meet next morning at 9:00. What I had learned was interesting, with some of it ripe for further investigation.

―――――――――

My choice of the first freeholder for development of a profile was Gladys Helms. "Gladdy was a very attractive fifty-one-year-old woman. The choice was easy to make because information was more readily available on the chairwoman of the governmental body.

―――――――――

Mrs. Helms's natural blonde hair, recently cut short, framed startling light blue eyes. Her pretty face seemed a bonus to her thin, athletically built body of 5'3". At age 50+, she still drew approving stares of men, especially in an evening gown at formal functions or poolside in her swimsuit. When revealed in a bikini while vacationing at the Cancun villa she and her husband shared, her body was even a greater treat for men aged thirty and above. Most people guessed her age as forty on first meeting her, prior to their more thorough inspections which noted the beginning wrinkles on her neck and the raised veins on her hands.

Gladys met Trent Helms, two years her senior, in 1971 while both were students at Boston College. At the time of their meeting, he was a junior majoring in finance, and she was a freshman. In the spring semester of that year, she declared her major as education. Upon his graduation and employment in the Boston office of Goldman Sachs, they were married. She reduced her course load in order to oversee the operation of their household and to be available for social events and for some of his business travel. She completed her degree in a total of five years, being four months pregnant and nearly late to graduation due to morning sickness. Sonja was born in November 1974, followed in 1979 by Trent Helms III.

Helms became very active in the Colts Neck Country Club, drawing satisfaction and support from a large group of women who reminded her of her mother's friends. In fact, occasionally when she reflected on her conversations at the end of the day, she had flashbacks to when she was a young teenager sitting quietly in the living room and listening to her mother as the latter talked with her friends during a luncheon in the sun room. The young wives drew solace from each other for the hardships of raising a family and keeping a husband happy. She also remained athletically active and won accolades as club singles tennis champion in 1977 and 1978 and doubles champion with best friend Penelope "Penny" Green for the years 1981-83. When she chose to end her competitive career and to continue to play only for recreation, she won chairwoman for the tournament in 1989 and kept that position to the present.

She also was a twenty-year member of the Spring Lake Garden Club and served as its president for five years until elected to the Ocean County Board of Chosen Freeholders in 1998. Her most public distinction was her wonderful generosity with her own time and with the household bank account in support of the Leukemia and Lymphoma Society. Society business had become a passionate cause after her best friend Penny Green died of lymphoma in 1987.

Gladdy was known both inside and outside her home as a tyrant with domestic help, a reputation which began with tempestuous tenures of a series of nine nannies, the first in 1976, during the sixteen years that her children were indulged by the individuals. The score was reported as five dismissed and four quit. The record for longest service was thirty years (one of the quitters), the shortest tenure having been two months (one of the dismissed). Trespasses among the dismissals included: failure to maintain the designated pattern of carpet nap while vacuuming, disappearance of the children's allowance money, talking back while being reprimanded, complaints by the children of inedible food on those nights when the parents were traveling or were out for the evening, and a pattern of tardy pickups from school and after-school music lessons and other activities. The pattern was repeated with a somewhat less frequent turnover rate among housekeepers who replaced the nannies when Trent III turned fourteen years of age. One of the dismissed housekeepers was angry enough to report to the IRS that Social Security and income tax payments had not always been paid by her employers for the nannies and housekeepers. *The Press* ran a brief article after confirming that the IRS had received the complaint, a copy of which was sent to the newspaper by an anonymous source. The investigation conducted by the IRS proved the complaint to be unfounded. The agency exonerated the family for maintaining a squeaky clean record and publicly chastised the housekeeper for her lies. Having been embarrassed by her firing and subsequently humiliated by the IRS report, the housekeeper threatened to "get even." The aggressive part of her character that supported the athletic prowess and that drove her leadership of organizations also encouraged the tyrant whose outlet became the careers of her household employees. At the same time, the quality made her a tough, yet effective Board of Freeholders president. She was tough in her castigation of County Executive Almwood and in her question to fellow Freeholder Ferguson about why he hadn't revealed his profession as environmental scientist. She also was fair when she gave advice to have special planned speakers be ready to go first during the public hearing so they wouldn't fall victim to time limits. She had been responsive when she recommended the county resident requirement be waived and when she asked County Executive Almwood to listen courteously to a member of public. She supported the board when she responded to a member of the public who suggested that freeholders act without thorough study. And she was decisive when she overruled a member of the public who wanted to debate with freeholders, when she used to get order, and when she held another to the two-minute time limit. She was a skilled politician when she turned my question of when the monitoring report of the frog population would be brought to the board into a request for me to share any information that I learned.

Second on my list for preparation of a profile was John Wilson, mostly bald with a fringe of white hair, forming a three-quarter halo from temple to temple. He fit my stereotype of an experienced, wise, friendly attorney. His age was sixty-one, having been born in 1941. He had been six feet tall, but now he likely was 5'10", as sitting at a desk, in courtrooms, and at thousands of lunches and dinners had taken its toll by curving his spine and tilting his head forward. Those lunches and dinners had had the additional impact of broadening his girth by about thirty percent from his playing days as linebacker for the Fighting Irish. He had waged a fierce battle against the spread of his waistline until he decided in his mid-thirties that the tool he needed to protect was not his body but his mind.

Born to working parents in Elizabeth, New Jersey, he learned as much on the streets as he did in school and in church. His father worked evenings at the docks while his mother worked the counter at Mendenhall's Deli, 6:00-2:00. Even with a schedule by which each worked while the other slept, they had spent enough time together to bring Jack and his four brothers and sisters into the world. While a parent was home at all times, although asleep for 6-8 hours of that time, the exercise of supervision wasn't close because most kids in the neighborhood were, in the morning, out of their row houses on the sidewalks jumping rope, playing games, and hanging out until dark. In summers when it was hot, the curfew was extended until 10:00 once you reached age eleven. Theirs had been neighborhood supervision, where anyone's parent was free to call out any other parent's child if a misdeed was observed, and where the limits of responsibility extended to include four, five, or six additional children if an emergency caused the absence of parents in the residence next door. Jack loved football and wrestling while in high school and distinguished himself in both. In the spring, he took a job at Leary's Grocery delivering on bicycle. Summers the shipping increased enough that he went to work with his dad as a sweeper in the warehouses.

Notre Dame became financially possible with an athletic scholarship to supplement what could be put away for college from the paychecks of Jack and both his parents. His football performance was good enough to maintain the scholarship but short of the level that brought stardom. It was in the classroom that stardom accorded him. He majored in history, learning for the first time that the memorized dates and funny-sounding place names from his high school classes could blend into exciting tales about common people whose achievements had been uncommon. He was fortunate that Father O'Brien had seen the intellectual spark during the required World History lecture course and that the good priest fanned it into flame by steering him into smaller classes and seminars. He graduated with academic honors. That record of achievement, together with distinguished scores on the qualifying exam, had earned him a scholarship to Seton Hall University Law School. The financial aid and his ability to live at home and commute by bus had opened the opportunity for graduate school. After receipt of his LB degree in 1966, on the recommendation of the dean of the Law School, he applied for and accepted a position as clerk for the Superior Court in Trenton. It was during that time that he came to the attention of the firm of Schmidt, Bartow, & Walters who hired him in 1968 and assigned him to their Toms River office, one of three new attorneys who would work among the superior courts in Toms River, Trenton, and Newark, as well as the probate courts in Philadelphia. He received some of the more difficult assignments because he had clerked for two years, while the other new hires were legitimate rookies.

Two high profile cases brought him into the public eye. One in 1971 was settlement of the Dover Township Homeowners v. Township of Dover. The other in 1975 became known as Mount Laurel and was the first of a series of cases regarding affordable housing.

Once his name and face were known, he remained in the limelight through the 90s. Near the start of that decade, in 1991, he was elected to the board of freeholders and had been re-elected regularly ever since. He had told the other senior partners two years before this story that he wanted to reduce his load for more time with his wife who had just completed radiation and chemotherapy to combat breast cancer. During that two-year span, her tests had been negative, and the two of them were enjoying their twelve grandchildren, the offspring of their own four children, and the oldest four grandchildren being the parents of the first five great-grandchildren. The proud progenitors also were faithfully following their plan for three international vacation trips per year.

It was a function of his age that he had questioned County Engineer Macintosh in regard to her somewhat technical presentation about the paving material, and it was a function of his wisdom that he had culled out and had understood the salient points from that presentation. Of course, it was a favorite ploy in business conferences and in the courtroom to feign lack of understanding in order to lull an adversary into smug complacency before springing a trap which displayed that he had understood from the outset.

There were only a few colleagues who discredited his professional record. In 1969, his third year out of law school, a convicted felon charged him with incompetent representation, Wilson being vulnerable due to his young age and relatively short list of courtroom victories. And as if the second charge of incompetent representation served as a bookend, his vulnerability in 2000 was due to advanced age. Although angered by both charges, the second launched a tirade, coming as it did after nearly thirty-five years of dedicated and tiring service to his clients. He was exonerated both times. Although acclaimed a kind man by his family members and close friends who knew him best, he took solace from the image of the complainants serving lengthy prison terms. The typical complaints to the local and state bar associations were that he had over-charged for services. Together the recorded complaints totaled less than ten, a rather extraordinary achievement for thirty-four years of service. His innocence had been upheld by every investigation conducted.

More bothersome complaints came from his involvement with organized politics; Republican candidates for public office targeted Wilson due to his great influence within the county and state Democratic party organizations. Within political circles, he was known as one of the "King Makers." His support could guarantee an eventual national appointment to a shining star on the county level. The other side of that coin was the assurance of a fiery tailspin to an ambitious local politician who was denied his support. And for that reason he had been the focus of some hard-fought battles within his own party. At the end of each fight, he always was able to proclaim himself "bloodied but still standing." Republicans charged that he was hiding in the smoke-filled back rooms, plotting strategies for their defeat without exposing himself to the choice of the electorate. When asked to respond to this charge, his response was, "I guess they're right. But then the campaigns I've been involved in only tell the truth. If I were defeated by the truth, I might—I emphasize might—have the same complaint."

Alberto Hernandez was a handsome man of short stature and athletic build. Features of his good looks included salt and pepper hair, brown eyes, pencil line mustache, perennial smile, and laugh lines near his eyes. New acquaintances and friends saw him as affable. Enemies and those he didn't trust knew his anger and tried to avoid his wrath.

His family's roots were deep in the soil of Guadalajara, Mexico where they were among the most successful farmers in the area. His father, Juan, immigrated to the US in 1939 at age eighteen and joined the US Army. He was shipped to Fort Dix, New Jersey for basic training where he showed an aptitude for driving trucks. His company served throughout the European theater and saw action in France and Germany. After the war, he returned to New Jersey and became a long-haul truck driver. Alberto, the first-born of Juan and Manuela, arrived in 1945, followed by Lenora in 1946, Hector in 1948,

Eduardo in 1949, and Rosalinda in 1952. His reputation as a skilled and safe driver who held the company record for most miles logged in a year made it relatively easy to land a job in 1948 as a local driver, a desirable position that kept him home to participate in raising his children. He opened a home renovation business in 1960, using money he received in settlement for a leg injury on the job.

Alberto, age fifteen at the time, became a valued worker after school and on Saturdays, except during football season when he was a star running back for four years. Although athletic scholarships were offered for some of the smaller colleges in the state, he turned them down to go into business full-time with his father in June of 1963. He loved the work and wanted to relieve his father from the long work days, six days per week. He attended Ocean County Junior College at night, taking business courses. With new ideas for advertising and for specialized training of workers in masonry and tile work, the business prospered. In 1971 his father made him a partner and turned over the management responsibilities. Shortly thereafter Alberto persuaded his father to agree to change the name of the company from Hernandez and Sons to J & AH Construction, Inc. He wasn't completely honest with his father, telling him that one of the reasons for the change was that the new name gave the appearance of a larger and more modern business. What he kept to himself was that the change also hid the identification of the principals as Hispanic. In the short time of five years, the number of employees doubled, while the revenue and profits tripled. Under Alberto's guidance, the focus of the business changed from renovation to additions. His reputation varied according to how people knew him. Customers were almost universally satisfied with the quality of the company's work. Employees were very loyal and told many stories of his assistance with paying medical bills for sick and injured family members and of his generosity at Christmas time. Competitors saw him as ruthless and heartless. Tales were rampant about his negotiation of lower prices in order to steal customers. The same competitors frequently claimed that he obtained reduced prices on materials as a result of entertainment of suppliers and completion without pay of work on their homes. Occasionally a story would arise that he gave gifts to building inspectors and union agents. As the company grew larger and more profitable, the complaints of competitors increased. Alberto moved the company into new home construction in the late 70s. The company flourished during a housing boom for the next several years, 1978-83. By the time the boom turned into a bust, reaching bottom in 1988, the company had changed direction again and was increasing commercial construction as it decreased its involvement in the housing industry. The next change was the addition of a new division for construction of government facilities, followed by another division for road and highway construction and renovation. The same dislike by competitors followed the company regardless of its direction. With larger stakes involved, the nature of challenges changed from stories and complaints to lawsuits. The company's powerful staff of attorneys enjoyed a batting average in the .900 range for courtroom victories.

The opinion of a typical member of the public was essentially benign because what the public heard and saw were reports by the company's PR division featuring genuine accomplishments of completion of work ahead of schedule and below budget; charitable contributions to hospitals, churches, and colleges, including OCC; and dedicated service on charitable organizations, service institutions, and corporate boards by Alberto and other company executives. His most visible donation was $8.5 million to build a state-of-the-art cancer center at Monmouth Hospital in memory of his mother Manuela. He was elected to the freeholders in 2000, following an election campaign which emphasized the cancer center donation and his generosity toward OCC in 1999 in the form of $5 million for expansion of the fine arts building and renovation of the building's heating and air conditioning system.

The public was intrigued by problems in Alberto's personal life throughout his rise to prominence and maintenance of star status, but they accepted them as missteps and not as flaws. General consensus is that a major disagreement about company practices in 1983 led to his father's sudden retirement from the company at age sixty-two. A handsome retirement package, the centerpiece of which was the contract for sale of his controlling share to Alberto over five years at the price of $10 million per year, maintained the silence of both sides. Rumors of marital infidelity had dogged Alberto toward the end of the two-year period of 1979-1980 when he and his first wife entertained the masses with a very public divorce case. The torturous twists and turns and innumerable delays suddenly came to an end after the allegations were made public. Although both sides were forbidden by the settlement from discussion of its terms, information that leaked out claimed that Emilia was awarded $13.4

million dollars, the home, and custody of the children. A widely held belief is that the divorce was a key factor in the falling-out of Alberto and Juan. Five years after the divorce, Alberto remarried. The new bride, maiden name Margo Fiedler, was fifteen years his junior at age twenty-five. "Trophy bride" was not a term in use at the time, but she filled the bill amply.

In 1998 Alberto was honored as the Person of the Year by the New Jersey Hispanic Business Association, for his assistance in promoting Hispanic business owners. The photograph published with the story of the award ceremony pictured Alberto receiving the award plaque from an owner he had assisted: Ramone Rivera, whose contracting company, Baja Paving Corporation, was noted for its practice of hiring Hispanic workers. "Assisted the owner" was a euphemism for having set Rivera up in business. Alberto leased the building, lent the money for equipment and vehicles, paid his own attorney to complete the legal documents for incorporation and to complete filings for registration with the state, hired Baja for its first job as a subcontractor to complete a parking lot at a commercial site where J & AH Construction, Inc. was the prime contractor, and introduced Ramone to other contractors. Baja Paving was a frequent subcontractor on J & AH jobs. Hernandez was a frequent contributor to the state and county Democratic party organizations. Rivera made contributions every time Hernandez did, albeit smaller amounts.

———

That completed the profiles of the freeholders who voted yes to pave the bridge and yes to award the contract to Baja Paving. My momentum carried me to the creation of thumbnail sketches of the remaining two freeholders.

Sam Ferguson was undistinguished in his appearance: average height, thin, pale, slight hunch to his shoulders, a thick head of dark brown hair which often was unkempt—at times touching the dark frames of his eyeglasses. Sam had grown up near Bethesda, Maryland, the son of an administrator in the National Security Administration. His father was a twenty-year navy veteran who had married at age forty-three, after retirement from the service. His strict and demanding interaction with his children had produced repression and a love-hate relationship.

Sam had been ridiculed as a geek during high school and college. His extra curricular interests in high school had included playing the violin and four years of participation in the school orchestra, holder of the office of class treasurer for his last two years, a member of the local chapter of People for the Ethical Treatment of Animals (PETA). He majored in environmental engineering at Virginia Tech. His hard work to meet his father's high expectations required him to avoid fraternity membership, partying, and intramural athletics. His first college date occurred in the spring of his junior year and led to his marriage of Nora Beaning four years later when she completed her MA program in mathematics.

Following graduation from his five-year program, Sam had gone to work for Harmonious World Environmental Engineering in Hammonton, New Jersey. Since Nora was three years younger than he, and with his two more years of undergraduate study and a planned third year of graduate work, the two had a commuting dating relationship. Following the receipt of her MA, Nora landed a job as an actuary in the Philadelphia home office of North Atlantic Life Insurance Company, requiring a short commuter rail ride of twenty minutes both morning and evening.

Three years before Sam had been elected to the freeholders, he had prepared a controversial study which concluded that there was no negative impact on the environment by the Oyster Creek nuclear power plant located in Lacey Township, New Jersey. The times at which he felt most powerful were those related to his field of expertise. Therefore, his statement of conclusions were worded strongly so that there would be no mistake about what he meant and no mistake about who was in control. The Oyster Creek study made it very plain that he was sure there was no leakage of radioactivity into the atmosphere or into the cooling water discharge to the surrounding wetlands, no excessively high temperatures of discharge water and, therefore, no threat to the safety and welfare of the flora and fauna of the wetlands, and no concern about the storage and transportation of spent fuel rods. The owners of the plant were ecstatic about the report, an emotion which was balanced by the conviction of its critics that the document was a "white wash." Environmental groups in particular lined up to fire their salvos of criticism. Local citizens who wished the plant to be shut down due to safety and health concerns for the people in the area were even more vocal. One leader had issued a threat of bodily harm and/or death to Sam: "Maybe we should anchor your body in the discharge area so you can be a part of that healthy and safe environment." With a mixture of some fear and a great deal of feeling insulted at the question of his professional performance, Sam had responded with one of his father's favorites, although his father's appearance was much more imposing: "You and who else?" The security personnel had moved toward the front of the room as the nature of the crowd's attitude had become apparent, and they quickly stationed themselves near Sam.

Sam had been encouraged to run for election to the Board of Chosen Freeholders by Gladys Helms who had come to know him through her association with Nora on the board of a local charity. Although Gladys was effusive and liked to be in control, while Nora was timid and preferred to follow the direction of others, they became friends. Gladys and husband Ralph invited Nora and Sam to several country club events where they all became acquainted and enjoyed the periodic parties. With the profiles of subsequent assignments being lowered, Sam's job had become more routine, and the query about running for election seemed like something he could handle. His performance as an engineer was always thorough, and clients were satisfied. Once on the Board of Freeholders, he was a steady worker and amiable colleague.

———————

Maggie Thomson, divorced at age thirty-five when her husband left her and three young daughters for a twenty-five-year-old secretary, had re-invented herself by earning an MA degree in public administration at NYU. She fulfilled the residency requirement while supporting herself and her children with the cash portion of the divorce settlement and while on a leave of absence from her position as an ICU nurse at the Jersey Shore Medical Center. She had known that if she had waited to begin her program or if she had begun her graduate studies on a part-time basis, the money would have been spent, the girls would be older and more demanding of her time, and she probably would have missed the opportunity to become fully independent. From some time during the third year of the marriage, she had handled the financial affairs of the household because her husband's wants were bigger than his wallet— the poster person for "champagne on a beer budget." The demands of her studies and of the commute, especially during the last three years of part-time study while she returned to a full-time job, had taken their toll. She resisted the allure of becoming a victim by focusing on her chronic fatigue, her steady weight loss, and the longer intervals between haircuts by telling herself she would be tougher— "lean and mean" was her favorite description. She often thought through her vision of a home with a room for each of the girls and a college fund to secure their futures. Her devotion to her children renewed her determination daily.

Her age now was forty-five. She had intentionally kept most of the lean physique, giving in to an occasional gourmet dinner out with female friends who had been available to talk her through the toughest times and had remained close despite their own satisfying marriages. They told her that the few extra pounds gave a healthier and softer look to her tall frame. Although she displayed a beautiful smile when pleased or amused, the usual downward turn of the corners of her mouth and worry lines across her forehead were "scars" which she had not yet shed. They gave her a studious look, a benefit in her career path.

She had dated occasionally during the ten years since her divorce, but she remained leery of men. Her father had been successful in his banking career, despite his alcoholism. The public and people in his office never witnessed the abusive language he vented on his wife and children. Leonard, her ex-husband, was another source of dissatisfaction with males in general, having seemed to change over the years—from doting husband who lavished her with expensive gifts and surprised her with exotic getaways, to an unpredictable house partner who alternated between an occasional bouquet of roses and days of communicating in only grunted "uh-huhs" and "huh-uhs," and then to an unresponsive house partner who often needed to work late. Maggie knew that a large part of the problem was her seizure of financial control after the first two years of marriage when the savings account had dwindled to $2,000 and both bank credit card balances were approaching maximum. Leonard had voiced the impact on him as an "emasculation." She explained her actions as a maternal instinct to protect her brood.

During her early years in the corporate medical world, she forced herself to become one of the "guys" at work, usually tolerating the crude jokes and sexual innuendos. When those lines of conversation passed over her limits of acceptance, she privately addressed the most vocal male and reminded him of the hospital policy on sexual harassment. Afterward she would enjoy one or two months before the men returned to their old ways. As the proportion of women in health care administration increased and as she rose through the ranks, the behavior of the men improved. Now, as assistant vice president for property acquisition within the Northeast Health System, she had enough responsibility and decision-making power to set the tone and to issue frequent reminders of the expected office climate. She was aware that behind her back there were references to her "frigidity." She didn't care, and the reputation discouraged invitations for cocktails after work or for a dinner date.

As she experienced increasing success with more responsible positions and salary increases, she became more confident and assertive. When ex-husband Leonard was dumped by his ex-secretary-turned-wife, he came around seeking sympathy. Her self-confidence had reached a level that made it easy for her to tell him to get lost.

Leonard initiated a nasty custody hearing from which details made their way into newspapers and TV news coverage. Both parties admitted to having yelled threats at each other during his appearance at her home to ask for expansion of his time with the girls. The embittered father testified that he had accused his former wife of "cutting off my balls" by taking control of the household finances during the early years of marriage. He reported that she had threatened, "I won't confine my cutting on your anatomy to below the waist."

Northeast Health System stood by their embattled vice president, completely satisfied with the groundwork she completed as the foundation for a sensational expansion of their holdings of hospitals, rehabilitation centers, walk-in emergency care facilities, and senior adult day care programs. Media coverage dried up with the disappearance of Leonard. A short investigation by the police was concluded after Maggie provided documentation of his similar disappearances over the years, a phenomenon which was supported during interviews with the daughters.

CHAPTER ELEVEN

When I finished emailing the profiles to Alex, I just wanted to get to bed and give my brain a break. So the minute I awoke the next day, questions started to pop into my head. It was a form of debriefing, one of my most effective tools, although I usually got a headache while going through it. An infinitesimal sense of doubt can trigger a review. On occasion in the past, that review had kept me from jumping to conclusions that would have blinded me to other alternative explanations of an event or series of events. The questions just kept on coming!

Had there been subsequent events which developed from the threat of the dismissed housekeeper to get even with Gladys Helms? Had she made foes by her assertive leadership as president of the freeholders?

While the appearance of John Wilson matched one of my stereotypes—successful and outgoing attorney—did his activities as a back-room political powerhouse fit another of my stereotypes —the no-holds-barred and good-of-the-party-at-any-cost power broker who directed the work of a posse of henchmen? Had there been follow-up interaction with a convicted former client after release from prison?

Were the stories of "gifts" by Alberto Hernandez to building inspectors and union agents, as well as the claims that he entertained suppliers and completed work on their houses in return for lower prices, only small parts of a pattern of bribes? Was Ramone Rivera an indentured cohort in possible illegal transactions, beyond being a grateful beneficiary, as a result of the largesse of Hernandez in helping to establish the Baja Paving Corporation? And had Emilia remained satisfied with the terms of the divorce agreement as J & AH Construction, Inc. had prospered and grown?

While I tended to think of environmentalists as the "good guys," had opposition to Sam Ferguson's report on Oyster Creek become violent opposition for one or some among those who publicly criticized and demonstrated against him? Specifically, had there been hostile interaction between Sam and the leader who issued the threat four years earlier?

Where was Leonard Thomson, ex-husband of Maggie, and what had he been doing since his disappearance three years ago? Had one or more of her workplace enemies gained influence over her as a result of knowledge he had?

My primary suspicion was that the yes voters may have been involved either in individual graft and corruption for financial gain or personal influence, or in political deals for payback of debts from the past or creation of new obligations for others to pay back at a future date. However, I couldn't deny the possibility that Ferguson as the no voter and Thomson as the abstention (possibly a disguised no voter) had taken the opportunity to oppose the controlling party or to win public favor, which might help to swing the majority to the Democrats in the next election. Politics was a game that I regarded sometimes with fascination and other times with disgust. I hated the thought that there always were explanations for politicians' votes which had nothing to do with the good of the voters or of the community.

I was feeling mental overload, even though I had been awake only five minutes! I was in the cabinet retrieving the Pop Tart box before I realized also that the weather was dreary. It looked like a mist was falling, and the temperature must have been in the 50s. I returned to my room for robe and slippers before starting the morning routine of reading email messages while simultaneously checking two TV news shows, at double time pace because I was anxious to talk with Alex in about ninety minutes. My dad may have been correct when on several occasions he declared me to be a "news junkie."

One advantage of a misty, cold, dark day was that the traffic was lighter than usual. I checked my watch against the clock at the bank and again against the clock behind Kim's desk, surprised as she was that I was ten minutes early. "You certainly are eager this morning!" was her greeting.

"I keep telling you: You can't keep me away!"

"You really have to do something about that all-work-and-no-play thing that we talked about. Alex himself, the one we call 'slave driver,' said that he worries about you sometimes, like when the time stamp on your emails are after 11:30 P.M. I hear the girls around the county are complaining they don't see you anymore."

I hesitated and then gave a try at countering her humor. "You're the woman I see the most, but that big rock on your finger means you're a prize I can't win. I just gave up!"

"You make me blush and want to cry at the same time. I'm just a wreck!" Then she gave me one of her A-rated flirty smiles and said, "I think you can go on in."

I don't think Alex's check of his watch was deliberate, but he appeared just as surprised to see me early as I was to be there. "I see you burned the midnight oil last night...or at least the 11:30 oil...huh?"

"Burst of energy," I explained while closing the door. Then I responded to his gesture by settling into my regular chair. Our routine was so prepared that I wondered when it would ever break down. Would he forget to gesture before I sat, or would I sit in a different chair following his gesture?

"Very interesting information in those—what do you call them? Profiles. You're always so thorough, and they read so smoothly. What's the next step?"

"If you're okay with my expenditure of more company time, I want to go further. The questions I have now are more significant than the ones that I answered in producing the profiles." Then I told him the ones which had come to mind that morning while getting my body to move. I had taken a few minutes at my computer at home to make a record and to print a copy for reference.

After I had finished, he said, "I agree with you about the significance of the new questions. As long as you continue to deliver with your other assignments as you've been doing, I have no complaints about you spending your time on more investigation."

"Thanks, boss. I'm into this series of events so far that I'd find it difficult to stop now."

"That's what a good reporter does—senses the possible leads and keeps digging"

When I didn't get up and leave immediately, he asked, "Is there something else?"

"Can you give me a few more minutes? This is personal business."

"Sure, I have the time for you."

"The experts would probably say it's a bad choice to talk with your boss about personal business. But I respect you greatly and see you as my mentor. I don't have a best buddy I could talk with about this, and my own father might get hung up on some of it. It's about dating and girlfriends. Something a nearly thirty-year old, like I am, shouldn't be worried about."

Alex reassured me of confidentiality. "It all stays here in this office with me. And if it's an issue that gets under your skin, it's probably unhealthy to try to leave it alone."

"I don't think I told you that I've been seeing the girl who's president of the Environmental Club. She's a wonderful person! She's bright. Works hard. Attractive. Has a close, supportive family. Very active in her church. Lives her values every day. I find it easy to talk to her. We started out with my phone calls to check information. Then we met for coffee a few times to talk about the club events and the paving problem. Our talk moved on to our opinions, hopes and dreams, plans for the future, you know. And we've gone out to dinner a few times on more formal dates. I'm welcome at her house. Her mom's a super person, and I really like her dad."

"I keep waiting for the word 'but.' The words you're saying make your situation sound great. The serious look on your face and your tone of voice don't match. What's the problem, besides the fact that you may have become a bit too close to the events you're reporting on?"

"Huh. Didn't know the disconnect between the words and my face is that obvious? There's a complication. I've met another person, Kate, and so far there's a feel at the start that hasn't happened with Roxanne."

"I see. Tell me about where your relationship is with each of them. And I don't need to know the bedroom details if there are any."

"If you're concerned about my getting a little too close to the events due to Rox, you'll be thrilled to know that Kate is the DEP Assistant Commissioner who is connected with the paving issue as well!"

"'I was happier before I knew all these details!" His chuckle seemed strained.

I continued, "I enjoy Rox's company. We have fun together. We hold hands when we walk. It's great when she wraps her arm around mine and leans into me. We kiss, sometimes tenderly and sometimes excitedly. Nothing physical has happened. And that may be part of my discontent…probably is part of it. Maybe is a large part of it! But I know with the depth of her religious beliefs and her values I just shouldn't try. Neither of us has said the word 'love.' Is that enough for you to go on?"

"If that's what there is to tell, there isn't any more. What about Kate?"

"I'd call Rox 'subdued' and Kate 'energized.' Part of it's a difference in appearance. Rox is African-American. With limited experience with others of that ethnic background, I may not be able to see the gradations…only the extremes. Do you know what I mean? I may not see any African-American woman as energized until I reach the extreme of someone who, if she were a white woman, I would call 'loud and brassy.' On the other hand, I react to Kate's red hair and freckles and sparkling green eyes as signs of spunk and sassiness in a good sense."

Interesting point. It might be good if you come to terms with that." Alex's response's reminded me of the clinical social worker my parents took me to see before they understood that all seventh grade boys are weird.

I forged ahead. "My 'relationship,' as you call it, with Kate is so new we haven't kissed. In fact, I met her for coffee yesterday afternoon, and it was awkward when we hugged as we parted. But the thing is…I want to kiss her, and I've thought about going beyond kissing. It was after spending time with her— just talking and laughing—that I got charged up enough to return to the office and finish the profiles. When we said goodbye yesterday, we both said that we want to get together soon." I stopped my rapid-fire talk.

"Do you have an equal comparative basis? For example, do you know anything about Kate's family? Are her parents together? How many siblings? How often does she see them? Does she acknowledge that the family has influenced her? If those things are important in your decision to develop the relationship in more depth, you probably want to know more. And you mentioned Rox's values. Do you have the same type of information or do you sense the same commitment to values when you're with Kate?"

"Point well taken. I guess I need to keep in mind that the quality of being new may add some of the excitement. I know you can see I'm confused. You've helped to give me some perspective on both relationships. I have to make sure that I'm not fantasizing Kate's attributes."

"I'm glad I was helpful," Alex replied with a smile as he adjusted from being partially reclined and let his chair return to upright. With a more serious look, "I need to return the conversation to your romantic, to some degree, relationships with people who are parts of a story you're investigating. The paper doesn't have a hard policy on this point. But you know from your earliest training in the field that objectivity is the hallmark of our trade because it assures as much as possible that the reporting is accurate and fair. Can you look me in the eye and tell me that you believe yourself capable of reporting publicly a misstep by either one of these women?

"Or...." he said with emphasis to cut off the start of my answer to his first question. "Or, if you have a nasty falling out with either of them, do you believe yourself capable of realizing your bias as you interpret an action that is on the borderline between misstep and correct step?"

He waved his hand to indicate he was finished and I was free to respond. "I can answer 'yes' to both those questions. I wrestled with my decision to become a reporter after having very nearly identical questions posed in the Media and Ethics' course. The difficulty increases with the degree to which we know the principal participants. I also wrestled with the question when I realized that my relationship with Rox might become more serious and even intimate."

"I'm confident that you are capable as you say. I wish you luck and a minimum of sleepless nights as you eliminate your dilemma. You're the only one who can resolve things." He stood, shook my hand, clapped me on the shoulder and left his hand there as he moved us both to his office door.

After Alex returned to his office, Kim asked, "All better now?" When I turned my eyes toward her with a look that must have indicated surprise, she explained, "You look better—less stressed than when you went in."

It was the first time I remember having seen her look ill at ease; I took some pleasure in that. I worked at not smiling when I said, "I'm glad you explained that. Alex is a good person to work for."

"I think that often," was all she offered. She could be serious. Perhaps the teasing and double meanings were the only way she knew to be friendly.

While I ate lunch, I made notes for a plan of what additional resources I would need in order to gain information to answer the questions regarding the profiles that I had created. Some answers would be found at the end of time-consuming searches of the newspaper's archives and web searches, but those would be easy. Others were going to require gaining the cooperation of the freeholders' acquaintances to tell what they knew from association as a friend or foe. I began a search for the friends and foes.

I phoned Kim, got past her with no quip, and asked Alex who he knew inside either political party who would be willing to talk to me off-record about the activities of John Wilson as a back-room leader. It occurred to me that our earlier discussion had awakened fatherly concerns, as he first warned me to be very careful and to tread lightly because an old-fashioned political boss was likely to be either your best friend or your worst enemy with little chance of a relationship in between those two extremes. He promised to confer with Griff Hess who would do a better job than him to guide me through the search, telling whom to avoid and whom to approach. He said no one was as well connected as John Wilson and a handful of others at his level of influence, but at the next level I would find Griff informed and respected. He suggested I come to his office the next day for part of the continental breakfast and meeting. My enthusiasm was all about the prospect of help and nothing about the need to get to the office by 7:00. Those people in high-level positions must get very little sleep! I told Alex that maybe Mr. Hess could also give advice on where to find information about trials of Wilson's clients who were convicted.

I turned to an old family friend for help with finding competitors of J & AH Construction who would be willing to talk to me off the record. While the information I would receive from someone talking on the record probably could have led directly to some useful information, off the record conversation would help to point me in the right direction for further investigation. In addition, off the record was my only hope for persuading people to talk with me. The family friend was Frank Melini, who had been business agent for the IBEW, the electrical workers union. Mr. Melini had secured summer jobs for me as electrical helper, so I felt comfortable calling him at the union. After I identified myself, he said he'd been keeping up with my career by reading my articles in the paper. He said, "I'm proud to tell people that the reporter worked for me as a kid. I tell them I wanted you in the union, but I guess you didn't want to get your hands dirty."

"It wasn't the dirty hands, Mr. Melini. It was too complicated for me to figure the right place on the conduit as the center of the bend so that the ninety degree corner fit just right. Those guys I worked with might not have known they were using math when they did that, but that's what it was, and they used it every day. I still have a lot of respect for electricians and other tradesmen. That's one of the things you did for me with the summer jobs, and I thank you."

"Always glad to help you, kid. Maybe some day you'll tell me what the other things were that I did for you. But you didn't call me to shoot the breeze, did you?"

"No, sir. You're right. I called to see if you would help me on the QT so I could get information for an article. I promise I won't use your name; I want to know the names of any of the competitors of Alberto Hernandez and his J & AH Construction Company who were angry enough about his tactics to steal customers that they might talk to me off the record and if you know of any building inspectors or officials of other trade unions who might have been paid off by him to keep quiet any possible illegal activities."

"Listen to you! Possible illegal activities! If it were Alberto Hernandez who was involved, you can substitute 'probable' for 'possible.' That's a tough assignment to give you those names. It's touchy, and I have to remember first: Can I get an agreement that you'll leave the IBEW out of this?"

"I'll be happy to leave the electrical workers out, if you can tell me that you know absolutely that there was no involvement."

"I can only vouch for my time there, and I'll guarantee that everyone remained clean. I don't know what happened since."

"Then as a reporter, I can't say I'll leave them alone if things come up. I certainly won't ask you about your own union. And I won't ever use your name."

"You're sure a tough one! That's why I wanted you in the trade... I tell you I'll give you what I can remember, but it's gonna take a couple a days."

I said, "Thanks a lot, Mr. Melini! This will be very helpful. Should I call you back in two days from now?"

"Yeah, that'll be good. Call me back. And, kid, be careful. You're moving to the big leagues of tough guys. They kill their own family members if they get in their way."

I pumped my left hand in the air after leaving his office.

═══════════════

I got wrapped up in my work again. Since I hadn't made any progress on paper, I took on the easiest of the three freeholders to check on: Gladys Helms.

My search to answer questions I had about her was generally unproductive. I learned that the housekeeper who threatened to get even after being fired was llanya Boichenko who didn't live in New Jersey now and whose daughter lived in Neptune. Helms had been party to a few disputes while serving as the assertive president of the freeholders. One conflict involved the student editor and faculty advisor of the newspaper who insisted on printing an editorial about apparent bias against gay students who were denied the requests they had made. The requests had been for establishment of a Gay Studies program, including the addition of one new course each year. A conference between the attorney representing the Student Press Rights Alliance and the dean of Campus Life for the college led to publication of the article, and then everyone forgot the issue. Helms also had been quoted in a news article about a representative of the American Federation of College Instructors who was trying to organize the school faculty into a union. She had said that the faculty seems happy with their pay and working conditions. A follow-up article reported that the rep left the campus after most part-time and adjunct faculty wouldn't sign the petition for union representation due to their unwillingness to pay dues with a portion of their paychecks. I found a letter to the editor about grading practices, sent by five students, which focused on Helms. Their allegation was that she had jumped on the grade-inflation bandwagon after discussion of the same topic at Princeton made the national news services. They also claimed that she pressured faculty to lower grades. No subsequent news article appeared in the archives. The last item with a hint of conflict was the follow-up to a quotation in an article about technology applications. She said, "The Board of Trustees takes a moderate position which is that technology can be a valuable tool for research and communication and can make operations more efficient, but we shouldn't purchase equipment just because the items are the latest products on the market." The quote became the topic of a letter to the editor from a student who said the equipment in place wasn't reliable and was often not available for use. If there were more serious problems, they didn't show up in the newspaper. Helms did not become a chief suspect. After my dismissal of Helms, there were two chief suspects: Hernandez and Wilson. I needed to think my way through Thomson and Ferguson. That wouldn't happen tonight.

Because I had other articles to write, I didn't leave the office till almost 7:00. On the way home I decided to take the night off from work. Following a quick check of the day's mail, mostly catalogues and business solicitations, I selected one of my favorite meals: peanut butter on rice cakes.

CHAPTER TWELVE

Before heading to bed I enjoyed the rare peace of mind that comes from assurance that I was too tired and muddle-headed to trust any work I might do. Every time even the suggestion of a work-related obligation or partially finished project began to slide along the side of my mind, I changed the channel or my chair or my sitting position, and the thought disappeared. When I turned out the light before going to sleep, I looked forward to more energy and a fresh take upon awakening tomorrow. During the night, there was no nightmare and no waking with my body in a sweat. Enjoying the refreshment resulting from a night of peace, I took time to stretch my back and legs before putting my feet on the floor the following morning.

My first thought about something other than myself and how well my life was going and how I would handle fortune as an award-winning journalist was the recognition of the sleepy voices of my compulsion and anxiety: *Shouldn't you finish your analysis of the board members at the college? Two of them are on the list of prime suspects; one you consider to not be a problem. You've got two left.*

After I swore at the thought that had invaded my reverie—pleasant consideration of my new life that would be free from worry and free from checking my multi-day to-do list and free from my top priority of pleasing others—the list of my obligations began to pull on the leash attached to the puritanical dog collar of my unfinished work. I strained to break free from the guilt trip my parents and teachers and bosses sent me on so many years ago.

No luck! I really should return to finishing the review of the last two freeholders. It would make the project so nice and polished to get the last two of five finished. That would give me more time to make phone calls and to talk with people. I couldn't stop the parade. *Finish the analysis. Make the calls. Talk with people. You can do that all before Noon if you stop lollygagging - stop smirking-stop feeling the best you have in years.* I gave up.

———————————

Maggie Thomson seemed an easier research project than Sam Ferguson. I read again the newspaper articles about the custody hearing. Somehow my first couple of readings had overlooked a lead which now leapt off the page at me. The attorney for Leonard, her ex-husband, as part of his attack on her character and fitness to raise the girls, had tried to introduce the failed lawsuit of one of the middle management males whom Maggie had left in her dust as she climbed the Northeast career ladder. The article included a passing reference to a restraining order issued against her, which had forbid her to make contact with the wannabe executive. The judge had ruled that information as inadmissible. While that line of research might have led to some interesting collateral information, I decided that to pursue the outside chance of finding a key to wrongdoing would use up some of the goodwill credit I enjoyed at the police department.

I decided that the vote on authorization of expenditures on the paving project might hold greater potential for damage to her reputation. Maggie's vote had been an abstention, but her comment indicated that she would have voted against the contract for paving had there not been the question about monitoring the frog population and their habitat under the bridge. In my initial analysis I had concluded that her motivation had been possibly to oppose the Republican majority and win public favor, which might be helpful in future elections. The only possible connection with the restraining order might be that the middle manager who had been passed over was in some way involved in the leadership of the Republican party. That didn't seem possible.

I puzzled my way through the disappearance of Leonard and what possible connection that might have in influencing Maggie's vote. The only rationale for an influence on her vote that made sense was if Leonard's disappearance was connected in some way to Hernandez or Rivera. And although Maggie would have wanted Leonard out of her life, if Hernandez or Rivera had engineered his disappearance, it didn't make sense that she would oppose award of the contract to Baja Paving. I added Thomson to Helms on my list of unlikely suspects.

That left only the analysis of Ferguson as a possible suspect. Sam Ferguson generally was undistinguished in all facets of his life. Although he had answered the threat of one of the opposition leaders during the demonstration which took place the evening he had presented his report on the human and environmental safety of the Oyster Creek nuclear plant, he was very much aware of the presence of the security personnel and had expected them to surround him if there was even a hint of trouble. It was very safe for him to goad his tormentor with a tough-guy remark.

That public exchange of words was the only hint of a problem. My question was had there been hostile interaction between Sam and this opposition leader during the intervening four years? Since an increasing number of local papers were maintaining archives of past issues, I spent the majority of my time searching them. I found the reference to the exchange in three different publications. One enthusiastic headline writer had crafted: "Environment of Meeting More Dangerous Than Nuke Plant." Sam made the most of Andy Warhol's promise: "In the future, everyone will be world-famous for 15 minutes." During the interview, which provided the basis for the article under the inflated headline, he played it cool and was quoted as having said: "When a person's brain falls short of the task, retreat to brawn is a frequent strategy. I permitted him to drag me down to that level, but I can compete in that arena also if necessary." The reporter had obtained contact information from the demonstrator at the conclusion of the meeting. She had been able to read the quote to him and ask for his reaction. It was, "OOOOOOOOOO!"

Fortunately, the reply to the reporter's follow-up question permitted me to close the book on the incident and on any further consideration of Ferguson as a suspect in wrongdoing.

After all the angst of gathering the information on the five freeholders and of completing a separate analysis of each of them, there were two primary suspects: John Wilson and Alberto Hernandez. Eliminating three made going forward easier.

Mr. Melini might have information that I could use to check Hernandez. I had an appointment just before noon to update Alex and Griffin Hess, and I could ask them if they had sources.

I was pleased that Kim was busy with a salesman when I arrived. She had time to say only, "Go right in. Mr. Speery told me he's expecting you." Alex and Attorney Hess were catching up on the latest developments in their lives when I knocked on the door frame. Alex waved me in as he said, "Come join us! Grab a bagel and whatever you choose to drink on your way. Griff was just telling me that his daughter has decided medicine will be her profession. I guess we can expect an increase in the hourly rate when we renegotiate our agreement. Tuition keeps climbing."

"Hi, Jeff." Hess extended his hand. I shook it as he began to close out the banter. "Cost of tuition is one expense which probably never will get cheaper. I thought fifteen thousand was a large charge for a year of law school about twenty-five years ago." He gave a hearty laugh and concluded, "I guess I should feel good that I won't be responsible for paying for college and graduate school for April's kid— whenever they're ready for continuing their educations. No telling where tuition costs will be then. April's my daughter."

Alex quickly quipped, "I can't imagine a successful attorney with several lucrative professional agreements escaping the costs of educating his grandchildren. It looks like you buy the grandkids some of their earliest books, start them reading at an early age, and then pay the tuition when they qualify for some of the most expensive universities in the world."

I stepped in at that point, "You wouldn't want anything other than that, I would guess. You may be able to recoup some of the investment when you live long enough that they take you in."

We all had a good laugh and took our seats as Alex moved the conversation to the day's business. "Jeff, this is my bi-weekly meeting with Griff to review developments in topics from past meetings and to explore whatever new has come up. It seemed like a fortuitous opportunity to get you in here to update us on your investigation, to make the request you mentioned to me for help finding sources for information, and to get advice from Griff. Let me get that started.

"Jeff is a persistent reporter. Reminds me of me at the same stage of my career. I kept the legal department busy also, but the degree of caution we must exercise now had no forerunner back then."

When Alex gave a big smile and Hess turned to look at me, I quietly said, "Thanks…if there's a compliment in the comments about running up the attorney billings." I worked hard at hiding my surprise by not changing the set of my face.

Hess took the lead at that point and asked, "Is this in regard to the case of the frog habitat and paving the bridge?"

"Yes, sir."

"Bring me up to date and then both of you tell me what you have in mind for me to do."

Alex spoke before I did, "You remember we last sought your advice in regard to the article Jeff had written. Since then, the Freeholders voted to award a contract to Baja Paving Company for the purpose of covering the existing bridge. I gave Jeff authorization to continue to look into the matter. He feels there may have been some personal agendas of Freeholders which swayed their contract votes. He did a great deal of research and created profiles of all five Freeholders. He also noted that they voted along political party lines. He needs to explore further and wants your assistance. Jeff, why don't you pick up from there."

Hess interjected, "Party line votes don't tell us much of anything because they're so frequent."

"I'm aware of a number of votes along party lines," I began as an acknowledgement of his downplay of the party-line outcome. "In this case, I think there may be more than the usual politics. The Republican yes votes reinforce their current power status. But there may be individual corruption and/or collusion. The Democratic no votes may have more to do with gaining positive public reaction than with doing what's best for the county. I'm particularly interested right now in John Wilson and Alberto Hernandez. I think you can contribute information about Wilson, and I hope you can suggest other people to talk to about him. I'm working with another source to help find people to talk to about Hernandez."

"I can help with information and sources regarding Wilson. I also hope you'll consider my plea for you to be very circumspect in your discussion with any sources who might supply information about either of these men. They're both very big players. John more with the existing, largely known political structure. With Hernandez, it's more with the underground criminal operation. Some people have gone so far as to call the people he's connected with the 'Mexican mafia.' I can't tell you often enough to watch yourself at all times and speak only with people whom other knowledgeable sources have assured you are safe."

When he paused, indicating the expectation that I respond, I said, "I've gotten the same picture and similar cautions from all others with whom I've spoken. I'll be very careful; I have no death wish."

"I don't mean to scare you, but at my age and with my interest in the good of the newspaper I feel strongly that I need to give advice and to try to get my clients to follow it. Let me start with the name of a Republican Party leader whom you can trust to keep your discussion confidential. I'll need to talk with him first. He's James Livermore, the treasurer for thirteen years. His father was a member of the leadership for twenty-six years, and James continues to be very influential. After I speak with him, I'll alert Alex who can notify you that it's okay to get in touch."

"Thank you, sir," I said with relief.

He continued to talk, "I can give you some general information based on my experience within the party. All of this is off the record. You can use it as a guide to further investigation, but you can't use what I'm going to tell you. Is that agreed?"

"Yes, sir. I'm grateful for all you're doing."

Hess turned to Alex and asked, "And how about with you? I've known you over the years to always keep a confidence. But my standing with the party leadership is slightly more important than our friendship. If that's bothersome to you, I apologize."

"No need to apologize. I understand completely and have complete faith that you are seeking my agreement because you need to." Alex's words were quite an endorsement; I had been a witness to his dismissal of a very important person who sought the same assurance of confidentiality. He had a reputation for being very assertive and very effective in frightening anyone who tried to gain influence over him

"John Wilson fits the stereotype of an Irish street fighter. He never runs from a fight, and he always fights to win. There were some pretty tough fights for control with losses on both sides, especially during his first years before he proved himself and earned respect and support of others in the party. He always had determination and accurate instincts about the weak points of his opponents, but he had to learn that he needed to win friends as well as defeat enemies.

"Through the years he's made plenty of accusations and been accused himself of lots of little things and some pretty serious ones. The most serious charge against him was misuse of party funds, a charge for which he was indicted and then ultimately acquitted. His accusers were drummed out of the party; two of them eventually left the state. Many of the losers in fights with him lost their political influence, some immediately and others in the next year or two. The difference between Irish and Italian gang leaders is that the former follow the rule: 'Finish the fight,' while the latter believe: 'Hold your friends close and your enemies closer. It's a matter of timing.

"Some onlookers have speculated that the nearly total absence of charges against Wilson is a result of the Republican control of most government offices in the county. Others attribute his avoidance of state and federal charges to his expansion of friendships beyond party boundaries. In recent years he appears to have slowed down and is said to be grooming a successor. You can bet money that he'll retain his influence, but his power will be less obvious. Who's to say who's wrong and who's right since both sides are meeting the obligations of their offices.

"Jeff, I can't tell you anything for certain. There have been rumors and innuendoes, the stuff that politics spawns and depends on. No one has made anything stick to him that has led to a conviction. Enemies were made, and political careers were stopped. He's either very skillful in not getting caught in violations of law, or he's a master at stopping just short of the limits. It's because I don't know which that I warn you one last time to be very careful."

"Thanks for your caution, sir. I know now better even than before that he's one of the all-time masters of influence.

"I have questions about complaints filed by convicted felons who were represented by Wilson. During my research, I read that two complaints were filed, but he was cleared in both of them. Do you have any information about whether either or both of them contacted Wilson once they were released from prison?"

"You were thorough in your research. I'm very impressed! Very little about the first complaint reached the papers. I don't know this for a fact, but I always thought the partners in the firm for which he worked had used their influence to quiet the potentially damaging accusation. No one was surprised at the conviction that led to the complaint. The perpetrator was a two-bit crook who came close to killing his victim. As I recall, he had a problem with the fiancé of a former girlfriend. I think the hoodlum's name was Ganello. Is that right?"

"Yes. Sammy 'The Enforcer' Ganello."

"Although the hearing on the complaint led to exoneration of Wilson I heard Ganello tried to blackmail Wilson after his release in 1984. As far as I know, he made only one attempt and then wasn't heard from again.

"What I know about the second complainant probably is no more than you found in your research. His name is Lester Lannon. He waited till he was released in 2000 after serving seven years for embezzlement before he filed his complaint. Wilson went a little nuts about it when he and Lannon crossed paths outside the courthouse, and that's what made it a news item. By that time he was a senior partner in the law firm, and it couldn't be hushed up. Although I would guess the other partners would have preferred to keep it quiet.

"As a result of Wilson's public explosion, the hearing was followed by the media. This kind of hearing is often interesting because the attorney who had defended the complainant is now in a position where his clearance depends on his subtle discrediting the former client. The attorney needs to show that the conviction was the result of the criminal's actions and not the result of a weak presentation of the evidence. In this case, Lannon appeared to be much more greedy than he was adept at his crime. After being cleared, Wilson repeated his earlier public remarks about years of dedicated service to his clients. You may be able to discover what happened to Lannon."

I was bursting with excitement about this new information, but I did my best to be cool. "This information will be very helpful. I will use it as a guide to additional research, and I promise not to use it directly. I thank you heartily! Do I understand that Alex will relay to me information from you about the opportunity to talk with Mr. Livermore?"

"All that is correct. I'm glad to have helped. Your work may help the people in general in this part of the state."

I rose and turned to Alex. "Thanks for allowing me to take some of your conference time. I'll keep you informed, as usual. I'll get out of your way so that you can get to other items on your agenda."

My enthusiasm got the better of me. After closing the door to Alex's office and before turning around, I pumped my fist in the air and whispered, "Yyyyyes!"

I turned around to find Kim watching me with her most coquettish smile. She quickly commented, "My, you're excited! I saw that same gesture by the Devils goalie last night as he got that little round black thing out of the way."

"You mean he got the puck out of the way," I said without thinking.

My instantaneous blush was the signal for her to move in and finish the victory: "No, he stayed right there. And that prevented the score." Her look was one of total satisfaction.

I know I was blushing again as I mumbled, "Good meeting. I got a lot done."

My nemesis called out as I hurried around the corner into the hallway, "Come back again soon. I always enjoy our discussions."

I returned to my desk and worked on locating The Enforcer and Lester. My search of public databases returned nothing for Samuel Ganello. I used all the ways I thought might yield some results: Google first as the easiest, NJ Department of Corrections, the state listing of deadbeat parents in case he owed child support, NJ Motor Vehicle Commission, archives of other newspapers using searches of news stories and of obituaries, several online white page phone directories, and people search services. I usually am able to find a person if he or she exists. I made note of the apparent disappearance for further consideration.

Lester Lannon was easy. He appeared on Google with information that he is a speaker to groups of released convicted criminals as a part of a transition program run by an ecumenical church program to ease the adaptation to life outside prison. The other databases provided other information: address and phone number, the name of his wife, and reference to an article in a weekly community "shopper" newspaper. I accessed the article and could tell that his new occupation was owner of a landscaping business and that he was a faithful member of the church. I dismissed his case as a possible concern in my research regarding Wilson.

CHAPTER THIRTEEN

Emerging into the midday haze, I checked my watch. It was a few minutes past noon. Other obligations and the need for lunch pushed their way through my exuberance at a new line which promised to lead somewhere with my investigation. Was I upholding the law or increasing newspaper circulation?

I chose to make a trip to Subway because the food was good, the service was fast, and the price was right. The Italian special once again won my vote. As much as I wanted to continue my quest with a phone call to Frank Melini, I had other article assignments: report of the CentraState's Celebration Ball recognizing Theodore Narozanick, the recent debate among the county politico's of whether the Democrats would gain their first seat on the Board of County Freeholders, and predictions that Ocean County would reach 625,000 residents by 2007. I needed to keep my high rating with Alex.

I'd been turning over in my mind the three articles and was able to finish and email all three by 3:15. Having completed that obligation, I quickly turned to continuing my frog fracas research. I was obsessed now.

My phone call to Frank Melini began with his usual effort to recruit me back to work as an electrician. I don't know if the attempts were sincere or were part of his remarkable people skills. It certainly made me feel good, and

I'm sure that he would find a place for me if I were to tell him that I wanted to resume work as an electrician.

"Okay, kid. You're a tough case. Sounds like you have your mind made up and you're gonna stay with the Horace Greeley routine. I guess you're calling today to get some names I promised you."

"Yes, sir. You know I like talking to you also, but you wouldn't believe me if I said that was the main reason I'm calling," I answered.

"I have five names for you. I can't guarantee that any of them will talk with you, although I think the competitors will. One is Jack Smalley, owner of Intercoastal Construction and Renovation, who was removed from a major restoration of the Breakers Hotel in Spring Lake. The hotel owner had several allegations against the company which are difficult to defend against. Smalley walked away rather than get tied up in court for a year or so. It was a time when he was already booked eighteen months out. Hernandez was awarded the new contract at a lesser cost. Smalley is sure his work was tampered with.

"Tim McGruder of TMC, Inc. was under-bid by Hernandez on three consecutive jobs. All were in Brielle, a town where Hernandez had never won a bid previously. McGruder said it was like Hernandez had knowledge of the other bids prior to the official openings.

"And Jason Leigh of Perfection Custom Homes was forced to withdraw from several projects when he couldn't get materials in time to meet the deadlines. Guess who won the re-bids."

"Would the name start with H and end with Z?" I asked with a laugh.

"What a smart boy! A building inspector is less likely to talk with you. I'm giving you two names. Axel Nelson was inspector for Neptune before he was convicted of fraud and collusion. He's out now and may talk with you because he was angry that the other side of the equation—Hernandez—was never even charged. I'm giving you the name of the widow of Larry Morison who was code enforcement director for Howell and died during the investigation following his indictment for taking bribes. Hernandez had worn a wire during three meetings with Morrison while he was cooperating with the investigative team. She may talk because the investigation was closed after the death so she has nothing to fear."

"This is all very helpful, Mr. Melini," I said with excitement. "Why wasn't this information compiled before now?"

"I've wondered the same thing. I guess no one was curious enough to ask the questions you asked. Remember that you can't use this information except as a guide to further checks."

"You have my word on that. I wouldn't do that to anyone because the reputation of keeping my word is one of the most important attributes for a successful reporter. Besides, you've been a very good friend for a long time."

He concluded the conversation with a warning and encouragement. "Watch yourself, my friend. And good luck while you dig up the truth."

"Thanks for both your thoughts. And goodbye."

I was able to make an appointment the following day with McGruder. I left messages for Smalley and Leigh, suggesting times the next day. If the suggested time would work in the schedule kept by each, then we could avoid a lot of phone calls back and forth. If it didn't, the prospect of me showing up is motivation for each to make a return call to work out another time. I also made arrangements for two days later to meet with Nelson and Mrs. Morison.

I did some planning of questions for my appointments the next day and got out of the office by 5:30. At home I phoned both Roz and Kate, being very careful to call each by the correct name. I enjoyed the phone calls but hated myself for postponing a decision on which one to gently remove from my life so I could concentrate on the other. Almost all my life I had dated only one girl at a time.

I had a restless night and awoke at 6:00, a half-hour before the setting on my alarm. Usually I would curse the loss of sleep. Today I thought it a good thing with all the tasks I wanted to complete

I checked my supply of flavors of Pop-Tarts: strawberry (My consistent favorite, unless I was temporarily satiated; I decided I was), brown sugar and cinnamon, chocolate, and blueberry. I chose the blueberry because I didn't care. A cup of coffee and OJ completed the menu.

I read the morning paper, checking particularly my articles to make certain they were the same as what I had put to bed yesterday. There were no surprises. I skimmed Alice Hopkins third article on the investigation into the embezzlement of $93,000 over four years by the treasurer for the Forked River Ambulance Corp. Although the theft of organizational funds was a relatively frequent crime across the country, I never understood why no fellow member had looked more closely into the monthly reports. If he had, he might have begun to wonder why the balance moved upward so slowly in the midst of re-peated fund-raising activities. Today's article reported an interesting discovery. The stepsister of the president's wife had been the auditor for the same four years during which the thefts had taken place. New York pro sports teams con-tinued to receive disproportionate coverage when compared to Philadelphia and New Jersey teams.

A couple of routine email messages were easy to handle, so I enjoyed a third cup of coffee and knocked off the daily jumble puzzle.

I made a practice of being early for appointments with sources who were new and who were seeing me at some inconvenience or risk to themselves. I was so accustomed to the coquettish looks and comments of Kim that I hesi-tated outside the office door to prepare myself for a verbal joust.

I relaxed immediately upon seeing that the secretary to the owner of Timo-thy McGruder Construction, Inc. was past middle age. With a gravelly voice in the lower range of pitches, she greeted me with, "You must be Mr. Stewart!"

"I'm Jeff Stewart. I want to look around for my father when you say 'Mr. Stewart," I said while I read her nameplate and quickly added, "Miss Jamison."

"Please be seated. Mr. McGruder is very punctual, and you're early. I ex-pect you'll be waiting for eleven or twelve minutes. I'll return with your coffee. Feel free to look at one of the magazines. Or, maybe newspaper reporters don't read magazines to relax?"

"I enjoy many magazines. I think it's because of their less frequent pub-lication that I find the style of writing to be less intense and more expansive. Not as much pressure to cover who, what, when, where, why, and how in one sentence. That kind of thing."

She disappeared into a space from the refreshment center to the left of her desk as I spoke my final words. "And here's your coffee," she began as she emerged from the refreshment area. When she saw that I had chosen *Home Music Choices* magazine, she asked, "Are you a music equipment officiando or a shopper?"

We small-talked about shopping and purchases in electronics and autos.

The phone on her desk rang, and she excused herself to answer. "Yes, he's here, and we've been having a nice talk. I'll bring him in, sir." She turned to me and said, "Jeff, Mr. McGruder is ready to see you, exactly on time. Bring your coffee if you like."

She walked ahead of me to the closed office door, opened it, entered, stood aside, and said, "Mr. McGruder, this is Mr. Stewart, although he prefers to be called Jeff.'"

McGruder had been moving toward us as we moved toward him. He shook my hand and said, "Jeff it is then. I'm pleased to meet you. I see Nellie fixed coffee for you. That's good because now I can have some as well. Nellie—"

She interrupted, "I'm on it, sir. Are you drinking high test or decaffeinated?"

"I'll go with your second choice."

"Now, Jeff, the information which Nellie passed on to me is that you're checking work of one of my competitors. I'll be honest with you, but what I'll tell you is only what I know for sure. I'm not gonna make any guesses. And I'm gonna make sure that I don't get sued. Understood?"

"That's exactly the way I want it. You tell me only what you know, what you're sure of, about Alberto Hernandez."

McGruder raised his eyebrows and looked momentarily at the ceiling. "You're taking on a tough one. That guy's been in on some shady projects. He's got no ethics! You can see what I think of him already. You tell me what you want to know."

"I hear you lost three jobs to him in Brielle because he underbid you. What can you tell me about that?"

"He never done no work in that town before, and I worked there many times. His bids were so close to mine and just a little below. It was like he had information about my bid before he turned his in. I started hand delivering mine just minutes before the deadline and staying in the town manager's office until the time was up. Then I followed the manager and his secretary into the bid opening.

"Once I started doing that, he stopped beating my low bids, and I got my share of work. Then some other owners started doing the same, and funniest thing, Hernandez got no more jobs there. Our attorneys talked with the town attorney, and pretty soon a clerk quit and moved away. I hear she has a lot nicer house than before. I don't care about her as long as the bid process looks like it's fair."

"Was there ever an investigation of possible collusion?"

"I never heard of any. He's in the right political party, and no one seems to want to look at what's been going on."

"Do you have a problem with my using this information if I get verification? I won't quote you as my source. I'll just report the facts."

"That's your job. I hope you get enough information to finish Hernandez." McGruder looked at his watch and stood up. "I got other stuff to do today, so that's all the time I can give you."

I said my thanks and left. Miss Jamison took my coffee cup and wished me good luck. She said she has a nephew who is a reporter so she knows how rough it can be.

Once outside the office building, I used my cell phone to check my messages back at work. Jack Smalley had called to confirm for 3:00 today and asked that I phone ahead of time to let his secretary know what the meeting was about. Griffin Hess had left a message that it was okay for me to talk with Livermore, but I would need to make an appointment. There was no message from Jason Leigh so I decided to drop in at his office at the 10:00 time I had suggested in the message I had left him the day before. While on my way to Leigh's office, I phoned Smalley's secretary—a male voice.

"I'm Jeff Stewart, calling to confirm an appointment with Mr. Smalley for 3:00 today."

"Yes, Mr. Stewart. Thank you for calling. I have you in the schedule for 3:00. Mr. Smalley asked what it is you want to interview him about."

I had become skilled at saying something that sounded sensible while I spoke but contained no information. "I'm gathering information about construction projects and want Mr. Smalley's views on the way in which competing companies influence the presence or absence of competition across the construction industry. Part of my interest is in what happens to the competitive atmosphere when a company gets too competitive."

"Thank you. I'm not sure I understand all that you said, but I'll do my best to pass it on to Mr. Smalley. And we'll see you at three o'clock."

Perfection Custom Homes occupied a modest red brick building set on a three-acre parcel with a small pond. While modest, the building was attractively landscaped with a variety of evergreen bushes and seasonal flowering mums. One portion of the pond contained swamp grass, while another portion was home to bamboo plants. A tasteful white sign with rust-colored letters was prominently positioned near the road.

An attractive receptionist welcomed me with a warm smile, "Welcome to Perfection. My name is Shaina. How may I help you?" Often a greeting of this type is expressed in a bored voice, which belies any semblance of welcome. Not so in this case; I felt that Shaina was truly glad I had arrived.

"Hi, Shaina. My name is Jeff. I left a message yesterday for Mr. Leigh, suggesting a meeting at 10:00 today and asking if that didn't work to let me know. I interpreted the lack of a return message as meaning that a 10:00 meeting is okay."

"Hi, Jeff. Do you represent a company?"

I pulled a business card from my wallet and said as I handed it to her, "I'm a reporter with *The Asbury Park Press*."

"Please be seated while I check with Mr. Smalley."

She rose and walked quickly through an open door into what obviously was a large office. I would describe her walk as business-like and not at all as provocative. Yet, the combination of her physically fit shape and the sway of her dress was very appealing. While I sat, I surveyed the waiting room: plaques announcing awards, including the best affordable design for the previous year, original artwork, displayed with prices for purchase; a large fichus tree; a fish tank, containing guppies and neon tetra (a colorful combination); a large glass-topped table with chrome legs, housing a number of trade publications, and matching chairs and couches which were simple and comfortable.

When Shaina returned to the reception area, she walked over to where I was seated and explained, "Mr. Smalley misunderstood your message and thought he should phone you if he was available to meet. He's completing work on a project that he must get to an assistant as soon as possible in order for it to be completed today. He said that he will meet with you in about fifteen minutes if you're willing to wait."

"Sure. I'll wait. That's no problem."

"How about something to drink—coffee, tea, soft drink, some juice?"

"My first choice is cranberry juice, and second choice water."

I watched her walk away again, still attracted by the movement of her green or teal clingy dress.

She returned with a big smile and a cup of cranberry juice. When she arrived, I told her I would retrieve my laptop from my car and return. She said that she could help me access the wireless network in the office if I needed it.

I spent the next fifteen minutes reviewing information that I had downloaded and then roughing out an article on trends in school classrooms this year. My concentration was broken by Shaina calling me.

I quickly saved my work and followed her into her boss's office where she introduced us and closed the door as she left.

Jason Leigh began the conversation. "Mr. Stewart...."

I interrupted, "Make it Jeff please."

With a large smile—my hoped for reaction—he began again, "Jeff, I only know that you're doing an article on some aspect of the construction industry. I guess I'll find out what aspect when you ask your questions."

"I'm going back a couple of years when your company had difficulty getting materials from suppliers and lost some projects for which you had won the bids. I believe Alberto Hernandez's company was awarded the jobs in all cases. Is that information correct?"

Leigh sat a little straighter in his chair as his face became more serious when I mentioned the name Hernandez. "Your information is accurate."

"That must have been a hard pill to swallow. Had you had problems with the suppliers previously?"

"Never. Not with any of them."

"Did they give you any reasons for the problems?"

"The reasons varied. Some had labor problems, like strikes or slow-downs. Some had estimated delivery dates wrong." As he spoke, the pupils in his eyes shrank, and his voice increased in volume. "Some had problems at the last minute with their shippers."

"Was Hernandez the only one who profited from these unusual difficulties?"

With a look of anger, he replied, "I don't understand your question."

"Was Hernandez the second place bidder in every case? Did any other company get the bid on a job from which you had to withdraw?"

"Smithson got one job, but then they had to withdraw."

I was surprised by this new revelation, as my response revealed. "What! That looks as suspicious as hell!"

"Where was your paper when that took place? I filed a complaint with the state, and nothing happened."

"I don't know, but I'm sure going to check. Did you give information to my paper?"

"I didn't call the paper because I was afraid that the publicity would cause problems with the handling of the complaint. What a fool I was about that! The state said that their investigation had shown unforeseeable circumstances were the cause of problems in both our cases and no one had done wrong."

"You're still in business. How did you recover from your supply problems?'

His eyes flashed as he replied, "I hope you don't really believe they were supply problems. They were thefts. Hernandez stole the business by somehow getting the suppliers to lie. I changed suppliers. Paid more. Made less profit. Had to lay off some of my best people. The man nearly ruined me." He rubbed his forehead with both hands and seemed to sink in his chair.

"Mr. Leigh, I know this has been painful for you to have to talk about these old events. I have one last question, if you'll oblige me."

"Sure, go ahead. You've done nothing wrong. It feels good to know that someone is interested in what that bastard has done. And if you talk to other people, you'll see that he did other things."

"Why did Smithson have to withdraw?"

"Supply problems with the same companies I dealt with."

"I hate to do this, but there's one more question which follows up your answer to the last one. Should I talk with someone at Smithson?"

"You could try Lawrence Smithson. When he retired last year, the company closed. I don't know if he'll be willing to talk."

"I'll do that. That's all of my questions, this time for real. I feel like I've intruded and ruined your day with these bad memories. Thank you so much. You've been very helpful. At this point, I don't know where this information will take me. I think it will be part of an article at least."

I gathered my things and left quickly. I took a last look at Shaina and her beautiful, clingy dress, and said goodbye.

CHAPTER FOURTEEN

Once inside my car, I took a deep breath and then exhaled slowly. This was exciting information for a young reporter. And it was frightening to hear a second victim tell the extent of the manipulations done by Hernandez. Last night I had been exhausted by information overload. My prediction then of even greater pressure today had proven accurate, and it was only 11:15.

As I drove to the office, I started to prioritize the other activities of the day. I needed to make appointments to interview James Livermore and Lawrence Smithson. I also needed to check with the county Better Business Bureau and to find ways to identify and talk with owners of property where Hernandez had completed work. I had three hours before leaving for my appointment with Smalley.

I was keyed up—a combination of excitement and anticipation of many things yet to do. A sandwich from the vending machine was acceptable under these conditions. I ate it, even though it wasn't noon yet, because if any surprise activity showed up, I wanted to be ready to go and not be delayed by the need to eat lunch.

I entered Better Business Bureau into a Google search, and within a few minutes was able to find J & AH Construction, the company controlled by Alberto Hernandez. A click on "Customer Complaint History" yielded a wealth of information. A total of nineteen complaints, covering a five-year period, were listed. Eight were indicated as having been resolved. Seven complaints were listed under the category "Work not completed to customer satisfaction." Details of these complaints included both failure to complete all work specified and quality of completed work not acceptable. Other categories were "Delayed completion of work" (5), "Cost overrun" (2), and "Failure to make repairs" (5).

The "Government action" tab provided some clarification. Both cost overrun cases were resolved after investigators from the office of the county prosecutor counseled Mr. Hernandez that fraud charges could be filed at the conclusion of their analysis of the incident. Four of the "Failure to complete work" category, presumably all for which the owners had filed an official complaint, were completed shortly after that filing. Two "Failure to make repairs" complaints were resolved at the conclusion of the questioning by the state's Consumer Advocate. The lesson to be learned is: Resolution follows some type of formal action by the owner of the property.

———

I had discovered earlier that the larger commercial and government customers who had complaints bypassed the Better Business Bureau and went straight to the courtroom. Once there, they had little success because the legal staff of the company were tough and skilled—another support for the "practice makes perfect" adage. The difference between the little customers and the big customers was the number of dollars involved. There were many cases of unsatisfactory work.

My mastery of the BBB website and online reports encouraged me to check out the company of Hernandez's friend and business associate Ramone Rivera, owner of the Baja Paving Corporation. At the time I discovered that Hernandez had set up Rivera in business, I thought there might be some spillover of unethical tactics. Another thirty minutes of searching lent credence to that suspicion.

The file on Baja Paving Corporation contained more individual items than the file for J & AH. There had been twenty-six complaints: seventeen due to "Dissatisfaction with the quality of work," five for "Delays beyond the agreed completion date," and four for "Cost overruns." I phoned the BBB in a search for further details and was told I might want to try the Ocean County Department of Consumer Affairs.

My phone call to Consumer Affairs was an educational experience. I learned that a member of the public could file a complaint online against any business operating within the county. A staff member will contact the business for information regarding the complaint and, if the complaint is evaluated as legitimate, will attempt to negotiate a settlement agreeable to the complainant. Any member of the public can call the department, provide the name of a business, and learn the history for the preceding two years, including the nature of complaints and status of resolved or pending cases. When the department is unable to negotiate a resolution, it informs the dissatisfied customer of his or her rights. One option is to go to small claims court. A Google search on the topic of small claims court introduced me to Nolo.com and njcourtsonline.com. The first of these is a resource for state limits on the amount per suit. How-to lists for preparation to go to small claims court, referrals to attorneys, and a number of other resources. The "Legal Resource Room" link on the second website leads to a service maintained by Rutgers University Law School, providing access to court decisions of the Supreme Court, from March 1994 and of the Superior Court Appellate Division and the Tax Court from September 1995.

I resisted my usual "student for life" propensity to read on from website to website due to short time and phoned Alex to ask if he would ask Griffin Hess to have his staff search for cases involving Baja Paving at any court level. I had to do a delay and a tap dance to get his agreement without a lengthy explanation of why I made the request. I pushed my luck and asked if the information could be available to me the first thing the next morning. With obvious unease in his voice, he agreed and stipulated that he would hand the results to me at a 7:00 A.M. meeting, after I had given a satisfactory explanation. I know seven o'clock worked well in his schedule, but it didn't fit the night owl hours of a reporter, whose information sources generally weren't available until ten o'clock and who spent normal business hours gathering information in order to compose articles after 5:00 P.M.

It was now forty-five minutes from my meeting with Smalley, and my priority list still contained phone calls. I was able to find phone numbers and make appointments with Livermore and Smithson. Thirty minutes later, I had just enough time left to gather my notes and other papers and to put the haphazard stack into my briefcase. I'd need to organize the information later while things were still straight enough in my mind to be able to reconstruct details if I found any gaps.

Intercoastal Construction and Renovation was located in a fine older home on State Route 35 across from the Belmar harbor marina and beach. It was attractively painted white with Kelly green trim and striped awnings which combined both colors, and a noticeable, yet tasteful, lawn sign of white with red lettering announced the company name and indicated a parking entrance accessible from the side street. The white and green reminded me of the traditional Irish population which had dominated the town in the past and which by now had shrunk as some of the larger clans had moved to somewhat more fashionable towns. As I entered the rear door from the parking area, I was greeted by a young man in dress shirt with tie. He looked up from his position at the desk and offered a charming smile as he said, "Mr. Stewart, I presume."

I took his outstretched hand and replied, "I doubt that you're old enough to have been taught about African explorers Livingston and Stanley, but that greeting format was once famous."

He continued to stand as he affirmed my supposition about his age. "I didn't know about the explorers but would be happy to learn about them."

I chose to give him the short version. "Dr. Livingston explored deeper and deeper into Africa and had been presumed dead until Stanley found him in 1871. Stanley's greeting is reported to have been, 'Dr. Livingston I presume.'"

"That sounds fascinating; I'll have to search for more information. Mr. Smalley is completing a phone call. May I get you some coffee, tea, or soda?"

"I'd like a soda, a diet cola if you have one. And please call me Jeff."

"Yes, Jeff. We do have soda. Please make yourself at home."

Having been in Leigh's office earlier in the day, I was prepared for the collection of trade journals. Fortunately for me, some of the titles were different. I began to look through *Regional Home Design Parade*. The palaces which were displayed in each series of photos were amazing. I marveled at the stone fireplaces surrounded by marble walls, at the glass walls overlooking forests or highlighting a mountain peak in the distance, and at the state-of-the-art kitchens filled with stainless appliances and hanging utensil racks. I looked for prices and found none. A passing thought was that while I looked at a form of entertainment to pass the waiting time, the primary purpose may have been to ratchet up the expectations of clients. Half the square footage of most homes on display would be four times the square footage of the nicest home of any of my parents' friends. Before I tired of ogling the way some of the top five percent lived, the host at the desk was asking me to follow him toward Jack Smalley's office.

Smalley was in the doorway, clothed for the GQ out-of-doors. His lips beneath a handlebar mustache were curved into a smile as he welcomed me with an apology for being late. My response was a "No need to apologize" and "I'm grateful for your willingness to see me."

"Bradley said you want to talk with me about the competitive nature of my field of work and the impact that an aggressive company can have. Do I have that right?"

I was dismayed by how accurately Bradley had interpreted my double-talk. My statement about gratitude for seeing me hadn't been nearly as sincere as my amazement that Smalley was seeing me now. My thoughts delayed my response by several seconds. "Bradley's summary is right on target."

"That's good! He is very efficient, quite the find as a half-year intern from Rutgers's architecture program." He paused, then, "It will be helpful to me to have you be somewhat more specific."

"Mr. Smalley, I'm gathering information about one of your competitors as part of an investigation of the decision by the Board of Freeholders to pave the H. George Buckwald Bridge on the OCC campus. I think the decisions made by some of the freeholders were guided by factors other than the public interest. I hope you'll tell me what you know about Alberto Hernandez."

I watched Smalley's face as I spoke. The first change was the disappearance of his smile, an expression which may be customary with him. Next came the furrows in his brow and a narrowing of the eye openings. He had nodded when I talked about factors other than public interest. The last changes were in his eyes—a widening of the openings and a flash of what could only be called "fire."

"I'll be glad to talk to you about that S.O.B.! I had hoped I was finished with him. But now maybe some good can come out of what I can tell you. The bottom line is he stole a major project bid from me. He forced me to back out of the project. To stay on the project and fight him legally would have cost me months of time and hundreds of thousands of dollars. I couldn't afford to do that, so I walked away. And then he gets positive press out of his stealing by convincing the owners of the hotel to waive the penalties for withdrawing because he could begin the work of his crews immediately.

"I was doing great, with eighteen months of work lined up. I was daydreaming about moving my company to the next level of success. Then that prospect disappeared." He paused as he wiped his eye with the side of his hand.

A minute later he resumed, "I know as sure as I've ever known anything that someone tampered with my work. There were collapses of some ceilings and breakage of water pipes. Three flights of stairs collapsed. My guys are all experienced in renovations. They would never do anything that would cause major failures like these. There was even some structural damage to the rear of one building, which obviously had been caused by a swing of one crane boom. And, of course, all this made my company look like we didn't know shit. The Breakers owners filed a brief for a lawsuit and filed a preliminary request for an injunction to prohibit my crews from entering the property.

"I was a madman, yelling and screaming at my staff and my family. I was stretched financially with start-up costs for this project and payment for materials for two other projects. The first payment wasn't due on the hotel renovation and my outlay on the other two jobs was fifty percent more than what I had received by the payment schedule. And add to that tuition payments for two kids in private universities."

He stopped again, stood, and said, "I have to excuse myself. I'll be right back." He walked rapidly through the door in the rear corner of his office.

About two minutes later Bradley appeared through the main door with some fresh fruit and another soda. He set them down near me and said, "Mr. Smalley will return shortly. He isn't feeling well."

"I could come back another day," I offered.

"Oh no. My boss wouldn't hear of that. Please stay here or he'll be upset with himself."

After approximately five minutes, Smalley returned and said with a strained smile, "I've talked quite a bit. I'm sure you get the picture. Maybe you have some questions."

"I find this very disturbing," I began. "Wasn't there some way you could prove that Hernandez was responsible for the damage?"

"There probably was some way. I watched a professional colleague go bankrupt as a result of his fight against charges brought by a client. He was sure someone had tampered with the work his company had done, and I'm sure he was right. He filed complaints with the police who said that they could find no evidence to support his allegations. He hired private investigators who worked for weeks and failed to produce evidence. He filed a lawsuit, and it was dismissed as lacking grounds. His family couldn't cope with the pressure and left him. And they never reconciled.

"I saw the same thing happening to me. It's scary to know what you should do and to know at the same time that you can't do it. I'm sure my life's better now than it would have been if I had tried to fight a dishonorable, immoral, destructive person and had lost."

He wiped another tear away and concluded with a smile, "My attorney did a good job working out the details with Hernandez's company. If he hadn't done so well, I would have paid penalties which equaled my profits for the last two years." He turned to me and with a look of relief said, "Well, kid, that's it from me. I won't even ask if you have questions because there isn't any more to tell."

For one of the few times in my career, I felt badly about asking questions. I stood to indicate my intention to leave soon and said, "Mr. Smalley, I thank you for the information, and I'm truly sorry to have caused you to relive such an awful chain of events. I've been in some situations where I've felt helpless, but nothing with such serious consequences as you were facing. I can't completely empathize with you because I don't have family responsibilities. I think you probably made the best choice, but it isn't fair."

"It helps to know you understand. I hope you don't mind me having called you a kid."

"No problem. Thanks for all your time."

Smalley walked me to the office door and said, "Brad, Jeff can find his way out. Please come in for a couple of assignments."

———————

I was relieved to be in the open air. I checked my cell phone and found one missed call. I pushed the button to see the call details and with great pleasure saw it was Kate's number. I hit the send button and heard, "Hi, Jeff." This was one of those times that I was surprised to have the receiver of the call know it was me. A good sign, though, that I was on her speed dial.

"Hi, Kate. It's good to hear your voice again."

"I'm glad to know you're pleased to talk with me. It's been awhile, and I was wondering if we're still friends."

"No need to wonder about that! What's up?"

"I've been in Monmouth County on business, and my next appointment is a meeting with the Jackson Planning Board. I have dinner hour free and would like to meet for dinner some place down your way."

"Wonderful!" I was a bit surprised at my exuberance. "When does your meeting start?"

"At 6:30."

"If you don't have a place in mind, I suggest we meet at Scorpio's Steakhouse on South Hope Chapel Road in Jackson. The food's good, and it's not too far to town hall."

"Sounds good. What time do you suggest?"

"5:00 would give us an hour with time for you to get to your meeting and settle in. Sound OK?"

"Sounds terrific! It'll be good to have company for dinner and especially to see you. I'll go easy on you for neglecting me the last few weeks."

"I wouldn't have neglected you without good reason. Do you want me to get a signed excuse from my boss?"

"Sure! Let's see if you can do that. I better let you go now so you can work on that. I tell you what. If you bring a signed note, I'll buy dinner."

Following a quick goodbye, I checked my watch. I had an hour and felt really relaxed. My next decision wasn't practical, but I also felt like having fun with Kate's challenge. I headed for work and placed a call to Alex's office.

———————————

Knowing that I would have to talk with Kim in order to talk with Alex was one of the impracticalities. Caller ID gave her a running start; she answered with, "Hello, stranger. Have I done something to make you angry?"

"I could never be angry with you. But I do get embarrassed sometimes when you flirt with me and tease me."

With an exaggerated tone of being hurt she replied, "Flirt? And tease? I'm always sincere. I can't be responsible for the meaning you supply to what I say. I guess the good news is that you could never be angry. My spirits are soaring like an eagle, while my heart flutters like a butterfly! But enough about us. Did you call to talk with Alex?"

"Yes, I did. Would you connect me please?" I did a mental gulp and re-phrased the last sentence, a feeble attempt to avoid some snappy comeback. "I mean please put me through to his phone."

"Now there you go again making the wrong choice on a double meaning! I'll try his line now."

I felt the warmth from my cheeks while I waited. Alex was on the line quickly. "Good afternoon, Jeff. Were you calling about our meeting in the morning?"

"No, boss. I'm headed to the office from an interview and want two mi-nutes of your time if you plan to be there for at least another twenty."

"I'll be here. What's on your mind?"

"Kate, my friend from the DEP. I want your help with a joke, and I'll ex-plain when I get there."

It wasn't exactly a sigh, but I could hear a release of tension in his voice as he said, "I'm glad to hear you're joking about something when you've been so busy and dealing with such a difficult project. I'm curious to hear your expla-nation."

"See you in twenty minutes or less."

After arriving at the office, I hurried to my desk and prepared the note for Alex to sign:

> *Please excuse Jeff Stewart for not keeping in touch with family and friends. He is a workaholic in need of rest and relaxation. Your help in reforming him would be much appreciated.*
>
> *Attest:*
> *Alex Speery*

Although I felt the pressure of time, I forced myself to walk up the stairs so that I was not breathless as I spoke to Kim. With tilted head, sparkling eyes, and a smirk formed by her lips she spoke first, "Jeff! My all-time favorite reporter. You're back among the living. Go right into Alex's office." She stood and extended her arm in the direction of the door.

My knock and entrance were quick as I escaped. Alex greeted me and pointed to my usual chair. I headed in that direction but didn't sit as I explained, "I spoke with Kate a little while ago, and we made arrangements to have dinner together before she has a meeting this evening. I dug myself a hole as I bantered with her—a much too frequent result of bantering with women—by offering to bring a note to excuse me from not staying in touch. This is what I prepared, and I ask that you sign it."

Alex said, "Hmm" a couple of times as he read and then looked up at me. "Why would I not sign this? I don't know Kate, but everything said here is true. If this is a sign of a new direction for you, then maybe she's helped already." He, with a flourish, took out a seal, which he sometimes used for special presentations, and embossed the paper with his name and title. "I love the work you do but fear you're going to burn out and find another profession."

I took the note from his extended hand and said, "Thank you, sir. I guess you and Kate have had some effect on me because I composed that note without help. I really must leave to get to the restaurant on time. I'll see you early in the morning. Good day."

As I breezed past Kim, she said, "You reminded me of the song lyrics: 'You come and go in a heated rush.'"

The heat was my cheeks again. Part way down the steps I shouted back, "Good to see you, Kim. I'll see you again in the morning.

CHAPTER FIFTEEN

The restaurant was in one of the smaller shopping malls in the area. Technically it fit the category of "storefront café," but the fresh look of a relatively new mall gave it a more upscale look. As I parked in a space facing the front door, I saw Kate enter.

Dodging a steady flow of traffic was one difference between a regular and a storefront restaurant. A common feature of this genre was a narrow entrance hallway created by either a full or a half wall. The hall served as a waiting area later in the evening. Kate and I were members of a very small group who chose to eat this early, so there would be no wait. Her faintly colored lips formed a warm smile beneath her dainty nose and dancing eyes. As I neared, both her hands were extended and a slight lean of her head toward me indicated that she expected a kiss on the cheek. I love to kiss a lady, any lady, when I meet her. I made this kiss linger a bit as her perfume awakened me.

After we were seated, I asked if she had been busy.

"No busier than usual. Mostly the same old stuff. Sometimes there's something new. Like the topics of tonight's meeting: new shopping center under consideration, the northern pine snake, and the eastern box turtle."

"Sounds exciting! I think I've heard of those two critters."

"Working for a newspaper, I'm sure you have. The two species are very common in this area and receive most of their attention when a construction project is proposed."

I encouraged her further, "So what good news do you have for the Jackson Planning Board?" I could listen to her talk about almost anything. She just gave off energy whatever she was doing. Her voice had a hoarse or gravelly sound, combined with a lyrical quality. At times she sounded as if she were almost singing.

"They're not going to like it, but I think they've had preliminary discussions with some environmental engineers and know what might be coming. They'll have to pay for a study by an expert who sets traps and does a designated number of hours of direct observation. The expert also uses some formulas based on the numbers and the size of the area under consideration and prepares a calculation that indicates if there is a habitat in the area."

She paused and addressed the waiter who had just arrived, "I've been talking too much. I'll stop, and we'll look at the menus. Could you come back in about five minutes?"

After making quick choices, Kate changed the topic. "What about you? There must be some explanation of why you haven't called. And, by the way, where's that note you promised?"

Her look of surprise was priceless as I handed her Alex's note. She immediately began to laugh as she read, "You're too much! It sounds like Mr. Speery and I have some work to do on you. Maybe you and I need to plan a recovery program."

"I don't know how much help you'll get from Alex. It's to the advantage of the newspaper for me to work a lot."

"Not if you burn out!" she said with care in her eyes and her lower lip pushing up slightly on its upper half.

As I laughed, I said, "I surrender! My mother, my boss, and now you have said the same thing. What do you have in mind for those ten steps?"

While the waiter placed our sodas and the basket of bread, Kate said, "I think we can put together at least part of the plan as we eat; but first I'm really interested in what's kept you so busy."

"There's not much I can tell you due to your official position. I've been gathering additional information on members of the Board of Freeholders. No details, but I'm not sure what went on with their votes to pave the bridge. I've been interviewing people who have information that probably will be useful, and I've checked records. I hope to be finished with this particular project

FROG GIG

in a couple of days. I have to finish this before I know what else remains with the big picture of the paving and the frogs."

"You look and sound tired," Kate commented with concern showing on her face. "Is it still exciting for you?"

"You're right; I am tired. And it is exciting, very exciting. I never know what's around the next corner 'til I get there." I ended my comments because our salads were delivered

Following the fresh ground pepper routine and the exit of the waiter, Kate began again: "Are we ready for planning the program for recovery from workaholism?"

"I can see you won't let it go until we do make a program. Where do we start? I've never done this before."

"We need to find things to substitute for work, such as having dinner with a good friend. Or talking on the phone with good friends."

"I detect a theme here. It's sharing activities with good friends."

"You can have family involved and friends in general," she said with a wink. "I started with good friends to make sure I was included at the top of the list." Then she gave me a combination smile and smirk.

My next words surprised me again. "Then we should have started with special friends."

The smirk disappeared and left a warm smile. "That's better yet! I think you're starting to get into the swing of this! That's good because I don't know what other things you like to do. You'll have to take the lead from here on,"

"Occasionally I go to movies. I like musical concerts."

"What kind of music?"

"About everything, except rap."

Kate had produced a slip of paper and pen and began to make a list of the activities. "Okay. I'm up to speed with this list. Your answer on type of music is kind of a cop-out. What three types of music do you prefer?"

I faked a look of dissatisfaction and said, "You're tough! I don't know the category names, so I'll tell you some of the people whose performances I've enjoyed: Back Street Boys, Live, Faith Hill, Wynton Marsalis, Linda Eder, and almost any symphony orchestra."

"I wrote down 'Anything.'"

"Thank you very much," I said with an exaggerated head bow. "I also like to go to professional sports events—baseball, basketball, football. I like to

143

kayak, raft, ride a bicycle, and hike. I like to go into Manhattan to see Broadway productions, although it's inconvenient and expensive. On rare occasions I enjoy museums. How am I doing with the list? There may be other things, but they don't come to mind now."

"You did well. If I count museums as one category and concerts as one and pro sports individually, I have a list of eleven items in addition to going out to eat and talking on the phone. A critical question is how many times have you done any of the eleven in the past six months?"

I didn't need the time to come up with the answer of two times, but I needed the time to decide how honest I wanted to be. I cocked my head slightly to the right, twisted my mouth, and looked at the ceiling. "Two or three."

She put down her pen and focused on my eyes. "You are a true workaholic. There are lots of things you like to do, but you choose not to. I think we have to start with a schedule in order to begin to break the habit of putting relaxation on your activity list below work, work, and work. That is, unless you don't want to change."

I gave a mental sigh of relief as the waiter brought our dinners. I could use the time to regroup. I'd like to conduct a study of the activities of waiters and waitresses as they place dinner dishes on a table. I'd use a video recorder to test my hypothesis that after they move the salad plates, bread plates, water glasses, vase, and salt and pepper shakers, everything is back where it started. I also think that waiters spend more times moving things than do waitresses.

After our guy finished his dance of the dishes, I was ready to change the topic. "Now that we have a clear path for a change in my life, let's get back to the snakes and the turtles."

A pretty woman with hypnotizing eyes has an unfair advantage over me in a verbal joust. She can get away with almost any move. Like taking an extra turn in determining the topic. "I'd like to let those snakes and turtles wait for another minute or two while you let me know if a schedule of some kind would work for you."

"You mean like a number of times per month as a target? Or do you mean setting up a timetable like the first and third Thursday?"

"Either would be a good start."

"What days and nights work best for you since I expect you to support me through this rehabilitation?"

With a facial expression to match the words, Kate said, "Oh! I didn't know you were headed in this direction. I'd like to see you more often. But I don't want you to commit to a schedule that includes only me. Maybe you need time to think further about the schedule."

I feared I had spooked her. "For now, then, let's leave it that I'll do something with someone twice a month. I know how to reach you to schedule one event at a time."

Relief was one thing I read on her face as she replied, "There you go! And the phone call will be a break from work—helping with the big goal. Now what's got you interested in the critters?"

"Let's say that a habitat is the conclusion. What's the acceptable course of action, besides abandoning the project?"

"Neither of these is an endangered specie. They're both classified as special interest species. If they're found, they usually get moved."

"Does that mean trapping them? And if it does, what prevents them from coming back?"

"It does mean trapping them. The preferred new location for a pine snake is a known habitat of the same species. The already existing habitat is attractive for the conditions of the soil and plants and for the identical society to which the snake has become accustomed."

Throughout the meal, we wandered from the initial topics to books we had been reading, movies we had seen, and local, state, national, and world events. She seemed as interested and as knowledgeable as I was. In short, we proved to be compatible over a longer period of time than our meetings at the demonstration and at the diner for afternoon coffee and pie.

After I signed the credit card receipt, Kate insisted on paying half. I lied with a low-ball but realistic amount. She handed me her money and glanced at her watch. As she did so, I realized that she wore very little jewelry: no ring, no bracelet, and only a simple necklace of thin gold chain and pendant. There was no distraction from her beauty. Her magnetic green eyes looked somewhat wistful as she sighed and said, "I hate to end this enjoyable break between appointments, but I must. I feel I know you much better now, and that's a pleasant outcome. And the food was very good—as promised."

"The way of all good things, I guess," I responded. "It seems we just got here. Time seems to go quickly with you. That's the essence of pleasure. We must do this again."

By this time we were out of our chairs and moving toward the door. She linked her arm to mine and said with a smile, "Yes, we must."

"We'll set the date during one of the calls I make to you frequently," I hurried to say.

"I'd say that you're making excellent progress!" she said as she took a quick step forward and away slightly so that she could look directly at me.

I followed her lead to her car. Once there, she dropped my arm, faced me, and rose on her toes. That was all I needed to take her shoulders in my hands and kiss her. It was too early in our developing relationship for passion, but our lips remained together longer than a friendly parting.

With a hint of laughter and twinkling eyes she said, "Goodnight, paper boy. I'm off to make people nervous about wildlife."

"So long, critter girl. You'll deliver the message with as much finesse as anyone."

I turned on the oldies radio station on my way home. I took as a message meant just for me the playing of "I'm Into Something Good" by Herman's Hermits. I sang every chorus from start to finish.

Once back at home, I decided that the most important task was preparing a summary of the information I had gathered about Hernandez and Wilson which might link to some underhanded reason for their votes to pave the bridge. I started with Wilson because I knew it would be a little easier. I ended with an outline:

- *Exoneration on charges of incompetent representation made by Ganello and Lannon*
- *Clearance by local and state bar association on complaints that he had overcharged for services*
- *Always the winner of hard-fought battles within the Republican Party*
- *Off the record I had been told by credible sources that:*
- *Accusations of misuse of party funds led to indictments and acquittals*
- *Accusers of misuse were forced out of party, 2 eventually left state*
- *Many losers in fights with him lost their political influence*

- *Republican control of most county government offices explained the almost total absence of charges resulting from Republican control.*
- *Existence of rumor that Sammy Ganello tried to blackmail Wilson after release from prison*
- *My search for whereabouts of Ganello came up empty*

The absence of Ganello was potentially the most damaging information on the list. The rest was rumor and speculation. The possibility that Wilson was responsible for that disappearance was also speculation.

I moved on to the creation of a similar summary for Hernandez. That outline, although incomplete, had multiple possibilities for criminal charges and lawsuits. The list was:

- *Competitors' stories of their customers having been stolen*
- *Competitors' claims that he obtained reduced prices on materials by entertaining suppliers and completing work on their homes at no charge*
- *Stories that he gave gifts to building inspectors and union agents*
- *Filing of lawsuits as the company grew and the stakes were larger, but the company legal staff had been very successful in defending against the conclusion that he forced his father out of the company due to major disagreement about company practices*
- *Rumors of marital infidelity preceded a very public divorce case*
- *Second marriage to a trophy bride*
- *Having set up paving company with puppet Ramone Rivera as owner and frequent funneling of business to Rivera*

Off the record I had been told by credible sources that:

- *Jack Smalley was certain that Hernandez tampered with his work on renovation of Breakers Hotel in Spring Lake, leading to cancellation of the contract, which was re-awarded to Hernandez.*
- *Tim McGruder suspected that Hernandez had knowledge of other bids before he underbid everybody on 3 jobs in Brielle after having never worked there before.*

- *Hernandez won the re-bids after Jason Leigh was forced to withdraw from several projects because he couldn't get materials.*
- *Building Inspector Axel Nelson was reported to have been angry because he was convicted of fraud and collusion and did prison time while Hernandez, as the other half, wasn't charged.*
- *Code Enforcement Director died following indictment for taking bribes after Hernandez cooperated with an investigation by wearing a wire to produce evidence.*
- *McGruder said Hernandez stopped underbidding him after McGruder began the practice of turning in bids just before deadline and staying with the town manager until after opening. Later a clerk quit and moved away to a much nicer house than she had before.*
- *Leigh said after suppliers reported that they could not supply materials, Hernandez got all re-bids but one and that the contractor who won that re-bid also had to withdraw for the same reason.*
- *Smalley said that collapses of ceilings, breaking pipes, and stairway collapses were the result of sabotage and that structural damage to rear of building was caused by swing of a crane boom.*
- *Smalley said that Hernandez then claimed publicly that he had convinced owners of hotel to drop their plan to file suit by agreeing to step in immediately.*
- *BBB record including 19 complaints over 5 years against J & AH—8 were resolved.*
- *Resolution of complaints shortly after both county prosecutor and state consumer advocate met with Hernandez.*
- *Existence of problems by the offshoot Baja Paving Corporation which Hernandez set up for Rivera, including:*
- *BBB file of 26 complaints in 5 years*
- *Possible additional information which might be available through Griffin Hess at a meeting the following day*

I decided to leave the Wilson dossier open and to concentrate my active investigation on Hernandez.

CHAPTER SIXTEEN

I expected a restless night due to excitement about the information, but it never happened. My alarm the next morning shocked me out of a sleep befitting the dead, surely the result of exhaustion after a busy day and two hours of concentration on my work to consolidate the investigation results. I skipped my breakfast of champions, substituting a stop at Terry's Not Just Bagels. I planned to be early for the meeting, but not the fifteen minutes that remained when I arrived. I took a seat in the outer office, relieved that Kim would not arrive for another hour, and set up for a picnic breakfast of the second half of the bagel and the second cup of coffee I had purchased. I was halfway through my speed-read of *The Times* when Alex arrived. My presence that early surprised him. "Jeff, do I have the wrong time for this meeting?"

I laughed and looked up. "That's not much encouragement to be punctual! I'm here early for the meeting at 7:00. Do I get extra credit I can spend when I'm late next time?"

He laughed also and replied, "No extra credit. But I do like the new leaf you've turned over. I need a few minutes to get settled. Come in with Griff when he gets here."

When Griffin Hess arrived, he announced himself by saying, "That looks like some other newspaper. Have you changed loyalties?"

"Good morning, Counselor," I said as I stood and held out my hand. "I like to read other papers. It's both pleasure and research. We never want to get too complacent in our product. Another news source may gain ground that online postings by newspapers are cutting into their own sales."

"We've had some discussions about that phenomenon in the Editorial Board meetings. We seem to be doing okay, but it bears watching. Do you know if Alex is ready for us?"

"He asked that I come in with you when you arrive." I had disposed of my breakfast trash and folded my newspaper as we talked. We entered together.

Alex rose from his desk and shook hands with both of us. "Good morning!" he said energetically. "Griff, it appears that Jeff is eager to receive whatever information you have."

As he took his seat and removed an envelope from his briefcase, Hess remarked, "I have some that may be useful. Although most members of the general public don't have easy access to this information, the separate pieces are considered to be parts of the public record." After setting his briefcase beside his chair, he faced me and said, "Jeff, I know you earlier found information about complaints, charges, and suits which have been made or brought against J & AH Construction. Most of the suits were covered by the press because of the large dollar figures. I found nothing beyond what you already have. I did, however, find some information about Baja Paving which you may not have."

I sat forward in my seat as he removed some pages from the envelope. "There were two cases handled in tax court. One involved failure to pay income taxes for some workers during a two-year period. That case was filed and settled two years ago. The second case involved failure to pay sales tax for an order of sealing supplies purchased from him by a customer. In both cases, taxes and penalties were paid. Those two cases were more serious than the other information my staff found. Six of the twenty-six cases in the record at the Better Business Bureau were settled in small claims courts with awards ranging from $1,400 to the state limit of $2,500."

"Thank you, sir," I said as he passed me the pages and the envelope. "Since Hernandez pretty much set up the business for Rivera, do these problems for Baja and the outcomes which appear to indicate that the company was guilty of wrongdoing cause problems for Hernandez?"

Hess nodded his head slightly as he responded, "It depends on whether you're talking legally or ethically. In most cases there's no legal prohibition against helping another person start a business. Exceptions to that would be use of the new company to commit illegal activities, such as money laundering or extortion, co-mingling the financial operations of two independent entities, and hiring undocumented foreign workers. On the ethical side, I guess he's guilty by association. If he was a good friend who cared, he would have provided the guidance that would have avoided the problems."

"I'm thinking that Hernandez pushed a lot of business to Rivera and used him a number of times as a subcontractor on jobs where Hernandez was the General Contractor. And with the business association, should Hernandez have voted on the award of the contract? I think he should have abstained or recused himself."

"You've got a point about the vote on the contract. That's something that may go to court. I would have expected the college attorney to intervene and advise Hernandez to recuse himself. I guess we'll have to wait and see on that one."

I was anxious to move to another item on my list for the day. "I know you have a number of other items to review, so I'll get out of the way."

Hess said, "Be careful what you do with the information and good luck with the remainder of your investigation."

Alex followed with, "Jeff, this looks like it's going to move to a more serious level. Keep me informed with each step."

It was only 7:30, so no confrontation with Kim would occur today. I took advantage of the situation to goad her via a note: "I was here. And you weren't. Jeff."

I hurried to my office to complete a quick check of the paper's archives on the trial and conviction of Axel Nelson, Building Inspector for Neptune. I had an 8:30 meeting with Nelson. The trial had been a major event at the time because the U.S. district attorney and the New Jersey attorney general had used it to further their political careers by citing their records of being tough on white-collar criminals. The state attorney general had been named a judge of the New Jersey Appellate Court just eighteen months later. The federal district attorney had been elected lieutenant governor of New York State two years later and then had been appointed to a vacant House of Representatives seat before his term expired as second in command in the state capitol.

Links from the archive database, which was accessible to the newspaper staff, permitted me to review articles in *The New York Times* and *The Washington*

Post. Nelson had been indicted for accepting a bribe and was sent to prison for failing to provide information to investigators from the district attorney's office. He had been indicted by a grand jury on the basis of information provided by staff members in his office who testified that they had heard him on his cell phone making arrangements to collect an undesignated sum of money from an unknown caller. The phone had been the disposable kind and was never found. Because it was disposable, it was likely that it could not be followed by GPS technology. He never took the stand at his trial. Without corroborating evidence, such as testimony by the payer of the bribe or telephone records which could confirm that he had been on the phone as reported by others under oath, there was insufficient evidence of his receipt of the bribe. There was circumstantial evidence of living a lifestyle beyond the means of his salary without a legitimate source of additional income, such as gambling winnings, an inheritance, or income from a second job. Nelson had told investigators that he was "a model for getting the most out of every cent I earn." I was amused by the comment and curious to see what he had to offer.

It was a short drive to Ocean Township where I had arranged to meet Nelson at General Plumbing Supplies where he worked the section of the counter reserved for the plumbers and contractors. The position was a natural for him. He had been a plumber early in his career and was well liked by his fellow tradesmen.

Based on a photo of Nelson being taken from court in handcuffs, I was able to pick him out of the three counter men engaged in conversation as I entered the parts department. His appearance had changed in minor ways: hair more gray and about twenty pounds spread from face to stomach. He sported a handlebar, mustache which was new since the photo.

He spoke first, "You must be Jeff from *The Press*," he said as he extended his hand and broadened his smile.

"You're right. You must be Axel. What gave me away?"

"No uniform or jeans, regular shoes, clean hands."

"And the waist of your pants worn above your hip bones," interrupted one of his colleagues.

We all laughed and Axel continued, "And you looked like you didn't know what to expect coming in here. Ninety percent of our customers are repeats. Come with me to the back office so we can sit and have some privacy."

———————

I matched his fast pace walking down an aisle of neat shelves and drawers. As we neared the end, he said, "Watch your step around the stuff on the floor, and don't get too close to the threading machines. They're oily."

Once I was beyond the end of the aisle, I saw we were passing through the shop—not as neat, but everything organized. I made my usual comment for a place like this: "Whenever I'm in a parts department—auto, electric, or plumbing—I marvel at how you guys remember numbers and where everything is."

"It's like anything else, a matter of practice. I bet you remember dates, people, and locations where significant events took place."

"That's true. I do.'

"My mind's not worth shit when it comes to dates. Ask my wife, and she'll give you an earful about birthdays and anniversaries." We had entered an office, and Nelson moved a newspaper off the chair where I was supposed to sit. He moved the phone and straightened a pile of papers that looked like invoices. I guessed the habits that produced orderly shelves carried over into all aspects of his life.

After he sat and rolled the desk chair into just the right spot, he asked, "Now what is it you want to ask me about?"

"I'm gathering information for an article, and that's got me checking into the activities of Alberto Hernandez."

"You better be careful who you check with if you want to avoid big trouble." The tone of his words matched his stern look.

"You're not the first person who told me that." -

"That doesn't surprise me. People either know him well and avoid crossing him, or they're fooled by the show he puts on and think he's wonderful. I haven't found many who are in the middle. It's probably better if you ask questions. That way I'll tell you what you want to know and avoid just complaining."

"I read the newspaper archives on your trial and conviction. I detected that you may have been victim to the political ambitions of the state and federal prosecutors. Did you ever suspect that?"

"Hell, yes! They both wanted to be seen as stomping out corruption. If you doubt that, just take a look at where they went afterward. That S.O.B. Fischer was lieutenant governor and now is in the House of Representatives, and DeMarco, that bastard, is now judge—appeals court, I think. They didn't care about who it was that they stepped on on their way up. I was just a stupid schmuck who took all the heat."

"How did Hernandez escape prosecution?"

"You tell me! You'd think it was a miracle that occurred when money allegedly gave me spending power beyond what was expected for a building inspector. It takes two to tango, always has and always will."

There was no doubt about the real meaning of what he was saying. I tried to ask the next question as diplomatically as possible. "Why did you choose to keep quiet, both when the investigators questioned you and when you stayed off the witness stand at trial?"

"I'll tell you what I told the investigators when they threatened that I could be convicted of withholding information and spend time in jail. I'd rather be sent to jail than sent to the undertaker."

"This may sound dumb, but I want to make sure I understand. Does that mean you felt threatened, that you would be killed if you told them Hernandez bribed you?"

"You got it."

"What about witness protection?"

"And be exiled to some out of the way place?" he asked in a louder voice. "And still be worried because the people with money and muscle can find anybody in any place? That would be second worst, right after being killed. I've spent all my life here. My parents and brothers and sisters are all in this area. My friends are here. And old friends and associates could maybe help me get a job...like they did."

"Didn't people shun you, stay away because of your conviction?"

"Sure they did. What I went through was bad, but it made my life simpler. I know who my real friends are, the people who care about me and not about them looking good while they associate with me. I have less money, so I have less crap around, and I get pleasure from other sources."

"Some of what you're saying sounds like the things people say after a religious conversion."

His eyes lit up, and he looked at me intensively. His speech was faster and a little louder. "It is like a religious experience! One place I find pleasure now is helping other people. I was always too busy to do that before. And I'm active in my church. I find time to read the Bible. I pray for others and not just myself."

I hoped he'd take me seriously as I said, "Would you recommend that others have the same experience?"

He hesitated in answering, and his look seemed to be questioning my sincerity. I guess he soon decided that I was serious and was not mocking him. "I just said what I went through was bad. At times it was hell—both for me and for my family. No, I wouldn't recommend that others go through the same thing. What I do recommend is that people take a long, hard look at themselves and decide if what they work so hard for is what's important to them when they think about what they really want."

I put away my pen and folded my note pad. I was excited and more at peace with the world than I had been for a long time. What I had dreaded going into it had turned out to be informative in more ways than one. I smiled intently at Nelson and said, "Hey, buddy, this has been an incredible experience for me. I thank you for being so open and honest about what you experienced. I'm really grateful for all your time. I know I'll be re-evaluating what's really important to me. That may be the best part of today, and that's not why I came to talk with you." I had stood at some point while talking, and now I extended my hand. He took it, and I squeezed his hand more firmly than usual. I wanted to reinforce the degree of my gratitude.

He had stood while reaching for my hand. "Can I count on you to not rat me out in whatever you say in any article you may write?"

"I give you my word that I'll use the information very carefully. You're a good man and shouldn't have to endure any more difficulty. I hope I see you again for some different reason."

The thought that kept recurring for several days was that I had been in the presence of a minister of God's word—although he didn't have an official title.

═══════════════

It was 9:00, so I decided to go a little early—something must have been in the air or in the water!—to James Livermore's office.

Livermore and Associates was an insurance brokerage firm with an excellent reputation and a large clientele. It was founded by his father in Asbury Park where the office remained for its first twenty-four years. An expansion of the professional and clerical staff was the occasion for its move to the more upscale Deal. The office for the company itself had been expanded twice in the subsequent thirty-two years, outward to include other commercial spaces for lease and upward to house additional company offices. The beige brick complex was situated along Main Street or Atlantic Avenue, depending on whether you entered from Long Branch or from Allenhurst. Livermore had kept his office on the ground floor in order to be more accessible to established and prospective clients.

I was greeted on my arrival by Margaret Stoner, James Livermore's secretary since the change of office location. Margaret—she insisted I address her that way—had a welcoming smile and warmth to her voice. In her early 50s, she was slightly overweight and dressed attractively in her definition of professional attire—a brown suit, pale green blouse, and low-heeled shoes which I usually designated as "clunky." Coffee was offered, but I declined. I had nearly finished reading an article on "Weighting Health Risks in Large Benefit Policies," printed in *Policy Parade*, when Margaret called my name and escorted me into Livermore's office.

After we shook hands and worked through "how-are-yous? and the "just-fine-and-you?", I made a play for amiability by saying, "I looked through one of your journals and discovered that there's quite a scientific base of information and greater application of actuarial tables in the determination of premium levels than I was aware of."

It wasn't immediately obvious if I had earned any brownie points, as Livermore displayed his business-only approach. "Mr. Stewart, what can I help you with today? Since you're from *The Press*, I'm reasonably sure it's not to sign up for a new insurance policy."

Because he chuckled following his remark, I did too. "I think Mr. Hess told you that I'm looking for information about John Wilson as an expansion of a project to build profiles of the OCC Board members. I think you can help with information about his role in the county Republican Party. What I've learned so far indicates that he's been a guiding force in the party and has had several detractors as well."

"Members of the Ocean County Republican Party through the years have been avid supporters or determined opponents of Wilson; there seems never to be a middle ground. Those on both sides of the love-hate relationship still talk about the most notorious demonstration of his power. Shortly after being named a senior partner, in 1982 he organized the campaign of James Allen and ran it from the back room as Allen successfully defeated Heaton Everest for nomination to the district seat in the U.S. House of Representatives. Allen was elected and served two full terms before returning to his legal practice. Everest's promising political career came to a halt. Everest's professional credentials were impeccable, including having served as editor of the Seton Hall Law Review, a position for which Wilson had been groomed by the two previous editors.

"There is widespread belief that the House seat election was Wilson's way of getting even for the defeat eighteen years earlier, an event which he considered an embarrassment. Some have said that the history of his powerful influence has populated a very large cemetery of promising political careers. Of course, he made both enemies and devotees. Many of those who enjoy his strong support also fear his wrath. The actual power he holds is awesome; the potential power is frightening. I respect that power from a distance."

"I'm sure you're aware that some of his critics go so far as to assert that he has arranged, or at least has encouraged, infliction of bodily harm, at the least, and commission of murder, at the most."

"I have no knowledge that he has conducted illegal acts. I do know that his beneath-the-radar leadership has made our party organization a powerhouse. I've told you all I can...all I know about John Wilson. Is there any other topic you want to discuss before we finish?"

"Yes, sir, there is. Alberto Hernandez is a member of the Ocean County Board of Chosen Freeholders and, I gather, active to some degree in the local Republican Party." Livermore shifted his position forward, almost imperceptibly but a move I noted as I continued, "He makes frequent contributions to the state and county Republican Party. His business associate, Ramone Rivera, makes a similar contribution each time Hernandez does. Has your position given you any insight into either or both of these men?"

"My remarks will be very brief. I've associated with both only to the extent that my party position requires. Hernandez volunteered for one of the least popular committee chairmanships two years ago, and he was appointed. Last year he had Rivera appointed to the same committee. My personal preference would be that Hernandez not be involved in any way with the party—not even be a member, but we can't bar him."

"May I ask the basis of your opposition?"

"I'd best make the explanation brief. A person who's a member of an ethnic minority is characteristically a member of the Democratic Party. I'm sure you've discovered that yourself. I believe Hernandez and his puppet Rivera are involved in the Republican Party because they want to gain social status through association with wealthier people. In addition, I've heard things I don't like about their business practices—reports of suspected bribery, indications of collusion to get bids for construction contracts, and use of inferior materials."

He glanced as his watch and with a hint of relief in his voice said, "I hope I've been somewhat helpful in increasing your knowledge of John Wilson, and I trust that you will respect my understanding that my remarks about Wilson, as well as about Hernandez and Rivera, have been off the record and will be denied by me if I'm questioned about them."

"Yes, sir. Your understanding and mine are the same. You have been very helpful, and I'm grateful." I stood as Livermore rose and moved around his desk and toward the door.

As he opened the door, he said, "I'm pleased to have met you, young man, and I'll be watching what you will write that is related to this conversation." We shook hands, and I left, waving to Margaret who was on the phone.

She said to her phone party, "Just a moment." And then she called to me, "Good day, young man." I waved again as she returned to her call.

CHAPTER SEVENTEEN

It was a few minutes before 10:30 as I began my trip back to the office. Once back at my desk, I took a mental step away from doing things on my agenda to ask if the agenda contained the right things to get the job done. Later the same day I had an appointment with Morison's widow; I expected that would corroborate what I had heard from others about bribery and possibly other corruption. If her information was contrary to what the others had said, then I would need to find another person to talk to. I needed to check for connections between the officers of J & AH and Baja. I knew I could do that by searching the NJ Treasury Department website, which lists that information for all companies doing business in the state. My alert signal went off when Livermore said that he had heard that the companies of Hernandez and Rivera used inferior materials. I needed a way to find the names and contact information for customers of the companies. These three activities moved to the top of the agenda.

I phoned the office of the municipal clerk and asked my question about the ability to review permits. A transfer to the office of the building inspector led to an affirmative answer. I could request information by date, by site of the work, and by contractor, but I would be required to make my request in person. Learning that I could find the information seemed like a victory in itself. I would go there after my 2:00 appointment with Mrs. Morison.

The immediate project was to look for overlaps between the companies of Hernandez and Rivera. The time spent in orientation to the treasury website and the hour's use of the people search database, to which *The Press* subscribed, found the relatives of the Baja officers. The brother of Hernandez's second wife is a vice president in the Baja organization. The wife of a junior partner in the law office on retainer by J & AH is the comptroller at Baja. The brother of Larry Morison's widow serves as the attorney for Baja. I decided the information might be useful later.

These ties provided evidence that the two companies, whose "owners" had chosen to file as separate entities, were in fact interconnected. This would be a problem for the general contractor on a government project where laws required that the lowest bidder be awarded the bid unless there were justifiable reasons to reject the low bid. While the legal requirements were not the same for projects in the private sector, it would seem that a reasonable expectation by the company paying the bills is that a general contractor would hire the low bidder.

My appointment with Melissa "Missy" Morison took me to Millstone Township, to one of the longer established homes built on an extensive lot before the area became attractive to new-money owners of private businesses and to thirty-something wannabes who had made some fast money with savvy (or lucky) investments and felt the pressure to live in a style which they expected to be able to afford sometime in the future.

A three-story, white frame house sat on a slight hill a quarter of a mile from the road at an elevation that was probably thirty feet above the level of the road. The driveway to the house first dropped to a brick-sided bridge over a small brook, which gurgled in gentle turns along the side of the road. Next the drive curved upward to find its way in front of the house and then turned past the side of the house, headed to the garage. As it passed the first corner of the house, it widened to permit an area for parking which allowed easy passage beyond at the same time.

The house was roofed in slate with five dormers spread across the front. The location on a hill, the number of dormers, and the front passage of the driveway combined to announce that this was "a large, substantial home with room for maximum comfort." The uniformity of identical drapes at all windows across the first floor was mirrored by identical lace curtains at every window on the second floor and in the third-floor dormer windows. Attractive evergreens, fronted by beds of blooming flowers, softened what otherwise may have been a cold look. A hunter green door with polished brass knocker protected the inside of the home.

I was surprised, as often I was when using a large, heavy knocker, by the volume of sound that was produced. Mrs. Morison promptly answered and with a small and tender voice checked my identity. "You must be Jeff. I'm not sure I have the correct last name."

"Stewart, like the actor Jimmy Stewart."

The movie star reference seemed to accomplish its purpose of putting her at ease. She smiled and opened the door wider as she moved backward a couple of steps. "Are you related to the actor? I always liked his movies. My favorites were *Rear Window* and *Mr. Hobbs Takes a Vacation*."

"No, I'm not related. I use that identification so that people will know how to spell my last name. *Rear Window* is one of my favorites, as are *How the West Was Won* and *The Big Sleep*."

"Oh, yes. I like the western but not your other favorite. It was too heavy for me."

By this time we were in a year-round sunroom whose three walls of windows looked out upon a magnificent yard landscaped with flower beds, some lining the fences and others spotted throughout the center of the property. A variety of mature trees also were positioned every ten yards or so in the center of the property. The pale yellow wicker couch, love seats, and chairs sat atop a braided hemp rug. Beneath each of the several tables in the room was a small area rug of white with royal blue border.

Following introductions, I said to the owner, "My, what a beautiful home, Mrs. Morison! From first sight on the road and up the driveway and now in this charming room and the view of a spectacular lawn."

"Thank you so much. This home belonged to my parents who let it go into disrepair. When they died, Larry negotiated a very reasonable price to buy out my brother and sister because they didn't plan to put into it the amount of money it would require to renovate. Larry was very handy himself and was able to barter some work using his carpentry skills for work by friends on the electrical system, plumbing, and tile walls and floors. Now, what were we going to talk about?"

"I know that your husband died of a heart attack while an investigation was taking place about accusations that he took bribes." Sadness settled over her face and caused her shoulders to droop.

I continued, "I know this is painful for you, and I'll try to keep my questions brief. I want your help because I'm interviewing a number of people who have information about Alberto Hernandez."

Her shoulders rose and her face lost its sadness. She began, "I hate that man! He lied to get my husband in trouble to take the attention off him. He worked with those investigators from the prosecutor who didn't care who got hurt or who died as long as they caught somebody who got convicted. Hernandez and those goons killed my husband! He never had heart trouble until the heart attack! That wouldn't have happened if they didn't indict him and continue with the investigation!" She broke down in tears for a few minutes. I didn't know what to do except offer my handkerchief.

As her tears and sobs subsided, she stood and offered refreshments. "I'll make some tea, and I have some pastries."

"I'm quite alright, Mrs. Morison. I don't need anything."

She gave a nervous laugh and said, "You may not need anything, but I need to fix something. I'm always most calm when I cook."

"Well, I need to help you. I hope you'll let me," I replied.

"You can help. Come with me."

"I can at least reach things and move things and carry them for you."

After ten minutes, we had our proper tea and scones. I doubt that cookies, especially the supermarket kind, were ever found in Mrs. Morison's kitchen. Once seated, I exclaimed, "What delicious tea, and the scones are just right! Sometimes scones are too dry and other times overly moist—not these."

"Why, thank you. It's rare, but nice for a man to comment on tea. It's lemon and chamomile to keep me calm."

I laughed lightly and said, "I hope it doesn't make me too calm. I still have several hours of work in front of me. May I ask you a question?"

Following her permission to do so, I asked a question and then followed with an explanation. "Did your husband on tape discuss taking money from Hernandez? An article from the newspaper archives quoted the prosecutor as saying that the month-long investigation had produced enough evidence to support the indictment."

"I don't know what Larry said. Hernandez may have tricked him into saying what he wanted. Or maybe the evidence was only the lies Hernandez told them. You know, they said that Hernandez had come to them after my Larry propositioned him. That word makes it sound like Hernandez was a prostitute; I think that's what he was and what he still is! But he doesn't just sell his body. He sells his soul and also his heart—if he has one."

"So it sounds like the prosecutor believed that Hernandez didn't take any money and that he didn't do anything wrong because he was just a protector of honesty. And after that the police asked him to tape record your husband's offers of money."

"That's what they want people to believe. And especially Hernandez wants people to believe that. I know it's not true because I know my Larry better than anybody does."

"Did you ever see your husband with more money than would be normal?"

"He usually had more money with him than other people do. But that's because he liked to gamble and he was good at it."

"Did he ever buy anything that you thought was unusual? A fancy car? An expensive piece of jewelry?" I tried to ask the questions in a manner that sounded like I was trying to help her remember details that would show he was innocent.

"He was always buying things, and sometimes it was a nice bracelet or necklace for me. The only time I thought that things might be unusual was when he bought our weekend and vacation home on Lake Wallenpaupack in the Poconos. I was never sure where that money came from, but I knew Larry would have gotten it honestly. Anyway, he always handled the money. I don't have a very good head for business. My son Eric takes care of business matters for me now."

"Did the investigators look at your bank accounts, income tax records, and any other financial data?"

"I don't know. If they did, they didn't tell me and didn't tell our attorney."

I debated with myself before asking the next question and then decided that in my quest for truth I must ask. "Mrs. Morison, did you ever wonder how you could buy this house, repair it, and maintain it on a single salary which only a few years ago reached the $100,000 mark and always before his promotion to code enforcement officer must have been less than $60,000?"

"Mr. Stewart, that question is your last! But I'll answer it. Larry always had odd jobs as a carpenter to supplement his income. I already told you that he did most of the repair work on this house and got the electrical, plumbing, and tile work through barter of his carpenter skill. He always handled the money, so I never had reason to check up on him or to ask questions."

"I can tell I upset you. I'm very sorry that I did that. I thank you for welcoming me into your beautiful home, for the tea made the proper way and the scones, and for giving me as much of your time as you did. I'm very grateful. It's time for me to go." I walked to the door in the lead so that I could escape as quickly as possible and could avoid a possible, ugly incident.

I let myself out and said a quick goodbye over my shoulder before pulling the door closed.

Once in my car, I sighed and thought, *Thank God that didn't go any worse.* I used the turn-around at the far front corner and then drove along the drive faster than when I had approached the house.

———————

I drove directly to the office of the building inspector in Dover Township so that I would have time enough to search the permits for names of customers. Baja Paving was now my target since the Board of Freeholders had issued the contract to that company. If I could get information that Baja's work had been substandard and add that to the connections between the companies to show Hernandez's conflict of interest when he voted to approve the contract, then perhaps the award could be overturned.

I completed the required forms and showed my driver's license. I checked the choice to search by contractor and specified Baja Paving, Inc. I also chose the interval of the years 1999 - 2002. It was necessary to search the first year by ledger entry since it predated the use of a new computerized system. Rose Marie Demartino was accomplished in running a homemade device down the sheets. As she moved the cutout portion of a file folder down each page, the name of the companies appeared through the window whose width matched the size of the contractor column. Each time she came to a Baja entry, she made note of the permit number. By the time she completed the first six months of the year, she had a list of 40-50 numbers.

"We're not going to be able to find the numbers for the full year and then check the permits this afternoon," she said as she turned the list of numbers in my direction for illustration. "Are you looking for some particular location or size of job?"

Smugly I answered, "I thought we might have this problem, so I have a possible course of action. I'm gathering information so that I know the experience of the company and can get an idea of its reliability. Let's choose two at random from each of the first six months."

With relief Rose Marie said, "Oh, that'll be good." She turned her list of numbers to face me and said, "You choose. I'll feel better. I hope you get the kind of information you want, but you might decide later that it isn't."

With no pattern I circled twelve numbers and moved the paper across the counter in her direction. "I hope the computerized database will be easier."

"It's much easier!" she exclaimed. "A piece of cake compared to this old method. The software permits a search by number, date, site of the work, contractor, and property owner. And the permit itself appears as a scanned document." She talked as she began to pull the twelve permits from the file cabinets.

I struck up a conversation by saying that her last name was of interest to me. "I remember a Frank Demartino from college who spelled his name in the same way,"

She turned abruptly and asked, "Where did you go to college?"

"Rutgers in New Brunswick."

"That's where my Frankie went. It's probably him you remember."

"The Frank I knew was a good athlete—I think football and baseball, although better in baseball."

"That's my Frankie! He was a starter at shortstop but was the third man back for the wide receiver position. He got some playing time in football, but usually when the other two were injured or on academic suspension.

I loved reliving my college days, and an interested listener could keep me going for a long time. "He had a hot glove and hit over three hundred his last year or last two years."

As she walked to the counter, Rose Marie said, "Here are the permits. I'm pleased you remember my son so well. He lives in St. Louis and distributes Budweiser. He made it to triple A ball and was called up twice for injured Cardinal infielders, once for ten days and the other time for three weeks. How do you want this information? Normally people write down whatever they want from the permits I show them. It may speed things up for both of us if I lay these down with the name and contact information showing for each one… What's the fancy computer name for that—'tiling?'—and then make photocopies for you. What do you think?"

"It sounds like everything worked out the best for Frankie," I said as she walked back to the counter. I glanced at the office clock, concerned about how much time remained before the end of her workday.

"No need to be worried," she said after seeing my check of the time. "I'll file the originals tomorrow, and the next three years really will go fast. Besides, my boss is gone for the day, and I don't mind staying a little late for a Rutgers Scarlet Knight. I didn't ask what your major was." She handed me the copies.

"Thanks. This will make my work a lot easier. I majored in English. All the practice I got writing papers for courses and my love of words are the things that led me into writing for a newspaper. How about Frankie; what was his major?"

"Business. It was both the baseball and the business degree that attracted Anheuser Busch to offer him a job. Now let's see what we find for the year 2000 when we search by the company name."

She struck a few keys and then announced, "Eighty-seven jobs that year. Which ones do you want me to highlight and print?"

"Start with the third one and then do every … Let's see what's easiest. Do every tenth one."

As the printer started, she said, "There we go. Now on to the next year."

"If the total number of jobs is more than 70 and less than 120, start with number 6 and do every tenth one. Then the following year will be the last one I ask you to search. The same total between 70 and 120, take the first one and every tenth."

She made a note of those directions and began. She had been right; it really was fast. It couldn't have been more than twenty minutes from start to finish for the three automated years. As she worked on those years, I looked at the copies of the twelve partial permits from the first year. There was enough variation in size of job, as indicated by price, to get a decent sample. Then I did the math and knew I was going to have information for about forty jobs across the four years. I needed a way to pick a sample from this sample.

"There you are!" Rose Marie interrupted my mental estimation of contract information and projection of how I would follow up. She flashed a satisfied smile as I took the pages from her. "I hope this gives you the information you need. You're a nice young man, and I've enjoyed talking with you."

"I can't begin to tell you how helpful this will be. You've been so helpful, and you've stayed here beyond your regular workday. I'll be able to decide if Baja is the kind of company I think it is."

"I'm glad to help. Don't worry a second about working a little longer. I have nobody at home waiting for me to fix dinner. My dog Wolfgang is happy to see me at any time."

CHAPTER EIGHTEEN

My ride home was about twenty-five minutes, including a trip through a Burger King drive up window. While driving, I had thoughts about avoiding people. The thought reminded me that I had been so intent on the investigation that I hadn't had contact with my friends. The recent dinner with Kate made her a special case, but she had commented on the absence of phone calls.

The thought of Kate aroused some guilt about Roxanne. Kate was new excitement while Rox was old comfort. I began another mental dialogue on the same topic: choosing between the two. If I concluded a dialogue with the choice again of Kate, which is what I thought probably would happen, I still had feelings of affection for Rox and lots of fond memories. It was too early with Kate to make a prediction of whether the initial excitement could lead to something more enduring. It may even have been too early with Rox to predict whether she and I could generate excitement once she had less to occupy her mind and once she had become more independent of her family. That is, if she could become independent of them. Rather than continue with that dialogue, I decided I should call Rox soon.

Thoughts about my friends brought to mind my statement earlier in the day to Axel Nelson that I knew I would be re-evaluating what was important to me. It was clear that friends and family were top priorities for Axel. I knew work controlled much of what I did. I had told myself that friends and family were next in importance. Now I wondered if in my case that was only something that sounded good.

One of my routines was to read the mail while eating dinner. That might have been some residual rebellion against the insistence in my parents' home that only things that took place during dinner were eating and talking about the latest in our lives. I couldn't resist popping three fries into my mouth as I walked to the closet. Likely more rebellion!

Time magazine was the one source of interest. I quickly scanned the listing of articles and regular features. I decided to read the short features: "People," "Entertainment," and "Science." I always have been attracted to predictions. I was not disappointed today. There was a prediction that John Kerry would be a candidate for president of the U.S. I also am always interested in female politicians, and this issue had a feature on Condoleezza Rice as national security advisor.

Half an hour later, I forced an end to my reading enjoyment. I had to prove to myself that I was on a new path regarding friends and family by sending an email to Vince. Thoughts of Kate and Rox and feelings of guilt had pulled his name into my head. I thought I should follow up our discussion about the demands on his time and his relationship with Crystal. I emailed because I didn't know which evenings he was working. My message said that I didn't know what he was up to and was curious about how he was doing. I said I'd like to hear from him.

In order to stay on top of my commitment to more frequently be in touch with friends, I phoned Rox, had an enjoyable conversation with Mr. Freeman, and then learned she was at a meeting. I asked to have her phone me when convenient for her.

I had two tasks that I should complete this evening. The first, the quicker one, was the addition of today's information to the notes on Wilson and Hernandez—Wilson in order to stay current with what I knew and Hernandez because I was pretty certain that I was on to something that would make the bridge paving at the college look pretty bad.

Essentially there was no new information on Wilson. I had discussed him only with Livermore who had commented off the record and had said that

Wilson had made the Republican Party a powerhouse, while effectively ending the political careers of those who opposed him. He had assured me that he had no knowledge of illegal activities.

Most of the information provided on Hernandez, and his alter ego Rivera, had been offered off the record. That information included much of what I already knew: Nelson kept quiet about Hernandez because he feared for his life. Livermore had heard reports that Hernandez and Rivera had taken bribes, had engaged in collusion to get bids for construction contracts, and used inferior materials on their jobs. Missy Morison couldn't account for the sources of income which resulted in her husband having enough money to renovate their beautiful home and to purchase a Pocono vacation home and believed that Hernandez had set up her husband to be convicted of taking bribes.

New factual information about the men and their businesses included: Rivera was involved in two cases settled in tax court and six cases settled in small claims court. The vice president, comptroller, and attorney of Baja have family or business connections to J & AH.

My motivation to expose Hernandez and Rivera was given a boost by what I had learned today. Selection of a manageable sample of the Baja customer lists was the second job. I had forty-one names of customers, from what had been a total of about 500. I knew that there had been a total of twenty-six complaints in five years, which had been submitted to the Better Business Bureau. If my estimate was that it was likely that at least twice that many customers had been unhappy, then the dissatisfaction rate was about one in ten. If the same rate applied to my customer list, then I would expect to find four or five. I was bummed out. I didn't have time to call forty-one people to find four or five. I was certain that some of the people would refuse to talk. Chances were that there would be less than four who were dissatisfied and who were willing to give me details.

I paced, and I munched on peanuts while I thought about this step. It really wasn't realistic to think I could find help to make the calls. Another reporter wouldn't have the time. Another person in general, if one were available, wouldn't have the experience needed to sort out responses and ask clarification questions, and I would have to give a lengthy explanation of why I was making the calls and of the topic investigation. I might get lucky and find several complaints early in my calling. But I couldn't count on that happening.

There might be different rates of dissatisfaction according to job size. It seemed that a large commercial establishment paying several hundred thousand dollars for a new parking lot would be the most demanding. On the other hand, a smaller commercial property owner, with limited funding, might expect more for his money. And, the individual homeowner might have higher appearance expectations.

1 reviewed the list, placing the letter "S" on jobs less than $10,000, the letter "M" on jobs in the range $10,000 – 100,000, and the letter "L" for job costing more than $100,000. There were eighteen jobs in the small category, sixteen medium, and seven large. I decided to go with the "pay the piper theory." The principle was that the more you paid, the higher the expectation for the quality of "the tune." Tomorrow at the office I'd call the large category first. If I hadn't found three or four who had complaints, and if I had the time to do so, I'd move to the medium category. Remaining tonight would be the job of finding as many phone numbers as I could.

As I worked to find phone numbers, my phone rang. As soon as I said hello, Vince said, "There must be something in the air. I thought all afternoon and evening that I should talk to you and then found your email at home. I know it's late, but can I come to your place? I need to tell you something."

As I hung up the phone, an alarm sounded in my head due to the pressure I read into his needing to tell me something. I smugly thought that I was on a new course. I'd sent an email and now I was hosting a friend. Most guys I know don't care much about neatness, but I straightened up some: dirty dishes in the dishwasher, dirty clothes in the laundry bag, old newspapers and magazines in the trash. After I checked to see if I had a clean bowl to put the peanuts in, I removed a dirty one from the dishwasher and washed it by hand.

I returned to my work. The commercial firms were easiest to find; most were in the phone book. Internet tools found the others. In case I changed my tactic or in the event I needed to extend my calls into the small category, I began to search for those numbers. Vince arrived after I found the fifth one.

I truly was glad to see him. "Hey, buddy! Good to see you!" I held the door open and then clapped him on the back as he entered. "Yeah, good to see you too!"

Because his face didn't quite match his words, I watched his expression closely. "You ready for that beer?"

"You bet." I couldn't read his face that time. "Peanuts, too?"

"Why not?"

"Have a seat and turn on the game or something if you want to," I said over my shoulder as I headed for the kitchen.

He called out, "I'll pass on the TV. There are at least ten sets going at all times at the store, often with someone trying out a speaker system. A time without broadcasts is what I need now."

As I returned to the living room with two beers in one hand and my clean dish containing peanuts in the other, I said, "You okay with the can or do you want a glass?"

"Can is fine. Just like home."

Vince still looked more serious than normal for him. "I see you're still working, and it sounds like the same place. Is it the same number of hours?"

"Yeah. I don't have a choice. I need the money for school and for my expenses."

This seemed like a good segue into a discussion of his girlfriend. "How are you and Crystal doing?"

"We're still together if that's what you mean. We're both busy with school, and I've got work besides. More time together would be wonderful. We wish we were married, but we're straight on school being our most important activity now." As he talked about the two of them, his face relaxed. "I thank you for helping me get my priorities in order."

His face turned serious again, and he leaned in my direction. "I wanted to come see you because I need advice. Again. You may think that's all I ever want. I've got to talk with someone. I don't want to get Crystal involved, and she'd just worry more about me. She already tells me I don't get enough sleep." He broke eye contact and looked down at the floor. "If I told her about this new thing, she wouldn't sleep."

"Man, you know I'll help. I really admire you for working as hard as you do. What's got you so uptight?"

He raised his eyes, sighed audibly, and sat back on the couch as he began. "Hunter, Rox, and I went under the Buchwald Bridge to check if there are frogs there and how many and just what it's like."

"When the hell did you do that?" I interrupted loudly. Vince flinched slightly at the volume of my voice, a volume that surprised me as well. "Are you guys out of your minds?"

Apologetically, Vince responded, "We did it the night before last—or really early yesterday morning. And we had good reason. Just let me tell it my way and then you can get angry and ask questions!" he said with his voice growing louder.

My surprise caused me to forget that I wanted to be supportive of my friend. His emotion shocked me back to that approach. "Sorry. I'll try to keep quiet."

"Hunter first introduced the idea, but Rox said absolutely not. Then after the Freeholders' decision to pave, we were so discouraged that we thought we had to do something drastic to try to change things. Hunter asked that we meet, and he brought up the idea again. I gave him strong support, and Rox agreed. We wanted to make sure there's something down there worth fighting for.

"Hunter had a plan so each of us checked ahead of time without going all the way under the bridge. And we checked the actual schedule of when the security patrols drove past the bridge so we could put together a better timetable. The value of his plan was shown when we didn't get caught.

"There are frogs down there. They're different than most people picture when they hear the word 'frog.' The problem is that we found something we didn't expect—a skeleton!"

"What!... Sorry. I said I'd keep quiet."

"You're surprised? Think of how we felt! It's muddy and mucky down there. It's more of a wetland or swamp environment than a stream neatly contained in a bed. I stepped on something and wanted to know what it was. When I reached down and pulled it up, we could see it looked like the large bone in the upper leg. My biology class taught me something useful. I carefully felt around and touched some other bones. That's the way we know it's a skeleton and not just an isolated bone."

There was a marked change from his earlier appearance as he told me about the exploration. His eyes were open wider. His speech was faster and louder. The pitch of his voice had gone up as well.

"I'm afraid of the consequences of having gone down there. There are restrictions against that sort of thing. But we can't be quiet about it. The police need to know what we found. We just don't know how to tell them. Hunter's asked to have his name kept out of it because he doesn't want a record. Rox is worried about the consequences for the Environmental Club. I guess I have the least to lose, but I don't want to be arrested. I need your advice." He stopped, and his body almost collapsed down into the couch pillow. He sighed again.

I waited a few seconds to respond, reminding myself that the activity had occurred already and that showing my emotion wasn't what Vince wanted. "Try deciding what to do by projecting what you stand to lose with each possible action. I think the choices are: don't report what you did, take some time and then report what you did, and report what you did immediately."

"I understand the first and last choices. What is the advantage of waiting before we report?"

"You can use the time to decide the best spokesperson, the best person to report to, the best method of reporting, and the best time to report."

"I see. I'm ready to work on figuring what we stand to lose with each approach."

"I want you to tell me. Then if I think of anything you missed, I'll add on."

"You have more confidence in me than I have in myself," he said with an expression that showed a half-smile on his lips and uncertainty in his eyes. "If we don't report it at all, it's possible that somehow someone finds out in the future. Then we've added failure to report a crime to commission of the crime. I don't know what the penalties are, but I guess it might include fines and possibly jail time. Do you see anything else?"

"If you did some minor wrong thing as a kid and experienced a guilty conscience, you may be able to imagine what that feels like and does to you when your wrongdoing is much more serious. You can lose concentration, sleep, friendships, just to name the most obvious. You run the risk that one of you decides he or she can't live with it any longer and reports what you did. Let's try what you stand to lose by reporting immediately."

"I guess part of what we lose is the ability to take control of the factors you mentioned when you explained what this option is."

"I don't see any others. Now when we get that control back with the delay, what are potential losses?"

Vince thought for nearly a minute before offering, "I guess we could be accused of withholding information during the period we delay. I don't know if that's a formal violation."

"It probably is. Or the violation is a temporary failure to report. It's likely that a formal charge can be avoided in an agreement at the time of reporting. However, one caution is that the delay must be short, a matter of a few days at most, in order for there to be any goodwill between you three and the police. The bottom line you already had figured out—you must report." I didn't know that I needed to, but I took the precaution of raising my voice and adding a stern tone.

"I feel better already," he offered. There was a look of relief in his eyes. "I need to talk with Rox and Hunter about the timing. Can I talk with you again if any of us has questions?"

I'll be happy to help you any way I can, except to be the one to report to the police." I laughed a little as I spoke the exception. Vince laughed a little also.

He continued, "I need to leave for home in a few minutes, but I do want to know what you're up to. What are you working on?"

"I'm still following up on the paving contract issued by the Freeholders. I've been doing some research about each of them; I may have something that could be of use in trying to overturn the vote, but I'm not ready to talk about it."

"And what's up with you and Rox? The last couple of times I've seen her I asked if she had heard from you. She said she hadn't and she seemed upset. I don't know if the upset was due to the pressure of everything lately or due to the lack of contact with you. I told her you must be busy at work. She said she hoped that's what's happening and not you getting more interested in Kate."

I don't know what showed on the outside, but mentally I winced at Rox's concern that Kate may have taken her place. "I have been busy at work, but I realized earlier today that I've been neglecting my friends."

Before I could continue, Vince said, "That thought is probably one reason you sent me an email. I'm curious if you tried to contact Rox as well. It's not really my business, but she's one of my very close friends."

"I did phone her home just to talk as a friend, but she wasn't there." It was my time to sigh. "I think it is your business when you're thinking about two friends—Rox and me. I'm pretty confused, and I've been feeling guilty because her fear about Kate is exactly what's going on."

Vince interrupted again, this time with anger in his look and in his voice. "Most of us who have gotten to know you could see what was happening between you and Kate. It might have started some time before the demonstration, but that day it was easy to see the attraction between the two of you. You need to make a decision and let Rox know what's going on."

"It's easy for you to say I should make a decision, but it's not easy for me to get the job done. I still have feelings of affection for Rox. And I don't want to hurt her, which is what I fear will happen if I leave her for Kate. Now that I need to take a look at my relationship with Rox, I wonder what the absence of sexual activity means. It's much too early for that with Kate, but I question why I've been willing to let that continue that way. Does it mean that I don't have that interest with Rox? Am I reading her right that she would resist an effort by me in that area? And if I am right, should I expect a frigid future if we continue as a couple?"

"You know, man, you can analyze anything to death!" Vince looked away, rubbed his hand on his forward, and waved his hand in disgust. "If you want to try to add some sex, and it sounds like you have wanted to in the past, just try it. Then if she tells you no, ask her why or then try to figure it out."

"I haven't tried because I respect her. Although we kiss sometimes like we were being sexually active, I sense there's a limit and I could lose her if I try to pass it.

"I felt an instant connection with Kate," I continued. "I feel an energy with her: a high level of enjoyment of doing things together. She initiates phone calls and activities sometimes. There's a tension within me of wanting to experience her body, while I'm cautious that I don't move too fast. Those same things don't exist with Rox. I'm Rox's friend wondering if I'll ever be her lover. I'm Kate's suitor hoping to be her lover soon."

"It sounds like you've already made up your mind. I don't like what it sounds like you've decided, but it's your decision to make. I have the conflict of being happy for one friend—you— that you're excited by a new love interest while I'm sad for another friend—Rox—that she's about to lose her current love interest. I hope you let her know soon."

"I haven't made the decision. If I make it right now, it goes against Rox, and that's why I'm going slowly—deliberately. Why I'm 'analyzing it to death,' as you said." I felt smug about answering his complaint with a reason that meant I was resisting letting go of Rox. I resumed my intellectual anguish over a largely emotion-driven choice. "Another issue that confuses me is the racial factor. Because Rox is African-American and I pride myself on being liberal in that area, I want to be sure that the difference in ethnic backgrounds of the two women is not a part of the rationale for my decision."

"Like I said, I've got to go home. And you're starting to drive me nuts with the debate between your feelings and your thoughts. You've been a great help to me again. I feel like I'm abandoning you when I should be helping. I know your decision is complex and tough. But maybe you should be more into it with your heart and less with your head."

"More times than not, that last statement of yours is running through my head. I hope my decision doesn't interfere with our friendship,

"It may in the short run, but I'm sure it won't in the long run. Thanks for the beer. And on the other topic, I'll meet with my co-conspirators, and we'll reach a decision about how to handle it."

He reached to shake my hand, and I grabbed him in a hug instead. We both laughed with embarrassment as we separated.

I drank a beer and went to bed, telling myself that I had too much on my plate to make this my number one concern.

CHAPTER NINETEEN

Despite Vince's information and our discussion, I awoke refreshed and ready to attack another big day. While I ate breakfast, I read some of the more substantial articles in this week's *Time* magazine. As I finished the fourth article, I finished my meal. After a quick shave, teeth brushing, and hair combing, I donned blue dress shirt, dark blue tie with small purple and red polka dots, and black slacks. I would carry my grey sport coat in order to be ready to attend a meeting. I had two scheduled for the day and would likely schedule others as the day progressed.

My first meeting was with Lawrence Smithson, retired former owner of Smithson General Construction. Our meeting was at the Colts Neck Country Club at 9:00 before his tee time of 10:00. My destination was the 19th hole grille, much less formal and much more comfortable. I parked my very modest, some may have said "shabby," car among the collection of Mercedes, Lexus, Infiniti, and Cadillac vehicles. I quickly surveyed the grille as I entered and decided that the mixed brown- and grey-haired man with yellow cotton slacks and green knit shirt was Smithson. I was correct, but I couldn't tell you why I chose him. My attire, especially the absences of a unique cap and golf shoes, gave me away, and Smithson waved at the same time he came into my view. He was leaning on the coffee bar, which would become a regular bar in an hour, engaged in a laughter-filled conversation. I noticed that his paunch, slightly smaller than and worn more stylishly than a "gut," was a sign of comfortable wealth he shared with half the others in the room.

As I got within earshot, Smithson called out, "You must be Stewart!" His was a commanding voice if ever there was one. Most of the conversations stopped momentarily as all eyes shifted my direction. When the sportsmen saw that their colleague addressed a young man who obviously was out of place, they resumed their noisy exchanges.

"That's right, and you're Mr. Smithson."

"Call me Larry. I'm sorry I don't remember your first name."

"It's Jeff."

"Okay. Then Jeff it is!" Spoken by him, those words sounded like the preliminary to a baptism, when the cleric asked the parents the name of their child and then repeated it for the congregation so that it gained a permanent status. "Let's go out on the deck. The noise should be less out there. We're all old friends and have lots of catching up to do even if we last saw each other as recently as two days ago." He hesitated until we moved outside and then lowered his voice. "Of course, we often tell the same things to the same people. It doesn't seem to matter because most times each of us doesn't remember the prior telling, and listeners don't either."

I joined his infectious laugh, and right then the ice of unfamiliarity was broken.

"Jeff, would you like coffee or tea? It's not time yet when I can offer a beer."

"A cup of coffee would be great."

"What do you take in it?"

"Milk and sugar, please."

Smithson waved his hand, and a waiter appeared so quickly that he was present to hear my preference.

"Isn't this a hell of a day! Beautiful weather and a super location!" Smithson waved his hand toward the course.

"They don't get much better than this." The warp-speed waiter returned with my coffee. "Oh, thank you."

Smithson's gaze gained in intensity as he continued to control the conversation. "I know you're from *The Press*, Jeff. And you must be working on some article. What is it that you want to get my views on?"

"I'm working on an article which concentrates on Alberto Hernandez. I understand you have some knowledge of his business practices."

"What's that son of a bitch done now? His name really blows my enjoyment of this beautiful day!" His initial few words were loud enough that a foursome toward the first tee turned their heads as if in response to a gunshot. He dialed down the volume. "What do you want to know? I'll tell you everything I know."

"It's a shame to spoil the morning. In advance, I thank you for your help. I know that Jason Leigh had to withdraw from several jobs because he had problems getting supplies when he needed them and that you got the new contract for one of those jobs and then had to withdraw. Was that because of problems with suppliers also?"

"I know you don't want to lead my answers with what you say in your questions, but that's a pretty sanitized version of illegal collusive activity! Yes, I had problems with suppliers for the first time as a company owner. Oh, there had been a few times when there was a strike that interrupted schedules, but there was no strike in this case. Hernandez forced the suppliers to cut me off." Shock and hatred had been replaced with a cool anger, determined to get his story out.

"Did you have proof that he had forced the suppliers?"

"No. Not proof. But I drew reasonable conclusions from what I saw and what I heard. When a few of the suppliers were willing to talk, what they felt comfortable in saying was: 'I had no choice.' After I sold my business, one of them told me he had been threatened with loss of his business or worse. But he said he would deny that if he were ever confronted. That may not be proof in the legal sense because he wouldn't be willing to testify, but it's ethical or moral proof enough for me."

"Are there others you think would talk with me?"

A short period of silence preceded his suggestion. "You may want to see Jimmy Owens, owner of American Eagle Construction. He found a way to stay in business and stay below Hernandez's radar."

"Why did you choose to not take that information to the authorities and let them take care of things? I'm pretty sure a prosecutor would love to have that kind of a start on a case."

Smithson laughed sarcastically. "Kid, you don't know what it would be like. It would be hell for me and my family. It would be hell for the guy who got the subpoena. And when it was all done, somehow or other Hernandez and his network would still be in operation."

"Doesn't it bother you that he used illegal means to get business you should have had and then you had to pay twice once with the lost income and again when you went out of business?" I felt strongly about what went on. I was more emotional than should be as a neutral or dispassionate reporter.

"Sure I was bothered, and for a long time. The way I deal with it now is what you're seeing today. I enjoy every day as much as I can. I tell myself that he did me a favor by forcing me out of the business. Instead of aging twice as fast during the years it would take to go through a trial and appeals, I'm aging half as fast because I'm relaxed and doing what I choose."

His voice changed to a happy, almost giddy, tone as he said, "Ah, I was once an idealist like you. I wanted to fight every battle that came along that in my view just wasn't right. I won some and felt great about those. I lost others and felt bad. And sometimes I got beaten up, sometimes physically, sometimes emotionally, sometimes ethically. Those last ones aged me and followed me through life for many years."

I looked him straight in the eye and asked, "Do you advise me to back off and give up on trying to make things right?"

"I'm not advising you at all. I'm telling you how my life evolved and my viewpoint changed. The world needs people who try to make things better, try to right the wrongs that are done. I've retired from that effort, and I leave it to you and others with the energy and the ideals to continue on. I wish you good fortune as you continue on with your battles and efforts to bring about improvement."

At that time, he rose out of his chair, extended his hand, and said, "Having made that speech, a surprise to me, I move on to one of life's greatest frustrations and yet one of its biggest pleasures—a round of golf with hours of kibitzing and periodic libation. I hope whatever you write will screw Hernandez to the wall!"

We shook hands. He flashed a huge smile. And he clapped me on my shoulder. Despite feeling overwhelmed, I managed to say, "Thank you. Right now I appreciate the information about Hernandez. I expect that at some time I'll appreciate your observations on life."

I drove away confused. What Hernandez had done to Smithson was wrong. There was no other way of judging it. Hernandez should be punished for what he had done—not just to Smithson, but to others as well! But the victim didn't want to seek punishment. His reason wasn't the biblical teaching of turn the other cheek; he didn't make his decision out of concern for his persecutor. I don't know if I'd be ready to accept that reason either. His reason was that he had been the victim once and didn't want to be the victim another time when Hernandez came after him for retribution for making a complaint.

So Smithson closed his business, stopped his income, and now spent his time playing golf and talking with friends. And he said that Hernandez did him a favor by forcing him out. Was that just lying to himself and putting up a front? Maybe there is a time when hard work has provided enough for a comfortable life and it's time to start enjoying that life. The time for me to make that decision was a long way in the future.

The rest of another busy day was staring me in the face and getting busier all the time. Now I had Jimmy Owens on the schedule. And while today marched on, yesterday was following me. There had been Nelson and his comments about true friends, my guilt feelings about avoidance of talking with people in order to rush ahead with work, talking with Vince, and guilty thoughts about my need to reach out to Rox. Smithson's comments could fit into the same theme—the value of spending time with friends. I knew I'd have to try again to reach Rox.

When I arrived back in the office and phoned American Eagle Construction Company, I was told by the secretary that I would have to leave my name and number because Mr. Owens was in a meeting. I did that and asked that she include in her note that I had gotten his name from Lawrence Smithson. Immediately her tone changed and she became more helpful. "Mr. Stewart, I'm Lucille Henry, Mr. Owen's assistant. The minute he's finished with his meeting, I'll ask him to phone you. He and Mr. Smithson have been very good friends for years."

Using the names from the building permits, I started the job of phoning former customers of Baja Paving. The responses were the usual assortment a reporter gets when searching for information. "The person you need to talk to isn't here now. May I take a message?" Of course, I always left my name (the fact that I am a reporter for *The Press*) and phone number. I expected to hear back from fewer than half.

When I was switched to the right person to answer my "inquiry," I usually heard: "We have no complaints about the work," or, "We don't comment on the quality of work that was performed. Our attorney recommends we not say anything—either good or bad." When did society get so frightened that we can't risk telling the truth?

One special response was, "I'm sorry, but there's no one who works here who is qualified to talk about that subject." After I had asked how that could be possible since the work was done only two years previously, the same answer was recited. It could be that this was a variation on having a policy of not providing the information. However, it did sound a little like the company didn't have anybody who knew what had happened when the work was done.

I did get lucky on the fourth call. Republic Federal Insurance and Securities, a company with a public image, had filed one of the complaints with the BBB. The Director of Maintenance and Security said that he filed the complaint because cracks began developing three months after the work was completed. At that time, he began regular monthly checks across the entire parking lot. He saw signs of excess wear and documented the progress of the wear with monthly photographs. When he complained to the GC, a new layer of asphalt was applied over the full site. The General Contractor was A & JH Construction.

At some time between my fourth and eleventh calls, I saw Rox's name on the screen of my cell phone when it rang. With the anticipation of pleasure, I answered, "Good morning! I'd hoped you'd call today."

With a hint of anxiety, her reply was, "It's been a long time. I was afraid that I had seen or heard the last from you, that is until Dad gave me your message. I'm calling between classes, but I wanted to let you know that I received your message. I'll call you this evening, if that's okay."

"I understand you're busy. I look forward to talking with you tonight. Have a good class."

"Thanks. Have a good day." The anxiety seemed to be gone from her voice as we finished the call.

I felt better after the call. Tonight would be better for both of us. We would've been rushed if she had called to talk right then. We had some serious stuff to talk about.

I returned to the list, and it was call number eleven that yielded more information. I was into the small company part of the list by then and had found a complete repair shop, Data Protection, who had settled with Baja in small claims court for the full amount charged for repaving the parking area. The owner had taken extensive photos which showed decomposition of the asphalt and cracks. With the money returned to him, he hired another company to redo the job completely and was satisfied with that result.

I was surprised to get a return call from one of the larger companies, in the category which I had phoned first. The facilities supervisor for Wayland Trucking refused to comment on the quality of work because Wayland had filed suit against Baja. He did answer my question about how much of the property had been paved, reporting that the paving covered all the company's property which was not covered by the building and which was not part of the retention areas. When I asked if he would consider me to be trespassing if I came on his property to check for myself, his answer was, "You probably won't be noticed because we have lots of drivers and forklift operators walking around. If you're going to take any pictures, use a very small camera and don't photograph any trucks or people. And we never had this conversation." A click informed me that we were done talking.

I didn't ever finish the list of forty-one properties because I ran out of time. One other conversation was productive. Frank Alesio, Director of Facilities for Corsican Kitchen and Bath Suppliers, returned an earlier call.

"Hey, Jeff. They tell me you want to talk about paving jobs. What's up?"

"Yeah, Frank, I see you had Baja Paving do a big job at your place and want to know how that worked out."

"Baja paved 90,000 square feet here, everything except the building footprint. I'm not allowed to talk about the work they did."

"Surely you can tell me if it was good, bad, or so-so." There was something about his manner that encouraged me to pressure a bit when I hadn't done so with spokespersons for other businesses. Perhaps it was his jovial manner and the instant familiarity he established.

"You can take one of those choices off the list because it doesn't match the work that was done. You read me?"

"I'll take the first one off if that's alright with you."

"I've got no problem with that."

I decided to push a little more. "Are you under court order?"

"The courts weren't involved. I understand that wasn't necessary because we have a new system of links between Corsican and Baja. Some of the Corsican family members who didn't do well in our management trainee program have now found employment in a less challenging field of employment."

―――――――――

Jimmy Owens, American Eagle Construction owner, phoned while I was making calls to property owners. He began the conversation gruffly, "My secretary called and said you used Smithson's name. How do you know him?"

"I spoke to him about this same investigation I'm doing."

Before I could say more, he continued with the questions, "And what investigation is that? Reporters used to write articles or stories and now you're all investigating."

"We still write articles, but with bigger subjects we need to check the facts. I'm investigating the activities of Alberto Hernandez and his company. The information is starting to look like he hasn't played by the same rules the rest of you do."

"And what did Smithson tell you?"

I didn't know what effect it would have on his answer, but I told him the truth. "He said that he closed his business so that he wouldn't have to deal with Hernandez but you found a way to stay open and stay out of Hernandez's way."

"Yeah, that's true." I thought I detected a change in tone of voice. "So what do you want to know from me?"

"Larry Smithson said that your problems with Hernandez started after you hired his former secretary. I guess that's Mrs. Henry. Did I understand that right?"

"Yes, sorta. I had a couple of problems when I sub-contracted under Hernandez. He wanted me to cut some corners, and I refused. So the friction started. It was because Lucille knew about those disagreements that she applied to fill the job opening I had for an administrative assistant. She had become more uncomfortable being a part of the Hernandez's operation and feared she might become guilty of some of the wrong things he was doing if she stayed."

"Didn't you think there might be problems with Hernandez if you stole his secretary?

"First of all, kid, I didn't steal her." The tone of voice was changing back to what it had been at the start of the conversation. "I had an opening, and she applied. I got a great assistant and haven't regretted hiring her for one minute. She and I weren't wrong; he was. And besides, I gave him the courtesy of phoning him and telling him that I was going to make her an offer."

"That was very ethical." A little flattery couldn't hurt. "And what did he say?"

"He said what I did was under-handed and I'd pay for it."

"He threatened you?"

"Yeah. But no risk. Nobody else was around, and I didn't tape record the call."

"How did he make you pay?"

"I didn't get more sub-contracts from him. Delivery of suppliers' orders got later and later. Jobs got held up by bullshit requirements of the building inspectors in Howell and Neptune. No one trusted me because I couldn't deliver a job on time."

"Near the beginning of our conversation you said that friction with Hernandez began prior to your hiring of Mrs. Henry. I believe that you said he wanted you to 'cut corners.' What did that involve?"

"Things like closing up some walls without inspection of the studs and wiring and plumbing behind them, leaving out cut-off and isolation valves on heating and air conditioning piping, direct-wiring fixtures without electrical boxes to connect them to, and re-using exit lights from prior renovation jobs."

I was glad we were on the phone because I'm sure my face said more than my mouth as I was shocked by this revelation. "Is that for real?"

"I'm not making it up."

"Some of those things are safety related. People could get hurt or be killed!"

"I know. That's why I didn't like it and refused to do it."

"How did he expect to get away with that?"

"I asked that question. He said gifts to the inspectors could get them to look the other way."

"Don't think I'm stupid. I just want to make sure I understand. Did you understand him to be talking about bribing inspectors?"

"I don't know any other meaning for his words."

I couldn't imagine that any of the other topics I had in mind would be nearly as important or that the answers would be any more revealing than what

I had just heard. But I asked anyway, "Smithson said you found a way to fly under Hernandez's radar. What was that?"

"I cut back operations and started going for the smaller jobs as the GC, no more sub-contracts with anybody."

"How did you keep Hernandez from ruining you completely? He sounds to me like a guy who doesn't give up until he's the undisputed winner."

"I was a little fish after I cut back. He had bigger fish to fry." The pugnacious edge to his side of the conversation had disappeared. It appeared that the opportunity to talk to someone about the major change in the commercial side of his life had been therapeutic.

"And did you learn things from Mrs. Henry that were helpful?" Nothing ventured, nothing gained.

"Yeah, I felt better because I knew the bastard's total life was rotten and full of trouble. Not just his business but his home life. It was all because the way he treated everybody like dirt. Lucille heard two loud arguments between him and his first wife. Her name was Amelia or something like that. She was crying about their divorce settlement. The money wasn't enough to keep her living like when they were married. He must not have done anything to give her more money because the next time they argued in the office, she yelled that she'd expose his treatment of her while they were married and his screwing around with other women and his illegal activities. He must've done something because Lucille never saw her again."

This conversation had one surprise after another. "Did you ever hear of her again?"

"No."

"Did you ever check to see if anyone knew where she was?"

"I'm not a detective, and I've managed to stay in business by avoiding Hernandez in every way. I had no special interest in his wife. Leave it to her family to watch out for her— brothers, sisters, cousins, aunts, uncles, somebody. But not me."

"Mr. Owens, our conversation has been very informative. I probably will use this information, but I won't attribute any of it to you. Thank you very much for your time and for being so forthright."

I stood as I finished my statement and extended my hand to him. He shook my hand and said, "I feel better. I never had talked about all these things with anybody. But be sure you keep my name out of your paper when you report from your investigation."

I quickly ended the conversation—not because I felt rushed or wanted to avoid contact with people, but because I was afraid he might tell me that he had changed his mind and was denying what he had said.

My reminiscence about illegal activities as I drove toward the Wayland Trucking Company site in Hamilton Township ended with a reminder of the reconnaissance adventure under the OCC Bridge by Rox, Vince, and Hunter. Although only a few years separated us in age, I thought how the whole college experience makes people stupid in some ways. You get so busy with books that you forget about life. The things that are important in the big picture, like safety and staying out of legal trouble, get pushed out of the way by important little picture things, like differences of two or three points on an exam. You also make commitments to ideas and ideals and have the freedom to pursue them. I felt the hope once again that the three of them would do right by reporting what they had done and would do it soon enough that they could avoid suspicion of covering it up until someone discovered what they had done.

As I approached Hamilton on the highway linking the NJ Turnpike with the Garden State Parkway, I reduced my speed remembering that state police trainees practiced detecting and apprehending speeders on this stretch of road with the State Police trainees. I support job training and enforcement of laws but want to avoid direct contribution to this effort.

The trucking headquarters was one of several freight transfer facilities which had begun to populate the connecting roadways near turnpike exits. Some of the warehouses were multiples of hundreds of thousands of square feet in size. They were greeted by supporters who welcomed the tax revenue and by opponents who protested the disruption of a rural way of life. Wayland's building was a large steel and concrete box with multiple loading docks. A paving contract for the apron of the box should be profitable. Perhaps not profitable enough for Baja.

Security at the facility was looser than I had anticipated. I dropped the name of Ron Anderson, telling the guard at the gate that I was his brother-in-law and knew where his office was.

Deterioration had been extensive. Edges had crumbled as much as eighteen inches into the body of the apron. Cracks of up to ten feet extended from building corners and yellow bumper posts near the loading docks. It was obvious why Wayland had filed suit.

Back at my office I chose to check on the employment connection which Frank Alesio had mentioned between Corsican Kitchen and Bath Supplies and Baja Paving. I used the NJ Treasury Department website to find the names of the Corsican officers. Most had the last name of either Bernard or Campoli. I phoned the Baja office and said that I had met one of the management people at a meeting and put his name on a list so that I could follow up with discussion we had because I have some work I need done. I said that my notes were confusing and I didn't know if his last name was Bernard or Campoli. The receptionist who answered the phone laughed and said that she wouldn't be of much help because there was a manager of each name working there.

I laughed also and said I would start with the first name alphabetically, with Mr. Bernard. When Bernard answered the phone, I told him the same lie which I had told the receptionist and then followed with the question, "Do I remember you saying that someone in your family works in the Corsican Kitchen and Bath Supplies company?"

He answered with a note of pride, "Yes, that's my dad. He's a vice president there."

I expected easily to take advantage of his pride. "I've heard about the wonderful reputation of that company. I had your name and a note about the connection to Corsican. Can you tell me his first name and possibly give me his phone number at work?" After he had met both requests, I asked, "I have another last name here which may be another connection to Corsican. It's Campoli. Is he related to someone your dad works with?"

"Yes, he is!" He seemed excited about the connection.

"Can you tell me the first name and phone number of that person at Corsican in case I can't get in touch with your dad?"

What a helpful guy! He gave me the information, and we had a nice chat about how good the product and services were at Corsican. I thanked him for his help, and we parted as if we were friends.

I made sketchy notes about J & AH and Baja before leaving the office.

While I had focused on Hernandez and his J & AH Construction company, the information which had turned up which created links with Rivera and Baja Paving company caused me to wonder if Ramone Rivera was an indentured business associate in possible illegal transactions. Was he an unwilling party based on his gratitude toward Hernandez? Had this relationship and common activities just developed as a result of the largesse of Hernandez in helping to establish the Baja Paving Corporation? Or was Rivera a willing party whose greed encouraged him to mimic his mentor?

CHAPTER TWENTY

I usually awaken feeling refreshed. Today was an exception to that pattern. The things on my mind must have prevented my usual deep sleep. These early morning meetings with Alex were messing with my preferred schedule of afternoon work on articles, evening appointments or attendance at evening meetings, and waking up about 9:00 with a leisurely breakfast while checking the news. On my way to our Frog Fracas update appointment, I decided I wouldn't inform Alex about my discussion with Vince—too many unknowns right now, especially about when to report to police.

I picked up a box of Munchkins—my breakfast, a polite offering to Alex, and a diversion of Kim's attention which might get me by her without losing another verbal joust.

"Ah, good morning! Are you the early bird looking for a worm?" was the gatekeeper's greeting.

A harmless enough beginning had the effect of diverting my attention; I replied, "No need for worms. After Alex makes his selection, you have your choice from this box of sugar and spice treats."

She put on a disappointed face and answered, "I guess you're telling me that I'm sour and dull. What a bummer! I thought we were building a great relationship which will pull us both from our dull cocoons to become prize butterflies."

I didn't know where this was going; I decided to end the repartee quickly. "You're quite the prize already!"

"I'll announce your arrival," she said with a twinkle in her eye as she swung her hips and blew me a kiss while crossing to the partially closed door. "Mr. Speery, it's the charming and delightful Jeff to see you!" she exclaimed with much exaggeration.

Alex began as I extended my hand holding the pastry box, "It sounds like you two are hitting it off nicely."

"You and I both wish!" I said and then moved into the conversation we were going to have. "I've talked with several people in positions to have detailed knowledge of the activities of both Hernandez and Wilson. I've also done online research and in one case visited the location onsite. I've got a lot of backup for my next article, just need your approval to write it."

Alex could be pensive, although he was decisive and held to original decisions. He thought an additional few seconds and then answered, "Not now. I want to be sure that what appear to be legitimate complaints and information, have corroboration."

I replied, "I think I have the corroboration through all the sources I used. Like my articles to be timely. And that's now!"

Alex appeared startled by my forcefulness. "I want you to put together the information, identifying your sources so I can decide if you do have corroboration, in fact. A second concern I have is possible endangerment of you and, frankly, of me. How long do you think it will take to prepare the information summary? If I agree that no more corroboration is necessary, I'll want you to provide the information to the police. Let the experts—the armed experts—decide what items need additional information and then let them get it."

"I can get it together by this afternoon. Do you want to meet sometime between 4:00 and 5:00?"

After studying his schedule, he answered, "My last appointment is at 4:00. I'll say 4:30. If it's a little later than that, I'm sure you and Kim can find things to talk about."

━━━━━━━━━━

I was okay with summarizing my notes about my investigative work. I should have prepared the summary earlier rather than leaving it in field note form after my visit to Wayland Trucking. My delay resulted from a combination of my push to check my suspicion regarding a connection between Baja

Paving and Corsican Kitchen and Bath supplies, my excitement at what I had learned about both those companies, and exhaustion at the pace of my schedule those past few days.

I went to my apartment to update the summary of information about J & AH and Baja because I keep my most sensitive notes there. The most time-consuming task was to gather the notes together and then to organize them so that there was a logical and complete record. I made a mental note to myself: Always finish the paperwork of one project before beginning the next project!

Following a two o'clock snack (in place of lunch), I word-processed a summary which I could add to my file and could hand a copy to Alex. I accepted the pressure that was created by hurrying home and then back to the office. I prided myself on confidentiality and had developed a paranoid streak when one of my colleagues at the Rutgers newspaper had beat me to the editor twice with a scoop article just minutes before I arrived. It made sense when I realized the connection to his expertise as a computer science major.

=======================================

Kim used my red face and heavy breathing, as I suspected she might, but I had no choice when I arrived at 4:40. "Here you are again—red-faced and out of breath! I wonder all the things you do when you're not here. Those things must be fun and exciting." she finished with a naughty smirk.

When I just smiled, she continued, "Oooh, I must be right since you don't want to talk about what you do."

As is often the case, Alex's entry ended Kim's fun and my flummoxed response. The following is the summary which I handed to Alex.

J & AH and Baja Connections

Lawrence Smithson had lost business and then went out of business when suppliers wouldn't deliver on time, that problem having started when Smithson was awarded the one re-bid which Hernandez had not been awarded after Jason Leigh lost work due to slow delivery by suppliers.

Most spokespersons for companies where Baja had completed paving work were either satisfied or reluctant to talk. A spokesman for Re-

public Federal Insurance said that cracks developed prematurely and a new layer was laid after he spoke with J & AH as general contractor. Corsican Kitchen and Bath Suppliers had been dissatisfied with the large paving job around its warehouse but hadn't pursued it after children of Corsican officers were given management jobs by Baja. Data Protection computer repair company had gone to small claims court and won a settlement due to decomposition of asphalt and cracks. I observed firsthand deterioration of the paving at the headquarters of Wayland Trucking Company, whose Facilities Overseer refused to talk but told me how to gain entry to the property. Damage was obvious in several locations.

Jimmy Owens had received several sub-contracts from Rivera of Baja and had refused to cut corners as Rivera had wanted. Eventually he had changed the focus of his business to smaller jobs after his company stopped getting subcontracts from Baja and had experienced delays from suppliers following Owens's hiring of the administrative assistant who had worked previously for Baja. The assistant had overhead arguments between Rivera and his first wife, and then the wife disappeared after threatening to expose her former husband for his treatment of her, his infidelity, and his illegal activities.

As Alex read, I fleshed out some of the information on the summary sheet, especially reinforcing the sources and their corroboration of each other. Then after he looked up, indicating that he had completed his reading, I added the questions I raised last night as I thought about the connections between Hernandez and Rivera: Which of them was in control, and had their connections developed innocently or had they plotted to work to their advantage at a cost to businesses and the rest of the world?

Alex put the paper on his desk and said, "Good work. As usual. It looks like you've dotted all the i's and crossed all the t's. Just a few questions, so that we can move ahead. I know you're anxious to publish an article on this. You and I need to get Griffin Hess's approval that we can't be held legally liable for the content if either of these guys files suit."

It was nearly 5:30 when Alex stood. I hope I didn't jump too fast to take the offered handshake. He said, "You've convinced me. I'll ask you to join Griffin Hess and me for our weekly breakfast meeting on Monday."

Kim had left for the day as I departed. Her absence was a relief because I think I may have done a skip step due to happiness. There was a good chance that an article published in the paper would support the Freeholders in rescinding the bridge paving contract.

That evening I phoned Vince and asked where he and his friends were in regard to reporting to the police. He replied, "I hate it when I'm leading a group working on a project and the others keep avoiding their responsibilities. Like in middle school or high school when we had to work in groups—develop interpersonal skills, build leadership ability, learn how groups function. Yeah, I know how groups function. The leader does all the project work while the others become more skilled interpersonally. I got all of us together at lunch the day after I came to your place and told you about checking under the bridge. I presented our three options. Well, actually, there were three then but now reporting immediately is no longer there because we've gone beyond the time boundary for immediate. Now I've talked to each of the other two on the phone at least once and individually in person at least once. I know that our best choice is to report as soon as possible, but they keep debating that and not reporting at all. Rox said she was going to call you tonight because you tried her last night while she was at choir practice. I'm asking you as my best friend to include in that call with her an attempt to persuade her to vote to report as soon as possible; I'm pretty sure that she'll be able to sell Hunter on that same choice."

"Okay. I'm glad to hear her plan is to call me. I want to try that relationship again."

I looked through the latest edition of *Time* magazine as I ate my favorite meal of peanut butter on rice cakes. I had a couple of bites left when the phone rang. It was Rox.

"Hi, Jeff," she said with a lilt in her voice. "Dad said you called last night. By the time we got home it was late enough that I didn't want to call you. So here I am. What's up?"

"I called to check on how you've been. I miss our talks and miss seeing you."

"I thought you had disappeared for good, and I've been worried you found a new girl to talk with and go places with. I've been kind of bummed out about loss of phone calls and talking in person. I think Mom and Dad miss that also; Dad was kind of excited when he told me you asked that I call. What've you been doing to fill your time?"

"Things are busy at work—many days much busier than I've wanted. Don't worry that I've stayed away from you. I've had no social life at all. It's just really hectic at work. I've had periods like this before, so I know that things will get easier some time."

In her voice I could hear the change in mood. "I'm glad to know that I didn't do anything to turn you away. What else is up with you besides work?"

"It's been all work. I recently realized that I've been neglecting friends and decided to do better. Kind of a New Year's resolution, although it's not a new year right now. We should go out soon, maybe this coming weekend. How about a movie and coffee afterward?"

Sounding coquettish (or at least that's the way I heard her voice —a change anyway), she answered, "There are several movies I haven't seen, and we can decide what to do afterward. There are lots of possibilities for afterward."

"Uh, ah, let's do that." I sounded like an idiot. "I'll look at the movies around—I haven't kept track of that either—and then we can talk again, maybe tomorrow. I'm curious. What's happening about reporting to the police what you and your two friends found when you went under the Buckwald Bridge?"

"Oh, is this the real reason you called me?" she said with a different tone.

"No, the real reason is to check on how you're doing. And you handed me a bonus of agreeing to go out. But the topic of reporting the discovery is very important to you—and the other two of course."

"I don't really know what to do. I don't want to get in trouble, but Jesus taught that we should confess our wrongdoings and take the consequences from those around us because God wants us to be honest and repentant."

I grabbed the opportunity. "It's always good to be honest. If nothing else, you sleep better when you're not hiding something that you did wrong."

When there was no reply, I continued, "You know the choices: report soon and don't report. I think everyone wins from the choice to report soon; I probably would have recommended that you three report immediately after the discovery, but that time has passed."

"I know you're right. I was leaning in that direction myself. I guess I just needed you to tip the balance beam. I know Vince wants Hunter and me to make a choice. I'll call Vince tonight, and we'll decide how to have Hunter make a choice."

With relief and some excitement I replied, "I'll make a couple of commitments myself. I'll find out what movies are around, and I'll phone you tomorrow night so we can decide together. What time is good?"

"How about 8:30? Dad goes to bed about 9:00 so the ringing phone won't disturb him, and I can get a good night's sleep myself."

"Tomorrow 8:30 it is! It's been great to hear your voice again. I'm looking forward to spending time with you."

"I'll think of some alternatives of what to do after the movie. A very good night to you!"

The next day Vince phoned while I was still at the office. "We finally have a decision about reporting to the police, and I think you're going to be in favor. We're going to report as soon as we can. But we need your help again, this time with a strategy of who to report to, how to set that up, and when. Do you have any contacts we can use?"

"This will probably sound strange to you. After telling you to report sooner than later, I'm telling you to wait until I can set up something that has the smallest risk to you three. Somehow I'll set up a meeting of the three of you, an attorney, and an officer in the police department. Just sit tight. Try not to appear nervous. And certainly none of you can talk about this with a parent or a friend."

"I'll follow your lead," Vince assured me. He continued, "I thank you for pushing the three of us to decide some course of action. I know, for myself, that I was so surprised at what we found and so afraid of what might happen to us when someone learned what we'd done that my brain was locked up. I think one of my psych instructors used the term 'enervated' in describing what can happen to you when you get so overloaded that you can't function."

We hung up shortly afterward. I squeezed my head with my two hands and muttered, "How do I always do this? I'm trying to decide about dating two girls, and I'm going two directions with frogs and paving the bridge. And I don't just hang around the edges; I freely put myself out front. Maybe I need counseling so I can change my life and simplify it."

As I started my research on what movies were around, I muttered, "I don't know. I'll think more next week about counseling."

Hidden among the collection of the usual B-grade movies—bad comedies, romances which all seem the same, and shoot-'em-ups—were only three better movies that interested me: *The Princess Diaries*, *Without a Paddle*, and *Manchurian Candidate*. The first was designated "romantic comedy." The second described as "comedy." The third was listed as "sci-fi, political." I liked *Manchurian Candidate* on the basis of the plot descriptions I found as well as due to the stars: Denzel Washington, always one of my favorites, and Meryl Streep, a traditional award nominee and winner.

———

The research had cleared my head and put away some of my frustrations before I phoned Rox. She answered with a flirty voice, "That's the model of on-time! Dad's clock just struck the half-hour. I hope your timing is the result of pleasant expectations and not the result of guilt for having ignored me for so long."

I'm glad she couldn't see my face because it felt warm to me. I recovered quickly and replied, "A pleasant time is always my expectation when you're involved."

"What movie did you choose?"

I answered, "I thought we would jointly choose. I have three possibilities." Then I listed them.

"You decide where we're going, so I can decide what we'll do after," she said almost with a light laugh.

"Then Manchurian Candidate it is!"

"My parents talked about maybe seeing that movie. That would be a rare activity for them. They tend to be suspicious that they may see things they won't approve of. What time?"

"Does 7:15 work for you?"

"I'll be ready then. Now I have less than twenty-four hours to plan for enjoyment afterward. See you, Big Guy."

"Sure…Beautiful Girl…" I stammered.

When I arrived at work the next day, I was glad that I had a full inbox of articles to write. I expected that the backlog would keep my mind off the three projects I was working on—almost to the exclusion of any other work: moving toward a decision about how to handle my dilemma of choosing one girlfriend, moving ahead with what I had learned about Hernandez, and encouraging the college kids to go to the police and tell them what they found under the bridge. My positive reaction to the work before me was not due to the topics of the assignments: fee increase for dog licenses in Bradley Beach; hearing for new parking meters for Belmar (write-up of notes taken by Allison Finch, whom Alex had assigned to me as a reporter trainee because he had reduced my expected production due to my investigations); beach replenishment developments in Seaside Park, another article on Allison's notes; and a new defensive driving course for senior citizens in Wall. I found time to ask Alex if my summary notes about Hernandez were okay to present to Griffin Hess and if he wanted me to get the notes to Hess this Friday before our Monday morning meeting. He told me to hand the notes to Hess only on Monday because they were best understood when combined with my narrative, in the manner I had presented them to him earlier. I knocked off early so that I could shower, shave, and take my time dressing for my date.

I was several minutes early in my arrival in Rox's neighborhood. I drove around aimlessly so that I would knock on the door at 8:28, a couple of minutes early to show my enthusiasm but not so early that it was completely out of character. Mr. Freeman opened the door with his magnetic smile and hand extended for a welcome. "My favorite reporter! You've stayed away too long. Roxie said you've been so busy that you had no time to come around. You shouldn't work so hard."

"Oh, thanks for your kind words. I'm happy to see you again."

"Come in. Come in. I know Grace wants to say hello and spend a couple of minutes with you as well—before Rox pulls you away."

"Daddy, take your time spending time with Jeff," Rox called down the stairs. "I found a spot on my sweater and need to change."

"Oh, my! A wardrobe malfunction," he chuckled and winked.

Mrs. Freeman walked toward us as we headed for the back room. She took my hand in both of hers, gave me her big smile, and said, "We always like to see you."

Rox announced as she came down, "I think we probably should leave now, so we can find our seats while the theater is dimly lit but not dark. I hate tripping over other people when it's pitch black."

On the way to the car, I took Rox's hand in mine, leaned closer to her, and said, "It's my lucky night with the problem with your sweater. This one's a knockout. I can't imagine the original one looked better on you."

I think she batted her eyes as she looked over at me. "Thanks for the compliment. We'll see later if you're lucky tonight."

The last glow of evening sun was not enough light to show the heat in my cheeks which I was feeling.

I was surprised midway through the movie when Rox moved my hand from holding hers to encircling her shoulders, and nuzzled her head next to my cheek. After a few seconds, I whispered, "You look spectacular and smell wonderful as well."

She replied in a whisper, "You make me feel like a queen." Then she kissed me quickly on my cheek.

We held hands through the main door as we exited. Then she linked her arm in mine and said, "Are you up to helping me find our way to a special place where I've never been, but I've heard many kids my age talking about? One of my girlfriends gave me directions, and I think I know the general area?"

"Sounds exciting, so sure!" Just before we reached the car I said, "I'm up for anything that keeps us together longer."

Another kiss on the cheek, followed this time by pulling my arm against her body, which included the softness of her breast. Mentally I exclaimed, *If that wasn't an accident, this could be an amazing evening!*

On the way, her directions included several turns which probably were unnecessary; a couple of times two lefts cancelled the right we had taken shortly before. I was uncertain if she was momentarily lost or if she was trying to mislead me. We drove up a short hill, giving us a magnificent view of a full moon. As we started down from the crest, the moon lit a secluded inlet from the harbor I recognized.

"I guess we needed to get here earlier before the others did," Rox said with animation.

"I'm sure we can find a place for us," I assured as I drove behind the second line of cars facing the water. "Here we go," I said happily, parking two car-widths away from our nearest neighbors—that car containing a couple in the front seat and another couple in the rear seat. I tried to keep the mood light. "I don't understand why they came all this way and then aren't looking at the beautiful scenery."

With a vamp in her tone and a gravelly sound in her voice, Rox replied softly, "It's obvious they're more interested in the scenery inside the car." As she finished, she moved closer, took my head in her hands, and asked, "Wha'd'ya think?"

"I think I better move nearer to you so that our lips can meet easily," were her next words. Our kisses excited me and seemed to have the same effect on her. After several minutes of sustained kissing, I moved my right hand holding her on the back to the added flesh beneath her armpit. She flinched initially and then opened her lips as I pushed harder with my tongue. I hoped the "hmmmmmm" I heard was real and not my imagination. I moved ahead on the assumption that it was real. I slowly moved my right hand downward, stopping first at her waist and next on her right thigh. I considered my next move as suave. By moving my hand in a generally circular motion, I was able to bunch up her skirt and move the hem to my hand. I wondered about the result as my hand touched skin and I began to move it higher on her thigh.

Suddenly, I felt her body stiffen. There was no stopping myself. And then, WHAM, and said with emotion, "No. Not yet! Take me home! Take me home...please!"

I stammered, "Sure. I'll do what you want. I guess I misread you. I thought you were enjoying this."

"I thought I was, too. Then your moves reminded me of a few other boys who tried the same things. I agree with the way I've been raised...with the advice of my mom...with the teachings of my church! A woman's body is a gift she gives to her husband on the wedding night. I can't be true to who I am if I give into moments of pleasure." After an awkward pause, during which I fumbled for my car keys which I had knocked out of the ignition with my knee as I pursued one of those moments of pleasure, she repeated, "I want to go home."

I started the car and without thinking turned on the headlights. Car horns sounded, and a few shouts of "Hey!" were heard until I killed the lights and navigated toward the driveway entrance.

I drove slowly, giving me the time to think and to phrase my words carefully. "Rox, I respect you and don't want you to compromise your values. I'm sorry for misunderstanding your affection as the lead to more pleasures." Then, after returning to the streets, I continued, "I still am very fond of you and hope you won't hold this against me the next time I ask you out."

"I'll try not to hold it against you. With time I may be able to return to where we were on the way into the movie. She looked out her side window for a short time, and then said, "I like you so much that I decided to try sex with you to see if I really want to wait for marriage." She sobbed, "My feelings about sex may change over time. Right now it's so much tied up with marriage and commitment that I couldn't enjoy it. I'm sorry for the encouragement I gave you with my comments, and my clothes and perfume, and my recent suggestive comments on the phone and on our date tonight."

Once she ended her sobbing, she said, " I wanted to try sex with you to see if I like it now. I don't like it when it's not part of a wedding night and life together. If you'll be patient with me, I'm sure when we both fall in love with each other and make the marriage commitment, I'll be ready to be your one and only sexual vixen. By waiting now, I'm sure we'll both be ecstatic as we enjoy ourselves and each other beginning on the wedding night and continuing for the rest of our lives." She turned toward me as she talked and ended by smiling as she said, "Dating, and courtship, and eventually marriage with me is no sex now and no holds barred later. Can you accept that?"

After a quick gathering of my thoughts, I replied, "We both have some soul searching to do now and then decide if those restraints...or...conditions fit us. I've never thought these issues through as you have. My home was different—little attention to these issues and no regular religious activity. You've brought me to a crossroads of sorts. We'll part tonight as good friends who have enjoyed getting to know each other and sharing some activities. I know you're willing to delay sexual pleasure with the promise of greater, sustained excitement in the future. I need to decide if that will work for me."

My mood the next day was general discomfort—not anything overwhelming or intense, just uneasiness. After surfing channels in search of TV sports, I realized that wouldn't pull me out of my funk. I paced around and even tried a brisk walk for exercise. Still no change! I finally rejected a passing thought of phoning Kate because I knew my problem was with what had happened last night with Rox. This could become a bigger source of frustration if my lousy mood about Rox led to problems with Kate. "Women!" I said in a whisper. In late afternoon, I lost myself in reviewing my notes for discussing an article about Hernandez with Jeff and Hess the next day.

After a restless sleep—couldn't seem to get comfortable with my mind racing through pieces of my girlfriend problems and the two investigations in which I was involved—at 3:00 A.M. I said to myself, "This is stupid. I need my sleep to be sharp for tomorrow, but the concerns about yesterday, today, and tomorrow won't relinquish their hold on my psyche."

"Crap!" I exclaimed when I decided to get up and read until I got sleepy. At 4:30 I turned out the lights, climbed back into bed, and finally fell asleep. The next thing I knew my alarm was sounding—more angrily by the second.

I was sure I looked as bad as I felt while rushing through breakfast, my commute, and up the stairs for the meeting Alex had arranged with Hess. I had steeled myself to ignore the quip which I expected from Kim. As I entered Alex's outer office, I was surprised to see an empty chair where Kim usually presided over her kingdom (or should it be "queendom?"). I called out, "Alex, it's Jeff."

In return I heard, "Come on in, Jeff. Griff and I are catching up on weekend sports and our activities. He continued as I passed through his door, "I know it's a rarity that Kim's not here. Rarer still is the reason: She's running late because she forgot to turn on her alarm,"

After I helped myself to pastry and coffee, I handed my typed notes to Hess and followed with the same presentation I had made last week to Alex. Hess was satisfied that there were enough indications of a collusive relationship to warrant an official investigation. He concluded, "That information surely provides a foundation that supports your...the paper's...suspicions that Hernandez is a bad guy—one from whom the Freeholders should stay away."

My mood got a boost from his conclusion. I sat forward. I'm sure I wore a wide smile. I said impatiently, "I'm ready to start writing. Do I understand that you're comfortable enough that we can publish an article about the preliminaries?"

"Not quite so fast. I appreciate your enthusiasm, one of the chief factors which drove you on with all the work you've put into this. We need input from law enforcement. I've been able to get that input occasionally from Major Sean Wilson who's the liaison to the community. He and I go back to high school times. If you'll hold off for a couple of days, I'll set up a meeting of the three of us and him."

"Jeff will hold off as long as you advise. I'll see to that because what we print has to go across my desk when it's this important and has potential for a defamation suit. Griff, you get back to me with a time we can meet with Major Wilson. Jeff, I know that with this encouragement, you'll be drafting an article. You can't discuss it with anyone—not with either of your girlfriends, not with the college kids whose work has sown the seed for this investigation. If your mother were alive, I'd include her on the same forbidden list. "Nobody' means 'Not any person outside this room as we speak.'"

I was surprised at the near lecture Alex had just delivered. "I get it," is all I felt comfortable saying.

Two days later, my day began again with a meeting with Alex. We were joined by Major Sean Wilson and Griffin Hess.

It must have been the uniform of Wilson that had silenced Kim who demurely said, "Good morning, Jeff. Go right on in."

I couldn't resist asking, "New alarm clock?"

"Funny guy!" was her brief reply.

I made the same report and handed out copies of the same typed information. The third time around I was very smooth.

Major Wilson commented at the end, "I'd seen the printed information when I met briefly with Mr. Speery. Your comments helped to fill in where I had a question or two. This should go to the best of our detective squad. Captain James McCann is the lead detective and will oversee the work. The lid is still on any publicity which results. Is that understood, Mr. Hess?" After an affirmative answer, he continued, "Mr. Speery? Mr. Stewart?"

I replied, "Yes, sir," in my most respectful voice. Nervously I asked, "Alex...Mr. Speery..."

"Alex is still fine when you address me," my boss interjected.

"Alex," I began again, "I was hoping we'd publish soon because this is a big scoop."

"It's because it's a big scoop—meaning that no one will expect it—that we're moving very carefully. And we always follow legal counsel; you've experienced that before. What's new is the guideline that we always follow direction from law enforcement."

"I understand. And I sure don't want to go counter to the advice we seek. But you know from your days as a reporter that when you found something big, you got juiced up and just seemed like your whole life, and sometimes like your next breath, was dependent on publication."

"Perhaps Major Wilson can assure us of exclusive coverage of this information and the outcomes of the investigation."

The major looked me in the eye and answered, "You've got my promise of an exclusive, and I can pretty nearly assure you that the chief will agree to it. We're appreciative of your insight and diligence which produced information of probably illegal activity. And we'll play ball with you."

While he talked, I settled back into a more comfortable posture in my chair. He finished with, "Is that okay with you, young man?"

I hoped the gulp I felt my throat take had not been audible before I replied, "That's certainly okay with me...and thank you for your encouraging compliments."

Before the meeting ended, we scheduled another conference the next afternoon to involve Captain McCann.

As I left, Kim gave a polite reply to my earlier question, "A new clock isn't required. Just a renewed commitment to faithfully use the existing one. Have a nice day!"

I certainly was surprised by the change in attitude. Perhaps with the frequent meetings and the law enforcement brass today, I would receive more respect going forward.

The next day as I entered the outer office, I tested the continuity of the new attitude. "Good morning, Pretty Kimie. Usually I see you in the morning, but here it is a few minutes before 4:00 and you're here, bright-eyed and still ready to conquer the world."

"You do make me blush when you talk so sweet. Go on in. You're on time, but they were early."

Major Wilson seemed in a hurry because he said my name as I entered and then introduced me to Capt. McCann. He pushed the agenda as he again turned in my direction, "Capt. McCann received your print summary yesterday, and I did the best I could to fill in your comments. Jimmie, bring us up to date with what you were able to do in the short time from yesterday about Noon until we left HQ today.

"And now is a good time for you to ask Mr. Stewart any questions."

"I'm pleased to meet all of you today. When all facets of a community work together, the citizens are best served. We can't possibly discover all the wrong things that occur. That's where we need help from the media and others. And then once some wrongdoing has occurred, or once there's a suspicion of illegal or unsafe events, we're the best prepared to investigate further and determine if and how the legal portion of the community should respond. The major has brought me up to speed. Here's what I've done so far. We're investigating reports of loud arguments between Rivera and his first wife because there may have been injury or death which led to her subsequent disappearance. We have an appointment to talk with Lucille Henry who works now for Jimmy Owens, the owner of American Eagle Construction. I'm sure you remember that she had previously worked for Rivera. Our second priority is to investigate the paving job at Wayland Trucking because it's the more recent inferior work which you identified. In a couple of days, we'll inspect the work at their headquarters, and we'll be following up in a meeting scheduled for later this week. We'll likely look into the other incidents you reported, but they're colder now. Since Wayland hasn't settled, we could use that to gain more information."

"I do have a question now to clarify some of the information. Do you have any specific details about the use of the cozy relationship between Rivera and the owners and families of Corsican Kitchen and Bath Supplies?"

I replied, "I think my notes end with the discovery of the relationship. I'll check to see if I have more intelligence." McCann gave me his business card and asked that I contact him directly regarding Corsican.

Major Wilson cut off that discussion and said, "Jimmie, we've got to get moving on the other matter we're following up. I could use a few minutes alone with the newspaper people if it's okay."

"Sure. Sure, boss. Whatever you want. I'll be outside. I'm looking forward to watching Mr. Speery's secretary." He looked my way, winked, and asked, "What's her name…Kirsten?"

Alex and I said at the same time, "Kim."

After the captain left, Wilson said, "We want the Freeholders to delay the start of work by Baja Paving. You should know that I'm going to speak off the record to Freeholder Sam Ferguson to inform him that we're investigating Baja Paving and to say that the Freeholders may be embarrassed if work by Baja proceeds. I think we can count on him to ask for a delay without giving a reason. It's to the advantage of our investigatory work to stop the paving for now, and we don't want Hernandez to gain information or to be spooked. I'm going to tell Jimmie to remember that we left today's meeting here at the same time."

Hess, who in the normal course of events would have had the opportunity to become better acquainted with Wilson, expressed appreciation from all of us, for letting us know about the contact the captain would make with Ferguson.

CHAPTER TWENTY-ONE

hoped for a more relaxed remainder of the day following the meeting. My first priority was to prepare a draft of the article about Hernandez and Rivera. Alex knew me all too well. That had its good side and its bad. The latest indicator was his lead into the admonition to not talk with anyone about the information I had uncovered about Hernandez and Rivera. He set the stage for the directive by saying: "Jeff, I know that with this encouragement, you'll be drafting an article." I anticipated using at least the remainder of the morning to work on that draft. As I headed for my office, I envisioned uninterrupted writing time.

I should have known better! I was partway through the second sentence of the draft and was certain it was the start of an American Press Association award winner, when Allison Finch appeared to ask her mentor (me) for advice regarding the organization of an article assigned by Community Editor Aldous Jones. I'm committed to the model of attentive listener as opposed to director. So what could have been a ten-minute event lasted twenty minutes. Then, Alli asked if I'd look through the notes she'd taken at three evening meetings which she was assigned. She feared taking more notes than she'd be able to cover in ten column-inches, the standard which she learned in her latest course, "Efficiency in Journalism." Being a proud teacher and an all around nice guy, I gave her twenty more minutes. Those interruptions were followed by a call from the Community News editor who was desperate to find an additional thirty inches of copy for the "Around the County" feature. I promised to send him half of what he was looking for by 2:00 P.M.

As I completed the remainder of the first paragraph of my draft, Detective David Jones phoned for clarification of one of my statements in the synopsis of the Hernandez-Rivera partnership. He asked for the name of the facilities manager for Wayland Trucking who had refused to talk with me and who had encouraged me to come see the damage myself. I gave him the information and hoped this was the last interruption.

Giving into the flow of the day, I put the draft aside and began work on my non-Hernandez assignments since those articles were easier to write in the midst of interruptions. I had learned early in my career the key "schedule first, then revise." It got the "little stuff" done in the midst of "little stuff distractions". It usually cleared a period for "big stuff" work later in the day.

What seemed ironic in the midst of all my internal debate, and what I came to regard as a fortunate coincidence, was a phone call from Kate while I was still at work. I answered the phone with a tired and overwhelmed, "Hello. This is Jeff Stewart."

"Well, Jeff Stewart, this is Kate McGuire. I hope you remember me."

"I...well, sure...of course I remember..." I was so surprised that I had a hard time coordinating my mouth with my brain. I gave up the fight and just blurted, "Hi Kate! It's good to hear your voice—great even! I guess you can tell I'm surprised to hear from you."

"You sound more shocked than surprised! I don't know how to process that."

"I've thought about you often recently."

"When I thought of you today, I phoned. You should try that sometime."

"Would you believe that it's been crazily busy at work?"

"That would be easier to believe if you had initiated this call. Considering that I picked up the phone and made the call, not so easy!"

"Can I do something to get on your good side again? It's more comfortable on that side."

"You played right into my trap. I'll tell you what you can do. I have another evening meeting over your way, and that makes me available for dinner this afternoon."

"To clear my name, I should tell you I'm busy. But to be honest, I'd love to have you as my dinner guest. Shall we meet where we last met—some time ago?"

"I can easily find my way there. But let's try some other quieter place that we can go to after we meet, some place that specializes in seafood."

"I'll be ready to lead the way. What time will you arrive?"

"Look for me about 4:00."

"I'll be there early—trying to redeem myself."

"See ya,'" she said just before hanging up.

Although the day was very busy already, I rushed through my other obligations and hurried home to shave, clean up, and dress in a sweater. After I finished early, I recalled that I had promised to be early at Nicholson's Grille. I was about thirty-five minutes away from there, so I left at 3:15. I felt like singing so I surfed the radio. I was listening for any favorite so I could sing along. I imagined Kate's beautiful face and smiled. I pulled into our rendezvous point at 3:50—pretty early, but I was determined to get there before she did. Ten minutes later Kate arrived. I exhaled and relaxed.

Before Kate opened her door, I was at the side of her car. "I'm impressed!" she exclaimed. "I want to see how other things go before I start betting on your actions."

"You're tough, but I'm hanging in." I couldn't read her reaction to that statement, so I continued on, "It's truly great to see you!"

She was still on guard as she replied, "I'm always suspicious of the sincerity of someone who throws in the word 'truly' as part of a compliment. But, I'll take it. Thank you. Since I'm the one who proposed this time together, I'll look for other signals to give me a read on your truthfulness."

I decided to recapture the lead in this verbal dance. "I didn't realize that this meeting is a test. We're going about eight blocks away to Finster's Seafood." I called, "Follow me as I returned to my car.

Once we exited our cars, Kate opened the conversation, "I apologize for being such a bitch there. I guess I want to be sure that your interest is as strong as mine. Okay with you to start over?"

"I'd welcome the opportunity. I can't tell you how disappointed I was with our 'greetings' back there. I was starting to fear that you had arranged this meeting solely for a free meal or for the opportunity to make me pay for your perception that I didn't care about you." She was looking at the ground and had slumped a bit by the time I had finished. "Hi, Kate. This is super that you have time to fit me into your busy schedule. How's your job? Which group are you meeting with tonight?"

"I thank you for telling me your reactions to what I'd said without you going on and on. I too welcome the opportunity to start over and to put behind us any preconceptions about the state of our relationship." She moved from her car, took my hand, turned toward the restaurant, and resumed the conversation, "My job's been good—sometimes boring and other times exciting. I still believe in the cause of the department I work in. Tonight I'm meeting with the Berkeley Township Planning Council. They feel caught between regulations. Much of the building going on will provide lower cost housing for senior citizens. We've been using the term 'affordable housing' in our written and phone conversations. Often the scope of a development runs contrary to regulations which protect endangered species and is in conflict with deforestation prohibitions because the number of trees to be removed from the northeastern edge of the Jersey Pinelands in order to permit the building would require planting replacements in sufficient numbers so as to be restrictive in cost and so as to create new forested areas which would reduce the lot size to the point that the new home would be unattractive."

This was a bit new to me. I replied, "I've never thought of those things being in conflict with each other. I'm all in favor of affordable housing, in favor of protection of endangered species of wildlife, and in favor of developers replacing trees. I'm so naïve that what you just said makes it look like we can't have all those good things at the same time and in the same location. So, what's to be done?"

"We keep talking and thinking and researching and thinking some more. Sometimes I think my most valuable characteristic is my ability to talk to other people in a manner which makes it clear that I care for them, their ideas, their fears, their hopes."

"I think you're right." We had slowed our pace as we talked, and now had stopped at the door. "Let's go in and sit where we can continue to talk."

After we were seated and had received our menus, I asked, "What kind of a schedule are you on this evening? I want to get you out of here in time that you can meet your commitment."

Kate checked her watch and replied, "I need to travel about twenty minutes more and should be there ten minutes early. The meeting's at 7:00. I need to be driving away at 6:30; it's just after 4:30 now, so we have a bit more than an hour and a half. Perhaps we should decide on our order now and give it to the waiter. That'll give the chef plenty of time, and we can talk all the while."

While waiting for dinner, we caught up on each other's life, job, personal events, her work with the Jackson Planning Board and the associated new shopping center, the northern pine snake, and the eastern box turtle, my investigation related to the decision of the Freeholders to pave the Buckwald Bridge, and my consultations with the leaders of the college Environmental Club.

After we finished the fried calamari and before our salads were served, Kate asked, "What're the latest activities of that core group who energize the Environmental Club and keep the members involved? Did they do anything after the Board of Freeholders approved the contract to pave the bridge? I've been monitoring the applications for work approvals in environmentally sensitive areas so that I can flag any application for the paving. I know that the project hasn't reached that stage yet."

I chose my words carefully. "You better believe they're watching what happens next. I think you could count on that spunky president giving you a call once the next thing happens."

"What's her name? Is it Rosalind?"

"Roxanne."

"Whoops. It's good I asked her name before I find myself on the phone with her."

"Most friends call her 'Rox.' She seems to have a full plate between school, a job, her church, and family."

"I'll make a point to give her a call in the next couple of weeks."

I changed the subject of our conversation in order to stay away from the hotspots that I couldn't talk about. "What do you do for fun? ...Watch movies?... Go to clubs for drinks and dancing?... Attend concerts or dance performances? I'd like to do something with you toward the end of this week or on the weekend."

With her usually attractive smile, Kate replied, "I thought you were so busy. Now you're not?"

I was caught off-guard. "...Work .. Relaxation and enjoyment are expected—maybe even are more critical—during regular living. All work and no play makes Jeff a dull boy."

"I'm glad to hear you endorse that guideline," she replied with the same winning smile. "To answer your question, I like to do all those things you asked about. It's not necessary to do something that's outside my home. I like to cook; I find it relaxing and fun."

"I didn't think 'til now that I could invite myself to your home for a meal."

"I can make this conversation easier," she said. "My place this Saturday at 8:00. I'll cook. You bring white wine. Okay?"

"Yes, I'm looking forward to an evening like that. Thank you for ending that negotiation."

Small talk about a variety of topics filled our eating time. At 6:20, Kate said, "I'm going to the ladies room to check makeup and get ready for my meeting."

That was my signal to call for and pay the check.

———————

Two days later, I phoned Kate primarily to show I had turned over a new leaf, and secondarily to coordinate my trip to her home to have dinner on Saturday. I needed to know her address and the time she had in mind for dinner.

I dressed safely—Docker pants, dress shirt with narrow red lines, blue blazer, but no necktie. She answered the door with an apron covering the front of her body, kissed me briefly on the lips, took the liter-and-a-half wine bottle, turned and headed to the kitchen with a quick, over-the-shoulder explanation: "I've got something heating in the kitchen and don't want it to burn. Make yourself at home in here," pointing to her right.

I noted the generally sparse furnishings, to which I reacted as "gender-neutral," one sectional, a coffee table, one easy chair, a side table, and a modern TV on top of the two shelves of books. I carefully studied each of the several framed photos on the tables so I would remember to refer to some of them during the meal. From the kitchen, she called, "Feel free to watch the TV; there's the weekly newspaper TV guide beside the remote."

After the study of the photos, I knelt on one knee to inspect the titles of the books—being the geek my young cousin accused me of. I pulled volume one of an aged encyclopedia set, checked the copyright, and began to thumb through. I paused to read what knowledge appeared in the section on "Atoms." I was still kneeling and reading when I heard Kate's voice, "A man kneeling in my living room! Somehow I had fanaticized this differently."

I began to reply as I turned in her direction, "I didn't take you for a bibliophile, but there's no reason to expect other—" I was taken aback when I saw her moving in my direction in a "little blue dress," a differently hued version of the well-known "little black dress." The color perfectly offset her shoulder-length red hair midway on her shoulder, emphasizing beautifully shaped legs. The neckline was a narrow circle of fabric, which connected at the top of the dress at a point above each breast, leaving an expanse of well-tanned skin which whet my imagination. From those two connections, the filmy fabric of her dress clung suggestively to her shapely curves in the relatively short distance to the bottom hem. She acknowledged that my eyes spoke for me as she approached. She asked, "Do you like this dress?" as she twirled, resulting in the exposure of more of her legs.

Words escaped me momentarily, "It's very ... You look so great!" I looked down as I realized that I must have been ogling.

Her next words were a welcome relief. She didn't expect me to say more. Perhaps I could regain my composure. "I bought it the other day for a special occasion, not knowing then what event that might be. I love the feel, but I debated if it was too dressy for a meal at home."

"You love the feel. I love the look. I had no idea that's what your apron covered earlier since all I could see was the topless back. I'm thrilled that you decided to go dressy in this way. Kind of makes me think I should go back to my place and dig out my tux."

"You look super the way you are," she replied in a manner meant to put me at ease. The jumble of thoughts in my head prohibited being at ease.

I pushed up from my kneeling position, carefully holding the "A" [volume] of the aged encyclopedia, my index finger carefully marking my place. As I approached her, I said, "Older books fascinate me—in fact, all books fascinate me." I kissed her lightly on her cheek and followed with, "What a contrast! This old, plainly covered book and your new, beautiful dress covering your... uh...attractive body." When her faced colored, I followed with, "Sooo, is dinner ready? Do you need me to open the wine?"

My spontaneity had been infectious, resulting in her reply: "Yes, please. The wine is the only thing being opened now. Follow me, please."

If her hips had swung so suggestively when we had been together at the demonstration, at our first dinner, or at dinner last week, I hadn't noticed. I concluded that the action hadn't been there before. Perhaps it was because it was the first time I had seen her dressed in heels.

The meal was delicious—a mixture of filet mignon slices, covered with a light sauce containing lump crabmeat. I'm not a fish-loving person, but the crab gave a novel taste which complemented the steak. Dessert was a chocolate mousse drizzled with a cognac sauce. Throughout the meal we shared information about our educations (including secondary and elementary schooling), our family members, and our fondest memories of childhood. From her answers, I learned that she had an older brother and younger sister, a commercial airline pilot father, and a classical artist mother. Her elementary education was followed by a private high school. Her mother wanted more art training for her than she would have received in a public school, and her father sought the moral atmosphere which put school and education first. Receipt of a BA in science from Oberlin College was followed by a masters in engineering awarded by New Jersey Institute of Technology. Her humble start in the NJ DEP lab was followed by a rapid ascent to her Field Representative current position. She attributed her advancement to the philosophy espoused by her father: "Take charge and shake up anyone in the way."

I helped with clearing the table, receiving praise for my mother's training of me. After the dishwasher was loaded, Kate suggested that we move to the living room for a "sipper of port." Port was the vintage wine, and a sipper was the stemless glass which included a built-in, curved "wine straw." It looked as if a glass blower had created a standard wine glass with stem and then had bent the stem upward and cut off the usual platform, leaving the "straw" slightly above the rim with an opening for sipping. The port was delicious, and the experience of using a straw made it unique.

As we sipped, soft mood music played in the background. I questioned her about the people in the framed photographs, going to a table, removing a frame and bringing it to her so that she would know who I was asking about. They were all family members, some extending beyond the nuclear family, as far as a great-great-great uncle who was reported to have been a soldier in the

Civil War. Each time I sat down, I moved slightly closer to Kate. She never moved, so we were thigh to thigh for the last couple of discussions. When I returned the last frame, she asked that I light a couple of candles in the room and that I turn out the last remaining lighted lamp.

When Kate directed me to sit at the end of the couch, I was initially confused since our exchange of innocent kisses throughout the evening produced great confidence that we were bonding as a couple. My heart began to beat harder as she rearranged her position so that she lay with her head in my lap. She picked a pillow from the floor where she had thrown it and placed it on my lap, causing her face to be elevated, bringing it closer to my face. After a gentle start, we simultaneously moved to hungry, prolonged kissing with both lips and tongues involved. When I moved my hand to her breast, she pressed her lips harder against my lips. The feel of the softness, contrasted to her hardened nipple confirmed my earlier suspicion that she was braless. After several moments of that stimulation, I moved my hand the short distance to the bare skin of her upper thigh. She opened her lips, and I responded by inserting my tongue. We then alternated tongue thrusts. While this continued, I moved my hand higher, finding fabric near her waist. Bingo, thong!

She turned her head slightly, moving her lips away from my tongue. She whispered, "My position is getting uncomfortable." She sat up, then stood up, and took my hand in hers. Her next words were, "Follow me." We walked through the dining area and kitchen and entered her bedroom. After turning on a dim nightlight, her next utterance was, "I may want to wear this dress again soon, so I better take it off." She turned her back to me, reached behind her back, lowered the zipper, and pulled the dress over her head. Her bare buttocks excited me even more. Then she turned to face me as she kicked off her shoes. Her body was exciting. Her beautiful legs accentuated by the tiny fabric of her thong, her flat stomach, and her luscious breasts, took my breath away. Then she said, "I feel like I'm on exhibition here—nearly naked while you're fully dressed."

I quickly removed my clothes, so flummoxed that I almost fell on my face while removing my shoes and then forgot to unzip my pants before trying to shed them. When I completed my activity, she said, "That's better—now only one bit of fabric each separating our bodies." She moved to the side of the bed and asked, "Will you help me?" as she took hold of a corner of the bedspread.

"This will go faster if you give a hand." I couldn't take my eyes from her magnificent breasts, athletic tummy, and exposed buttocks as we quickly gained access to the bed. She held out her hand from across the bed and crooked her index finger, moving it so as to make a come hither sign. I eagerly mounted the bed and crawled across. She began to laugh heartily, causing her breasts to shake—exciting me further. We kissed while I still knelt on the bed.

Next she took hold of the waistband on my shorts and declared, "It will be easier for me to do this before we lie down." As she pulled down, I stepped down to stand on the floor.

I hooked by thumbs inside the thin slice of fabric at her hips and said, "Let me return the favor!"

"My, my!" she said. "Look how you have grown!"

We fell onto the bed and wasted little time completing the sex act. Afterward, we lay in each other's arms.

The next sound that registered with me the following morning was Kate's whistling as she went about straightening up—emptying the dishwasher, using an old-fashioned powerless carpet sweeper, and washing the port sippers. I put on my shorts and pants to be safe, hoping there would be a need to remove them once I saw what she was wearing. I was disappointed after opening the door and observing that she was wearing a sweatsuit.

"Good morning, sleepy head," she said with flitting voice. "I'm pleased that I wore you out so completely!"

I walked to where she stood, took her in my arms, and gave her a forceful kiss on the lips. "You may be as happy as me about that...but I have my doubts."

During a breakfast of store-bought muffins and coffee, she said "I don't do breakfast unless it's at a restaurant."

"You don't need to do breakfast, especially after you did so well with dinner, port sipping, and sex!"

"I just wanted you to know in the event that we wake up again in my place."

"I'm hoping that we do so often."

"You seem a bit impulsive—we enjoyed talking when we met at the college demonstration, went to dinner before one of my meetings, then silence set in, then a phone call again, a pre-meeting dinner again, last night dinner plus, and now saying you want in the future to repeat last night."

"You may be right about all that. Can you live with my impulsivity, or is it a complete turn-off?"

"I think I can adjust as long as you find time to stay in touch. My forwardness last night was a first for me. I never seduced a man and never went to bed on a first date. I want to make sure that you have lots of motivation to stick around."

"This conversation is pretty heavy for first thing in the morning. But here I am, and I'm looking forward to coming back." I took her in my arms, kissed her on her ear, and whispered, "Believe me. I'm motivated to stick around."

We separated and stood awkwardly before she said, "This is a strange question after the earlier parts of our conversation. But, here goes. What do you have in mind for today?"

"I have some open projects which I need to spend a great amount of time on. Does that mess up your plans for us?"

With relief written on her face, Kate said, "Yesterday I hadn't thought beyond last night. Before right now I hadn't thought beyond earlier this morning. But now I know I have work that needs to be completed by tomorrow morning."

After the previous fifteen hours, it was tough to say goodbye and leave. But I had committed to giving her attention, and I intended it to be frequent attention.

The sky seemed bluer, and the sun shone brighter and warmer. I whistled while walking to my car. I drove a little slower. My thoughts gradually turned to work. I needed to talk with Alex and Griffin about the skeleton find. I decided to send an email to Alex asking to have the first few minutes of his meeting with Hess on Monday.

On Sunday afternoon, I got down to work again. I pulled up the draft article about the investigation of Hernandez and Rivera. Generally, the draft reported that the police were investigating the fulfillment of contract terms by Ramon Rivera, owner of Baja Paving; that a record of complaints of failure to complete work as promised in signed contracts had been uncovered by the

Asbury Park Press; that the information from APP's investigation was being checked by fraud experts; that the propriety of the business ties between Rivera and Alberto Hernandez, owner of J & AH Construction, founded by Jose Hernandez and currently owned by his son, Alberto Hernandez, a member of the Board of County Freeholders who had been questioned during the APP investigation; and that collusive business practices between Hernandez and other contractors was a second focus of investigation by the police.

I made a note to check through Alex and Hess on what progress had been made on a possible reconsideration by the Freeholders of the contract they had approved for the road paving to be completed by Baja Paving.

I tried my best to keep my Sunday evening free so I could watch whatever teams the NFL and TV networks had scheduled to play at that time. As my attention drifted during time-outs and commercials, I replayed my preceding night's and today's early morning activities and conversation. Kate had been so smooth with the staging and direction of the events—right down to her seductive clothing—that I periodically doubted that it was her first experience with seduction. The flow of activities was flawless. I wondered if she were a sexual addict. Or, had she set out to gain power over me through arousal of my prurient interests?

Each time those or similar thoughts came to mind, I felt guilty that they had occurred. I shook my head or walked around and then concentrated on the game.

Another line of thought was a pleasant reliving of the events. At those times praised myself for how smooth I had been, and I became aroused as I thought of the most thrilling activities: my hand on her breast and then on her upper thigh, the realization that she wore no bra and the feel of the abbreviated fabric of her thong, watching her shed her dress, removing her thong while she removed my shorts, even the sway of her dress in rhythm with her hip movement while she had on all her clothes! Was I so in control that I took advantage—at the same time that she acquiesced, reinforcing my power?

After a night of delight, my mind made the memories an agony. I finally downed the last of my Coors Light, gave up on the football broadcast, picked up where I had stopped my engrossing read of *Bury My Heart at Wounded Knee* by Dee Brown, and drank two more Lights. The combination of three beers and some enjoyable reading prepared me for a good night's sleep.

The next morning I was up early to join the weekly meeting of Alex and Hess. I didn't feel like eating cereal again, cooking an egg, or settling for a bagel. So I drove through at Burger King for one of their breakfast sandwiches. I arrived right on time.

"The third week in a row of attending Alex's meetings with Mr. Hess looks like you've become a member of the inner sanctum!" was Kim's greeting as I arrived in her part of the boss's office the next day.

I was feeling sorry for myself, so I replied, "I could do without the interruption of my regular sleep time."

"Early to bed, early to rise make a man healthy, wealthy, and wise. If you have a wild weekend, you gotta pay your dues," she replied with a smirk.

Kim announced my arrival. I sat for only a couple of minutes before Alex opened the door and asked me in. After I sat, Hess began on his assumption of why I was there. "Young man, I know you're excited about the Rivera paving, Hernandez investigation and the exclusive story promised to you. However, once information is given to the police for further investigation, the development is on their time schedule—often seeming to drag before something pops and then the whole affair is closed out quickly."

When he paused to breathe, I jumped in. "I'm not here about Hernandez-Rivera. I have a different piece of the same frog saga. Three of the college kids found what they think is a human leg bone, and they guess it has something to do with the other happenings."

The lower jaws of Alex and Hess dropped in perfect unison. They both began to talk at the same time. Alex won the verbal contest and repeated his question, "A human bone? Where was it found?"

"Under the Buckwald Bridge."

While Hess shook his head in disbelief, Alex asked, "What were they doing there?"

"They went to check if the rare frogs existed so that they could decide whether their cause was protecting anything."

"Did they find frogs?" Hess followed up on Alex's question.

"Yes, there are frogs there, and they're the endangered type," I replied.

Alex took the practical approach, as usual. "I'm guessing they didn't report the find because you haven't been bugging me about writing an article."

"You're right about that, and that's why I'm here," I stated. "They want to go to the police as soon as possible, but they want to avoid being charged with withholding information. I think you guys may be able to facilitate the reporting by arranging a meeting with one or more police representatives."

The upshot of several more minutes of discussion was a plan to set up a meeting of the three of us and Major Wilson within the next day or two.

I took two steps toward the door before I remembered the question about what progress had been made on a possible reconsideration by the Freeholders of the contract they had approved for the road paving to be completed by Baja Paving.

Alex said they would ask that question when the meeting with Major Wilson took place.

As I left, thanking them for their willingness to become involved, Hess said, "Kid, you're a real pistol—a go-getter. You smell out a good story and then turn it into two stories. I'm glad you're only one; if there were others of you, we may not report any regular news."

The next afternoon was the meet5ing with the major.

I reminded myself several times before going to Alex's office for the meeting that Maior Wilson appeared to be all business, so I would make my flip comment by Kim reinforced my thought that the presence of the major had a quieting effect on her.

Alex appeared to be in a hurry also, skipping introductions and any small talk, before saying, "Jeff, fill in the major on what you told Griff and me."

"I've become friends with three of the college students," I began. I must have been nervous because I felt the need to clear my throat a couple of times. "My friends told me a short time ago that they were feeling the heat of their crusade and wanted to know if there were frogs under the bridge. They found frogs and also stepped on something that they're sure is a human thigh bone. They want to report their finding to the police but don't know how to do it."

Wilson replied, "One or all of them could have come to police headquarters. How long ago was their escapade? "

"It was about two weeks ago."

"And they're just now wanting to report it? How long ago did they tell you?"

I nervously answered, "They told me about two weeks ago and hadn't agreed on whether to not report, report immediately, or wait to report it later. One of their concerns was that they may have committed a crime by going under the bridge, regardless of what they found. I pushed them for a decision, but you know how college students are—inexperienced, too busy, mostly thinking about school and romance and part-time jobs. It took a week for them to agree to report it as soon as possible."

The major's face expressed concern for the delay as he asked, "So that's been about a week ago that they agreed. Why the delay until today?"

I think I squirmed some in my chair as I started my explanation, "I was glad that they decided to report their experience. They said they know that they should have reported immediately and were worried that they would be charged with withholding information. I had just met you in this same office a day or so before they told me their decision, so I advised them to wait until I could talk with you and make an appeal to not charge them with withholding information."

"The report of the discovery should not have been delayed. That's cut and dried," were the initial words. Then he changed his facial expression and continued, "From their perspective, I can understand the dilemma. Do they admit trespass under the bridge in order to avoid withholding information? Or, realizing later that the trespass would be nothing in comparison with withholding information, how could they avoid being charged with something?" He paused, then concluded with, "A reporter needs to be curious and energetic to get the job done of recognizing leads and pursuing them. But, Jeff, maybe you're too curious or too energetic. I've got to think about this more. We'll probably need a meeting of you and me and maybe your two mentors here and, certainly, the three college kids and some of my staff. If you want to prevent the delay in reporting from blowing up in your face, you can't do a story on this yet."

Major Wilson paused, made a brief note in the pad he carried with him for reminders, and then looked first at Alex and next at Mr. Hess. "I'm likely to develop a twitch when I hear your names. Or maybe I should say I don't know you and some other member of my department will need to come to any meeting here. I gotta go now. There's other stuff I have to attend to. In a day or two I'll decide on how to handle this and will let Mr. Hess know so he can pass it along."

———————————————

The next day I heard from Hess that Wilson wouldn't charge Rox and Vince and Hunter as long as I would wait for his okay to publish an article. Relief!

CHAPTER TWENTY-TWO

I was relieved and wanted to tell Vince the good news. As soon as he answered the phone, I blurted, "Hey, brother! It's Jeff, and I've got really good news for you." I continued with an abbreviated account of my meeting in Alex's office with Wilson and Hess. I finished with: "We'll need to be ready to meet with the cops on short notice. When they give me date, time, and place, the three of you need to clear your schedules and show up. Until after we meet with them, it's a possibility—not likely, but possible—that Wilson will change his mind and charge you guys with withholding information or obstruction of justice."

His "okay" was not enough of a commitment for me, so I added, "I hope you remember how frightened you guys were until you and I spoke last time. Maintaining Wilson's benevolence means a big difference in the quality of our future lives—that includes my life as well."

"I said 'okay,'" he repeated.

"I'll leave it to you to deliver that message to Roxanne and Hunter."

I realized I hate to be the "bad guy" who's always telling others what to do. While I was proud of my new commitment to attending to friends, I chose to cut this call short because it already was loaded with emotion. "I'll get back to you when I know date, time, and location."

It was pretty scary for the student leaders of the Environmental Club to report their trespass. No one, and that included me, could tell the students what punishment might be connected to an unapproved trip into the frog habitat. The students expected me, probably because I was a few years older than the oldest of them, to run interference for the need to report which I had ingrained in them. They knew they had taken a risk of being booked by the police for wanting to learn the answer to the question of whether they had acted in haste to know if their community rally, the meetings which they had held, and the testimony made to the Board of Education and the Trustees were completed in their secret haste to gain an answer to their question. The students approached me and asked that I protect them from what I referred to as their "impetuous haste" to attack once again the actions of a special interest of adults whom they believed to have hidden their heads in the sand of: "They're young and jump to conclusions primarily due to the gap in average age between themselves and us—people the age of their parents."

Included in my presentation to the police department was my statement of: "Environmental Club officers had done the frog community and the general community a favor because they had answered two questions which remained and had saved the Toms River community from a long, hard-fought court case. The questions are: Is this an empty debate, or are there, in fact, members of an endangered species which the Trustees are committed to protect? Such a commitment carries with it the obligation to not threaten the safety of the frogs."

The meeting happened two days later. Knowing how anxious the kids were, I was afraid that one or two of them would find an excuse to miss the event. In individual conversations, I extended invitations to each one to go to lunch with me and to let me drive each of them to the APP office. After all had accepted, I told each that we would go as a group. Food works wonders to win support from college students, and, I'm told, the same is true also with senior citizens!

The plan was to meet in Alex's office with Griffin Hess present to protect the legal interests of the newspaper. Others designated were all from the Toms River Police Department: Major Sean Wilson and Captain Jimmie McCann.

Griffin Hess's absence was explained by Alex at the start of the meeting. "Mr. Hess is not available this afternoon—contrary to what both he and I had anticipated. There are so many of us who need to be involved, and we need to move so quickly that I decided to hold this meeting without Griff. Initially he was opposed, but I promised to stipulate—and that's what I'm doing now— that all decisions made this afternoon are tentative until he has reviewed them and has voiced his agreement. Jeff, will you please serve as recorder during this meeting?" As I looked his way and began to open my mouth, Alex said, "Jeff, I expect that you will participate in this meeting with the same opportunity as the rest of us to speak and the same obligation to voice any concerns and ideas that may be helpful in our decisions." After I closed my mouth, he asked, "Okay with you, Jeff?"

I answered in the affirmative and followed with, "I expect that you want me to be available to Mr. Hess to answer questions as he reviews our decisions."

I was surprised to hear Alex say, "None of you here, other than Jeff and I, are aware of how simpatico the two of us, he and I, have become. We anticipate each other's responses and sometimes operate as if we can communicate silently. His statement just now anticipated the request I had planned to make of him."

I nodded vigorously.

There was lively participation and give-and-take for about twenty minutes. Then I made notes as Wilson outlined his understanding of our decisions.

The following are my notes from the meeting:

- *The parties to the meeting during which decisions were made, as reported below, are: Major Sean Wilson (TRPD), Captain Jimmie McCann (TRPD), Alex Speery, R.F., V.F., H.M., and Jeff Stewart.*
- *The discovery of a frog habitat was made as the group of three passed through a portion of the property of the Ocean County College in an effort to determine if the Pine Barrens tree frogs continued to maintain their habitat in the same location as known before.*
- *The three individuals were uncertain about the course of action which they should take following this discovery.*
- *Following some deliberation on their part, they have voluntarily provided information to representatives of the Toms River Police Department.*

- *It is the intention of the TRPD that members of that department, and any other persons who may be needed to satisfactorily investigate, shall replicate the movement of the three individuals through the same portion of the property belonging to Ocean County College.*

- *The first objective is to look for any members of the tree frogs community. A second objective of the search team is to retrieve as many skeletal bones as is possible. It is expected that achievement of the first objective will be completed very quickly. The second objective must be pursued with great care and with a longer timeline.*

- *This investigatory activity shall be closed to the general public. The first information released will be in regard to the existence of the frogs. Gaining data in regard to the second objective likely will require more time. Therefore, information from the search will be released at two very different times.*

- *Although the expectation normally would be that knowledge of an illegal activity (or potentially illegal activity) should be reported immediately to the law enforcement agency with jurisdiction over the location at which the activity had taken place, that expectation has been deemed as moot for a number of reasons.*

- *There will be no formal, legal action taken in regard to the three individuals who discovered the habitat of the tree frogs and discovered the apparently human bone and then delayed until now in the reporting of the discovery,*

- *In advance of the start of the investigation, in the morning edition of the Asbury Park Press (which shall be published and distributed on that date and perhaps published and distributed on one or two days earlier if possible), there shall appear prominently an article reporting the existence of police activity, the purpose of the publication of the article in that specific edition of the newspaper being to formally give notice to the public of the investigation and of the probable disruption of traffic and other activities on the road through the specific portion of the property belonging to Ocean County College.*

- *The Toms River Police Department expresses its gratitude to the individuals R.F., V.F., and H.M. for reporting their discovery.*

- *There will be no formal, legal action taken in regard to the three individuals who discovered the apparently human bone and then delayed until now in the reporting of the discovery.*

- *The Toms River Police Department expresses its gratitude to the individuals R.F., V.F., and H.M. for reporting their discoveries.*

Major Wilson requested that all individuals present at the meeting sign their initials to the notes, indicating their agreement to the accuracy. All parties complied.

Major Wilson requested, "Captain McCann, Mr. Sperry, and Mr. Stewart please remain after the others have left this office so that we may confer in private."

As none of us wanted to be at odds with the major, we all voiced or nodded assent.

Vince turned to me inauspiciously, held out his hands, and hunched his shoulders as he mouthed the words "What is this?"

I shook my head and made the same, inquisitive hunching move. I knew he would have the opportunity to ask what had taken place before he exited my car in the parking lot at OCC.

Comments from the three students were mixed as we traveled to the college: "That was scary!" "I thought it was interesting." "It was pretty neat to be a part of a meeting to plan a criminal investigation!" "I was afraid that we might be called on to speak." "I was glad we weren't called on."

As I began to talk, I had the same thought as I had recently upon realizing that I often accepted the role of telling others what to do. I said, "As scary or as cool as you may think that was, you must not *under any circumstance* talk about it, make comments about it, or write about it. I reported your information to the major and to the captain in such a way that they both agreed that there would be no charges filed against any one of you or against all of you. Now don't blow that and run your mouth and set all of you—and me— up for trouble from the police!"

Despite the unanimous head shaking and grunts of "Uh-huh," I asked the specific question of each in turn: "Do you agree to keep this to yourself and to refrain from telling any details associated with it to your best friend, a parent, your love interest, or any other person?"

Of course, they each said, "Yes. I agree to what you just asked."

Vince hung back as the others hurried to class or to their cars. When they were beyond earshot, he asked, "Did they talk about potentially filing charges in the future?"

"No. The purpose in staying behind was to discuss a tentative calendar and the personnel they would need to deploy for the investigation. They seem to be short handed with their usual activities. I can understand they have a lot on their plate: patrolling, responding to traffic accidents, occasional arguments which sometimes include punches being thrown, responding to 911 calls, together with their more serious enforcement issues of burglaries, investigation of assaults, and drug trafficking and overdoses. Working through the staffing concerns likely will delay the start of this investigation. You and I never had this conversation."

———————

Mr. Hess phoned later that afternoon. "Sorry I missed our meeting this morning. A judge before whom I was required to appear had to reschedule."

"No problem. From what I hear, you high-powered attorneys often have your schedules revised by a judge or the opposing attorney. That's one item that would drive me nuts if I ever dared to practice law."

"I've gotten used to it. The reasons for this call are to say 'Good job with the notes. They're very clear and concise,' and to give you the opportunity to add anything that you want me to know before I give approval."

"The only thing I'll add is my take on the conference at the end which involved Alex, Major Wilson, and Captain McCann."

"Alex referred briefly to an addendum after the main meeting. I didn't get clear who was present. From your reference just now, I understand it was only the four whom you mentioned now. Is that right?"

"Yes. I don't know the reason for the secrecy."

"What was said?"

"The police department is experiencing a shortage of personnel, and the shortage may delay pursuit of this investigation."

"That's the same I understood from Alex. In respect to you and the three students, as well as in consideration of the possible urgency to complete an investigation so that identification of any killer or killers could proceed before the perpetrators disappear, I'd like to get them to move quickly on this."

"I'd sure like to see a rapid disposition," I added presumptuously.

"For a long time now, one of my friends, a retired detective, and I have discussed the formation of a cold case squad to provide a source of temporary manpower to the TRPD. I should talk with Sean about that. He can put a bug in the ear of Chief Dennis Hughes." After a brief hesitation, he said, "Sometimes I think better aloud. Please forget what I just said since there are lots of steps involved before something like that happens."

I smiled as I replied, "I didn't hear you say anything just now."

"Good man," he answered. Then continued, "To sum up, I'm going to contact Alex and Major McCann and tell them I'm in favor of the strategies contained in your notes. I'll also tell them that you were a top-notch scribe. Are we done?"

"We're done."

After we ended the conversation, I pumped my hand and mouthed the words, "All right." I was greatly relieved that my young friends wouldn't be charged. At the same time, I would await word from Alex before telling Vince, Rox, and Hunter.

When Alex phoned me with the official version of the approval by Hess, he asked that I join a meeting in his office the next morning with Wilson and McCann for an update on the Hernandez-Rivera case. After hanging up the phone, I thought, "When am I going to get a 'normal' start to a day?"

If there were to be a normal day, the start to the next day, a Wednesday, was not that. The alarm jarred me out of a pleasant dream extension of the reality of dinner and overnight with Kate. We were on the way to her bedroom; she was wearing that same sexy, blue dress, and her hips were swaying suggestively. I grabbed the clock with my index and middle fingers placed as I would to throw a baseball. A flash memory of a previous incident of throwing a clock stopped the motion midway to release. There was no hope of getting back into the fantasy after that interruption. There was only once that I could recall when I was able to re-enter a dream. That earlier experience occurred while I was in the midst of being hired into my current position. I decided that last night's thought related to the 'old normal,' while the start of today and of several days prior was the 'new normal.'"

I told myself, *Enough of this anger and reverie regarding my dream-life! Get up and get going so I can advance in my pursuit of a Pulitzer Prize.* Maybe it was the stress I was experiencing that caused me to think, *Screw it!* in response to the fleeting consideration of stopping to pick up some pastry on the way to *The Press* building. I put coffee on to brew as I went to shave. I skimmed the morning newspapers as I downed a cup.

When I rushed through the door to Kim's part of the office, she announced, "And Beetle Bomb."

I had pushed hard to get there on time, and I wasn't about to have her take away that accomplishment. I looked dismayed and said, "What do you mean? I still have thirty seconds. I deserve to be treated as being in the pack."

"Well, Spike, Beetle Bomb was in the pack all the way through the race, just in the back of the pack most of the time, including when he crossed the finish line. Go on in. You may have missed the bragging about who has the best looking child or grandchild."

I rushed through the door to Alex's office and shook hands all around. It must be etiquette to start a meeting quickly when police brass are involved because Alex cleared his throat as I entered the office and began when I was shaking the last hand and engaging in small talk. "Thanks to all for coming here once again. I understand this to be an update on the investigation of the county paving contract with Baja Paving with a review of the known facts regarding Baja's owner Ramone Rivera and his mentor Alberto Hernandez, owner of J & AH Construction. Do I turn the meeting over to you, Sean, or to your colleague, Jimmie?"

Sean answered, "I want to set the parameters for the meeting and then turn to Jimmie for his presentation." Without an opportunity for a response or interruption, he continued, "Based on the research by reporter Stewart and on the questions he raised in his fact-sheet of the business activities and relationships of the two company owners, our detective squad, under the able guidance of Captain McCann, has pursued the most potentially serious and the most easily accessible components. They have reached a point where action is being contemplated. The purpose in involving personnel from the *Asbury*

Park Press is to keep them informed because the paper was the initial source of data."

Jimmie presented the most critical facts and conclusions before announcing the final decision. "Reporter Stewart, you were thorough in your investigation and kept your records in enough detail that we could easily pursue this case. We thank you for your quality work. You were perceptive in your evaluation of your data. The two companies, J & AH Construction (formerly Hernandez and Sons) and Baja Paving Corporation, are essentially the same company— a reality that is hidden in their paperwork filings with the state, in which they certify their independence. We have alerted the interested state agencies who await additional data from us as we continue to move forward. In addition to the fraudulent filings, the mixing of receipts raises tax issues and permits the companies to hide what otherwise would be regarded as collusive practices. That provides one basis for the owners' arrests. One of the business owners who were your sources of information has agreed to testify on the involvement of Hernandez in the cancellation of supply orders so the owner with the low bid on the job would fail to meet completion deadlines which appeared in the contracts for his work. The result was that the contract was nullified, and then Hernandez stepped forward to negotiate a contract for his company to complete the work at a premium cost due to compressed timelines. It appears that this was a common practice for Hernandez, a practice which has "collusion" written all over it because he coerced the suppliers to declare that the supplies were not available, which caused the contractor to stop work and pay a penalty, opening the door for Hernandez to ride in as the hero and complete at a premium price due to the faster schedule on a job for which he was not the original low bidder. This provides the second basis for his arrest. We pursued the disappearance of Hernandez's first wife, thinking initially that she may have been killed or otherwise disposed of by Hernandez since there was an abundance of evidence of the conflicts between them. Due to our extensive resources in the field of personnel location, we were able to discover that she is alive and living in Mexico, now as Mrs. Emilia Sanchez. She and her present husband live in a large home on a large ranch with a very profitable business of raising cattle. She refuses to appear voluntarily as a witness. She wanted to escape her abusive first husband and has nothing much to report except hearsay and suspicions. We have discontinued our investigation in this area. Bottom line is that we have now confirmed two of Hernandez's actions which justify his arrest. We are delaying that arrest until we have completed further investigation that may provide reinforcement of our conclusions or may provide new bases for arrest."

Alex beat me to the punch as he addressed Wilson in asking, "Sean, did someone supply information to a Freeholder about the investigation of Hernandez and was that information linked to Hernandez's motion to approve the Rivera contract? The apparent de facto collusion between Hernandez and Rivera possibly could be used in a court case to overturn the contract, dragging the Freeholders' reputations through the mud."

Wilson replied cagily, "I don't have full information related to your question. However, I must say that I was surprised to learn that Rivera had sent a letter to the Board of Freeholders in which he asked that the contract be nullified."

McCann, addressing Wilson, said, "That's one of the mysteries surrounding this case. Another is that some of our staff working on this case reported that members of the state and local Republican Party organizations confronted them initially with questions regarding the reasons for their investigation and with suggestions that evidence was made up. Someone must have provided some information to the heads of both organizations because they backed off quickly."

Wilson added, "Now is as good a time as any to caution that all people in this meeting are prohibited by law from informing any other person of today's discussion." After a pause, he continued, "There won't be any arrest made soon because we're short of staff and we're making assignments based on the degree of threat to public safety."

Hess spoke, "Excuse the interruption, Sean and Jimmie. I had heard by the grapevine that there is a personnel shortage. Some of my retired police officer friends might jump at the opportunity to provide a cold case squad, which could be called on to supplement regular personnel—at greatly reduced wages, I might add.

Wilson spoke appreciatively, "Griff, that may be the key to several logjams we have and may prevent logjams in the future. Hmmmmmm. Give me a day or two to plot what that may look like and to take it to Chief Hughes. Thanks! If I can present this in the right way, you will have done a great service to the community."

"Call me if you need my help, in any way," Hess replied with a smile.

"I think we're done here for today —with the bonus of a possible solution to a growing problem," Wilson finished.

Hess asked to extend the meeting to discuss a different subject. All finished gathering their papers and other belongings and sat down again. Hess then turned to me and said, "I wasn't available for a prior meeting on the topic of the bone found under the Buckwald Bridge by three rambunctious students. You subsequently shared the initialed notes from that meeting. I have reviewed them and talked by phone with you. I have concluded that the decisions made that day do not constitute a legal complication for the college. I bring up this other issue which derived from the consideration by the Board of Chosen Freeholders of paving the Buckwald Bridge so that all parties here are aware of my conclusion. I also bring it up now because there is a potential solution to the problem of too few detectives."

With a large smile Wilson asked, "Griff, are you the business agent for the potential cold case squad, finding cases in order to keep them employed?"

While everyone laughed, Wilson clapped Hess on his back and said, "Of course I'm kidding; I feel like joking because you've presented a good idea for a solution for a problem we've been dealing with for a few months."

As Wilson and McCann were on their way out the door, I made my request: "Alex, Mr. Hess, may I have about five more minutes of your time?"

Alex answered first, "Sure."

Hess was in a rush, saying, "I can give you about three minutes. I'm about 45 minutes late for an appointment at my office."

"I'll make this fast," I promised. "Because there's potential that the bone investigation may start with little notice, I prefer to create the article, the one that will serve as a notice of possible traffic problems, as soon as possible so that it can be reviewed by both of you in advance of the police work. Do you agree?"

Both agreed. Hess, an attorney through-and-through, offered advice, "As you write, keep in mind the concepts of 'slander' and 'libel.' Both have to do with making untrue claims about a person's character. Slander involves the spoken word, while libel involves written accusations. As such, slander provides some wiggle room because the speaker can always say that he had used the words but intended a different meaning. Libel is much more cut-and-dried because the words are there in print and the usual meanings are assumed."

"I'll get started this evening. When finished, I'll run it by Alex who can run it past you, Mr. Hess. That's all the time I need."

"Thanks for accommodating me," Hess said as he hurried away.

After dinner I phoned Rox to tell her that I had been assigned to write an article on a temporary closure of the bridge. "The college and police administrations want the article to serve as a public notice in regard to traffic movement," I commented.

"Does it have anything to do with an investigation about our discovery of a probable human bone?" she asked quickly.

"I'm not at liberty to provide any more information."

"When will the survey begin?"

"I'm not sure. I think no one knows at this time." I replied. "I want it ready to go in advance since I had promised to write the article. I phoned because I want you to be aware of what's happening since you were one of the discoverers. If you were to hear about it at the same time that the general public will hear, you might be suspicious that your discovery had been made…or soon would be made…public."

She responded, "If you need to create some cover to forestall the development of any rumors which may lead to the release of information about our unwitting crime, you've got my permission to make up any quote of me which you think will be helpful."

"Good idea! I hadn't thought of using the article to give cover for the un-approved search. I've got to get to work on this assignment, and I want to do the work because I'm really pumped!"

The draft I prepared that evening was printed eventually—exactly as it came out of my printer. It read as follows:

Police Investigation Threatens Traffic Flow at College

Traffic on H. George Buckwald Drive will be diverted, starting today (or another date - to be determined) to permit the Toms River Police Department to conduct a safety survey in the area of the H. George Buckwald Bridge. A recent decision by the Ocean County Board of Chosen Freeholders to pave the bridge has triggered protests both on and off campus. The protests and the paving were not cited in the notice circulated in advance of the road closing.

Roxanne Freeman, President of the OCC Environmental Club, could not provide additional information. "The Environmental Club was not notified in advance. I'm somewhat hopeful that whatever information is developed by the police activities will support the club's positions that the bridge should not be paved and that not paving it will have no negative impact on the traffic flow. A delay will allow more time to find solutions to the problems which have been announced as a primary reason for paving the bridge, such as a solution of wooden pegs, which hold the bridge together, being vibrated out of the plank surface."

I'm very cautious when I write an article that serves two or more purposes and when I include a quotation. The article received approval from Rox, Alex, and Hess.

CHAPTER TWENTY-THREE

When I picked up Kate on Saturday night, I was struck by her beauty. I always thought of myself as a good catch, but she was so pretty, I considered her in a different league. Her soft, low-pitched voice was a perfect match for an almost constant smile. I sometimes wondered if everyone got that smile or if it was special for me. I usually dropped the question using two rationales. I told myself it was for me, and it didn't make a difference if other people got it because they weren't around when I was. I took her hand in mine as we walked to the car. She squeezed my hand hard and held onto my arm with her free hand, sometimes leaning into me as she laughed at my stupid, old jokes. I knew they were old and stupid, but she was such a good date that she laughed. Her laughter was the reason I told those jokes.

After I closed her door behind her entry and entered myself from the other side, she scooted closer, fumbling for the middle seat belt and the designated buckle. We solved that problem, some of it arousing me as more than once her butt landed on my palm-up, open hand as I tried to help. I fought a successful battle with myself to avoid moving my hand or fingers until after she pulled herself up and I moved my hand away.

Laughing, I said quietly, "You know, we may not get to the movie theater if that continues to happen."

She replied with a sorrowful look, "I've got bad news for you big guy. It's that time of the month for me. I knew it would be touch and…er, I should say it was a close call, starting late this afternoon. So, it would be best for you to avoid becoming aroused."

I'm sure I blushed. I was thankful that it was dark already. I answered, "You have many endearing qualities in addition to a luscious body. I hope you'll give me a rain check."

She playfully pushed my right upper arm and said, "I like you to pursue my body, but I'm glad to know there are other things you like about me."

We caught each other up on our jobs, finishing as I turned into a parking space close to the theater. She clung to me as we walked to the entrance to the shopping mall, which housed the theater, but she didn't lean into me with the same force as earlier.

The mall was busy for a Saturday night. I saw several people I knew and called to and waved at them. Just after I realized—with some surprise—how many friends showed up at the same time, I saw Rox and Colleen approaching ahead of us. I turned to Kate and reminded her of their names. We both waved and called their names. They were carrying a couple of bags each, telling me they had been shopping for some time.

"Hey, guys. I hope you left some merchandise in the stores because if you didn't all these other people are going to be unhappy."

They laughed politely while Kate let go of my hand and said, "I remember you from the demonstration. Colleen, you picked up nicely on the excitement to capture the energy among the crowd. That momentum inspired more energy. And, Rox, I frequently use you as an example of organization and hutzpah. That event was super from start to finish. I've never seen such success in any other event like it."

Both girls responded with smiles and quiet "thank yous."

Rox asked, "Are you shopping for something special?"

Kate replied, "We're headed for a movie." Turning to me, she continued, "What did you choose?"

I was glad to get a chance to speak in hopes it would dispel some of my anxiety about the nature of this situation. "I'm hoping you're willing to watch *Friday Night Lights*. It's getting good reviews and making a lot of money."

"I don't know what else is showing," Kate began, "but I like to watch sports. That should be good."

I glanced at my watch, and Rox said, "You guys should keep moving. I'd hate to be the reason you miss the beginning."

"Didn't you date Rox some of the time?" Kate asked as we walked.

"Yes. Yes, I did…but not lately," I answered as I took her hand again. When I had her hand in mine, I looked her way and got that big, beautiful smile once more. My anxiety disappeared.

The movie was super! Kate seemed to like it also. On the way to the car, I blurted, "Since we're not going to make love, how about a coffee for old time's sake?"

"Surely, there must be more to your life than sex and caffeine!"

"I didn't say that very well did I?" I offered half an apology.

"You could have done better…or, I hope you could."

"Well, at least you know I heard what you said earlier and will respect your wishes to hold off on the sex."

She smiled wryly and said, "You're backing yourself into a corner. We don't have to avoid all sexual activity. Only the conclusion." She continued after a slight pause, "Now I'm the one that offered too much information."

As we drove out of the parking lot, Kate suggested, "We can save our money by going to my place for the coffee preliminary, since it sounds like we both would like to engage in some arousing activities."

And so that's what we did. My rating on a scale of 1-10 is that we lived a 5—fun until it stopped, yet necessarily frustrating.

Our kisses were as passionate as they had been a couple of weeks ago. We both talked in the future tense throughout our time together.

The following Tuesday evening, I was surprised by a phone call from Rox.

After I picked up, she said, "Hi. I was glad to see you the other night… glad to see Kate also. Hope the movie was to your liking."

"The movie was good. Did you shop much more?"

"A little more, then we ate a late dinner at Applebee's."

Following an awkward pause, she continued, "It took all the internal conversation with myself that I could muster for me to make this call. Not long ago, I would have considered this call as forward. You know, 'Girls don't call boys.' But after seeing you with Kate, I decided I must call."

I started to cut in, "I have no problem—"

"Please don't make this any more difficult; let me keep talking before I get cold feet again. I want to go out with you—I don't care where or for what purpose. Then I want you to have your way with me. I won't stop you…won't stop us from whatever you choose to do." Following a sigh of relief, she finished, "That's all. I'm finished with my appeal. I ask that you call me Thursday night after I get home from choir practice with a plan for the reason we're going out. I need the call and the plan for my parents' sakes. Now, goodnight. I hope my call won't keep you awake." She hung up before I could gather my wits so I could tell her goodnight.

On Thursday, I phoned as she requested. She expected my call and answered on the second ring.

"I hope I'm not calling too late," I began.

Out of breath, she replied, "No…not too late…Mom and I…just returned. How are you?"

"I'm good. Busy at work, which often means busy at home also with the same things." I paused then continued, "Saturday evening still good for you?"

"Yes. I'm good," she replied then changed her voice to a whisper, "and looking forward to everything we may do."

I was caught off-guard by the whisper before remembering that her parents were around. "I'll be at your house at 6:00. We'll go to dinner at the Olive Garden and then to see *13 Going On 30*. It might be kind of silly, but I like Jennifer Garner. Sound okay?"

"Yeah, sounds good. I guess we end at your place for awhile."

"That's it. I started cleaning up this evening. First load of wash is in now. I hadn't appreciated enough until today how convenient it is to have a laundry room in the apartment complex."

I heard her father call out in the background, "Tell Jeff 'hi' if that's him!"

"It's him, Daddy!"

I added, "Tell him 'hi' and that I'll be at your home a few minutes before 6:00 so he and I can catch up on the off-season trades by the Yankees, Mets, and Phillies."

"Will do," she promised. "Now I have to get to some studying. First test in Econ. 330. Goodnight."

"Goodnight. I'm excited about being with you in less than forty-eight hours now."

Talking with Mr. Freeman was enjoyable. He's an avid fan, but he knows from years of experience that the early promise of a team can be side-tracked by injuries, team dynamics, and improvements among the opponents. So he was hopeful about his Mets and jokingly put down my Phillies. I laughed at his put-downs of the Phillies although past seasons of fizzling performance starting before the All Star break made some of my laughter uncomfortable.

Dinner was good—not gourmet, but consistently good at an affordable price. The Olive Garden had established its place in a market of many choices. I enjoyed the movie. I find Jennifer Garner to be sexy in a "girl next door" way. There were some funny scenes. Rox took my hand early and then rested her head on my shoulder. She even kissed me on the cheek as we first sat and then again at the end of the movie.

I followed the kiss at the end with the remark, "That's nice! I guess you're ready to go to my place?"

She squeezed my hand and sounded assent quietly with a slow "Uhhh, hunhhh."

After we were outside and away from the crowd, I pulled her to me and kissed her long and passionately. She seemed to enjoy closing her lips on my tongue.

Before unlocking my door, I warned, "I cleaned thoroughly—even washed the glasses and glass vase. But this is still a guy's place—without a mother to give direction. There may be a stray sock or pair of jeans lying somewhere that's the wrong place. Bottom line is: Don't expect perfection, not the neat and just-polished look you and your mother give your home. Okay?"

"Okay! I'm not expecting miracles, and probably half of my neatness as a housekeeper is to please my mother. Your place can't be as bad as the warning prepared me for. Now let's go in."

Once inside, after we both shed our jackets, she stepped in front of me, reached her hands to my cheeks, and pulled me closer. This time my lips closed on her tongue. I fought my inclination to start removing her clothes and throwing each piece in the air.

I excused myself in order to start the stereo with the most romantic FM station I was able to find a couple of hours earlier. As I walked away, Rox asked, "After I use your powder room, could I have a cocktail."

"One cocktail coming up. You surprise me with that request."

"I'm fortifying myself for doing something completely new—as I give myself to you."

To myself I said, "Yessss!" and made the abbreviated version of a fist pump.

We sat on the couch, soft music playing in the background, and drank our Dark and Stormy cocktails, while reviewing the evening. We both liked the movie. I knew that watching the star was a key to my reaction, and I suspected that the remainder was supplied by anticipating the end of the night. As we consumed the last of the drinks, I said, "We can remain out here on the couch, or we can go to my bed which is a lot more comfortable. Your choice."

In a seductive tone, with desire in her look, she answered, "I chose you when I made my phone call on Tuesday. You choose the location."

"Okay, the bedroom!" I blurted.

She had seen the room when she used the bathroom earlier, so she led the way. After arriving beside the bed, she said, "I'm all yours. I know you don't want to do this part, so I'll get us started." She raised her skirt and began to work on removing her pantyhose. I kicked off my shoes and removed my belt. She turned to me, joined her hands behind my neck, and said, "I'm all yours."

In my head I cautioned myself to go slowly. I unbuttoned her sweater and looked at her standing in front of me, wearing skirt, panties, and camisole. She leaned toward me, and we kissed passionately. She stopped me from undressing myself and then proceeded with removing my shirt and slacks. We kissed again as we both worked to remove the last pieces of clothing of each other.

When I stepped back so that I could look at her nude body, her eyes started from the floor and moved upward to survey my body. Escaping her throat was an "Uhhhh!" sound as she paused her scan near my waist. As we hugged, I moved my erection to the side for our mutual comfort. When our bodies reached the end of the fall onto the bed, we already were busy with our hands. As I started my maneuver so that I could enter her, her body tensed. I slowed, looked at her, and she turned her face away.

I was surprised by what I said next, and I guess she was just as unprepared: "I sense you're not ready for this."

"No. You don't need to stop. I said I want you to have your way."

"It's no good for me if you're not enjoying what we're doing," I whispered as I moved a short distance away.

We lay there silently for what seemed to be ten minutes or more. Then I said, "We should stop. I won't get full pleasure if I'm forcing you. You'll hate yourself, and maybe me, in the morning. We've been good friends, and I don't want to ruin that. I want us to get dressed and then we should talk in the living room."

Once seated together on the couch, I said, "Rox, I consider you to be one of my best friends—such a good friend that I don't want to give that up. I'll think of tonight as a trial, an attempt to see if there can be more to our friendship than respect for and protection of each other. I have my answer. I hope you're okay with us remaining good friends."

"I care for you also, Jeff. In a way it's similar to the way I care for my parents. I'm relieved that you feel the way you do because I think if we had continued, my feelings tomorrow would have driven us apart. I don't think there are many guys around who would do what you did and then understand it as you do. I'm more than okay with us remaining good friends—in fact, remaining best friends forever." She cemented the sincerity of her words with a large, wet, noisy kiss on my cheek.

On Monday, I dug out my article about the traffic slowdown on Buckwald Drive. I made a couple of small changes—probably insignificant changes. I concluded, once again—like my suspicions a couple of times before—that I probably would want to revise anything I had in hand after having not worked on it for a few days or longer. I made myself stop, reread what I now considered as the final version, and took it to Alex for the planned publication the following Saturday.

I phoned Kate next and recommended that we get away for a long weekend including Friday through late Sunday. We flew to Charleston and rented a car. After a full day in Charleston, we drove to Savannah for the last day and a half before flying home again. We both loved both cities. We took the ferry to Fort Sumter in Charleston; Saturday evening we took one of the famed ghost tours of one of Savannah's neighborhoods. The homes in both cities were charming. However, the strong community feeling we experienced in several of Savannah's neighborhoods made it our favorite of the two. Intimacy continued to develop and to contribute to the bond forming between us.

On Monday it was back to my other love: covering the news. I couldn't resist driving across Church Street to check on the traffic congestion. Thanks to a strong police presence at the college entrance at the north end of Buck-wald Drive, and perhaps partially due to the article in *The Press*, there was less congestion. It appeared that fewer people were traveling in the vicinity. Those who did go there benefitted from the change of the traffic light to flashing yellow and the personal direction of the police officers.

I turned south at Hooper Avenue and then right again onto College Drive to check the other end of Buckwald Drive. Things were not as pretty.

CHAPTER TWENTY-FOUR

Capt. McCann had called and asked me to attend a meeting with the newly formed Cold Case Squad. I entered the meeting pumped up because the captain had praised my work two days ago, and I now felt my work was finally paying off—not just for me but for the public in general. I thought of the breakthrough search and reporting of Woodward and Bernstein.

I also welcomed the opportunity to observe firsthand the interaction of this historically significant squad. When I arrived, McCann was present with a slightly older man in a suit. McCann shook my hand and turned to his colleague. "Dick, here's the hot-shot reporter whose investigation has produced leads that we need to run down. It's his work—along with the curiosity of some OCC students—that produced the final straw that pushed the number of unassigned cases over the tolerable limit and that then produced the suggestion to try a Cold Case Squad. I guess you could say that his work brought you and your two cohorts out of retirement."

Investigator Richard Ericson's face softened some from his almost permanent scowl as he extended his hand and said, "Hiya, kid. Glad to meet you. I don't know yet if I'm going to like the work ahead of us. I guess it's wait and see. Can't be any tougher than helping the wife corral the three grandkids."

"You and your fellow CCS members must be super sleuths," I said with a big smile as I shook his hand vigorously. "I'm honored to meet you!"

"Better see what we can deliver before you get too excited," he mumbled as he looked at the floor.

Just then Investigator David Jones and Lead Investigator James Kelly arrived. Following short introductions, McCann began, "The regular detectives have sorted through the praiseworthy work of our new friend Jeff. They've completed additional investigation of the most serious offenses and a few minor offenses which were included with the others or which emerged as collateral findings and were easy to pursue. They have a list of charges on which they could easily arrest Hernandez and Rivera. I'm assigning you three to continue their work and to conclude it. That will closeout this part of Jeff's work. I'd like to see that done within the week. Dick, I want you to take the lead on this because my decision will be to leave to you the final wrap up, the hand-off to the prosecutor's staff, and any continuation of communication in regard to testimony. At the same time, I anticipate pulling Jim and Dave to begin the skeletal recovery and to serve as liaison to the prosecutor in regard to that case. Eventually, Dick, you'll join your buddies on the other case, as opposed to the frog case. All of that clear to the three of you?"

Kelly and Jones nodded. Ericson appeared confused as he replied, "Will this mean a higher grade of pay for me? I understood your explanation when I pointed out that of the three of us, I'm earning the least. Your explanation then made sense that since we are paid an hourly rate based on our last pay grade prior to retirement and since the pay scale at Dover Township was higher than the Brick Town pay scale, I'll be paid the least. But in this case, I'll be doing both more difficult and more valuable service."

Kelly and Jones took hold of Ericson's suit jacket and guided him backward. While they did that, Kelly said, "Dick, give it a rest. You know this isn't going anywhere. Every penny we make is gravy because we still collect pension and Social Security."

Ericson moved his upper body from side to side until the other two let go. "You two think you're gonna lose out if I go to a higher pay grade? What happened to 'one for all and all for one'?"

Jones replied, "That kind of support still works for me. But the Three Musketeers didn't have a union and weren't working with a pay scale. Come on now, and be a team player."

Ericson smoothed his shirt and suit jacket as he mumbled, "Easier for you to say than me."

McCann intervened, "I'll rephrase: Dick, do you understand what your assignment will be?"

A nearly silent "yup" came from Ericson.

"And are you capable of doing those things?" McCann pursued.

"Yes, sir," was a clearer utterance.

Attempting to smooth the waters, McCann closed the uncomfortable outburst: "I need you guys, the Chief needs you guys, and the community needs you guys. We've got to move along this investigation and then get you three back to the really cold cases. We're using you here because this case has potential for breaking out into the open. And what good would it do to start clearing the cold ones while letting a current case get more complicated?"

"Okay. Okay," Ericson said with force. "I won't screw things up. I've always been a team player...often while sacrificing my own interests."

McCann shook his head and continued, "The purpose of this meeting is to give you three guys the opportunity to hear from Mr. Stewart and the opportunity to ask him for any clarification that's necessary. Jeff, I know you brought notes from your investigation. And you earlier shared your information with our regular detectives. Although the regular investigative squad has put together a list of potential charges, we're reviewing your work to make sure that nothing has fallen through the cracks. I hope today that you can review that information with the CCS so that they'll be able to decide where to intensify the department's work. This is what the squad was formed to do—to concentrate on areas of cases because they have the time without the pressure to process new cases. I think you brought along a printed version of your findings which you can distribute at any time you want. This is your opportunity to shine the spotlight on certain components, and it's our opportunity to identify where to dig in. This is your stage."

"Thank you, Captain," I began. "I'll give a quick overview and then pass out the printed stuff.

"I need to say at the beginning that much of my information was given to me off the record. Hernandez and Rivera have enjoyed very low-profile reputations because people who know a piece here and a piece there are frightened. I think the key to gaining additional intelligence is either that you can take a few leads from my work and dig more deeply so that some or all of those leads become serious enough that charges will stick and witnesses won't be afraid, or, as another key, that the combination of those leads produce some patterns which taken together amount to more serious offenses and witnesses won't be afraid.

I began, "I've arranged my notes for this presentation in the same pattern that I've used in organizing the written information that I'll distribute at the end of the presentation. The first bits of information are about Hernandez as a single individual.

"Witnesses reported several instances of Hernandez obtaining contracts to perform work which previously had been awarded to lower bidders. In some instances, the low-bid contractor suddenly was told that a critical supplier was not able to provide goods in time for the deadline to be met, and in these instances, J & AH Construction was awarded the bid at a higher total price due to the accelerated schedule he would be required to meet. There was one instance that I uncovered in which a second contractor who had beaten out Hernandez also could not get delivery on time and lost the contract to Hernandez when he also was unable to get delivery of materials. Hernandez was able to charge a premium due to a short timeline."

"Excuse me for interrupting, but I have a question," Ericson interjected with his hand raised as if he were in a classroom.

"Yes, Investigator Ericson," I replied, then continued, "What is your question?"

"It'd be easier for all of us in understanding now, and eventually understanding after we've left here today, if this information was in written form."

The other three groaned.

"Yes, it would be easier, and that's why I prepared written details for distribution at the conclusion of today's conference. The purpose of my comments now is to give you an overview so that you get a feel for all of the data and so that you can more readily understand my notes as you read them," I replied in what I hoped was an even tone that didn't reveal my annoyance with his conclusion that I'm stupid enough to give them such important data only in oral format.

Kelly said loudly and with impatience, "Dick, the guy's trying to help us learn the details. Give him a chance!"

"If things aren't clear when he finishes, then ask questions. God knows you always have a thousand questions anyway," Jones added.

Ericson looked at his two partners and said, "Okay. Okay, I'll wait. I was just trying to save time! But I can see the advantage of receiving the information through listening and through reading." He then looked at me and said, "I'll hold my questions to the end."

Jones replied, "I'll bet ten bucks he won't wait 'til the end to ask another question." He laughed primarily to himself and closed with, "He's never in his whole life waited to ask a dumb question."

McCann silenced the others when he said, "Jeff, I apologize. Please continue."

I began again, "I was listing the information I obtained in my investigation which either show or suggest that Hernandez persuaded suppliers to not deliver materials on time which caused construction companies to cancel their contracts which often resulted in Hernandez performing the work at a premium charge. I'll continue from there with other information."

I continued on with information about Hernandez and then switched to Rivera. The last part of my comments turned to the apparent overlapping administrations of two companies which filed reports as independent entities. "There is a pattern of interconnections among relatives in key positions in the two companies. The brother of Hernandez's second wife is vice president in the Baja organization. The wife of a junior partner in the law office on retainer by J & AH is the comptroller at Baja. The brother of Larry Morrison's widow is the attorney for Baja. Although she declared she hates Hernandez because she sees the deadly heart attack suffered by her husband as directly linked to the pressure from the legal case which developed around Hernandez's report that Larry offered him a bribe. Her brother as legal advisor to Hernandez seems strange."

"It's interesting that you stopped with your observation about the unusual character of the brother serving as legal counsel to an enemy of the woman," Jones began. When I turned to look at him, he resumed, "We have to analyze all of our information in regard to its legality. We can't make decisions on the basis that he or she sees something that he or she considers unusual." Both colleagues nodded agreement.

I wondered how challenging this assignment would prove to be, and then I replied, "Point well taken. I assume that you three and the other investigators in your department will sift reports and other sources of information through a legal consideration. I know what things don't seem right, and it was that standard which led my experience to evaluate their importance legally, and that's what has brought us together." Each of the three investigators gave signals of their acceptance of what I had said—a visible sigh, a drop of shoulders or a slouch, a smile.

I took a swig from my water bottle and continued, "This is probably as good a time as any for me to give you the packets of my notes which will provide more detail to my comments. I hope all of the details will be useful. And I hope the packet will give you additional information which you will need."

Kelly spoke for the squad, "This is quite a bit of information for us to digest at one time. I propose that we meet again early tomorrow so that we can walk through point by-point and ask you for clarification. You must have things you need to do with other parts of your work as a reporter. Is the plan good for you? And is 9:30 tomorrow morning a time when you can meet?"

"Yes to both of those. Where shall we meet? One place is as good as another."

"Can you get us a conference room at the newspaper headquarters?"

"Can do."

"The major likes to think we're in the field most of our time. If he doesn't see us, he'll assume that's where we are. And if he questions us, we can tell him where we were and what we were doing. Dick, you'll lead us tomorrow since you're going to be the head of this project. Everybody okay with all that?"

When there was no answer, he said, "Speak now or hold your peace."

―――――――――――――――

As I left the building, I realized that I was hungry. Here it was 1:30, and I'd had no lunch. My stomach was screaming, "Burger and Fries!" After including sharing the most important details, I picked through the hardcopy mail and my voice messages. It was like a jolt of electricity that shot through me as I heard Kate's voice. I think she was being gentle with me as she quietly reminded me that I was going to call regularly. She said she had hoped for a call before today. I made a commitment to myself to phone at her home tonight during the time period she suggested. I also set up a brief, late afternoon meeting with my trainee, Allison Finch.

As I thought ahead to my meeting the next day with the Cold Case Squad, I suddenly realized that all three of them will be raising questions and challenging my conclusions. I needed to be prepared to respond in order to help them prepare for their next steps. I decided a color code would speed my ability to locate the specific data which supported each potential charge regarding Hernandez:

- Collusion by H. with suppliers to force cancellation of contracts for projects on which he had not been the low bidder and subsequent winning premium price contracts on the same projects,
- Collusion by H. with Planning Board employees to obtain prior information from bid packages submitted by competitors,
- Complaints of criminal trespass and physical damage to partially completed work at job sites by associates hired by H. A complaint about quality of work by H's company which were resolved after investigators from office of the County Prosecutor counseled H. that charges could be filed,
- A complaint of fraud against H was settled after complainant filed charge with Consumer Advocate.
- 4 complaints of failure to make repairs resolved by H's company were removed when the repairs were completed following the filings,
- An abnormal number of filings with the BBB by clients,
- A report of bribery by entertaining suppliers and completing work on their homes at no charge in order to obtain reduced prices on materials,
- A report of bribery by H giving gifts to building inspectors and union agents,
- A report that H set up the building inspector with false claims of fraud and collusion, which resulted in the inspector choosing to not testify and to take time in prison rather than be murdered,
- A report by the widow of a code enforcement director that the director died following indictment on false charges obtained by H wearing a wire,
- H's vote as Freeholder to approve Baja Paving to complete the project of paving the Buckwald Drive Bridge, despite the fact that companies of H and R were intertwined through officers and employees.

I used a similar color code in regard to potential charges against Rivera. The evidence included:

- Poor quality of work, in at least one case, which was repaired only after court intervention, and in another case the complaint was dropped after R gave jobs to children of the complaining company's officers
- Report by subcontractor that R stopped using him after that contractor hired R's administrative assistant,
- Court case settlement for failure to pay income tax for some employees,
- Court case settlement for failure to pay sales tax on some supplies,
- Six of the 26 cases in the record at the Better Business Bureau were settled in Small Claims courts with awards ranging from $1400 to the state limit of $2500.

I left the office later than I had planned after intern Allison Finch appeared at my office asking for guidance.

"Thanks for scheduling this time to help me. I'm sure you're busy, but I need some advice."

I felt good about completing my analysis of the information about Hernandez and Rivera and about my upcoming call to Kate. In that good mood, I replied, "Come on in and find a place to sit." I looked at my watch as encouragement for her to make our conversation short.

"I interviewed Jack Krenshaw about his championship win in the New Jersey State 8-Ball Tournament. The interview was pretty dull for someone, like me, who has no prior knowledge of the game of 8-Ball. But he told me that his game improved dramatically since he began using a special chalk he imports from China. Then he said that I shouldn't include that information in my article. I asked friends who play pool frequently if there are tournament regulations which deal with the brand or other specifications regarding the type of chalk that's used. Based on their replies that the type of chalk can have a major impact on the fairness of a game, I requested a copy of the regulations for the state tournament he won."

I interrupted at this point, "That's very resourceful. I'm impressed!"

She concluded her explanation of why she asked to talk with me: "Thanks for the positive feedback. I understand the regulations to say that use of any chalk other than the two types and brands listed is prohibited. My dilemma is that he gave me the information about the chalk before he told me to not use it. Am I bound by his request in these circumstances? Or should I ignore his request?"

"I'll answer your question in a minute. But first I'm curious about how you would use his statement about the chalk."

"I keep thinking I have a choice between using it in a factual way or making the information the heart of the article. I imagine two very different articles: one has a headline like 'Local Man Wins State Tournament,' and the other has the headline 'Prohibited Chalk May Change Tournament Results.'"

"That's a good way to put the issue into perspective. If you report his statement in the more factual article, it's likely that the information'll get into the hands of a competitor, and then the brown stuff hits the fan anyway. And, either way, the champ's going to be angry with you. So, I guess the decision becomes to either report the championship without information about the chalk or report the information and let things develop."

"If I report the chalk information in a factual way, my motive is unclear. While if I report it as a breach of the regulations, it's clear that my motive is to detract from his win."

I knew that Allison and I were on the same wavelength, "Okay. We have the same understanding of the problem. Now, I need to give you an answer to your original question. If it were me, I'd include the information in a factual way with a calm headline. Then if he's unhappy with me, the disagreement is about when he told me to not use the information. As I understand you, he told you after he had given you the information. That's too late. The common understanding would be that unless the request to not use comes before the sharing of the information, anything said by the interviewee is said in the context of the spoken or silent agreement to talk."

"Oh, thank you! That's how I had planned to report, but decided to get your recommendation."

"Hold on. Don't start writing until you get the okay from Mr. Speery ... from Alex. He has the final say on those types of issues, and it's always better to get that say in advance—especially when you're not a regular employee and are in an internship position. If Alex says don't include the chalk statement, then see your faculty advisor in your OCC program."

I stuck out my hand for a shake and got a gigantic hug. Then she almost danced out of my office.

I was relieved that Allison showed good judgment in recognizing there was a potential problem in the situation and showed initiative in her way of handling it. I had been worried that she may not have the character to develop into a self-reliant reporter. In this case, she knew that there was a potential problem and figured out a way to deal with it and carried through. Another positive to carry into my phone call of the girl I had decided to pursue!

Since I was rushing to get to my phone, I stopped at the neighborhood pizza parlor and picked up two slices for dinner. Because Kate recognized my phone number, she answered. "How amazing! A call from my favorite—my absolutely most favorite—reporter."

I was getting faster with my answers—probably my encounters with Kim served as speed training: "That sounds like you have lots of reporters in your life."

She was one step ahead: "Sometimes in my line of work I talk with lots of reporters. But in my personal life [Here she slowed her speech and did her best at a Southern accent], there's only you. And it's you in a big way!"

"I'm guessing you'll say yes to my invitation to go out this week."

"Aren't you a clever detective, as well as a skilled reporter!"

"I suggest Saturday evening. I'm ready to take you to any place you want."

"How about you choose a nice, romantic restaurant—don't make it too expensive. I'll do some housework, and we can come back here and see what comes up."

"You know how to please me! Shall I pick you up at 7:00?"

"I'll be ready—ready and waiting."

Fortunately, the next couple of days went fast with all that was happening with my investigation. Each busy day made the time shorter till Saturday.

The following morning could have been a late start for me, but I woke up early in a dream about Kate and I—a dream I would have liked to complete because she had just turned out the lights and was walking with swinging hips toward the couch where I was waiting after lighting the candles as requested. I said out loud, "What the hell! I can knock off some of the things I saw that had accumulated in my inbox for a couple of days." I knew I needed to stay busy through the end of the week.

The CCS arrived together. I met them at the entrance and walked them to the conference room, which Alex was happy to provide because I told him that the meeting would move us closer to the goal of the DSPD completing its investigation so that we could print an exclusive story.

Ericson pulled multiple yellow pads from his briefcase, a weathered container bravely showing scratches, stains, and nicks—with a stubborn locking mechanism which resisted the owner's first few efforts to gain access.

Jones took advantage of his colleague's difficulties with the quip, "It'd probably be quicker if I took that thing and a paperclip over to the county jail and held a contest with the petty theft experts."

Ericson stared at Kelly who interpreted the look as an appeal for support against his frequent nemesis. Kelly said, "Keep at it. But it'll help to keep your eyes on what you're working on."

Ericson uttered an audible sigh, followed by a smile when his next effort produced access.

Kelly looked at Ericson and asked, "Dick, are you ready to lead us ahead?"

"That's why I've been fighting this tired old lock! I did my homework and have several comments and questions."

"Fire away," I replied. "I guess that's safe to say to an armed person who also is a defender of the law."

"The jury's out on that in this case," Jones responded.

"Dick get us started...please!" Kelly declared.

"I choose to first eliminate items which are simply assertions, since there are no witnesses referenced and there are no citations of ordinances or laws. I include in that group most of the reports that Hernandez obtained contracts outside the standard bidding procedures..." He paused and looked at me. I returned his stare and waited for him to continue. "... complaints which were subsequently resolved through interventions of public officials, filings with the Better Business Bureau which were never pursued in court, the claim of false reporting by a business owner who decided he preferred to be convicted and to do time, a similar claim by the widow of a Code Enforcement director who died of a heart attack after being booked on charges provided by Hernandez. That leaves possible bribery of building inspectors and union agents, bribery of business owners to obtain lower prices on supplies, and his vote as a Free-holder to approve a paving contract with his buddy Rivera."

Ericson continued with a general question, "Are there any comments? ... Questions?... Rebuttals?... Challenges to my conclusions?" He looked at each of us, hesitating before moving on to the next person. "In regard to Rivera, my conclusions are that we should not pursue any of the cases in which property owners dropped their initial complaints after the owners were satisfied with action taken himself by Rivera, the report by a subcontractor that he was no longer hired to do work after the subcontractor hired Rivera's administrative assistant, the two tax cases which were settled by court order, and the cases which were settled in small claims courts. It appears to me that Rivera has been a more savvy operator than Hernandez and has been able to avoid legal challenges. We might want to check further ourselves on the remaining twenty of the twenty-six BBB filings which Mr. Stewart chose to not follow any further." He stopped his presentation while taking a drink of his coffee. Then he asked if there were questions or differences of opinion.

When there were none of the follow-ups he suggested, he said, "That leaves us with the very sticky issue of the interconnections of the owners and officers of the two companies. I raise the question: 'Is it a crime to merely have these interconnections, or do the laws permit such a web to exist as long as there is no violation of other laws?'

When I opened my mouth immediately to reply, Ericson spoke more quickly, "I believe that we should certainly look for legal violations which may be an outgrowth from that network. Now, Mr. Stewart, I'm finished."

Kelly and Jones began to reply until I raised the volume of my voice and talked over them. After a couple of words from me, they stopped trying to talk and, by their body language, indicated they were listening. "I believe there is virtual control of Baja Paving Company by J & AH Corporation. Hernandez's brother-in-law is the vice president of Baja. The secretary of Baja is the wife of the vice president of J & AH. The son of the comptroller of J & AH is the treasurer of Baja. This isn't surprising because Hernandez befriended Rivera and set him up as a company."

Kelly challenged this statement, "Where is there proof to that effect?"

"Hernandez won a Chamber of Commerce award for setting up Rivera as owner and mentoring him. The archives of my newspaper contain a feature

article with photo. In addition, the two other connections between voting officers can be found by names in the official filings of the two companies, and
then an online search using those names will provide information about relatives of each."

"So, how do we know that the connections have led to illegal activities?"
Jones asked.

With these connections in existence, it's easy for Hernandez to tell his VP
and his comptroller to take action through Baja to provide influence, such as
to hire some thugs to take action against a company which ultimately will
benefit J & AH, to delay deliveries of materials to an enemy, or a wide range
of activities which are illegal and contribute to J & AH's bottom line."

"I guess you mean that these relationships provide the means for crimes
to have been committed? And what we need to do is investigate some of the
other reports you received?" Ericson asked.

"And don't forget the reports of bribes by Hernandez and his vote to approve a county contract with Baja, which can now be seen as a conflict of interest when the points of influence become clear," I concluded.

"Kid, you're smart and thorough. I hope you know we had to challenge
so that we're sure that all the non-indictable information is removed from our
assignment and sure that there's a high probability of Hernandez—and perhaps
Rivera—being charged."

"No problem. I'm glad that my work has led this far."

CHAPTER TWENTY-FIVE

The south end of Buckwald Drive was a cacophony of noise and anger where police officers took turns in signaling drivers to turn into the large parking lot, telling them to turn around, and denying the access to their usual path going toward the college. Try as I might to block from my awareness the ugly facial expressions and the blare of scores of car horns honking at the same time, those factors left me frazzled. Although my thoughts kept turning to Kate and her recommendation of two months without lovemaking, I wanted to remain positive the morning after—"D Day" for the start of the search for the endangered Tree Frogs, but eventually I gave in and leaned on my car horn and made gestures with my free hand. I curtailed my rude behavior in order to not draw the attention of the police officers because my top goal was to get closer to the "traffic survey" which was being conducted a short way north of where the officer stood waving to follow the others into the parking lot. Unusual events to a reporter were like a flame to a moth.

I rolled down both front windows and stuck an arm and my head out the driver side opening. The officer was annoyed that he had to deal with one of the nerds who was playing ignorant of the police force's intention. He walked to my car while moving his right arm in a circle. When he was close enough that I certainly would hear his voice, he shouted, "Keep it moving, buddy. We've all got to play together."

Because I didn't move as he had signaled, he closed the complete distance to my car. I began before he could make any comment or ask why I thought I was different from everyone today. "Sir, I'm here to see Captain James McCann. I know he must be here to oversee this operation." The officer—by this time I had read the name of "P. Innis" on his name tag—slowed his pace and changed his expression from angry to inquisitive

"What's your name? It makes little sense that the captain would schedule an appointment for the first few hours of work today."

"My name is Jeff Stewart. Is it okay if I reach into my pocket to get my driver's license and press credentials?"

"Yeah. Go ahead. I'll send them up the line to his position ahead. Although I doubt he wants some nosey reporter poking around here. This is an active project site."

As I took my license and APP pass out of my wallet, I responded, "I think he expects me. I know for sure he won't turn me away."

"I hear that every day, kid. I'll take those, and you turn off your ignition. No need to expose my colleagues and me to more pollution."

While waiting, I jotted down some questions I wanted to be sure to cover while talking with McCann. The next time I glanced up the road, I observed Officer Innis walking quickly toward me and waving his arms to indicate I should come to him. I almost started my car then decided I was being set up to drive without a license. Not wanting to appear uncooperative, I opened the door and began to get out. "I don't want you to walk up the road to the captain. I want you to drive."

My reply made sense to me. "I was afraid to drive without my license—especially while being observed by an officer of the law."

Perhaps it was my smile which Innis may not have been able to read that set him off. "Are you for real? Do you think I've been standing here in the glaring sun so that I could trick an unsuspecting individual into driving without a license? Well, I wasn't! I'm devoted to protection of citizens and facilitating police projects to which I've been assigned. I'm too damned busy with legitimate responsibilities to make you a martyr for being tricked into driving illegally."

I meekly pulled my foot into the car, tried quietly to close the door, and waited for him to blow himself out.

That wasn't what he wanted either. He said, scowling, "I asked you some questions. and I didn't hear your answers."

"I thought you were doing a pretty good job with both the questions and the answers. Which question do you want me to begin with?"

I offered a subdued comment as we went in different directions. "Thank you for your help. I hope your day gets better."

———————

Capt. James McCann walked to me, checking his watch just before arriving at my car. "Mr. Stewart, are you here to see me? I've got to keep circulating until that racket is eliminated. I understood that you wrote the article which identified the expected traffic congestion. I wonder why you chose to not stay away."

As a reporter, I want to check up on the media releases for accuracy. And besides," I decided to become charming, "I can't stay away from all the excitement."

"You better believe I'd choose to stay away if I could. Stay out of the way, get your excitement fix, and then move on. If you'll stay close to me, you can park over in that wide spot ahead on the right and walk to where the real action is."

"Real action" was euphemistic. We passed the vehicles parked in a helter skelter formation—some on the road and others in the grass, still others were half on the road and half on the grass. Some of the larger trucks seemed to have made an attempt to park off the road and failed miserably. Much talking was going on, with an occasional shout of a command or warning standing out above the general buzz. After we passed most of the vehicles, I was able to focus on the near-end of the bridge. The size of the crowd and the slow-turning and mixing reminded me of a tailgate party at an outdoor athletic event.

I'm sure my expression showed my surprise. As if audio clues were necessary, I commented, "I've never seen so many people on and near this end of the bridge. Did any emergency employee go to his regular job today?"

The captain replied, "This is the center of the universe for emergency workers in Dover Township today. Probably a lot of accumulated, favorable credit was spent to get assignments here today." After the next few paces, he continued, "Why not offer to cover the event? The sun's shining. The temperature is unseasonably warm. And the excitement and mystery here is like a shot of adrenalin on a typical start of the work week."

After McCann returned from a hushed conversation with his counterpart from the fire department, I couldn't resist asking, "Are you and other leaders expecting the bridge or the woods to catch fire?

Although he laughed at the question, he gave me the public information answer: "The modern firefighter does more than just fight fires. He's expected to be flexible in meeting the needs of the public—crowd control, a source of information to reply to questions, general clean up, as well as being prepared to stop and mop up after chemical and sewage spills to maintain a healthy atmosphere. Just like it's not just cops-and-robbers for the police force, it's not just Smokey the Forest Fire Bear and Dalmatians riding on the truck for the fire department."

I had pulled my small notebook from my rear pants pocket and a pen from my shirt pocket and had started to jot down snatches of his comments. He replied, "You can quote me on that if you want to."

I always had hundreds of questions and never hesitated to ask them. I know at times, people—even friends, and especially family—found me to be a pest with my insatiable curiosity. I slipped into my question mode and asked, "Captain, can you give me some background on how this investigation got to this point?"

He spread his feet apart a bit, and hooked his thumbs into belt loops, pushed his chest (and belly) forward, and pulled his head back. I knew I had struck pay dirt!

His monologue included much of the following information, some information reported research I completed in order to supplement and clarify the captain's narrative. The cooperation between the DEP and the TRPD was a rough road. There were more speed bumps and potholes than there was smooth surface. The DEP insisted on a survey of the number of frogs. The police chief was willing to agree to the survey but wanted a one-week deadline. Such a survey typically is conducted by a forensic naturalist, a person who has completed graduate work in an environmental science, knows how to identify the wildlife under consideration, is familiar with accepted techniques for counting a sample and extrapolating a full population estimate, and has the disposition to sit for hours while constantly scanning a designated territory. Needless to say, the low-bid regulations guiding the operations of government entities had to be set aside as an emergency to permit employment of one of the animal counting specialists. The Freeholders engaged in an extended debate regarding the qualification of the current situation as an emergency. Following a vote of three yes and two abstain for the appointment of a naturalist who was available on short notice, rainy weather of two days caused a delay which added to the tension. Other issues included the number of pairs of feet allowed in the habitat at one time, the establishment of a priority condition under which the frogs had first claim on a location and those under which the humans had first claim, the type and size of tools and equipment to be used in the exhumation, temporary installment of fencing to maintain an agreed distance between the site work and onlookers, monitoring of noise levels in the vicinity of the project, limits on the amount of time any one internal combustion engine could run or idle in the area, and choice of one combination monitor/supervisor/ombudsman by each department. The ultimate agreement on a notebook of protocols and rules was truly miraculous. I was told that the time to reach agreement had consumed two very full days.

The major result of all the activity, both today and prior to today, was to establish that there was a habitat of Pine Barrens Tree Frogs existing under the Buckwald Bridge. That fact, by itself, should be enough to say to the Freeholders: "Stay out of there, and take no action in regard to the bridge, and especially under it." Whether they would get to that same position remained to be seen.

Regardless of the future decisions of the Board of Chosen Freeholders, one of its members—Alberto Hernandez—could be charged with failure to recuse himself from the vote to take action. In fact, the offense of Hernandez was made all the more obvious by his two motions to pave the bridge—his motion to put the repaving to a vote and his motion to approve the repaving. He not only cast his vote in favor of the repaving, his name appeared in the minutes as the person who made the motion to repave. He was not just passively involved, he was active in bringing the vote to its conclusion.

Hernandez put himself in position to be considered a major player in the re-pavement consideration, an action which placed the Freeholders in opposition to their earlier CAFRA agreement to protect the frogs—even to the extent of a large expenditure for the purpose of protection. And the vote included the benefit to Rivera of the cost of re-pavement. This directed even more attention to the interwoven personnel of both corporations. My predictions of exposure of the illegal filings was handed to the citizens of Ocean County.

POSTLUDE FOR FROG GIG

While the book *Frog Gig* has ended, the story goes on in the book *When It Rains....* because the search for the frog habitat also found evidence of another crime, one which is more serious because it involved an apparent double murder of a young female and her unborn fetus.

The threesome from the Environmental Club went under the bridge to search for the Pine Barren Tree Frogs. Their efforts were originally planned to determine if the efforts to protect the rumored wildlife had a purpose. The original study identifying the frogs had taken place so many years in advance—at the time the bridge was built—with no subsequent study results on file anywhere, that there were numbers of people in the community who questioned the current status of the habitat of the fabled endangered species. The proponents of protection of wildlife argued with the residents who spoke of their protection as an unwanted expense. Although three members of the Environmental Club had conducted the unapproved exploration under the bridge in the late night hours, they did so because the arguments on both sides of the issue were threatening the toleration of the array of clubs offered by the college. One of them had said to the other two, "These arguments which question the club's existence also question the existence of all the clubs. Therefore, some individual or small group should look under the bridge to determine if the wildlife exists or if it has moved on during the time since their protection was instituted." One of them had replied, "While we see the clubs as wonderful opportunities to put into action the things we learn in class, there are others who want to withdraw their support of the club program." It was in the spirit of protecting the club program that the three did their research of the times that the campus security force inspected the area and then planned the descent into the muck and mire at a time when most of their friends slept. While they observed the tree frogs, they also "stumbled" upon a hard object, which appeared to be a human leg bone.

After finding the bone and apparent smaller bones of a skeleton, one from their small group informed a reporter from the newspaper which reported on local stories. I am that reporter. I had doubts that I could persuade the group to report their find due to the fear they had and which I shared. From the first time I heard of the find, I encouraged one of the threesome who appeared to be most likely to make the report. After the lapse of approximately two weeks, the group agreed to report to the police. I was pleased that they asked if I could help them to avoid being punished. Through the intercession of my editor-in-chief with an officer in the police department, we were able to negotiate a confessional meeting where the information would be shared with an officer high in the ranks who had already agreed to work to recognize their contributions to the community and to represent their findings and subsequent consideration of punishment in the most favorable light.

This book worked up to the identification of the habitat of the endangered species. It was easier for the newspaper and the police to explain that the blockage of the roads was due to the decision to repave the road. At the same time the publicity would hide from the public the exhumation of the skeletons. Everyone knew that the truth would some day be told about the skeleton. The college gained through an immediate cover-up of the fact and then would let the police department determine if the public should know about the discovery by the three officers of the Environmental Club, those three then likely to benefit from their dutiful report to the police. At the same time, the police could get some planning time to prepare for the search to find the murderer.